A Touch of Gold & Madness

Book Cover by Bianca Bordianu at Moonpress Designs

Edited by Kirsty McQuarrie at Let's Get Proofed

First edition November 2023

For all the Anakin, Damon, Draco, and Erik Northman lovers out there—
For always rooting for the redemption in the villain. For those who know
that our trauma shapes us, but it doesn't define us. It's never too late.
You're worthy.
And for my parabatai, soul-sister, Tory.

Disclaimer

The themes in *A Touch of Gold and Madness* are heavy and could be potentially triggering or harmful to those unprepared to read it. It is important to the author that the reader is informed of the most triggering content before diving into this story about trauma and healing. This is by no means a complete and comprehensive list, as it is nearly impossible to list everything that could be potentially triggering to every individual. What may be sensitive to one person may not be to another, as everyone has traumas that have affected them in different ways.

Suicidal ideation, mentions of child abuse, scene alluding to child sexual abuse (not shown), mental and emotional abuse, domestic violence, drug use, alcohol consumption for coping, death (blood, gore, torture, beheading, etc.), a side character is found having committed suicide, anxiety, depression, grief from loss of a partner, vulgar language, explicit adult scenes 18+, mentions of human trafficking, bullying, the word "rape" is explicitly said in later chapters, and kidnapping.

Introduction

F or over a millennium, two magical races have lived amongst the humans, hiding away and blending into obscurity amongst their civilizations. Over time, their origins have been lost to their people, as they made Earth—otherwise known as Terraguard—their home.

The two races have co-existed with one another over the years, but every now and then, they'd have a dispute that would bleed over into human society. Such an incident occurred ten years ago in the year 2015, when a war broke out between the two races—Elementals and Kinetics—igniting a series of events to occur amongst the human population.

News broadcasters and the government knew what truly was happening, but they passed off the attacks as terrorist attacks, natural disasters, and wrongfully blaming mental illness.

Three years into the war, the Kinetic King, King Forest, made a public appearance, announcing the existence of the races and warning the humans of the dangers of the Elementals, telling them they needed to prepare for the worst.

So, they did. Humans built underground bunkers where they readied for the apocalypse that they always feared.

Two years later, on April 24th, 2020, an unfathomable EMP struck the world. It was strong enough to eradicate the entire world's power grids in one blow, wiping out over three-quarters of the human population. This was coined Devolution Day by the surviving humans.

Now, five years after Devolution Day, humans live underground while Kinetics and Elementals are still at war, desperate to take their world back.

Glossary

Currents - The colorful electrical currents that race up and down the arms and necks of Kinetics. Specific colors denote which energetic source on the electromagnetic spectrum they derive their magic from.

Glamour - The ability to hide the physical characteristics of Kinetics and Elementals. For Kinetics, silver, magnetic bracelets hide their physical traits, as well as suppressing their magical abilities. For Elementals, black-crystal infused bracelets hide physical traits, as well as suppressing their magical abilities.

Speakeasy - The underground bars, or taverns, built by humans prior to Devolution Day. This is where they congregate to escape from the bleak reality that is topside. Typically, they are marked by a makeshift wooden cross in a field.

Revel - Royal celebrations amongst Kinetics.

Scorse - Human trading posts that offer essential living needs to barter. However, scorses also offer the darker side of the underground trading system, where illicit drugs, human trafficking, death matches, and prostitution are prevalent.

Deplete - When Elementals replenish their magical reserves, they must feed off the energy coming from a living being's aura. To drain it completely, kills the living being, resulting in being thrust into the devolution of becoming Endarkened. Also means to drain one's magical well.

Endarkened - Elementals who have depleted three auras and are now mindless, rabid beings that only seek out depleting the next aura. They prefer strong magical auras which increase their power.

Domain - Regions amongst the Kinetics are split up into domains all over the world.

The Royal Domain - The domain that's central to all Kinetic domains worldwide where the king resides and rules. It is based in Atlanta, Georgia, where they live in a luxury high-rise hotel to blend in with the humans.

The King's Palace - The high-rise hotel that houses the royal Kinetic family and those in the Atlanta region.

Hollows - Small communities throughout the world hidden further from civilization that house Elementals.

Mushweed - A herb created by Elementals over a millennia ago in small villages that speeds up the replenishment process to help reduce the risk of depleting an aura.

Kinetic Powers

Kinetics derive their magic from energy based on one of the energetic waves from the electromagnetic spectrum. Each energetic source is depicted by the color of the Kinetic's currents. Most Kinetics who share the same source of energy will wield their magic in unique ways specific to them.

<u>**Sonic**</u> - Kinetics who derive their magic from sound waves are able to control, manipulate, or cancel out all sound. Highly experienced Sonic Kinetics are able to pinpoint a specific target and control what they can or cannot hear.
Currents: Blue

<u>**Light**</u> - Kinetics who derive their magic from visible light waves are able to control, manipulate, or cancel out all sight. Highly experienced Light Kinetics are able to pinpoint a specific target and control what they can or cannot see.
Currents: Gold

<u>**Thermal**</u> - Kinetics who derive their magic from thermal waves are able to control, manipulate, or create heat. Most Thermal Kinetics wield this ability by controlling their opponents' internal body heat. They can also control external temperature, as well.
Currents: Yellow

Microwave - Kinetics who derive their magic from microwave radiation are able to control, manipulate, or absorb microwave energies. This ability is most used for intelligence purposes. It can also be used in the form of blasts, which can fry an individual from the outside in.

Currents: Green

Gamma - Kinetics who derive their magic from gamma waves are able to control, manipulate, or absorb gamma energies. This ability is especially dangerous as it's usually wielded as a poison because it's a form of radiation. Gamma Kinetics can control how fast it affects their target.

Currents: White

X-rays - Kinetics who derive their magic from X-ray waves are able to see with X-ray vision and/or are able to emit X-ray radiation, poisoning their targets.

Currents: Black

Ultraviolet - Kinetics who derive their magic from ultraviolet waves have the ability to emit ultraviolet light from their body or create ultraviolet burns.

Currents: Red

Infrared - Kinetics who derive their magic from infrared waves have the ability to track, see, or emit heat on a specific target by controlling external heat to their surroundings.

Currents: Orange

Nuclear - Kinetics who derive their magic from nuclear waves are able to create electricity.

Currents: Purple

Electromagnetic Pulses - Kinetics who derive their magic from electro-magnetic waves are able to control pulses either electronically or through pressurized blasts, and can create electricity. It is the rarest of all the abilities amongst Kinetics.

Currents: Silver

Chapter 1

GRAY

The militia woman's skull slammed into the hardened earth, bone crunching upon impact. Yet, she didn't relent in her fight. I straddled her bucking hips from behind, her legs thrashing beneath me and fists swinging in desperation at my face to no avail.

I adjusted my position, pinning her pelvis to the ground while digging my knees into her sides as I reached for my dagger. I usually avoided fighting humans, but she'd recognized me and attacked. She needed to be contained before she blew my cover and mission.

The woman's head swiveled to the side, searching for the gun I'd dislodged from her moments ago. I spotted it several feet away, a chuckle bubbling from my chest. "I don't know why you humans insist on using guns against us," I said, her body stilling as I pressed the edge of the dagger to her throat. "You know they're useless against our kind. We'll just heal from it in a matter of minutes." Once the bullet was removed, that was.

Her upper lip peeled back from her teeth as defiance shone in her eyes. "So you think," she spat. It was her turn to chuckle, "Don't think for a second I don't know who you are." My dagger bobbed and nicked the delicate skin, a trickle of dark liquid seeping from beneath the blade. "You think just because you hide your Kinetic nature, you go unseen, but it doesn't change the fact that you're evil on the inside. Your kind needs to be eradicated." She glanced down at the silver bracelet donning my wrist, letting on to the fact she was aware of my glamour.

"You're angry with the wrong side. It was the Elementals that..."

"Bullshit! Your kind destroyed everything," she hissed through clenched teeth. "And when I inform the speakeasy below of your presence, you'll be dead before you ever set foot..."

No.

I jerked my blade across her throat, a deep gash on her trachea that silenced her threat. "Can't let you do that," I huffed and sat back, the lead weight of guilt instantly dropping from my chest to my core.

I rolled the limp corpse over onto her back; arms clad in military camo plopped to the ground with a thud. The tall grass of the open field would obscure her body for only a brief time. The human rebel's glazed eyes stared into the starless night as dark crimson cascaded from the gaping line slashed across her throat.

Despite the cloudy sky, the moon cast its illuminating glow, providing just a sliver of light in this bleak world. A chilled breeze sent a shiver down my spine as the seasons transitioned between the rigorous summer months into autumn, blowing ice-blonde strands of my hair into my eye.

I rummaged through her weapons belt, searching for any human weapon or ammunition to trade. A loaded magazine clip belonging to the woman's pistol reflected off the moonlight in my fist before I shoved it into my weapons belt. Three feet away lay the fallen gun where the barrel dug into the soil. I checked the safety and forced it tightly into my belt.

Why did she believe that attacking me was a good decision? It wasn't like the poor woman stood a chance against my training anyways.

Crouching beside the woman's head, I brushed her eyelids closed with my fingertips, her dark lashes resting against her sunbaked skin. "Consider yourself one of the lucky ones who gets to leave this hellhole," I murmured more to myself, my head drooping forward. Instinctively, I clutched the black stone hanging from the leather strap around my neck to bring me comfort.

I breathed in the crisp air scented with nature's decay. It soothed my lungs and eased the tension a fraction, enough to lighten the burden in my chest.

I peered at the dead woman again. Except when I laid my eyes upon her corpse, I no longer saw the human rebel. Instead, I envisioned Slate's dark, ashy hair and lifeless hazel eyes. Grief at his loss slithered around my heart and squeezed.

A ringing sang in my ears, sounding the alarm of impending emotion threatening to pull me under again. I clenched my jaw until it ached, trying to swallow past the lump in my throat. Crying was weak. Emotions were dangerous. I worked to shut them down, just as I'd been trained to do my entire life.

I blew out a breath, forcing my mind back to the task at hand. To kill the man who was not only responsible for the collapse of modern society but also for Slate's death. I let the anger simmer and burn into a furious inferno, gearing me up for the hit of a lifetime. The only hit that mattered in more ways than one.

This mission wasn't just an assignment; it was my own personal vendetta against the man who took away the only light I had in my life. Slate had been my rock, my anchor—a reminder to turn the hatred I received from my people into a strength.

And Griffin Silas robbed me of that, leaving behind a hardened princess assassin in his wake.

Hating every second of it, I began to strip the woman of her faded military fatigues, swapping out my black leather gear for hers instead. I strapped my weapons belt underneath the loose uniform to hide it from view while managing to stash a few Kinetic knives and daggers in the pockets and up the sleeve.

The silver magnetic bracelet engraved with intricate Kinetic sigils suppressed my magic, as well as the luminescent blue currents that usually raced up and down my arms and neck. I effectively appeared human.

The glamour concealed my dual-toned, black-and-white waves that were marbled together to appear gray, earning my name. It was a Kinetic custom that no one escaped. Unsurprisingly, my father couldn't have cared enough to give me one of the more creative names among our people.

After double-checking that my bracelet was intact and my glamour was in place, I rose, turning away from the nearly naked corpse at my feet. I couldn't fail. Too much was at stake. Despite the fact I bore twenty-four kill marks on my arms, this was Griffin Silas—the ruthless and cunning Elemental prince. The man who ignited the war between our two races nine years ago by infiltrating the King's Palace and murdering many of our top Kinetic warriors. He blamed the Kinetics for the deaths of his parents. In his quest for misguided retribution, he sparked a war that led to the demise of modern society only a few years later, known to everyone as Devolution Day.

The most notable death on the day of his insurgence was our legendary Chrome Freyr. He was the only person with at least twice as many Elemental kill marks than me. He had been considered infallible. Our beloved hero's death was almost enough to declare war.

Many Kinetic assassins have tried and failed to kill Griffin, all falling prey to the same fate: death. Now, it was my turn. It wasn't solely vengeance I sought. If I killed Griffin, maybe, just maybe, I could earn my father's respect.

The king's parting words echoed in my mind as I cut through the field, getting used to the feel of the loose military fatigues instead of the tight black leather. *"If you return and he is not dead, there will be consequences of the likes to which you've yet to experience, child."*

Memories of the ricocheting pain in my skull from his fists had a knot forming in my stomach. I hated him. And I hated that I wanted to make him proud. But for now, we shared a common goal: Griffin's death.

I couldn't fail.

Mounted in its ironic glory before me stood a wooden cross in an abandoned farm field, marking an underground bar. I observed the hand-crafted structure and the ground it sat in, reminding me of the days when cars worked, and crosses signified the crash site of a loved one.

Rounding the bereft cross, I stood off to the side, careful not to stand on the door. I pushed it several feet to the right, watching as the earth opened beneath me, revealing a set of wooden stairs.

Leading up to the world's collapse, during the height of the Elemental and Kinetic war, humans went into prep mode, bracing for the apocalypse they had long since feared.

Underground homes and bartering businesses were constructed. But the most common were the speakeasies, where the humans gathered to drink moonshine and unwind.

They also were told to be Griffin's favorite haunts.

I descended a few of the warped steps into the tight vertical tunnel. It left me in a dank void. The wooden stairs were attached to the somehow sturdy concrete walls.

Thankfully, with our heightened vision, I could see through the pitch-blackness. Not even the magnetic magic-inhibiting bracelet could suppress that trait.

The makeshift stairwell dropped at least twenty-five feet into the earth, the air growing thicker the further down I went, with the musty scent of Georgia red clay permeating the confined space. Once I landed at the bottom, ventilated air from the pipe system the humans had built filled my lungs.

Muffled laughter and raucous voices sounded from the other side of the wall. I followed the tunnel leading to the speakeasy's entrance.

Reaching the end of the tunnel, I pulled open the thick, weighty door made of unpolished wood. The speakeasy held an old rustic vibe reminiscent of the 1920s. With no electricity due to the powerful EMP strike five years ago on Devolution Day, candles and lanterns provided the light source. It was what I imagined an old pirate tavern would have looked like.

I searched for my formidable target through the mass of men and women crowded around makeshift tables, gathering in a jovial nature that I envied. The humans were in high spirits tonight as they decompressed from life topside.

My attention landed on a man in tattered jeans and a grungy tee playing an upbeat pop song on a beaten guitar before catching on a cloaked figure sitting in a rear corner. His back was to me, facing the wooden barrels that lined the backside of the U-shaped bar. Cases upon cases of colorful moonshine in glass jars lined the stone wall on wooden crates.

Most of the patrons in the establishment were disheveled like the guitar player. But standing out amongst the unkempt, militia rebels could be seen mingling with the rest, dressed in faded and stained military fatigues.

Blending in as a rebel, I walked to the bar toward the back of the speakeasy, squeezing past drunken couples before raising a casual hand to snag the runner's attention. From the opposite end of the bar, he acknowledged me with an upward tilt of his head, making his way toward me. He tossed a dingy rag over his shoulder and wiped the sweat from his brow with his arm. "How can I help ya?"

Leaning on the unlacquered bartop with my forearms, I smiled. "Whatever you got."

The speakeasy runner didn't try to hide his roaming eyes. I wasn't sure how he could check out a woman in this baggy uniform, but he seemed pleased with what he saw. He nodded, walked to the crates nailed into the wall, and reached up, grabbing a glass jar filled with blue moonshine.

When he returned, he set it down and sighed. Scratching his thick beard, he asked, "I hate to do this, but what's the trade, darlin'?"

Summoning my inner femininity, I shook my head and waved him off. "Oh, of course." I pulled the loaded magazine clip and pistol from the holster at my waist. "Will this do?"

The speakeasy runner's eyes widened. "That's a hefty price for some 'shine. The magazine will do just fine, sweetheart." Having no use for a fucking gun, I shook my head. "No, I insist. It's the least I can do," I said innocently, sliding the pistol and clip across the bar. "I can always get another one at the compound," I said with a shrug.

The runner looked skeptical, but he relented. "I owe you another drink then." As tempting as that was, I declined. My only aim here was to find Griffin and kill him, not get lit off moonshine. "Just one is fine. Thank you, though...um, I don't think I caught your name?" I replied with a forced aura of flirtation.

"Jensen." He held out his hand and offered a smile.

I closed my fingers over his rough palm. He gave it a gentle squeeze. "This place yours?"

With a nod, he answered, "It is. My parents had it built before Devolution Day. When they died, it became mine." Jensen busied himself behind the bar, putting away the gun and magazine clip underneath the counter. In this world, humans could never have too many weapons.

"I'm sorry about your parents," I said, studying my laced fingers on the bar before pulling back and taking a sip of my drink. The alcohol content was strong enough to make one breathe fire.

Jensen shrugged. "It happened on Devolution Day. They were on a flight."

"Fuck," I whispered over the rim of my Mason jar before taking another sip. I'd grown accustomed to the harsh burn the past five years, seeing as there wasn't much variety in alcoholic drinks these days.

After Devolution Day, bootleg moonshiners created a booming business for themselves. They thrived in their trade as well as the farmers. While beer and other liquors were made, moonshine became the most prominent alcoholic drink in our post-modern era.

Jensen wiped down the bar and met my eyes. "Let me know if you need anything, ya hear?"

I nodded. "Thanks, Jensen. See you around." With a small smile, I pushed away from the bar, taking my drink with me and weaving through the crowd in the direction of the man cloaked in darkness in the corner.

Griffin.

As an assassin, I could be swift, discreet—in and out before anyone knew they had a dead body in the speakeasy and pieced together that I was the culprit. The majority of humans tended to their business anyway, paying me no mind as I pushed through.

The cold glass in my hand would be in the way; I knew I needed to ditch it. I got it solely to maintain the façade I was part of the human militia. I couldn't afford a misstep that would make me stand out in a negative way. Hopefully, getting rid of it wouldn't raise any suspicion.

A man sitting on a tall wooden barrel eyed me as I approached. I stopped at the table and mustered a genuine smile, offering the strong drink to him. "I'm not feeling too great. You want this?" I asked, channeling that nauseating feminine charm to produce a sweet smile.

With a suspicious furrow of his brow, he studied the drink. "What's the trade?"

"No trade. I just don't want it. Can't bring myself to waste it either."

After giving it a sniff, contemplating whether it was contaminated, he must've decided the risk was worth it because he eventually shrugged and held his hand out. I gave the Mason jar to him with a nod, to which he returned, and set my sights back on the lone figure in the corner.

After tailing him for three weeks, I could identify him anywhere, especially as he stood out in the room of unkempt humans in his black pixie-style cloak. Even relaxed and slouched over the table, he still held a swagger in his shoulders that showed he wasn't concerned about being surrounded by militia members.

Maneuvering around another couple, I eased my boots along the planked floor as I came within inches from Griffin's lean back. The black hood draped over his raven locks, only a few strands dangling around his jawline. He tilted his head back to take a sip of his drink. I was astounded by his arrogance.

I seized the chance to take advantage of his exposed throat. Slipping a knife from my sleeve, I quickly wrapped my left arm around his shoulder from behind, pressing the blade against his trachea. Griffin Silas's throat bobbed. I pushed harder.

Not seeming bothered by the threat, he angled his head to look over his right shoulder. As he met my eyes, a thin trail of blood slid down his throat. My breath hitched at the unexpected beauty of the merciless killer in my grasp. I'd seen plenty of photos of the prince taken prior to Devolution Day as he became the most wanted being in living history. But he'd been younger, and seeing him this close, with his Elemental gilded skin that reflected the warm glow in the speakeasy, I hesitated.

Holy shit, he was fucking ethereal.

I stood captivated by his beauty and stunned by a familiarity emanating from him like an itch I couldn't scratch that went deeper than simply recognizing his face. Silver irises that swirled like molten metal gave him a sense of *other*, drawing me in. The gold was deceptively beautiful, meant to lure you in before the Elemental depleted your soul's energy. That was my theory, anyway.

An excited gleam sparkled in his abnormal eyes, an unhinged grin accompanying it. "Come on out, little savage," he said in a husky baritone. "I wanna see you play."

I snapped out of my initial shock, poised to slice a deep line across his throat. Lighting fast, his hand shot out and gripped my gloved wrist, stopping me. "Princess Gray," he drawled. "I've been wondering when you'd make your move."

Cold fear seized me as its hostage. "You've known I've been following you?"

Griffin laughed, showcasing his straight, white teeth. "I've quite enjoyed your distant company." With a jolt, he pivoted out of the chair so fast it knocked over, then shoved my back against the wall. Pressing his front against mine with his knee between my thighs, he pinned my hands to the wall above me, the knife still clutched in my fist.

Griffin leaned in to where his breath caressed the shell of my ear and whispered, "I thought you wanted to play, little princess."

My heart felt like it wanted to beat out my chest. "Fuck you."

"Mmm…" he groaned, the sound reverberating through my bones. Without touching me, his nose traced down my neck, the warmth from his breath sending tingles down my spine.

I wished I could access my magic. Its electric nature crackled in my veins, begging me to set it free. A small zap to his hands would be enough to give me the space I needed to fight back, but within the tight confines of a speakeasy, any indication that I wasn't human would spell disaster of epic proportions. Most humans blamed the magical species for ruining their world, so giving them a reason to attack me in their domain wasn't wise. Which begged the question, *why wasn't Griffin glamouring his Elemental traits?*

I needed to give myself some time to think.

"So," I said breathlessly. "Was your misplaced vendetta for your parents' death worth the destruction of our world?"

"Who says I'm the one responsible?"

"Literally everybody."

"Define 'everybody.' Because if that involves your father, it doesn't count." When I didn't say anything, he continued, "Let me guess. Consensus is that I killed your boyfriend, too?"

White flames burned away the icy fear at the mention of Slate's murder. "Don't fucking talk about him."

Griffin chuckled. "I'm just going off the rumor mill, little princess."

"So, you're claiming you didn't kill him?"

"I'm saying it's a high possibility. Can't be sure."

Liar.

I'd been so caught up in the conversation with Griffin that I hadn't noticed when silence fell over the speakeasy. With a glance over his shoulder, I saw every human glaring in our direction. Rebels had their guns drawn and aimed at us. Griffin seemed unphased.

"Well, this has been fun, Princess, but I'm afraid it's time we finally part ways." With a speed I didn't know was possible, he snatched my knife without the use of his hands, and a millisecond later, the knife was lodged in my thigh. He stepped back, and my knee crashed against the hard floor, sending another sharp pain through my leg.

Almost immediately, the wound began to burn where the blade touched, the singe increasing with each breath.

That shouldn't be happening.

"See ya around, Gray." With a wink, he spun and strolled with a self-assured air through the speakeasy, calling out to the humans who were three seconds away from removing my head, "Let her go free. She's *mine.*"

My only thought aside from the pain was, *why would the humans listen to him? He's supposed to be their enemy.*

I dropped my backpack on the floor of the empty train car, ignoring the loud echo that made my head throb. Ran by Kinetics and our energetic magic, freight trains were the most efficient mode of transportation since Devolution Day, saving me days of trekking back to Atlanta. At the rate my wound was healing—or *wasn't*—I didn't think I'd make it.

Kinetic blades were meant to poison Elementals. The imbued black crystal within the blade was lethal to them if strong enough, while the redfern infused in Elemental blades served as the equivalent to Kinetics. We didn't train with Kinetic blades, as we didn't want to risk our resources by wasting them on ourselves.

A wooden bench that sat jammed against the rusted aluminum wall called to me. I crawled onto it, lying on my back. The tourniquet I'd fashioned for the wound was drenched in blood, prompting my head to swim. I bit my lower lip as the burning sensation in my thigh slowly radiated throughout my body. The half-mile walk to the nearest train station had done me no favors.

I lost him. I failed. And I wanted to vomit either from the pain or the shame of my shortcomings. Maybe both; I couldn't be sure.

This failure only gave those in the Kinetic court more of a reason to disparage me. I could only assume they'd flaunt their disapproval at my annual birthday revel tomorrow night. This was the perfect ammunition for my father and Amethyst—spinning more lies to keep me separate from the others.

The burning pain in my organs intensified as my limbs began to numb. My vision tunneled as I fought the impending blackout indicated by the ringing in my ears. It was a relentless pain unlike anything I'd ever felt before.

Was I dying?

As the blackness snatched me under, I willingly fell into its depths, weary from the fight.

At the least, I proved my father right in one regard. I lived to disappoint.

Chapter 2

GRIFFIN

The roar of the train was loud enough to almost silence the fucking voice in my head. Almost.

Kill her.

She's a threat.

Take what's ours.

I did my best to ignore it as I paced back and forth in the train car, trying to outrun the restlessness pulsing through my body, begging me to act—to kill the Kinetic Princess in the train car next to me.

That fucking magic of hers.

Mm, so strong.

She's a threat.

At least, that's what *he* kept telling me. I wished to fuck it was anyone else's voice.

Shaking my hands at my sides, I continued to pace.

It could all be yours. The whole world at your feet, Prince.

My head wasn't big enough for the two of us. I shook it from side to side as a feral growl erupted from my chest. When the attempt to expel the voice from my mind didn't work, I shoved my hands in my hair and yanked at the roots. As if I could remove this shit from my brain by pulling it out by the strands. I knew better. This...*affliction* had been with me long enough to know that the only reprieve I got was temporary at best.

Kill.

Kill.

Kill.

A mantra on repeat. A war drum of impending death that had me disgusted yet exhilarated. These days, it was getting harder to tell which thoughts were actually mine and what came from the affliction. It didn't help that my memories were being erased with each passing day, taking the man I once was with it. Not that I'd been all that honorable before...

But right now, *he* was louder and chattier than usual—worked up over the girl. A girl who was most peculiar. If I didn't need her alive, I'd have left her to die in the speakeasy.

The little assassin thought she'd been discreet in following me for the past three weeks. She had no clue about the monster she'd been tailing. I'd felt her...and not the energy of her aura. No, no. I felt *her*. In ways I didn't usually feel others.

Familiar. That ice-blonde hair was so damn familiar. I couldn't tell if I wanted to fist it for a fuck or beat it into a wall. But I knew I'd seen that hair.

The strangest thing about her was the fact that *he* started to clear out of my head whenever I was near her. It was part of the reason I hadn't made a move against her until tonight. I wanted to savor what little peace I could manage while I was able to, without consuming any substances or drinking obscene amounts of moonshine. But time was running out, and I needed to force her hand.

I could've taken her after I gifted her thigh one of her blades, but I needed to get my shit together before I did. Had I taken her, I would've killed her. And then the plan would be dead. Dead. Dead. Dead. Just like...

I screamed, slamming my fist into the wall at the vision of honey-colored eyes and a beaming smile flashing in my mind's eye.

Don't forget what's at stake. What they took from you.

"I don't need your shitty reminders!" My voice, vicious and deep, boomed off the aluminum walls as I rammed my fist into the deep ridges again and again. I stood stiff and heaving, wanting to hit something else. The gaping dents showed me just how much control I'd lost. There had been a time I could've knocked a hole in that wall with my bare fist in a single punch.

I could've fixed the wall, but I liked it better broken.

I glared at the almost holes in the wall before me, ignoring the shattered knuckles in my fist. *Almost-hole. Almost whole.* Like me. How poetic.

Physical pain, I'd take. It was my companion. If I thought it'd work, I'd trade physical agony for eternity over the fracturing of my mind any day.

All that work I'd done on myself. Gone. For nothing.

I wasn't sure how much longer I could hide it from everyone. It had to be until Forest was dead and the Kinetics no longer controlled the fate of this world. I could let the cards fall as they may after that. But until then, I had to keep it together.

As if it personally wronged me, I remained glaring at the wall. But then I felt her. A vibration tugged on my heart, followed by a sense of unbridled fear crashing into my chest. The feeling clawed deeper into my mind, knocking me back several steps. Like a tether, it yanked me to the wall. I felt her giving up.

She was dying.

No, not yet, little assassin.

Not till you've served my purposes.

Her fear was waning, and in its place came resignation—the hope of freedom. *No.*

Well, shit. So much for not alerting the conductor of my presence. The energetic signature my magic emitted would be a beacon. Cursing my shaking hands, it seemed to take a fucking eternity to unclasp the black bracelet suppressing my Elemental magic. I basked in the sensation of feeling solid and grounded in the brief moments when my magic returned. Reaching out a hand, I felt for the metal and worked it to my will, blasting out the ceiling of the container above me.

Wind from the high speed of the train rushed me. Cold. Cold like my insides. Like my blood. Like my soul.

Using my magic, I forced dents big enough to form hand and footholds for me to climb to the top. The action helped ease the anxiousness surging through me, putting my body to use instead of leaving my thoughts alone with *him*. Scaling my way upward, I pulled myself onto the thin edge and rose with careful balance against the wind's onslaught.

Damn, I wish I were an air elemental right about now.

The prospect of being thrown to my death didn't scare me. A part of me longed to be put out of my misery, but I had important shit to accomplish first—starting with saving the little assassin princess against all temptation to snuff out her vibrant life force.

I tight-walked the thin edge of the moving train car, then leaped to the metal box ahead. Dropping into a crouch, I removed my dagger and stabbed it into the metal. I called on my element to weaken the material, making it easier to carve a circular hole large enough to accommodate my frame. Falling through the gap, aluminum clanked against the floor before I dropped in behind it.

I silenced my landing, immediately spotting the unconscious princess sprawled on the makeshift bench against the wall, the pain from the poisoned blade bringing her to the brink of death. My heightened eyesight could see through the darkness enough to spot the ghastly pale hue painting her tanned complexion. Her chest rose and fell in shallow and uneven breaths with a pinched expression of pain on her face.

Kill her.

I squeezed my eyes shut, doing my best to fight the urge to slice open her throat. Gods, it was so strong. Yet, a part of me felt repulsed by the idea. I didn't know which one was true. I ignored them both and focused on the task at hand.

Reaching into one of my pants pockets, I retrieved a syringe, holding it up to the faint sliver of light streaming in through the hole I'd created above me. The vial was full.

I took measured steps toward the assassin, allowing myself to be guided to her waning life force. Each step brought an emotional strike to my chest, one I felt I should know the cause of, but couldn't for the life of me remember.

She's a threat to everything. Must die.

"Shut the fuck up," I murmured to the quiet darkness as I knelt beside her.

She was beautiful. In a hardened and lethal kind of way, but she had a vulnerability to her that I could tell she worked to hide. A little warrior. Too bad she had to die eventually.

Taking the syringe in my right hand, I brushed aside the stray hair that had fallen loose around her neck. The moment my skin made contact with hers, I was bombarded with...*peace*. The inner turmoil that raged within me at all hours melted away. The voice silenced. A flashback hit me of a little girl in her school uniform with iced-blonde strands, lying in the fetal position on the playground as all the other kids fled from her.

I gasped, snatching my hand away from her like it was a searing burn. It was a memory I didn't remember.

What the fuck was that? The normalcy of my fractured mind and soul returned at the loss of contact.

She's a threat. Kill her! Kill her, now!

No. She was a threat to *him*, somehow, which piqued my interest in her more. I didn't trust myself to do something I wouldn't regret if I sat there and pondered what had just happened. Before I could overthink things, I took the syringe, jammed it into the frenetic vein that clung to life on her neck, and emptied its contents into her bloodstream.

Rocking back on my heels, I shoved the emptied vial into a pocket before rising to my feet, already missing what momentary reprieve I'd experienced. Because now, the affliction was coming back at me tenfold, and I needed to get off the train before I killed my only chance of hope.

I forced myself away from the girl, angling toward the sliding door of the train car. The need to take, take, and take gouged deep cuts into my mind. Pushing it open just enough for me to fit through, I jumped to the gravel below. It was time to hunt for a Kinetic to take from this world while I waited for my next run-in with the princess.

Chapter 3

GRAY

"Nobody else knows about this, Forest." An exasperated sigh followed. "I mean, did you expect anything different from her?"

I awoke in my bed. Anxiety seized control of my chest with a vicious hold. Amethyst Freyr's refined tone rang throughout the King's Quarters—my father's personal suite that made up the entire top floor. The luxury hotel housed the Kinetics in this region, or what we called a domain. He gifted me my own suite within the King's Quarters once I'd turned twenty-one. It was just enough space to afford me privacy, but close enough for him to keep a watchful eye on me.

So many questions raced through my mind.

How did I end up here? How am I alive?

I cringed, remembering the burning pain that had seared my insides. How I'd healed was beyond me. My body shouldn't have reacted the way it did to the Kinetic blade. As a Kinetic, our bodies didn't respond to the black-crystal infused in the blades that were meant to harm Elementals—it should've been just a typical stab wound for me.

The innate healing abilities of both races should've healed the injury within seconds of the knife's removal. That left me with even more questions: who'd healed me? And how? Maybe Hazel or Scarlett knew something.

I expected a brutal punishment. It would be long and tortuous, as always. Most likely, my father would take liberties to create his own form of art on my body with different types of blades, but I knew I'd be getting off easy if that were the case. My father's previous warning promised the worst if I failed my mission.

The weaker part of me wished I was already dead.

I needed my sketchpad and pencils to draw Griffin's face, wanting to commit to memory the details of the man I'd failed to kill—a reminder to keep the fuel alive regardless of the outcome of my father's retribution.

Their voices grew louder outside my bedroom door, halting me from grabbing the pad from my nightstand. Drawing was the one thing I had my father couldn't control, so I'd kept it to myself. I squeezed my eyes shut and pulled in a deep breath to brace for the inevitable. There was no escaping the impending confrontation.

I eyed the cream-colored double doors as they swung open and banged into the wainscoting, rattling the walls. I fought the urge to flinch as King Forest stalked into the room with an energy dipped in malice. Amethyst sauntered close behind him with her dark grace and deceptive beauty.

My father appeared aged in his late thirties. He was much older, but Kinetics and Elementals could slow their aging process at whatever age they chose. We had much longer lifespans than humans–extending for almost two centuries–so most of us looked forever youthful.

The rich green of my father's beard flinched with a tick of his jaw. His immaculate dark suit was pressed to perfection as he glared at me from the doorway. My stomach roiled. That look was murderous.

I cocked an eyebrow at the verdant-haired king before tilting my head to take in Amethyst, my father's Hand and mother of the late-Chrome Freyr. Her face held a bored expression. Pulled into a pin-straight ponytail, her deep violet hair stood in stark contrast to my father's forest-green coif.

"You failed." The king's authoritative baritone sunk into my chest.

"I'm alive, aren't I?" I remarked with a shrug, followed by a smirk, refusing to show the inner turmoil within me. "You're welcome."

Depthless brown eyes zeroed in on me. "It appears you don't seem to think consequences apply to you, daughter." He turned his gaze to his hand as he rotated the thick silver on his ring finger. "I should've known you were incapable of following simple instructions. You prove time and again how inept you are." Spinning the ring on his finger with a casual twist, he went on, "*Kill him,* child. That was the order. Or did you miss that part?" He looked up from his ring to pin me to the bed with the weight of his disgust. "I suppose being Slate's murderer wasn't enough motivation?"

I sighed. "If you had such little confidence in me, then why even bother sending me on that mission in the first place?" I leveled him with a flat expression while my palms ached from the sharp sting of my nails.

Amethyst stepped forward to join his side and cleared her throat. Her dark plum lips pursed in thought as she arched a single, sharp eyebrow. She snatched her gaze from my closet door, appraising my weakened state with the tilt of her lip and a smug grin. "We had hoped you'd be able to step up this time with the right motivation, but I suppose no one will ever be able to live up to my Chrome's accomplishments." She sniffled and cast her head to the side in feigned sadness.

I rolled my eyes at her display. Her son's death had always been her trump card, helping her garner sympathy from our people to mask her wicked personality. The low-cut, A-line plum dress exposed her shoulders and arms, showcasing her wild, red currents. She tapped a claw-like nail against her crossed arm as she pretended to gather her emotions.

Despite living in the same space for fourteen years before his death, I'd never met Chrome—much to my dismay. He was a legend and the best warrior in recent history. I had wanted to learn from him. I'd suggested to my father once that it would be a great idea for us to train together. His response was prolonged agony, ensuring I never questioned that he knew what was best for me again.

Opulent earrings dangled from Amethyst's ears while she absentmindedly fiddled with the inlaid ruby. "But it's quite all right," she added, her tone perking up. "Tonight is your birthday revel. The least we can do is publicly honor our heir to the throne just this one night." Casting a sideways glance at the king, she elaborated, "Before she must deal with the repercussions for her failure at a later date." Her tone, dipped in poisoned honey, made my stomach churn. *So* fake.

Internally, I groaned at the prospect of the upcoming "celebration" for my twenty-fourth birthday.

My father angled his head to narrow his eyes at Amethyst. She smirked, dropping her hands to rest on her hips as the two Kinetic leaders fell into a silent form of communication. The dark suit the king wore accentuated his strong physical prowess while hiding his white currents.

Every Kinetic bore currents that glowed a different luminescent color. Each color represented the form of external energy based on the electromagnetic spectrum that their magic controlled. White—in the king's case—represented gamma rays, which he wielded as poisonous radiation, while Amethyst's red currents represented the power over the ultraviolet. My blue ones, however, meant I was supposed to wield the power of sound waves, but my magic didn't behave accordingly in the slightest. It was an enigma that just made me stand out more from my kind in ways I didn't want.

Women flocked to the charming looks and charisma of King Forest Monroe. They came and went from the King's Quarters multiple times a week, but Amethyst was never one of them. Her husband, Grim—as depraved as he was—seemed to satisfy her needs. I didn't care to find out what that entailed.

King Forest broke the silence and trained his attention on me. "Fine. But don't think for a second that this is settled, Gray. You have three hours to get ready for this evening. Don't fucking embarrass me."

Amethyst's stormy-blue eyes landed on me next. A devious grin pulled at the edges of her plum lips, a sinister promise hidden behind her sharp beauty. "Happy Birthday, Princess," she said with false admiration. "Let's hope it's a night you won't forget. You never know when it could be your last in your line of work."

I held her stare, challenging her to do her worst. "Oh, I assure you, Amethyst. I don't need your well wishes to enjoy myself."

Amethyst smirked once again before turning a knowing smile on my father. The sounds of her lethal stilettos trailed from my bedroom suite, easing the tension in my chest just a fraction.

King Forest remained behind, his hands shoved into the front pockets of his trousers in a casual display, exuding his overbearing energy. I held his stare, waiting for him to excuse himself from my presence. "Hazel will bring your dress. At least try to look like royalty and not a wild heathen. That includes fixing your hair," he said, crinkling his nose as he appraised my rugged state. "It looks like a pair of pterodactyls copulated and then fought to the death in there."

"Of course, Your Majesty." My voice was flat as I fought the urge to give him the middle finger...or a dagger to his chest.

"Wait!" I called out as he reached for the door. He paused, glancing over his shoulder. "What happened to me?"

The king's upper lip curled back as he directed his gaze on the spot where my knife had stabbed me. The silence threatened to crush me under the weight of his stare.

His voice held no emotion as he said, "You're weak. A defect."

Not giving me a chance to respond, he swept from the suite, leaving me feeling like the broken little girl I'd left behind years ago.

"Ugh, Hazel. I hate this thing. This is such horseshit," I said. "Leave it to heels to be the death trap that'll take my life." The stilettos were vicious, my feet and ankles already aching from the steep arch.

Hazel giggled as she pinned another strand of hair back from my face before taking a step back to observe my updo in its entirety.

I eyed my reflection in the floor-length mirror, noting the haltered gold dress that shimmered from the glinting light. All my curves were defined, and the olive beneath my tan complexion glowed in perfect contrast. The halter revealed my toned physique and the royal crest branded on the nape of my neck—a crescent moon fitted within a sun, the mark of the Monroe line—the ruling family of Kinetics dating back centuries.

"Oh, hush, Gray. It'd take much more than a stiletto to kill you," Hazel Helair said, chiding me as we readied for the revel.

Twenty-four small kill marks—a diagonal number two with a slash through its center—were branded vertically from my shoulder to elbow, marking the number of Elemental kills I'd made. Because our currents rejected tattoos, we used brands to showcase our body art. Whenever our currents passed through them, the raised skin lit up, creating a colorful display on our bodies.

The royalty brand lit up blue with my passing currents on my right biceps—a thick band lined with diamonds on the top and bottom encircling my arm, allowing every Kinetic to know my rank and power within our hierarchy. I wanted to cut it off.

Every Kinetic branded their family's crest to their body part of choice. They branded their position or rank on the right biceps while their accomplishments were on the left, such as my kill marks.

With a sigh, she slid a lock of her bronze, metallic hair behind her ear. "You know...if Slate was here, he wouldn't be able to resist you. He'd purposefully grope you in front of me just to make me want to vomit in the corner." A bemused eye-roll revealed she missed her brother's ridiculous antics.

I chuckled, turning my head to look out the window to peer at the decrepit Atlanta skyline, allowing those fond memories to taunt me.

When Slate Helair was alive, he made it his life's mission to build me up when everyone else tore me down. I was fourteen when he'd won my heart and instilled a sense of confidence that I had never been allowed to have. I could still hear his firm, but loving voice say, *"Princesses don't cower. Others cower at you. Never forget that, beautiful."*

"You know he's still here with you, right?" Hazel asked as her reassuring hand stroked my bare arm in a comforting gesture, sliding over my brands and currents. "He'd never leave your side, Gray. Not even death could pull him away from you. Let that give you the strength to get you through the revel, yeah?" Hazel rested her hand on my marked biceps, imparting a mixed expression of hope and despair. No doubt she still grieved his loss as well.

I nodded and studied the white carpet. The emotional void would engulf me if I stayed with my thoughts about Slate too long.

Shaking away the longing in my heart, I returned my gaze to my reflection. Hazel was right. No matter how most Kinetics showed me their disdain, her older brother would have stuck by my side and showed me off to the world with pride.

I double-checked my appearance one last time. The loose knot that held my hair displayed the marbled black and white strands. Shimmering gold eyeshadow painted my lids, enhanced by a smoky effect.

"You look dangerously beautiful. Now, let's go before you're late," Hazel said with a pointed look, knowing I would purposefully be late to my own revel to spite my father. It was her job to ensure that I wasn't.

I sagged my shoulders, poking out my bottom lip in the mirror at Hazel's reflection. "But that's boring, Hazel. Scarlett would agree with me."

Hazel rolled her eyes and shook her head, likely wondering why she had to be the responsible one between the three of us.

I turned away from the mirror to face her. "Oh!" My face lit up, remembering I had questions. "I meant to ask you—have you overheard anything from Amethyst about how I ended up back here?"

Hazel raised her brows and tilted her head. Soft green eyes peered at me in concern. "Not really. Amethyst has kept me on a short leash these past few weeks, only letting me in her office to deliver her daily schedules or to send me on errands." Irritation laced her tone toward her boss—who was also her aunt.

I found her disclosure odd. Amethyst always kept Hazel glued to her side, using her as a tape recorder and information manager. "Well, that's disturbingly out of the ordinary," I said, puzzled.

Hazel nodded, worry painting her soft porcelain features. She averted her gaze to the analogue clock with Roman numerals. "We should go before your father adds to your punishment."

I released an exasperated sigh, knowing she was right. A heavy weight sank to the bottom of my gut at the fast-approaching event. "Right," I said, conceding to my fate. "Let's get this over with."

Hazel trailed behind me as I walked to the double doors, adhering to royal protocol. Her calming presence was always welcome, and I basked in it as we cut through the sitting area. Reaching the threshold, I paused, hesitant to turn the handle, attempting to garner enough fortitude to face the night ahead of me.

"He's right here with you, Gray. Draw on your strength from knowing that," Hazel whispered over my shoulder.

I sucked in a deep breath, my nails digging into my palms, allowing the oxygen to wash away my fear. Large crowds gave me crippling anxiety. Perhaps it had something to do with the fact that they typically ostracized me. But these people would *never* see that side of me.

Chapter 4

GRIFFIN

"Name?" The bearded human standing at three times my width glared at me. With bulging biceps and a lifelessness in his eyes, I gathered he'd rather be in the ring than out here in charge of tonight's sign-up for the fights.

"Trevor. Former black ops," I lied, meeting his empty gaze with one of my own, shoving down my rage and hunger for death so I'd appear less feral.

The beefy man roamed his eyes down my body, a smirk tinting his expression. My body type didn't say "steroids," so apparently, that meant I was a lost cause. Going incognito was thrilling. I loved it when people underestimated me.

"Preference?" he asked.

"Kinetic."

"Alright, Trevor," he said and jotted my fake name and preference down on the sign-up sheet. He slipped me a piece of paper with the number forty-two marked on it. "Head to the back and get ready. They'll call your number when it's time."

Without a word, I took my leave and pushed past the man into the abandoned warehouse. The interior of the expansive space was dark, empty.

Dust and trash cluttered the area, but that was to be expected. I walked to the back and opened the metal door that led to the stairwell, descending the steps to the basement. Several floors beneath the earth, I allowed the voice to continue his death mantra, hyping me up for the fight to come.

The only ones I permitted myself to kill were Kinetics. Not that I had a vendetta against all of them, but I couldn't bring myself to kill humans. They'd suffered enough from the fallout of our war. And obviously, I couldn't kill my people. So, Kinetics sated the uncontrollable drive and hunger for now.

Finally, I reached the bottom of the stairwell and took in the scent of blood and dust. The place was grimy, and mold began to infest the walls and ceiling of the underground establishment. Unlike the speakeasies that held a sense of camaraderie and hope, this place was dank with death, despair, and hatred.

I just managed to catch this scorse before it moved on. Thankfully, a human rebel with ties to Hogan informed me at the last minute. Scorses were known for hosting the underbelly of humanity while trading every-day items, but this event was one of the darkest parts of it. Sergeant Hogan was the owner of this one, but even he had no say when these particular trades came through. He had even less of a say in whether to host them.

I beat on the door with my fist five times to the specific rhythm required to gain entry. One, two-three, four, long pause, five.

Kill.

Kill.

Kill.

The metal bar on the other side of the door screeched in protest as the human guard slid it back. A red-headed man with a gun casually poised in his fist met me on the other side. With a sneer, he appraised me with amusement like the beefy man at the front.

Gracing him with a grin I was sure appeared manic, I headed into the crowd of criminals. There was a bar off to the right. The temptation to grab a glass of moonshine called to me, but I pushed it away, not wanting to silence the darkness tonight.

Scantily clad women leered at me as I passed through the crowd, and too often, one of them attempted to seduce me with a swipe at my arms or shoulders. Some nights, it'd work with the hopes to expel this unrelenting madness. This time, however, I didn't need sex.

I caught a group of people snorting lines of white powder off of jagged mirrors. Another glimpse showed others nearby shoving needles in their arms and going slack in their seats. Their eyes rolled back into their heads from the euphoria. Women sat in men's laps with tight postures and haunted eyes. Slaves.

Okay, there were *some* humans I wouldn't mind killing. Slowly. Gruesomely. And in ways that made their torture tactics pale in comparison. The ones trading women and children in the sex trafficking circuits deserved me in my most depraved state.

Another surge of rage powered through me. Closing my hands into tight fists, I forced myself to walk past the degenerates, proceeding toward the back where the fight cages stood.

A deafening cheer went up in the crowd ahead. The prime-time cage sat in the center of the vast room, where the vilest of humanity watched with rapt attention, calling for blood—for death.

Silence quickly descended upon the crowd as bone crunched against bone. Nearing the cage, I caught a glimpse over the top of the crowd's heads. One shirtless man beat another to disfiguration. Blood coated the cement floor they fought on. The one on the losing end of the fight lay unconscious, his face swollen and glistening in his ruby life force. The one on top kept swinging, not stopping as he pummeled in desperation to finish the job.

The human trafficking portion of this new world saw value in Kinetics and Elementals. They'd capture them and restrict their magic, selling their kind into the circuit as slaves to fight these underground death matches—usually against humans.

Judging by the crowds' collective disgust, it appeared the Elemental won this fight.

I forced my way closer to the cage, hoping I'd recognize the Elemental slave. I didn't, but it wouldn't stop me from freeing him at the end of the night. Once the human was deemed dead, the Elemental dropped his head to his bare chest, bruises already forming on his skin. Remorse coated his expression as he despondently stared at his work.

The crowd came back to life, shouting jeers of hatred at the Elemental that claimed one of their own. They hadn't come to watch their fellow man die—they wanted to see Elemental or Kinetic blood.

A burly man made his way into the cage, snatching the Elemental to his feet. Drained, he swayed, unable to heal his wounds. Who knew how long he'd had his magic suppressed by the black bracelet on his wrist, weakening him further?

Another man, clad in black—gloves included—entered the cage and dragged the dead human out by his ankle, leaving a nasty blood trail in his wake. A voice came over the underground scorse, echoing off the cement walls. "Number forty-two. Take your place in the main cage."

Everywhere else in the world, with the exception of Kinetic Domains and Elemental Hollows who ran on magic, was void of electricity. These specific human activities functioned on rare solar-powered generators. It's bullshit how the innocent suffered the most.

Posing as a human, I walked toward the main cage. People studied me as I passed, gauging whether I stood a chance in the fight. It didn't matter what they thought—I wasn't here for their approval. I needed something. And the only way to get it was to win. I'd kill a Kinetic as a bonus while feeding this unhinged affliction within me.

I was a fucking time bomb. And all it really took at this point was for someone to touch or look at me in the wrong way, and I'd go off. This fight was a necessity in more ways than one.

With each step I took, the darkness hyped me with promises of violence, retribution, and death. Promises to take, take, take. Kill, kill, kill.

Humans parted for me, shifting out of my path as I neared the cage, like they sensed something wasn't quite right with me. If only they knew the truth about who they allowed to walk amongst them.

Climbing the cinder block steps, I ascended into the prime-time cage. Someone finished cleaning the pool of blood from the previous fight, leaving the ring as I entered. Like the last two men, I would be shirtless. It was a requirement in these venues to ensure there was no cheating or disguised Elementals or Kinetics amongst the humans—like me.

Before I'd entered the abandoned warehouse, I'd had to get creative with my magic-suppressing bracelet. Contact with skin was required to hide the physical traits and shut down our magic. My gilded skin and swirling silver irises would be a dead giveaway. I simply strapped it to my thigh beneath my pants with a scrap from a discarded weapons belt. Easy.

The cage was empty, so I picked a corner with a chair, stripped until my torso was bare, and began stretching. The tattoos marking my neck, arms, and chest were a mixture of Elemental sigils and normal human tattoos I had gotten a few years back. Thankfully, the bracelet hid the sigils and left the ink tattoos visible.

I wasn't nervous—not even a little. Bending to one side, my hamstrings strained before I stood up and pulled my arm across my chest, feeling my back and shoulder muscles loosen. Curious chatter of "the new guy in the cage" echoed throughout the crowd. If only they knew.

The darkness ratcheted up tenfold the longer I waited, crying out for blood and death. The affliction's bloodlust needed the tension. *I* needed the release. The anxious energy had me bouncing on my feet impatiently.

Too lost in my headspace, I didn't notice the huge Kinetic slave brought into the cage. Must've been a captured warrior. Good. More of a challenge.

"Ladies and gents!" the male voice speaking over the loudspeaker announced theatrically. "Prepare yourselves for a match between disgraced Kinetic Warrior, Matte, and ex-black ops, Trevor!"

I wasn't sure how much longer I could hold off the intensity buzzing through me.

Kill.

Kill.

Kill.

Finally, a whistle screeched, signaling the start. We squared up our bare chests and fists. This Kinetic appeared familiar, but I didn't recognize him. He, however, looked horrified, judging by the paleness of his skin and widened eyes. He knew exactly who I was.

With his fists blocking his face in its defensive stance, he asked, "How?"

I shrugged. "I have my ways." Then I jabbed him four quick times in his ribs, making him back up before I threw a kick to his thigh.

Matte grunted but soon recovered. He went on the offensive, striking for my jaw as a misdirection to land a blow in my gut, which he did. The air knocked from my lungs, but I smiled anyway.

Lunging at Matte, I jumped at an angle, dropping my shoulders to where my body inverted. Locking my ankles around his neck, I twisted, snatching him to the ground as I rotated and caught myself on my hands.

I quickly scrambled to pull him in an ironclad chokehold. He was pinned, almost to the point of passing out. But while I held him down and blocked his airflow from the side, I jammed my knee wherever it would strike. Just before he lost consciousness, I let him go and shot to my feet. Lightning-quick, I straddled his chest and began punching his face, feeling the darkness take the first real drop of blood to feed its frenzy.

I didn't stop. Matte tried to fight back, but it was no use. I had him, and I was rabid. Each drop of blood made me want more, more, more.

Take. Take. Take. Fucking take it all!

I tried. I wanted to paint a beautiful scarlet picture of Kinetic death on this floor. I wanted him suffering. Whimpering. Screaming. It was music to my fucking ears. I needed...I needed...

I didn't know how much time had passed as I wailed on the face of Matte's corpse. I only came back to myself when I was hauled off his body. He was no longer recognizable. Mutilated.

And I smiled at the sight, feeling like a possessed madman. I could imagine how garish I appeared. My black hair clashed with the bright blood smearing my face and upper body. I absorbed the fervor, the rage, not one shred of guilt for the Kinetic death at my feet.

Contentment.

The darkness lifted enough to offer a slight reprieve. Although the hunger and rage still hung heavy over my soul, I could form deeper thoughts aside from the "Take. Take. Take" mantra. It'd never be fully satisfied, but at least it wasn't suffocating me at this point.

Standing in the trading booths deeper within the compound, a woman with skin as pale as snow gazed up at me from the table she manned. Sensual hunger gleamed in her eyes as she roamed over my savage appearance. Sex was another form of currency in these parts. "Congrats. Wanna celebrate in a bit?" she asked before flashing a knowing smile.

I licked my lips and cocked my head to the side. "As tempting as the offer is, I need to be on my way."

She visibly pouted and slumped in her seat. "Are you sure? We can make it quick..."

I leaned over and stroked the backs of my knuckles down the creamy skin of her cheek, "I can promise you, I wouldn't be quick," I whispered.

Her breath caught and her eyes glazed with desire, but I only offered her a small smile before pulling away. "I'm here to collect my reward for the win. And then I gotta go." But not before I freed the Elemental that'd won earlier.

The woman seemed to shake herself from her lustful state and cleared her throat. "Right. What is it you want?"

"Cocaine and chloroform," I said, thinking of the princess that would surely give me hell when I moved to take her.

Chapter 5

GRAY

The ballroom doors swung open upon my arrival. The Royal Domain's Supreme Trainer, Smokey Valor, greeted me at the threshold, standing rigid and astute. Beyond his stern exterior, I swore there was a hint of regret looming in the depths of his eyes. Hazel drifted close by, offering the comfort I needed to make it through the suffocating speech that I was forced to endure.

"Happy Birthday, Princess Gray," Smokey said with a respectful bow. His smoke-gray hair was cropped short on the sides, and he was dressed in his guild finery that blocked his blue currents. I met his deep brown eyes that were continuously haunted by grief. He didn't look a day over thirty-five.

I fought to breathe but I managed enough inhales to stay on my feet. A set of invisible chains squeezed my chest, growing tighter with each pair of eyes, threatening to shatter my bones.

Upon my entrance, silence swept across the elaborate ballroom. White marble walls shone with pristine beauty, and lavish crystal chandeliers draped high and low from an arched ceiling that depicted fresco paintings of reveling and feasting Kinetics.

A posh bar spanned an entire wall, beckoning me with an endless supply of moonshine. I planned to plant myself there for the night, eventually. The reprieve only alcohol could provide would be my saving grace.

The polished black floor glittered with a majestic radiance. Draped, floor-to-ceiling blue and gray tapestries depicting the Monroe royal crest were spaced with precision along the far wall, blocking the windows that overlooked the abandoned city. Baroque candelabras cast an eerie glow against the white walls that bled black veins.

In unison, all the Kinetics dropped to one knee and bowed their heads. I hated it; I hated how the lack of sincerity was clear in many of their tight postures. Not *everyone* was full of disdain. Those that weren't scrutinizing me cast pitying gazes. Yet, they feared the king's reproach if they got too close or acknowledged how fucked up my entire situation was. My father had worked hard to successfully isolate me from our people, and he'd succeeded.

A white raised dais loomed ahead of me, flanked on either side by an orchestral band. King Forest's embellished throne perched atop it, primed to cradle his oversized ego.

I straightened my back and tilted my chin upward. My teeth felt like they'd shatter from my clenched jaw. Surveying the people who knelt before me, I avoided eye contact with any of them.

I felt like an intruder in my own home as the tang of bitter resentment combined with hopeless pity cascaded off them, promising to swallow me whole.

I offered a faint smile to the supreme trainer in thanks. Smokey Valor wasn't the warmest of Kinetics, but he'd never been outwardly disrespectful toward me. Being the top-ranked trainer, my father had delegated him to oversee my training during my teen years to prepare me as an assassin. He was a warrior at heart, honorable but not the most personable. I could relate.

With the shocking disappearance of his only son, Onyx, several years before, his stiff demeanor took a dark turn. No one knew what had happened to the well-respected son of the supreme trainer, but we grieved his loss all the same, accepting that death claimed him. The loss turned Smokey into a shell of the valiant man he once was. I couldn't fathom the sort of grief that accompanied a missing child, so I regarded Smokey with a softness I didn't lend to others.

Revelers parted a pathway in unison, so the blue runner rug guided me to the dais. I feigned impassiveness as I glided past each disdainful face. Maintaining the pompous air I'd perfected over the years, I dared anyone to challenge me. My upper lip curled into a subtle snarl, showing my distaste for them in return.

Those that believed my father and Amethyst's lies didn't like me—yet they wouldn't outwardly fuck with me, either. Not anymore, at least. Nearly every day for the past two years, many tried proving to our people that I was a fraud and not worthy as their princess. Emboldened by my father's unsupportive behavior, some cowards would jump me in groups or ambush me when I was alone. But after I brought enough of them close to death's door and left them disfigured or disabled, they'd left me alone. In the end, I didn't "prove" anything except that I wanted my people dead—according to the rumors. It became the widespread belief that I was the one initiating the fights as lies deepened their distrust

Naturally, each Kinetic I gravely injured only pissed off my father. My success in self-defense earned me brutal punishments for the public to witness. The king claimed it was all in the name of justice and to set the example that even royalty wasn't exempt from our laws. But he knew what message it sent. That he didn't stand with me.

I faced the crowd once I reached the dais. Hazel placed a simple, silver diadem on the crown of my head, as was the custom of Kinetic royalty. The live orchestral band waned from the slow, melodious tune that sounded my arrival, signaling everyone in the crowd to rise to their feet and bow as one.

King Forest stood to my left. His broad chest puffed out in glory and egotism. A smile curled at the edges as if he held in an inside joke that I wasn't privy to. Clad in a charcoal suit and a blood-red tie, he stood immaculately in front of his people. His notable forest-green hair and beard drew everyone's attention as he stood stalwart and proud. I forced a breath in. His captivating energy sucked all the oxygen from the room while he basked in the effect.

"Good evening, my *electrifying* Kinetics," Father's baritone voice boomed off the palatial walls. The crowd remained awestruck at their alluring and charismatic leader, gazing at him as if he were a hallucination. "Tonight, we gather for my beloved daughter's birthday revel to celebrate her twenty-four years of blessed life. She has devoted many of her short years to fighting for our kind with the *hope*," he said, letting the moment hang before he slid in the subtle insult, "to one day become your next outstanding leader in my steed." It seemed only I could pick out the imperceptible sarcasm.

I forced a smile at my father's duplicitous claims. My cheeks ached and trembled from the falsity of it.

Why he adopted me to only detest my existence remained an unsolved mystery.

The king enunciated the long pause before he continued. No one dared to breathe as they clung to his energy like they were his puppets, bending to his every whim. "Tonight," he resumed, relishing in the unified trance that swayed back and forth, as if enchanting his marionettes to life. "Princess Gray Monroe may not be of my blood, yet she is more than a biological daughter could ever be. She is willing to forfeit her life *every* time she steps beyond these walls in order to seek out Elementals and eradicate them." The king's bottomless mahogany eyes cut in my direction, a silent reminder of my recent shortcomings.

I remained standing like a hostage for sale on the chopping block.

One of the personal cooks in the King's Quarters rumored my father adopted me because he needed an heir. She'd explained how the love of his life died in childbirth, giving birth to a stillborn baby. He apparently loved her so much that he could never settle for another woman.

According to my father, my birth parents were murdered by a pair of Endarkened Elementals in their frenzied need to deplete their energetic life forces or auras. I was only an infant when the monstrous creatures attacked my parents. They hid me behind a dumpster, which spared my life, only to be found by Amethyst in the aftermath, providing my father with a solution to his childless predicament.

I held my father's pointed stare. The various hues of the burnt umber flecks contrasted against the darker, earthier shades of his irises as I studied him. So many secrets taunted me behind those eyes. Anger, concealed by a fireproof cloak, roared with fierce flames. Even from a distance, the heat from their intensity licked my skin.

The king dropped all pretenses as he bore the full weight of his authority upon me, determined to make me submit to his will as the silent tension deepened. Because it was custom, he wanted me to bow before him to our people. To cower. To show that I could be managed. Controlled. And if I didn't, his glare ensured I'd pay for it. But I wouldn't be swayed by him—never again, no matter how much pain he inflicted upon me.

I stood my ground, tilting my head back in defiance, anchoring my stilettos to the marble dais beneath my feet while refusing to bow. Instead, I gifted him a wicked grin, taunting him to do his worst.

His rich green beard pulsed with a life of its own as he clenched his jaw, unable to react in such a public and traditional forum. It'd tarnish his charming image. He broke the muted exchange to face the stunned crowd once again. The weight of the shocked silence was all-consuming. No one defied the king publicly.

I joined my father in gazing at the crowd, focusing my attention on the varying colors of the exposed currents. Red, purple, blue, white, orange, yellow, and green glowed and snaked up and down arms and necks. Although many of our people regarded me with disdain, I couldn't help but appreciate our unfounded beauty.

Subconsciously, I searched the crowd for a particular Kinetic with slate-colored hair and gold currents. My stomach sank just as fast as I woke up to the late realization that I wouldn't find Slate or his gold currents that represented his light magic. Longing and sadness settled in my chest as I wished he were here more than anything tonight.

In our natural form, our hair color stood to be a multitude of bizarre colors. At some point in our history, it became our custom to name our children based on the unusual hues. Most Kinetics bore monotone shades, but there were the rare exceptions. I was one of them with my black-and-white strands blended to appear gray. The crowd soon recovered from the shock of witnessing their king challenged as he droned on in a bloated speech. They once again became entranced as I fell hypnotized by the colorful currents charging the room.

"Let's revel!" my father said, snapping me from my dissociative state.

I wasn't sure how much time had passed. Only that my ankles and feet were locked up from the unhinged stilettos they forced me to wear. Taking a step, I hissed from the pain.

"Ay! Revel!" a cacophony of cheers chorused, echoing off the marble walls. As if we weren't living in post-apocalyptic times, everyone began shedding their propriety the moment the formalities ended.

I felt the heat of my father's glare upon my profile. Turning to face him, I found he'd already made for the direction of his throne on the dais. I moved to take my leave, but something stopped me mid-stride. Pivoting, I watched as the king lowered himself onto the throne with predatory grace, placing his electrified hands on the armrests—a vicious gleam glimmered in his dark eyes.

I spotted Hazel wedged between Amethyst and Forest. Her amber eyes locked with mine. The grave expression she gave me caused my heart to sink to the depths of my bowels. Her porcelain skin paled three shades lighter. Hazel knew something, but she was locked by their sides the entire night as Amethyst's assistant.

My fingernails dug into my palms. I surveyed the joyous revelers breaking off into groups, hoping to find anything suspicious. Nothing stood out that might cause alarm, but the alarm bells blared in my head, anyway.

Something was wrong.

At the King's Palace, danger was laced with opulence and hidden behind perfect smiles. The wolves were out tonight, and I was the hunted.

Chapter 6

GRAY

"Happy Birthday, Stoney!" A jarring punch to my biceps snatched me from paranoid thoughts, rolling my eyes at the play on my name.

"Scarlett," I greeted with faux disinterest. "You've lost your touch while I've been gone." I smirked at my ruby-haired friend, who looked every bit as fiery as her personality.

With a snort, she tossed her long, deep red ringlets over her shoulder. "I wouldn't be cocky about that if I were you. Golden's been teaching me some new techniques," she said with a flirtatious grin.

Scarlett Kittle was a male and female's fantasy. She stood tall with a deep tan, her green eyes stark against her long red tresses. The violet dress showcased her hourglass figure that slit from the ankle to her hip. She wore her confidence like a badge of honor, and I loved her for it.

"Ew. Thanks for making me nauseous," I muttered loud enough for her to hear. She deepened her smirk. "Speaking of nauseous," I said, eyeing her from my side, "where's the 'shine? I'm going to need it to get through this shit."

Scarlett chuckled, pointing to the bar at the back of the ballroom. "Let's cause a fucking scene, Stoney. It's your birthday, and you can cry if you want to. Or vomit on the throne. Either will do."

Against my better judgment, the idea of pissing off Forest and most of the Kinetic kind highly appealed to me. A smile crept up my cheeks as I envisioned the night's antics.

I felt the stares prodding me as we walked through the raucous crowd in our straight shot to the bar. Their gazes slithered over my body, threatening to penetrate the inner armor I'd constructed. The call for alcohol grew stronger.

Revels were a favored tradition amongst Kinetics. It was an excuse to dress up in formal attire and then party until our hearts combusted. Most times, they grew wild and lewd as the night progressed. I'd never been a fan of the duplicity.

The lighting dimmed, leaving behind a soft illumination from the candelabras, casting a sensual mood in the ballroom. Bodies writhed against one another to the gritty classical music. Bright colors from the currents added a multi-hued glow that emanated a club-like feel. Couples and throuples were only stopped by a layer of clothing from relishing each other's bodies. It wasn't fifteen minutes into the revel, and it was already quickly approaching pornographic.

Scarlett and I found ourselves lost in the mass of writhing bodies and heady energies during our trek to the bar. At the center of the dancefloor, Scarlett smacked her palm against a male's ass while he ground his pelvis against a woman with neon-green hair. He snapped his head around to look at Scarlett with lustful eyes. Dark, swarthy skin contrasted with fiery orange hair. The neon-haired female sent Scarlett a scathing look. I noticed the orange currents zipping up her arms and neck, indicating her infrared heat magic.

Shit. I grimaced, snatching Scarlett along to our destination.

We clawed our way through the gyrating bodies. The pulsating beat of tribal drums only increased the animalistic fervor with which they moved. I felt the rhythm in my bloodstream, beckoning me to get lost in the seductive madness. Surrendering my body to the melody is a freedom I was rarely afforded. I planned to make it happen tonight with the hopes of forgetting all the recent events and what was to come.

We reached the bar at last after forcing our way through an opening at the edge of the dancefloor. Our hands clasped one another's as our bodies were thrust against the bartop. Meeting each other's eyes, we burst into stomach-clenching laughter.

Scarlett and I weren't always friends. When I first began my training at age thirteen, she held the same misconceptions about me as the rest of our people. But one day, she stumbled across a private beating my father imparted upon me and realized how wrong she'd been. She took a few days to come to terms with what she'd witnessed and overheard. It had fucked up her reality and what she'd believed to be true. But with a heartfelt apology, we soon grew close during our training, making her my only friend for a few years until I met Slate and Hazel.

Scarlett's role as the Royal Domain Emissary required her to be highly trained in combat. She was as fierce as they came with a saucy attitude to match it. As emissary, she traveled the lands to different domains through-out the continent. It was dangerous. Especially during dark times, causing the emissary position to become the most replaced in recent years.

A poke nudged my ribs. "Look at Cardinal over there," she said, nodding in the direction of her older brother. Judging by the way he leaned into a man's ear, he worked to pick up a hot and beefy warrior with lavender-col-ored hair. Cardinal bore a close resemblance to Scarlett, his short-cropped hair only a shade lighter than hers. "I bet he strikes out," she laughed. "He can't stand that I pull more dick than him."

I shook my head and refaced the bar.

Scarlett slapped her hand on the bartop in quick succession to alert the bartender behind the counter. The pink-haired male looked up "Two apple pies, barkeep! We got a royal revel to blow up tonight. And you, kind sir, are going to be the detonator." Scarlett gave him her most wicked grin.

The bartender studied us with apprehension. I watched him gauge the risk of punishment if he indulged in our plans of debauchery. Analyzing him, I searched for any cracks to exploit, refusing to be deterred from my night of fun. Noticing the green currents illuminating through the fabric of the white button-up sleeves, an idea formed.

"Hey," I said, capturing his attention. His hazel eyes shifted to peer at me. In a lazy gesture, I propped my elbow onto the bartop while cradling my jaw in my palm. "You're of microwave magic, right?"

The bartender nodded, his nervous eyes shifting about.

"Well, how about you let us cause a scene by continuing to shoot us some 'shine, even if you have to sneak it..." I said, noting Scarlett next to me, casting him flirtatious looks with her green eyes. "And I'll ensure you a secure role within the guilds where your magic would be most useful." I watched him put his thought process on display, weighing the risks of the choice I offered. "What do ya say?"

The bartender wiped his palms against his pants. He kept glancing in nervous anticipation to where the king sat perched on his throne. "Uh..." he said and then bit his bottom lip. His deliberation tested my frayed patience. Finally, he resigned himself to a harsh breath and a sag of his shoulders. He nodded. "Fuck it. But if you get caught, it's not my doing. I've been instructed to keep you sober."

I rolled my eyes, not surprised to learn my father and Amethyst wanted to keep me sober at *my* birthday revel. "Got a name?"

"Vermillion. Vermillion Pringle, Your Highness. Most people just call me Mills." Mills ran his fingers through his salmon-colored fringe, pushing it out of his eyes. He reached under the counter where he grabbed two stout tumblers.

"Pleasure doing business with you, Mills," I said as I pushed myself off the bartop, straightening my posture. "I'm sure these drinks will be extra potent, yeah?"

Mills paused his search through the stacked crates of human-made moonshine. The names of various flavors labeled the Mason jars we traded as goods. "Didn't you say two apple pies?"

"Aw. He's cute, smart, and he listens. Can I keep him, Gray?" Scarlett squinted her eyes, cocking her head to the side as she made a show of appraising him, clearly envisioning him on top of her.

I chuckled at the pink tint painting Mills's ears. "Scarlett," I said, shoving an elbow into her ribs. "Leave the man alone. He's got enough going against him as it is."

Scarlett huffed out a dramatic sigh, disappointed in my response, but leaned into me and said, "I can just stick him in my pocket. Nobody will know. I swear."

I snorted, shaking my head. "Gods above, Scar. Control your ovaries, would you?"

"Fine," she whined. "They're contained," she said, resigned before sighing again as she checked out the tight-fitting, black slacks that hugged his ass.

Scarlett and I waited for Mills as he retrieved our drinks. After my failure with Griffin and the impending punishment from my father, I craved just one night of fun. One night, when regret or anxiety didn't bombard me. The alcohol couldn't come fast enough.

A strong energy joined us from behind. Before I could turn to investigate, Scarlett lunged for the male, throwing her arms around his neck. I leaned my back against the bar to avoid being shoved off-balance by her. A flash of hair the color of fresh snow garnered my attention.

"Cotton!" Scarlett buried her face into the side of his neck as she assaulted him with friendly affection.

With a rare smile, Cotton Sjodin embraced Scarlett in a warm hug. He stepped back to examine her at arm's length. Olive irises darted over her face and then her body, searching Scarlett for...something. I wasn't sure. When he appeared satisfied, he met her sea-green eyes and arched a questioning white eyebrow.

Scarlett nodded, her blood-red curls bouncing with the movement. "Yeah, I'm good, Cotton. Just happy to see my oldest friend."

With a tilted grin, Cotton mussed the top of her hair, earning him a punch to the gut. "Cotton! Do you have any fucking idea how long it took to get my hair like this?" Scarlett growled as she fixed her tresses with a tender touch. Cotton stood in silent amusement, content with the reaction he sought from the spitfire.

"Two apple pies for the princess and—her friend," Mills interrupted from behind.

I spun on my heels to meet the nervous bartender and said, "Careful with her, Mills. She's cute at first, but she can be a bit stabby if poked in the wrong places."

I snagged the tumbler closest to me, gulping down the moonshine's liquid fire. It seemed Mills followed through and provided me with an extra potent drink. I winced as it scorched my throat but welcomed the warmth it brought my body as it settled in my stomach. A sense of calmness began to ease through me, and I sighed from the relief.

Mills bore an appalled expression at my statement. I shrugged and turned back to join Scarlett and Cotton.

Cotton was mute. No one knew why or how he'd lost his ability to speak, and I never knew him well enough to ask. I wasn't social, so we never developed much of a friendship. We were both close with Scarlett, and that was where our bond ended.

Most people were unnerved by Cotton. Being mute heightened his observational skills, which made people feel seen on a deeper level that made them uncomfortable. It's one of the reasons he was the Royal Domain's Inquisitor. But coupled with his ability to see how body heat changed according to emotions during questioning, it essentially made him a living lie detector. No doubt he knew people's secrets just from observing them.

As if noticing my presence for the first time since his arrival, he wrapped his right arm across his midsection and folded himself at the waist in a respectful bow. I offered him a grateful smile and a small wave. "Hey, Cotton."

I tuned out Scarlett while she gushed about her training room escapades with Golden Figgaro. Cotton's pinched expression said he shared in my disgust on the matter. Fuck Golden. He was such a pious prick so far up my father's ass that if he wasn't careful, he'd serve as an enema. I wished Scarlett would choose literally anyone else to get dirty with.

I tossed back large swigs from my drink, my attention drifting towards the revel. It grew more raucous and salacious with each passing moment. Couples and small groups removed themselves from the dancefloor, huddling in corners or at tables lining the opposite wall while devouring one another. They fed off each other's energy to fuel their own, heightening their drunken and erotic euphoria.

I scanned the ballroom, finding Hazel still held hostage at Amethyst's side. Remembering the look she'd given me, I wondered what she knew. I needed to separate her from Amethyst and find out.

I drained my drink before I realized it and turned around to request another from Mills. If I hoped to make the statement I intended for tonight, I needed much more liquid courage.

"Hey, Mills!" I called to his back.

He granted me his attention, so I raised the empty tumbler in the air and shook it so the ice clinked against the glass.

Mills nodded, his pink fringe straying into his eye, and returned to the crates stacked against the marble wall behind the bar.

As I waited, my thoughts trailed off and replayed my epic failure involving Griffin, trying to make sense of it all. It was clear there were a few loose screws in his head, judging by his unstable behavior. None of our interactions was supposed to have happened. He should be dead.

It unsettled me that I couldn't figure out why he felt familiar, too. There was no way we'd ever met before. I wouldn't forget a man like that. Those molten silver eyes peered at me in my mind, reminding me of my weakness. But the most plaguing question of last night was my body's reaction to my dagger. It shouldn't have affected me. And how the fuck had I suddenly healed, seeing as I had been in death's embrace on the train?

A slow tingle began to spread in my limbs. I shook out my arms and adjusted my stance to help my blood flow. What was taking Mills so long? My mouth was drying up like a smoker's skin with every breath.

And then, everything spiraled.

I gripped a numbing hand to my constricting chest as I struggled to force air into my vacuous lungs. My innards heated with each passing second. They were ablaze, every nerve-ending feeling singed.

Finally, Mills slid the tumbler of apple pie moonshine down the bar to me, his brows pinched in concern. "Thanks," I wheezed out before I guzzled down the liquid fire to sate the severe thirst. It didn't help. Given Mills's worried expression, I assumed I looked as shitty as I felt.

Tunnel vision threatened to close in, while my head felt like it was in a vacuum. My muscles turned to mush, making standing an intense challenge as I barely held on to the bartop with my declining strength.

I cursed to myself as my knees buckled. Twenty-four hours hadn't even passed since I was stabbed and recovered from the injury. What was happening to me?

My ears rang, blocking out the music and boisterous revelers. The beat morphed into my desperate pulse that throbbed in my ears, pounding the death knell of my fading life force. A hard surface slammed into my kneecaps before it caught my face. My body was numb, but like on the train, my insides felt like they were being incinerated.

I was blind, and the only sound I heard was the hammering in my head. All I could do was focus on slowing my labored breathing as panic set in. Every time I tried to grasp onto a single thought, it slipped from my reach, leaving me wheezing for its return.

I caught distorted and muffled voices through the beating drums in my ears. "Gray..." I heard. "Help me get her, Cotton..." It was difficult to place the familiar voice, mainly because it sounded like it was melting.

The darkness once again tried to claim me with a vicious snatch to its depths—more determined this time. It wouldn't fail; its willpower was potent. The shadows' claws sank into my soul and yanked, not before I heard a melting voice drip the words, "She was poisoned by the king."

Chapter 7

GRIFFIN

"**B**e ready."

"I'm here, aren't I?" I drawled, taking in the deserted cityscape around us where lichen climbed the buildings. We stood between decaying skyscrapers, shielded by the shade from the setting sun. Both of our hoods were pulled far over our faces, blocking us from anyone's view.

The man next to me snorted. "She's gonna breeze right by here, completely oblivious to her surroundings. She'll be sporadic, so watch out," he said as if he knew her, as if he'd trained with the princess in the past.

I knew I should've remembered him—trusted him, even. I understood he was important to the plan, and I was aware of what his current role was, but trying to place him from the past and his significance to the part he played today was like trying to grasp air as more memories faded.

I'd received a message that morning indicating a rendezvous point in the alley between the former banking and telecommunications buildings. The madness nearly pulled me under as I had wracked my brain for hours trying to recognize the sender of the message. It seemed like the harder I tried to place him in my memories, the more my mind threatened to fracture for good. The sharp pain slicing through my skull was enough to bring me to my knees, my palms grasping my head.

As I stood next to him now, one thing was for sure: the familiar stranger was a Kinetic.

"Valik wanted me to assure you to have patience. Once everything..."

"What are you talking about?" *Valik?* I kept my focus straight ahead, staring at the deserted street with weeds growing up through the cracks. A worn shoe lay discarded a few feet away from a hunk of metal on the sidewalk.

"You know..." the man said, apprehension lacing his tone, "with your situation..."

No. I had no idea. "Be more specific," I snapped.

"Shit. Never mind, man," he said as if this was information I should know. Was he talking about my affliction? No one knew about that, so I doubted that was the case. Another surge of frustration heated my chest at the loss of memories. Deciding not to push the issue, he added, "Just hurry. I'll do what I can to help speed things along and get her out here sooner."

I nodded. "Yeah, do that. I'm ready to go home." Damn, I missed the serenity of the Hollow. It eased my suffering just enough to be able to hide my spiraling from everyone.

"Just stay out of sight and do what you gotta do. Everything's at stake."

With only a nod, I kicked off the wall I had been leaning against and strode away to lie in wait for the princess.

Several hours passed as I hid in an abandoned hookah shop nestled within the city six blocks from the King's Palace. The blue couch was stiff, dusty, and ridden with bullet holes—pretty sure that was dried blood to my left, too. I leaned forward on the splintered wooden table. It offered enough of a flat surface to get the job done.

After swiping off the dust and debris, I lined up the white powder along the blade of a knife with unsteady hands. I took the wooden straw I'd kept from the Hollow—made by some of the earth wielders who specialized in wood—and snorted a third line within a five-minute span. A numbness swelled in my chest, face, and mind as relief then adrenaline flooded me, pushing the affliction aside. My only thoughts consisted of getting the princess and going home—and killing the king. It seemed the only reprieve I could get from my spiraling state was resorting to extreme measures.

The voice was still there, chattering away in the background, but for now, a barrier blocked him from my central focus, acting as a temporary band-aid. The powder clouded the unwanted thoughts while defining the notions I needed to sort through.

Taking a deep breath, I hummed on the exhalation, savoring the brief euphoria that warmed my chest. I sank back into the couch, relaxing my muscles and slumping low into the stiff cushion. A low chuckle rumbled from my diaphram. It built and built, rising to hit the peak of hysterical laughter. I gripped my stomach from the cramp, but it only fueled me to laugh harder.

On the outside, my cackling made no sense. I probably seemed fucking insane in all honesty. But I understood it. All the restraint I had been clinging onto for the past few weeks dissipated with the rush of the powder as it swam in my veins.

After several minutes of unprovoked laughter, my breaths finally began to slow and some of the weight lifted from my chest and shoulders. I licked my lips. Good. They were numb; I needed all the parts of me that mattered to remain that way.

Aside from the buzzing in my head, the echoes of quietude caressed the inner recesses of my mind. Taunts from the darkness were effectively shut out, and I couldn't help but be grateful for the powder. I had never been one to indulge in drugs in the past, but it helped numb my mind and deathly urges, allowing me the chance to think. To form a plan. *Slow* down. Prepare.

I wasn't sure how long I'd need to wait for the princess to flee, but I knew eventually she would. The king wouldn't tolerate her failure to kill me. Too many Kinetics waited for the moment she lapsed—to the point that her life was no longer worthwhile. The Kinetics were cold with their own people in that way.

A wave of instinctual anger boiled to the surface. I had no reason to feel any sense of protectiveness toward the woman, but yet, the thought of others harming her pissed me the fuck off. I clenched my fists and jaw, angling my head from side to side, cracks popping down my neck from the action.

I hadn't thought much about that moment I had with her on the train. The one where a potential lost memory surfaced by the contact of her skin, that was. Could that even be called a *moment* when she was unconscious and unaware of my presence? The memory was probably something fabricated by the voice to control me, to fuck with my head even more in order to push me over the edge at long last.

Glass crunched near the front door, eradicating the silence in the deserted hookah shop. I stilled, waiting for the intruder to approach me. Adjusting the grip on the knife in my fist, a slow grin began to pull up at the edges of my mouth, feeling my inner predator rise.

"There you are." The teenage boy rounded the corner, and upon seeing me, his eyes went wide in response to the feral grin on my face. "Uh...why do you look excited to murder me?"

"Didn't know it was you," I said, shoulders dropping and turning toward the table again. "Now I'm sad."

"Sorry to disappoint," Dash said, sighing as he moved to take a seat beside me on the couch. "Hogan sent me with the radio so you can monitor her movements."

With a nod, I straightened and focused on the teen boy next to me who'd far surpassed anybody's expectations of him amongst the human rebels. Like most humans, he'd lost a lot, including his youth and innocence at a young age. Now, he was the best shot in Hogan's crew. "You come to keep me company, kid?"

His small, unruly afro bounced with the overdramatic snort he released. "Please, Griffin." Crossing his arms, he leaned back into the couch and met my gaze with a deadpanned stare. His huge brown eyes were magnified by thick-rimmed glasses as he said, "As much of a stud as you are, I prefer company of the feminine variety."

I rolled my eyes. "Do you even know how to be around females?"

Affronted, Dash scoffed. "Of course! They love a man with confidence. Flattery goes a long way, ya know. Like, you pick one of their features and just basically smother them with how much it turns your dick hard. You don't leave any room for them to question whether they like you or not."

"Oh, for fuck's sake," I said, pinching the bridge of my nose. Gods, I felt bad for women these days. With the dwindling population, men were becoming desperate—even more so than they had been before Devolution Day. "Dash, you're about to become my prime source of entertainment." My voice was muffled in my hands as I cradled my face with a shake of my head.

Thankfully, I had no desire to procreate and bring a child into this fucked-up world, while simultaneously damning them to share in my genetics. And I had no intention to burden a woman to love a man as monstrous as myself. I mean, there'd have to be something seriously twisted within her if *I* was what she wanted.

I hadn't always been this way. In fact, I had worked my ass off healing myself from my past, but this affliction had muddied my mind and emotions to the point I didn't know what was real or not half the time—and that was the scary part. I could turn on my loved ones any day because the demon convinced me they were a threat.

"Take notes, Griff-Daddy," Dash said, pulling me from my inner thoughts, "Watch and learn. This is a new era, old man. Chivalry died with half the population on D-Day."

Oh, how well I knew that to be true. "Yeah, you have no idea, kid."

Chapter 8

GRAY

"Speak!" Jacob Smart, my personal bully, screamed at me.

My ribs felt broken. The bruises from my father this morning only intensified the pain. It hurt to breathe, much less to speak.

After a long silence, Jacob spoke again. "Fine. I'll make you, then."

I braced for the next wave of pain. My eyes squeezed shut, and I tightened my hold on my ailing ribs.

Sudden agony erupted from my shin like someone slammed the hilt of a warrior's sword into the bone. But it was merely the toe of Jacob's boot—such a strong kick for an eight-year-old human.

A scream tore from my already raw throat.

Twice in one day. It wasn't exactly a record, but it wasn't common. Usually, I had time to heal between beatings. I hadn't been so lucky that day.

Even without our magic awakened, our bodies healed faster than a human's. However, it was slower than a Kinetic with manifested powers.

It became difficult to breathe as silent tears streamed down my dirty cheeks. All I could do was hope it wouldn't last long.

Where were the teachers? How come they never stopped this?

I waited for the next assault to come, but the surrounding voices became fewer and quieter. I lay in the sandbox for what seemed like an eternity, humiliated. But no more blows came. I opened my eyes with apprehension.

Everyone had disappeared, including Jacob. In his place stood a boy I'd never seen before. He looked about two years older than me, perhaps a fifth grader. With short black hair and striking blue eyes, he gazed down at me with a frown. As beautiful as the blue eyes were, they didn't feel like they belonged to him, more like they were a disguise.

"Are you okay?" asked the boy. Secrets hid behind those eyes, yet a strange familiarity resonated within me. I recognized the masked emotion: pain. Others might see rage, but me? I saw his suffering. It mirrored my own.

I took a shaky breath and nodded my head. "Yeah. Wh—where did they all go?" I swallowed, cringing as the built-up saliva took bits of sand with it, scraping my throat on the way down.

"They left. I don't think they'll be bothering you anymore," the boy said as he crouched down to eye-level with me. "Next time, I'll beat their ass."

"She can't stay here. He'll never give up." Hushed voices drifted into my frail consciousness.

I struggled to open my oppressed eyes, weighted down from exhaustion. A bright light stabbed my eyeballs through the cracks in my lids, forcing me to snap them shut again. I tested my limbs to see if movement had returned to my body. Using my remaining strength, I lifted my arm inches from the mattress, only for it to plop back onto the sheet.

My body tried to heal, but my magic reserves were detrimental, not allowing the healing to happen as it needed to. Weak and depleted, I released a pained groan as I remembered the events that led me here—wherever *here* was.

The memory of fire scorching my veins and organs was the first to come to mind. The blackness that engulfed me was a shade that didn't exist in this reality. No light could penetrate it as it seeped into my soul, tainting it with despair.

Whispers quieted at the sound of my groan.

Footsteps approached my side. "Gray?" a commanding feminine voice cut through the room.

I rolled my pounding head to face Scarlett's direction, every fiber of my body aching.

"Shit, Gray," Scarlett said, worry mixed with relief in her tone. "You can't move?"

"Of course, she can't, Kittle. Her energy was spent purging the remaining redfern from her system. She needs to replenish, but she doesn't even have the energy to absorb on her own right now." Hazel's usual calming tone was clipped, but it was the mention of redfern that piqued my attention.

After several failed attempts, I opened a squinted eye. I hoped these two had the answers I needed.

"Ww...what...happened?" I asked, the deep scratchiness making my voice unrecognizable.

"Hazel," Scarlett snapped. "I think you should start explaining a few fucking things to the princess. *Now.*" She crossed her arms over her chest. Her long, vibrant curls were pulled into a messy bun on top of her head. Somehow, she still looked stunning.

My vision cleared the longer I lay in the foreign bed. And once both eyes were fully open, I tried to place my location. I lay in a small, bare room with large windows that gazed into the pitch night. No photos or art decorated the cream walls, and only essential black furniture occupied the space. The bed I rested on was hard and felt unused, judging by the lack of sheets and the one blanket that draped over me.

"Fine," Hazel said with a sigh. Her bronze hair was still in its updo from the revel, but she was alert and focused as she led this operation. "Let me share some of my energy with her first. She needs to be present for this, and I'm sure she'll have a ton of questions." She paused. "You two might want to join me."

My leaden body wouldn't allow me to scan the room. I shifted my gaze to spot the third person, but whoever it was remained out of my line of sight, only increasing my curiosity.

"Okay, but hurry. We don't have much time, Helair," Scarlett said, failing to mask her impatience.

The edge of the bed dipped with the weight of Hazel's delicate figure. She offered a gentle smile before wrapping her warm hands around my ice-cold ones. Energy waves emanated from her body, her black currents pulsating up her pale arms as she pushed her energy into my aura for me to absorb. Hers was the embodiment of warm comfort as it washed over my icy body.

I was ravenous, so I drew on the energy she offered and took it for my own. I couldn't feel the effects right away, as deprived as I was. Several minutes passed before I began to feel lighter.

"That's enough. I need to keep some for myself," Hazel said, breathless. She cleared her throat and looked up at our ruby-haired friend. "Scarlett?"

The warmth of Hazel's hands disappeared, and I shivered in their absence. She rose from the bed to stand nearby. Despite returning to a baseline level, I was still low enough that my healing couldn't do what it needed. Energy-sharing would be the fastest way to replenish my magic reserves.

Scarlett dropped into Hazel's vacated spot on the mattress, jolting my aching body. "Damnit, Scar," I grumbled in irritation. She flashed me a smirk as she grabbed my hands in a firm grip.

The high-voltage energy of her nuclear magic electrified me. As I did with Hazel's energy, I absorbed Scarlett's, adding a tremendous boost to the baseline Hazel had provided me. I no longer felt trapped in quicksand, and my healing began to ease the aches plaguing my bones.

I moaned at the reprieve and gave Scarlett's hand a slight squeeze in appreciation. She continued to share, and I continued taking. "All right, Stoney," she said in a gentle tone. "I think that's enough." Scarlett released my hands. The bed shifted as she rose to join Hazel.

With my body's functionality returned, I could better scan the room. An ash-gray carpet lined the floor. There were no lamps or curtains that gave personality to the space. My bed pressed against the far wall of the room, and a chest of drawers sat at the foot in the corner.

Although I felt much lighter, lethargy still weighed me down. Scarlett's form of magic should've made me ready to run three miles, but I wasn't anywhere near that point.

Remembering there was a third person, I snapped my head to the left, feeling the strong aura that always caught me off-guard. "Cotton?" Surprise coated my features from his presence. In all honesty, Cotton looked like he belonged on a GQ cover—back when GQ existed, at least. His short white hair remained combed to the side, and his suit didn't have a wrinkle in sight.

The Royal Domain's Inquisitor dipped his head in silent acknowledgment. Scarlett and Hazel flanked either side of him, exuding their unique aura in their own ways.

Scarlett stood in fierce determination; her violet dress now ripped up both sides of her legs instead of just one. On Cotton's right stood Hazel, emitting a solemn strength that was neither physical nor visible.

"What happened?" I asked, looking at the three of them.

Hazel shook her head. "No. Absorb some of Cotton's energy before we get into everything."

I rolled my eyes. "I always wondered what it'd be like to have a mom."

The faintest of smiles appeared on Cotton's hardened expression before tilting his head. He glanced down at my hands, then arched a brow, asking for my permission to touch me. "Yeah. Hands are fine, Cotton. Thanks."

With careful precision, Cotton wrapped his palms over mine. His yellow currents glowed on the backs of his pale hands. The energy from Cotton's thermal-based magic warmed me to my bones. I didn't waste time absorbing it into my aura, allowing it to top off my reserves.

The deep warmth from his energy made me moan. It was revitalizing. I wanted to take it all as my insides tingled with small jolts of arousal in my core caused by his brand of magic.

Cotton snatched his hands from mine, severing the influx of warmth that flooded me.

"Give a girl a warning before you surprise her with feelings like *that*, Cotton," I said, fanning myself. I attempted to simmer down the tingling sensation with deep breaths. "Quite the gift you have there, Inquisitor."

Cotton winked, a knowing smirk teasing one corner of his lips. He stuck his hands into the front pockets of his trousers and rocked back on his heels. I'd never seen him look so smug.

I felt replenished, so I sat up to be present with the others.

Scarlett snorted, smacking him on the shoulder. "Gods above, Cotton. It was just an energy bump, not an orgasm. Chill."

"If he'd let me keep going, I totally would've orgasmed," I said with a shrug. "Now I'm tempted to take care of myself, with or without you all here."

Hazel's pale face pinked as she looked out the window into the night. I could've bet three diamond rings she was remembering the time she'd walked in on Slate and me. I chose not to tease her about it this time.

Scarlett chuckled, her cat eyes crinkling in the corners. "Don't threaten me with a good time, Princess."

My expression deadpanned. "Maybe another time, Scar," I joked, "but I need some answers." I swung my legs over the side of the bed to face my friends.

A weight hung from my neck down to my chest. I peered down, spotting the sentimental black stone suspended by a leather string. The large polished piece rarely ever came off me. I wasn't able to wear it to the revel because of the haltered dress. Having once belonged to my biological mother, I hated not having it on at all times. So, how did I end up with it now?

Scarlett cut me off from asking. "Welcome back, Gray. You scared the shit out of us, dude." She closed the distance to wrap me in a bear hug. I'd never been much of a hugger, but Scarlett couldn't be stopped. Plus, she gave great hugs.

"Thanks," I said, pulling away to look at each of my friends. "To all of you. I don't know what happened or what you guys went through to help me, but I'm beyond grateful for you." I let the weight of my appreciation settle. "So," I said, turning to the topic I'd been most eager to get to. "What does redfern have to do with any of this?"

Hazel forced out a breath and took a seat on the bed beside me with a careful grace. She laced her fingers together in her lap, appearing to gather her thoughts.

I turned my attention to Scarlett and Cotton, who stood shoulder to shoulder in front of us. "So where am I?" I asked, looking around the empty room.

Scarlett angled her head to glance upward at Cotton. She jabbed a thumb in his direction. "His suite. This is his spare room."

"Oh." Surprise rang through me. I'd never been close to Cotton, so for him to freely offer his residence warmed my heart.

"We needed a place that neither the king nor Amethyst would suspect you to be. We figured it would buy us a few hours," Scarlett explained.

I furrowed my brow, wondering why I needed to be hidden from my father and Amethyst.

Cotton placed a hand on Scarlett's shoulder. He glanced at the door and held up one finger. Scarlett understood. "Okay, thanks," she said, nodding before Cotton turned and exited the room, not bothering to close the door behind him.

Hazel leaned over, wrapping her arms around my shoulders in a hug. "I'm so glad you're okay, Gray. I was so scared I was about to lose you, too." She rested her head on my shoulder while my hand reassuringly settled on her arm.

Moments later, Cotton appeared in the doorway carrying two black leather chairs. Once he reached Scarlett's side, he dropped them to the carpet, arranging them to face us.

Scarlett thanked the Inquisitor as they dropped onto the seats to settle in for our conversation.

Scarlett cleared her throat, "So, when we said we were going to cause a scene, Stoney, I didn't mean for you to nearly die."

I huffed out a laugh. Running my fingers through my hair, I searched for the pins that barely held it up. "It was a spectacle, wasn't it?" I winced.

Hazel sighed. "You could say that." She sat up straight and looked at me. "Between Scarlett threatening the bartender and Cotton carrying you out, we're lucky you're here with us and not with the healers," she said with a reproachful look toward Scarlett who shrugged, uncaring. "Everyone witnessed you collapse. And your screams..." She shuddered at the memory.

"I wish I could say that it'll never happen again, but..." I said, trailing off, noticing a pattern of nearly dying beginning to form.

"But what?" Hazel asked.

"This sort of thing keeps happening to me," I said with a shrug.

"The king poisoned you with redfern, Stoney," Scarlett said, getting to the crux of it.

I halted the probing in my hair, freezing at her words. "He what?"

"He poisoned you. He tried to kill you."

I wasn't sure what I was expecting, but that wasn't it. To hear that my father, adopted or not, tried to kill me, left me feeling like I'd had my feet kicked out from underneath me. The others let the truth settle before pushing onward. "I knew he would punish me, but I was expecting the usual beating or whatever. Not...*death.*"

"Punish you for what?" Scarlett asked, her head cocking to the side.

Running my palms over my face, I answered, "I failed to kill Griffin." I dropped my hands and rested my elbows on my knees. The silken gold fabric of the dress suddenly felt suffocating, the color reminding me of him. "He'd promised me that if I failed, I'd suffer 'consequences unlike any I've experienced.'"

"There's more to it than that," Hazel said. She straightened her posture in willful determination.

I cocked my head and narrowed my eyes at her, fear seeping in at her tone.

"All right," she started, leveling me with a serious expression. "The day before Slate left for his mission, he came to me." Hazel's doe eyes met mine, a sadness creeping in at the mention of her brother.

"What does Slate have to do with this?" I asked, frowning in confusion.

"Kind of—um—a lot?" she responded in an apologetic tone.

"Okay?" I prompted, glancing at Scarlett, who wouldn't look at us.

"You know how much Slate hated the way your father treated you—well, he'd always suspected he was hiding something." Hazel took a deep breath to press forward. "He began doing some digging behind his back every chance he got. He'd eavesdrop on conversations, sneak into Aunt Amethyst's office, go through files, books, ledgers, drawers...anything. One day, he discovered some stuff that rocked him. I don't know the details of what it was, but he told me they'd been up to something. It was huge, and apparently, it'd been a long time in the making. And you were at the heart of it." Hazel paused, allowing time for me to process.

My heart beat wildly in my chest, and once again, I worked to control my breathing. "Just tell me, Hazel," I snapped and then squeezed my eyes shut. "Please," I added in a softer tone, to ease my unintended harshness.

Hazel nodded. "Evidently, the king and my aunt have plans that could destroy everything, but you're needed for them. Somehow. However," she said, biting her bottom lip in hesitation, "if you failed to prove useful, they planned to eliminate you, as they'd consider you a liability."

My palms stung from my nails. I focused on the pain and pressed harder, distracting myself from my whirring thoughts. "Did he say what those plans were?" I asked, my voice almost as soft as a whisper. How had they kept me in the dark for so long?

Hazel shook her head. "No. Slate came to me in an awful state on the day he left. He said he'd tell me everything once he returned from the mission..." she trailed off and closed her eyes, wringing her fingers together in her lap. She took a deep breath before continuing, "Before he left, he made me promise to look out for you, to keep you as safe as possible. No matter what it took."

"I guess my usefulness has run out, then?" I asked. "Failing to kill Griffin was my last chance."

Hazel nodded solemnly. "Yeah, and when he nearly killed you, that sealed the deal," she said, dropping her eyes to her lap.

"It's still unclear what happened," I mused. "Is it possible for Kinetic blades to affect us?" I asked, glancing back and forth at the three of them with hope.

A look of shared confusion passed between them. "What are you talking about, Stoney?"

I peered at Hazel. "You mean you didn't know I almost died from a Kinetic blade?"

Hazel's face paled and horror hung from her features. "No, Gray. No one told me that part."

I relayed the events that occurred between Griffin and me, explaining how close I came to death on the train and then awoke healed in my bed.

"Black crystal and Kinetic-infused magic should not affect you like that. There has to be more to this than we're seeing," Hazel said, her brows pinched low as she thought out loud.

Despite the new information that Hazel passed along, I was left with more questions than answers. What were my father and Amethyst up to? And where did I fit into this? Why did Slate not warn me when he was alive? And where the fuck were the king and Amethyst now? Surely, they were searching for me.

It didn't entirely surprise me to learn the king wanted me dead. Another part, the part of me who had always sought her father's affection and approval, felt betrayed...and angry.

That part was the loudest.

"How did the king poison me with redfern at the revel without affecting others?" I asked.

"Mills," Scarlett scoffed, her own form of betrayal coloring her stark features. She shook her head in disappointment. "It's so sad because I had such high hopes for him." Her expression then shifted to something akin to approval. "Although, I didn't think he had it in him to pull something like that off. Peculiar little guy, huh?"

Hazel, Cotton, and I leveled her with flat expressions. Hazel rolled her eyes at our friend's overactive sex drive. "I overheard the king inform

Amethyst that 'the boy' would lace your drinks, as he predicted you'd rebel and get drunk tonight."

The pieces clicked together. All the signs had been there the entire time. Amethyst had been all too eager this morning to allow me a good time at my revel. I knew there'd been ulterior motives, but murder wasn't on my list.

"I assume you swiped a dose of the antidote?" I asked, my brows raised.

Hazel nodded, looking pretty happy with herself. "Yeah, I stole a syringe of blended nickel from my aunt's office. I saw it on her desk this morning, which I found odd."

"I forgot how brutal it is to watch the nickel work the redfern from your body. We had to restrain you to keep you from hurting yourself," Scarlett said, a haunted expression on her face.

Cotton sat in his usual stiff silence, his jaw flexing.

I nodded and thanked them, realizing where my hoarse voice came from.

"If people spotted you and Cotton carrying me from the ballroom," I said, looking at Scarlett, "then, won't my father and Amethyst know you two are involved?"

"Not necessarily," Hazel answered. "They left just before you collapsed. That's how I was freed up to join y'all. It was chaos. But of course, there were a few people who took notice."

A heavy silence fell over the four of us, while my anger rose with each beat of my heart.

"I'm going to fucking kill him," I said. I stared at the gray carpet, mentally praising Cotton for how clean it was, despite my growing anger. "And that psychopathic bitch, too."

"I'm pretty sure I don't need to list all the reasons why that's a terrible idea," Scarlett said.

I stood up, unable to contain the sea of emotions raging within my body. "And I'm pretty sure you know why I don't give a shit." I returned my hands to the back of my head and snatched the remaining pins loose. My marbled hair fell in matted waves down my shoulders. "I'm done, Scarlett. And I'm done falling in line. I don't have to anymore. He needs to die, if only to protect others from whatever insane plans he has for the world. He has done nothing but put me through hell my entire life. But now, I can fight back. And I'm fucking done playing his games."

"We understand, Gray," Hazel consoled, moving to stand beside me. She placed a gentle hand on my forearm. "And you have every right to be upset right now. I can't imagine what you must be feeling, but you shouldn't act rashly here. It could play right into his hands."

"So, what are you saying? I'm supposed to walk around here and pretend my father didn't just try to kill me? That he's probably pissed I survived this attempt? Am I supposed to just sit around and wait for him to try again?" My voice rose with each question, my breaths coming in harsh. The longer I remained in this room, the more trapped I felt.

"Absolutely not," Hazel said, looking at Scarlett then Cotton. A silent communication transpired before me as they spoke through their eyes and facial expressions.

I watched the odd scene unfold. After enough time had passed, I cleared my throat to garner their attention. "Well?"

Hazel quirked the corner of her lip and a single eyebrow. "We're getting you the fuck out of here."

Chapter 9

GRIFFIN

My veins itched at the absence of magic my bracelet stole from me. I needed my power back. The effects of the white powder I'd inhaled earlier began to wane, leaving me jittery. The drug didn't take it all away, but it helped give my thoughts some concrete direction and shut out the taunting voice that never ceased to shut up.

I needed my violin to channel my fracturing thoughts and emotions. That always seemed to bring me some peace.

I wasn't one to fear much of anything. Yet, claws of panic sunk deeper and deeper into my chest at the impending mind-shatter that threatened to overtake me again. Not having my magic to blow off some steam was only fueling the rapid rate.

All my coke was gone. I'd sniffed it whenever Dash would leave the room to receive messages on the ham radio in the front of the shop. Night had fallen hours ago. Now, it was merely a waiting game. And I hoped I could hold out long enough to capture the prize.

My thoughts drifted to my people at the Hollow—to my responsibility. I was their leader, no longer an official prince since the entirety of the Elemental kingdom fell at the death of the king and queen twenty-seven years ago. Beneath the madness shredding my mind to tatters, I cared deeply for them and would do anything to keep them safe.

But it was getting harder and harder to put on the front that I wasn't spiraling. My people looked to me for guidance, strength, and friendship. And the progression of my apathy in every regard intensified as I continued to lose the memories that made my relationships special. I kept trying to grasp onto any recollections, but they would just slip through my fingers like smoke. Once they were all gone, I feared for those closest to me.

"Our source told us that the king tried to kill her." Dash's deep voice made me jump. Beads of sweat began to slide down my temples, but I shivered, feeling the cold emptiness within me returning to exact its vengeance. "Apparently, he attempted to poison her at her own birthday revel. So, it shouldn't be much longer before she tries to make her escape."

While I wasn't surprised by Forest's merciless action to kill his own daughter, I was surprised by the vicious rage that turned my frigid soul into an inferno at the mention of it. My breaths came in ragged, my nostrils flaring as I worked hard not to show any reaction to the news. How could I possibly explain why it bothered me whether she was harmed or not when I couldn't even understand it myself?

Clearing my throat after forcing air deep into my lungs, I said, "Good. Once you get word that she's out of the King's Palace, I'll need to tail her."

"I'm coming with you, Griffin," Dash said. I spun around to face his stubborn stance, his back straight and arms crossed over his scrawny chest. "You don't get to have all the fun. I don't give a damn if you're an Elemental or not."

My eyebrows shot to my hairline. "No." With my voice firm, I went on, "You're too young. The princess may not be able to defeat me, but she can easily kill you. She's one of the best, Dash. Probably trained to be ruthless like her father," I explained, hoping to convince him to rethink this terrible idea. "You're not ready."

Dash shook his head. "No, I'm a part of this with you. I can help. And I *am* ready."

"No, you're not. You're good, but she's a Kinetic. Highly trained and feared amongst her people." I rose to my feet from the couch to reach my full height. "She'll kill you if she suspects you're anything more than a straggling human trying to survive. Even then, she might not even give you the courtesy."

"Well, I'll just need to be really convincing." Dash grinned deviously before turning his sharp brown gaze into an innocent puppy-dog look. My mouth dropped at the convincing display of him morphing into a pitiful and harmless teenager.

I narrowed my eyes, assessing his acting abilities. "Have you been practicing?"

Dash broke character with a knowing smirk. "It's good, right?"

With a sigh, I ran a hand through my hair, still fighting off the darkness that loomed closer and closer. The voice was returning, urging the usual: kill, kill, kill. "Fine, but there's still no guarantee that she won't kill you upon sight."

Dash rolled his eyes. "Listen, it'll be the perfect plan. I can earn her trust by appearing to be a harmless kid. I could lead her to the compound, then you can grab her and take her to the Hollow."

I chewed on my lip, doing my best to mull over all angles of this scenario through my foggy brain. It could go terribly wrong in many ways. However, it could also go right and make my job that much easier.

I lost track of time. It was past midnight. I knew that much, but I had no idea beyond that fact. The cold burrowing within the confines of my skin numbed me, and my mind was a blur of maniacal thoughts. My energy was spent trying to fight off the madness, while it should've been spent trying to remain hidden and watchful.

Dash and I split up, moving closer to the King's Palace grounds, just out of reach of the alarms. We moved ahead of the skyrise hotel in the direction we anticipated the princess would run upon her escape. Buildings served as cover in the pitch-blackness of the night. As usual, I blended in with the shadows, allowing the depths of their darkness to embrace me.

The numbness allowed me to remain preternaturally still while I tried to focus on any movement surrounding us. With my magic suppressed, my senses were slightly inhibited. So, I relied on my training, which was, thankfully, like second nature.

The hair began to rise along the nape of my neck just before a muted exhalation reached my ears.

Kill, kill, kill. I ignored the voice in my head and remained frozen in my spot, listening to each quiet step the intruder took toward me.

I waited as he crept closer until I could feel the whispers of his breath against my skin from behind. Sensing only millimeters separating us before I heard the rustle of his clothing, presumably him raising a blade of some sort.

The moment his weapon nearly pierced my throat, I spun. And with that motion, I released a dagger from my belt, ready to strike. His eyes widened with recognition upon seeing my face. "You're..."

My dagger carved across his throat, silencing his next words as he gaped at me, horrified. His body thudded to the concrete in a heap as he gurgled on his blood.

I turned away from the Kinetic Warrior as his life slowly faded from him. *Good.* The violence only seemed to excite the darkness within me, and now, the incessant call of bloodshed raged like a war drum in my mind, unrelenting.

The crinkle of footsteps on loose pebbles echoed in the alleyway to my left while I caught a swift shadow to my right. I rolled my neck, a grin inching up the sides of my face for an actual fight.

An ear-splitting shriek pierced my ears, and I immediately cupped them with my hands. I knew all too well that it was a sonic augmentation ability, where Kinetics could create sound waves that weren't there. Highly skilled ones could isolate their magic to a specific target, which I presumed was the case right now. The octaves climbed higher, bringing me to my knees on the hard cement.

The only positive was it silenced the nasty voice that never shut up. But at what cost? With my attention forced to endure the sonic torture, my senses were drowned out to everything else. Caught by surprise, a blast whipped me into a stucco wall several feet away. The shrill screech never let up.

With a groan, I didn't allow myself to remain on the ground for long. Without my magic, this wasn't a fair fight, and they knew it.

Cowards.

Killing them with my bare hands would be much more satisfying, anyhow. The beast within me roared over the screeching in my mind, overriding the sonic shrill with its barbarity and thirst for bloodshed. While my head threatened to explode, I felt a surge of power thrum in my veins, egging me on to submit to the consuming corruption.

Despite the darkness, I could see the shadowy forms looming closer, approaching me from every angle. One leaped from the top of the building above, landing at my side with a thud. I shook off the blow, while two others closed in on me from each end of the alleyway.

My vision blinked out, plunging me into a void of nothingness, briefly startling me, but this wasn't new to me. A Kinetic who channeled the power of light energy manipulated my vision, robbing me of my sight. It wasn't the first time, and I was sure as hell it wouldn't be the last.

Using the only two remaining senses, I gauged their approach. I couldn't hear them over the roaring in my mind that kept the screeching at bay, so I honed in my olfactory and tactile senses. As their scents loomed closer, the air whispered across my skin, and pebbles bounced off my boots from their careless steps. The grin that overtook my face was savage at best as I reveled in the challenge.

Distantly, I wondered how Dash fared and if he was being tag-teamed, too. I couldn't hear if there were any gunshots in the distance, so I had no way of knowing. I just hoped the kid could handle himself long enough for me to get to him.

My intention was never to set out to protect the Kinetic Princess from her own people. I chuckled to myself at the irony that I was doing just that by clearing the way for her inevitable escape.

I felt the static charge from the man to my left, preparing for an attack. With my smile intact, I took the microwave blast to my gut, allowing its power to zing through my body. Again, I slammed into the wall. Fallen stucco clattered to the ground around me from my body's impact, and this time, I basked in the pain.

Chapter 10

GRAY

We all had our roles; mine proved the riskiest. While Scarlett gathered weapons for me and Cotton distracted the guards, Hazel would be sneaking into Amethyst's office to find the invaluable antidotes. In order for her to do that, my father needed to be distracted.

Everyone protested, but there was no other way to keep King Forest occupied while the others did their part. Plus, it would give me a chance to confront the man I called Father.

My stomach churned at the prospect of entering the King's Quarters. I stood before the door, steeling my nerves to enter the luxurious space. I punched the code into the keypad and pushed the handle down with a click. The creak from the heavy door screamed into the silent foyer.

With a deep breath to snuff out my fear, I crossed the threshold and called upon the darkest parts of myself as I walked toward the living area.

My father's brand of poisonous energy radiated from the living room, and I didn't mean his magic.

"Where've you been?" King Forest's refined voice reached me as I approached the white carpet. He stood with his back to me, dressed in the same charcoal suit from the revel as he oversaw his ruined city.

Through the glass doors leading to the balcony, the sun rose over the decrepit Atlanta skyline. Moss and greenery climbed the buildings as their structures began to crumble.

I wouldn't cower, but I'd be lying if I said I wasn't nervous. He had ultimate power in this world. Who was I to stop him?

I observed his bored stance from behind. The thought of blasting him through the balcony doors crossed my mind. It was tempting. I could level the entire building and not feel a thing aside from unequivocal rage, but that wasn't my current goal.

Ice cubes clinked in a crystal glass, chilling aged whiskey from pre-Devolution Day. Like a statue holding long-buried secrets, the Kinetic King stood proud while he stared at the enlarged painting of the beautiful, pink-haired woman that hung by the porcelain fireplace. Whenever I inquired about the woman's identity, he told me it was only a model. I never believed him.

I kicked off my heels, and they clicked against the marble floor of the foyer before rolling to land on the carpet. "I had a bit too much to drink last night. Had to sleep it off somewhere or...with *someone*," I answered dryly, both of us aware of the lie. Antagonize him, that was my plan.

"I didn't realize that being a drunken whore was in a princess's job description," he snapped and turned to face me. A sour expression engulfed his genteel face as he took in my disheveled state. "Though I shouldn't be surprised. You were always too eager to please others."

I sneered, "Well, they please me between my thighs, so I call it a win."

"That fucking mouth of yours is a dick sedative," my father spat, his upper lip peeling back. "I'm sure you even fail in that department."

I chuckled and took soft steps into the living room, the plush carpet squeezing between my toes, cushioning the soles of my feet. Inches separated us. I only came chest-level with him, but I held his glare all the same. The bottomless depths of his eyes threatened to swallow me whole. "And I'm sure you need a dick reviver, old man. However..." I drawled, taunting him. "The men I please *love* my filthy fucking mouth."

His fist struck my cheekbone. It was a powerful blow that had me reeling from the impact. I stumbled back a few steps and clutched the sharp, bruising pain. My smile turned feral.

I wanted this. I had hoped for a reason to brawl with the king. To have a chance to kill him, slowly and painfully. Even if that wasn't the main goal, it would be a lovely bonus. Forcing him to crack his composed exterior was the way to do it.

"Strike a nerve, did I, Father?" I asked, followed by an unhinged chuckle. The urge to unleash years of pent-up resentment and emotional pain ravaged me. For a brief moment, I could understand Griffin's madness.

The king shook his head and closed his eyes, pinching the bridge of his nose. "You were a mistake, Gray."

"I'm pretty sure the daily beatings for the past fifteen years have instilled that point."

The king stiffened and straightened his cufflinks in nonchalance, regaining his composure. "You've always been such an obstinate learner, my dear."

"My apologies for failing to be the perfect little child soldier you've always dreamt of," I said, struggling to keep the emotion from my voice. I squared my shoulders and held my palms facing outwards at my sides. Oh, how hard I'd tried to be the next Chrome Freyr for him. In the end, it was never enough.

I drew energy into my aura, building my reserves for a substantial electric blast. I was grateful Scarlett, Cotton, and Hazel lent their energies to me, but I would need more in order to best my father.

"It's a little late for apologies, daughter," the king said in a condescending tone. "Don't you think?" A strand of his perfectly styled, deep-green hair fell across his eye. The blue undertones caught on the rays of the rising sun. He calmly pushed it back into place with delicate precision.

"Perhaps." My palms vibrated from the energy waves I absorbed. The air cooled, and the lights dimmed as I stole the electricity for myself.

Father looked around the room with a knowing smirk, able to sense my absorption fueling the strength of my magic. "Still being defiant, I see."

I ground my teeth and thrust out my palms, expecting a large blast to slam into him. My heart dropped to the floor when nothing happened.

My magic vanished. It was just gone.

And that could only mean...

"Grim..." Dread sunk deep into my core. I shook my head, realizing that I'd walked right into his trap—another failure.

Grim Valor, the husband of Amethyst, stood behind me. I could only guess that he'd been lying in wait for me to make a move. His dark, empty energy consumed my magic the closer he drew. "Hello, Princess. It's been a while."

"Not quite long enough."

Grim's loafers screeched against the marble tile as he approached. The cold void of his energetic aura suffocated me. Every second left me feeling more barren. He leaned into my ear and murmured, "Nah. It's been too long, little one. Too long."

Ice froze my veins when his rancid breath forced its way from my ear down my neck. I peered at my father, who stood pompous with his arms crossing his chest.

I imagined Grim's predatory gleam that hovered behind me. I could almost see the layer of grease that always burnished his long black hair, his beady eyes preying upon weakness, and his sharp nose hooking to a gruesome right as if permanently damaged. I never understood what Amethyst saw in him. Maybe it was his corrupted soul that mirrored her own.

"As I said, Gray. You were a mistake," my father said as Grim's poisonous fingers trailed down my arms.

I knew better than to shake him off so I didn't flinch. "Like what you see, Grim? Amethyst must be holding out on you."

Cold hands ensnared my wrists, pinning them behind my back. I struggled against them, but a dark chuckle sounded in my right ear. "We'll see who holds out, Princess."

"What is this, Father?" I demanded.

I thrashed in Grim's hold. He yanked on my wrists, causing me to stumble in my struggle. Father leered at me. He believed he'd won.

I slipped an arm loose and bashed my elbow into Grim's ribcage. The blow forced him to loosen his grip on my other wrist. Freed from his hold, I spun around and punched his pallid jaw. A grunt escaped him as he stumbled. Grabbing his wrist, I thrust my knee upward, nailing him between his thighs. He dropped to the carpet with a thud.

Hatred simmered in his dark eyes as he strained on the floor, cupping himself. "You fucking bitch!" he shouted, spit flying from his thin lips.

I went for a throat jab, but I was snatched backward by my hair. A knife quickly pushed against my throat. I froze. Pain radiated from my scalp. Each breath pressed my esophagus further into the blade, singeing me with a sharp sting, and sending a trail of blood sliding down my skin. A strong arm wrapped around me, binding me to a broad chest.

Shit, shit, shit.

"Well, that was rather fun," Father taunted from behind. "Grim, get the cuffs."

With a grunt, Grim straightened his back, running his fingers through greasy hair as he rose on wobbly legs. He retreated from the room with a limp, and I couldn't stop the fleeting sense of pride that washed through me. I grinned despite the knife against my throat.

"You failed, Gray," my father said. "Can't say I didn't warn you."

I swallowed, my throat bobbing against the blade. "Well, I guess that was the ultimate disappointment."

"Indeed."

A silence overcame the suite, smothering the oxygen in the room.

Grim returned with the magnetic metal wrist cuffs moments later. He grumbled as he hobbled toward us, still aggravated by my assault.

"Hold out your hands," the king instructed.

I rolled my eyes and offered Grim my wrists in annoyance. "Is this how you like your victims, Grim?" I sneered. "Bound and powerless?"

Grim's nostrils flared. He backhanded my cheek with a resounding crack. My skull knocked into my father's shoulder, furthering the blinding

migraine from his previous attack. I snickered despite the searing pain.
The injuries only seemed to fuel my fire.

"Is that all you got, Grim?" The metallic taste of blood coated my
tongue. Gathering it all, I spat on his face. Blood and saliva oozed down
his crooked nose, deep crimson splattering his cheeks and forehead,
giving him an even more garish look.

The knife dug deeper into my throat. "Go ahead, Father," I taunted.
"Please, cut out the foreplay already and just kill me, for fuck's sake."

"But, Gray, you know how I do things. I like to take my time," King
Forest said in a soft, yet unsettling tone.

I snorted. "You're only wasting valuable time that could be spent
doing more important things. But be my guest."

"You can't trust others to do the dirty work for you," he said, the thick
metal cuffs locking into place. My magic snuffed out in my veins. "I have
to do everything of importance myself. And *this* is very important to me,
daughter." With a shove to my back, the king walked to the door with
Grim at his side. He guided me forward, my hands stiffly cuffed in front
of me.

My gut sank as I realized where he planned to take me. The prison
cells were utilized for more than retaining traitors, Elementals, or Endarkened. The king used them to torture his prisoners, and he always
ensured he was present for those events.

The elevator jolted to a stop.

Grim, having swapped positions with my father behind me, shoved me
forward while the king walked alongside me. We made our way through
the underground level of the prison. Dim lighting barely lit our way, and
shallow cracks slithered along the concrete floor from years of wear.

The moist, frigid air crept into my bones, chilling me to the marrow.
The oxygen was thicker as I fought to maintain even breaths and slow my

mind. It was difficult, given that I fought back gags from the horrendous stench of decomposition and bodily waste.

The prison was a sprawling myriad of interconnected cell blocks. As we approached, groans and growls drifted through the metal bars, making the hair on my skin prickle with unease.

Morbid curiosity got the best of me, so I stole a glimpse inside a cell. Obscured in the shadows, a woman stared at me with wide and distant eyes. Her long, oily hair sat matted to her skull in bald patches. The silver irises of an Elemental stared back at me. The gold layer of skin cracked and peeled away in large swathes, while the remaining layers paled a ghastly dull hue, depriving her of all vitality. I looked on in horror at the shadows that painted her gaunt features as she reached her frail arm through the space between the bars.

Then, in an act that stunned me, the Endarkened woman dropped onto one knee, her breaths raspy. She said nothing. But when she pressed her forehead against her knee, I faltered in my steps at the foreign custom.

Grim and my father strolled past her as if she weren't there as they guided me past prisoners of different varieties. Most huddled against the wall, not acknowledging us as we passed.

We reached the end of the corridor, and a heavy metal door loomed above. My father typed in a code, followed by a jarring buzz that cut through the miserable silence. Like a death knell, a hard click echoed off the concrete.

Another hard shove to my back thrust me into the interrogation room, the cuffs digging into my wrists. I stumbled forward.

I needed to escape. Otherwise, I'd die in this dank dungeon. I couldn't hand my father that victory.

I'd always had supreme vision, even amongst Kinetics. So, despite the void in the room, I saw their movements. I'd never disclosed this minor fact to the king, and I was currently grateful for that decision.

"Grim, I need some light. Back off some," the king said as Grim's magic absorbed any illumination in the room. They believed it gave them an advantage.

But if I allowed them to have light, it would destroy any hope of getting out alive. I didn't plan to stick around in their chamber of horrors.

Taking advantage of the brief upper hand, I threw an elbow into Grim's nose with all my strength. My wrists were still cuffed, but I wouldn't let that stop me from fighting. My father heard the impact and lunged for me. I saw his silhouette and stepped aside. He collided with Grim, who fell to the putrid floor. Enraged, the king spun around to face the spot I'd previously stood, but I'd moved behind him.

With him unaware of my position, I silently snagged the knife my father held to my throat. With my wrists bound, I slashed it across the nape of his neck, then plunged it deep into his lower back. I missed his spinal cord, but still, the king crumpled to his knees.

"You defiant fucking bitch," Forest ground out.

I couldn't linger long enough for the king to heal. Taking hasty steps toward the door, something grabbed my ankle. I lurched forward, slapping my palms on the cold floor. "Don't *fucking* touch me," I said in a growl, slamming my heel into Grim's temple.

I scrambled to my feet, ignoring the bruising on my knees and the stinging in my palms. I struggled to reach the door within my view.

"No." The king's labored voice reached my ears from within the darkness, still hindered by the stab wound. "Not you, too."

His words *almost* stopped me in my tracks.

"I'm sure we'll meet again, Father," I spat, keeping it short and sweet.

At last, I reached the door and punched in the code, silently thanking Cotton for thinking ahead when he had written it down for me to memorize in the event things went wrong—which they had. I yanked it open.

I winced. The dim light in the corridor blinded me as my eyes adjusted from the emptiness of the interrogation room.

But then I ran.

I sprinted past the cells that detained decaying prisoners and ignored their pleas for freedom.

The elevator loomed ahead, so I pushed my body to its brink to reach it. I didn't look behind me, fearing Grim or my father were on my heels. The cuffs needed to be removed as soon as possible.

If I could get to Cotton...

I pounded the elevator button in violent desperation, wishing I could coerce the defective box to move at the speed I needed it to. I bounced on the soles of my bare feet while I waited, still wearing the gold dress from the revel.

The heavy door boomed at the end of the corridor. Startled, I jerked my head to glance over my shoulder. My heart lurched to my throat at the sight of Grim sprinting toward me with blood flowing from his nose, painting his throat.

There were only five more floors before the elevator reached me. I tightened my grip on the knife's hilt and spun to face Grim. I couldn't allow him to catch me by surprise again.

He continued to close the distance. Although my wrists were bound in front of me, I fell into a defensive stance,

The elevator dinged—the biggest fucking mercy I'd received since the moment I confronted Griffin Silas. I backed myself into the metal box, focused on the racing Grim. My heart hammered in my chest as I watched him draw closer.

The elevator doors inched shut with a metallic clang. I slapped the button for one floor above, to the basement where I was to meet Scarlett.

I let air fill my lungs and dropped my head against the elevator wall during the brief ride to the training room. The king hadn't had time to alert the guards, so I'd be free to grab the needed supplies. With my magic inhibited, I wasn't able to signal Scarlett, Cotton, and Hazel that my task was done.

I hoped to find them and get what I needed to flee. And if not, then I'd do what I did best: go at it alone.

Chapter 11

GRAY

I dashed from the elevator in search of Scarlett.

Guards patrolled each floor of the King's Palace, so I remained vigilant, knowing my bound wrists would raise suspicion.

In the training room, several Kinetics warmed up on dummies, sharpened their blades, and built up their energetic magic in designated areas. I disregarded them as I jogged past. But paranoia soon set in as I felt each set of eyes land on me. Their scrutinizing stares slid over my cuffed wrists as I ran in a haphazard frenzy. Time was running out.

Scarlett said she'd be where the blades were stored, so I cut through the aisle leading to the weapons. I had been held up with my father and Grim for almost an hour, well past the timeframe I was due to meet up with her. I prayed she was still there.

The blades were stationed at the opposite end of the training room. I couldn't help but wonder what I looked like to the random Kinetic, with sweat smearing my makeup and dried blood caking my skin. My hair looked as if it housed a family of armadillos—not exactly a princessly look.

I reached the end of the training room. To my right, a stout warrior—with pink and white dual-toned hair pulled back into a low bun—stood watch. He spotted me and paused his movements with an unnatural grace for a man his size. Neither of us flinched. We stood frozen in silence, daring the other to make the first move. I noticed the sword strapped to his back and glanced down at my cuffed wrists.

Fuck.

"Gray!" Scarlett's voice snatched me from the silent standoff. "Oh, for shit's sake! Where have you been?" Scarlett spun me around by the shoulders to face her. It only took a glimpse of my stiff posture for her attention to land on my wrists.

With a quiet curse, Scarlett grabbed my biceps and dragged me away.

"Hey!" the warrior called to our backs.

We didn't stop, not even to glance over our shoulders at the skeptical warrior looming behind us. "Stop!"

"Fuck off, you brute!" Scarlett said without hitching a step.

A low-grade burn simmered on my skin, like a light sunburn but soon built into agonizing pain. I stumbled and cried out, dropping to a knee.

Scarlett, still holding onto my arm, fared little better. She gritted her teeth, a pain-filled groan escaping her. "Fucking ultraviolet magic."

In my desperation to escape, I never noticed the red currents dancing up the warrior's arms. The burn on my back continued to increase. "I can't do...anything with these fucking cuffs."

Scarlett clenched her eyes shut as she withstood the pain.

The warrior descended upon us. Metal rang out as he withdrew his sword.

My mind raced for a plan, but the heat on my back threatened to melt the silk dress into my skin. I battled the gut-wrenching scream that fought to erupt.

The warrior's shadow loomed over me. Blue glowed from the sigils on his sword, illuminating the surrounding floor.

I braced for the impact—for my death.

A burst of violet electricity shot past me, slamming into the warrior. Scarlett's magic forced him to release control of his power, allowing the ultraviolet burn to ebb in its intensity.

The high voltage locked up the warrior's body in uncontrolled convulsions. His eyes bulged from his skull as he forced out guttural grunts. My insides twisted at the sound.

Scarlett continued to unleash her visceral power onto him, even after he collapsed to the cement floor with a thud.

"Scarlett!" The warrior's eyes glazed over with lifelessness. "He's dead. Stop!" Scarlett would expend all her magic on a godsdamned corpse; she was lost to it. Some Kinetics' powers were more addictive than others due to the volatile nature of its energy source. Scarlett's was one of them.

I shifted my attention from the body wrapped in purple volts to Scarlett. Her green eyes were unfocused, lost in the trance of her nuclear-powered magic. Violet streams of electricity poured from her outstretched palms into the dead warrior. My shouts fell on deaf ears. "Scar!" I tried again. "Let it go!"

All the commotion attracted the attention of the surrounding Kinetics in the training room. Voices drew closer, and my only option was to snap Scarlett out of her trance. The warrior's body smoked from the electricity charring his flesh, and its stench made my stomach roil.

Scarlett's magic attacked anyone who touched her skin while she wielded her power. I braced for more pain as I swung my bound hands into her jaw. Upon impact, I seized up in my own electrical onslaught. Purple volts bridged my fists and her face while she still unleashed upon the warrior.

My body spasmed as I grunted from the high-voltage currents; my veins and arteries fried. I had seconds before I succumbed to her power, considering I had no way to fight back.

The pain came in quick waves as the electricity moved to my organs. I wanted to either climb out of my skin or freeze in place, which created an insufferable dichotomy.

The irony that I would die by Scarlett's hands while trying to flee from my father didn't escape me.

Scarlett suddenly collapsed to the floor in a pool of red hair. The purple volts receded back into her currents. Sweat glistened on her skin from the fluorescent lights, indicating the amount of effort she used to wield her magic.

I crumpled to my side, weakened from the pain and strain of my muscles. A whimper fell from my lips at the sight of a pair of polished black boots that stepped into view. Through my hazy vision, I focused on the Kinetic in front of me.

I imagined Grim standing there, ready to haul me back to the interrogation room one level below. I was too weak to fight back. Too much had happened in such a short time.

I lay on the cold, hard floor, waiting for another round of agony to kick-start me alive. Erratic breaths clawed their way from my lungs to keep me afloat. Miraculously, I remained somewhat conscious.

The man squatted in front of me. I barely made out his silhouette, but the sleek boots were at the forefront. Gentle fingers pressed on my carotid artery for several beats before they retreated. But then, the Kinetic moved to my cuffed wrists.

A flash of white hair caught my attention. "C—Cotton?"

There was no verbal response, but I felt his hands fiddling with the manacles. I was still in pain from the warrior and Scarlett's magic, but I'd heal faster once the cuffs were removed. They didn't entirely suppress our healing abilities; instead, they only slowed them down.

Cotton jiggled my wrists, not even bothering to be gentle. My body protested; every fiber screamed in torment. He didn't appear apologetic about it. He simply offered a shrug.

My wrists finally broke loose from the magic-restricting cuffs. A firm hand grabbed my forearm and yanked me to my unsteady feet. With my magic freed, my healing abilities kicked in and began to cool the burned areas of my body.

Cotton bent down to scoop Scarlett up and started toward the elevators. Curious gazes landed on us as we passed, but we avoided them on our trek. I wondered how much time Cotton had bought us with the guards.

Scarlett lay limp in Cotton's arms while we waited for the elevator. I bounced on the balls of my feet, impatience gnawing away at me from precious seconds wasted. I fought off the growing urge to panic at the slow elevator. I hated that the fate of our lives hung in the hands of an inanimate object.

No one approached while paranoia swallowed us whole. Every few seconds, one of us would glance over our shoulder to ensure we weren't being followed.

The elevator *finally* sounded its arrival. Cotton's breaths grew labored from carrying Scarlett's dead weight as we stepped into the lift. His physical strength hid behind his tall, slender physique, and the hardness in his facial expression gave people pause. Yet, it seemed Scarlett was the only one able to break through it.

I soaked in the brief quietude that always existed in Cotton's presence. He appeared calm and composed, but the heaviness in his eyes exposed his anxiety.

We were safe for the moment, but I wasn't sure how long it would last. I used the reprieve to take deep, slow breaths and to savor my magic's return.

I shook my wrists where the cuffs had bound me. Plan A was an absolute failure. I was only meant to prevent Forest from sending a search party after me while Cotton held off the guards and Scarlett got weapons, but that plan got turned sideways with Grim.

The elevator came to a standstill.

I braced for any surprises waiting on the other side of the doors. The doors ground open, and...thank the gods, no one was there to ambush us.

Cotton glanced at me and nodded, signaling for me to take the lead. I didn't hesitate.

Running feet sounded levels below. But with our limited time, we were clear.

Ascending to only a few floors below the King's Suite, I knew we were on Cotton's floor, where the higher-ranking Kinetics resided. After having left his suite only an hour earlier, I recognized that the door at the end of the hallway belonged to him.

Struggling to balance Scarlett in his arms, he typed in the code on the keypad to his suite.

Once inside, I followed Cotton into the guest room, where he laid Scarlett on the bed I'd previously occupied.

"Is she okay?" I asked, walking up to the bedside and taking in her unconscious form. The reality of what we had just gone through hit me as I gazed at her.

After one final scan, Cotton nodded and exited the room. He beckoned me to follow him with a wave over his shoulder.

Cotton padded through the spotless suite to the main bedroom. Like the rest of the King's Palace, it was lavish, with a white marble kitchen floor, high-end appliances, and fine furniture from the renovations pre-Devolution Day. It was much smaller than the King's Suite but larger than the commoner's because of his inquisitor position.

I stopped in the doorway of his bedroom, observing his living space. Like the guest room, it was bare of anything with personal value.

I didn't comment as he rummaged through his closet. Moments later, he reappeared with a stuffed duffel bag and shoved it in my arms. He nodded to the bag, indicating for me to inspect the contents.

I found black leathers, cowls, and fingerless gloves that I usually wore for missions. Scarves, thin hoodies, and combat boots were shoved in there to accompany them. Mixed in were comfort clothes like leggings and tees I'd need to blend in amongst humans. They'd also stuffed other essential amenities within the smaller pockets. Hidden at the bottom were my weapons of choice: Kinetic daggers and throwing knives designed to weaken and kill Elementals, along with magnetic bracelets to hide my nature.

I looked up at Cotton, relief pouring through me. Cotton dipped his head in response before brushing past me into the kitchen. I trailed him to the counter, where he scrawled on a pad of yellow paper.

The guards are cleared. I threw them off course. Told them to watch the east exit. At least, that's where they were heading before I found you in the training room. You need to leave now.

I nodded in agreement but noted the ruined dress that clung to me in tatters. I needed to change. Cotton understood and pointed in the direction of the bathroom.

Rummaging through the duffle, I snagged the leathers and mission gear before jogging to the washroom. After about five minutes, I was finished and returned feeling much more capable of facing whatever obstacles lay ahead.

I studied his profile. His light olive gaze found mine. Hardened lines ingrained his forehead from frowning in thought as if he was always looking between the lines. A silver scar marred the crease of his lips in an inward arc. It was the first time I'd noticed it, and I wondered what the cause had been.

"Is it possible for me to absorb some energy before I leave? I have a feeling I'm going to need it," I asked, redirecting my attention back to his intense gaze.

Cotton furrowed his brows and looked up at the ceiling. He pointed a finger at the lights as though questioning whether that would suffice or not.

I nodded. "Yeah, that's perfect. Thanks." Scarlett would need his energy to help heal once she regained consciousness, so I didn't blame him for not wanting to energy-share.

Taking a deep breath, I focused on the light waves that emitted from the LED bulbs in the fixtures and absorbed them. The lights in the room flickered and dimmed before blacking out for several breaths. I turned my focus to the ultraviolet light streaming in from the windows until I felt another rush of energy rejuvenate me. Sunlight was always a potent source, but I had the unusual luxury of being able to absorb different forms of energy on the spectrum to replenish. And finally, I listened for the hum of the electricity and drew it into my aura.

With my energetic magic fully restored, blue currents sped up and down my arms.

I let out a sensual moan at the euphoric feeling, forgetting where I was. I peeked an eye open. Cotton sported the smallest of smiles, which transformed his face into the attractive man he truly was.

I cleared my throat and looked away. Cotton's knowing smirk teased me, furthering my embarrassment. "Okay," I said, holding up a hand. "Just because you're exceptionally great at reading people doesn't mean you can taunt me like that. It's been a while since I've had a good fuck."

Cotton bit his bottom lip while running a hand over his mouth to hide his smile. This would be the second time within a three-hour time span I'd gotten aroused in his presence. He was going to get the wrong idea if I wasn't careful.

Selfishly, I wished he could talk so I didn't feel compelled to. Squeezing my thighs together, I looked at the door as if it would save me from this humiliating situation.

But reality doused me with ice water at what awaited behind that door. Cotton's expression returned to its stern intensity, washing the attractive smile from his face.

"I'm leaving. Wish me luck. I appreciate your help more than you know."

A quick nod is all I got in response.

I met his perceptive eyes. "Let Scar know I said thanks for everything." Another nod. "And tell the king I forced your help if he suspects anything. Don't get in trouble on my behalf. Convince him I'm the reason she's unconscious."

His furrowed brow deepened with confusion.

"I'm sure, Cotton," I promised. "He already wants me dead. That won't change. Having you two on his list doesn't help matters at all. Just...do it, okay? Swear it."

Cotton dropped his gaze to the floor, not fond of betraying me to the king after all he'd sacrificed to help me flee, but he conceded with a clenched jaw and an upward tilt of his chin.

"Okay," I said, blowing out a breath. "Thanks." I hoisted the black duffel over my shoulder, striding to the door without another glance.

Instead of focusing on what could go wrong, I focused on my freedom. I centered on my magic that kept me anchored. And I imagined returning one day to finish off the king. Not only for his demise and my revenge but to retrieve the few Kinetics I cared about.

I reached for the darkness that was bred to exist within me. As a child, the damaged part of myself formed a mask to hide my weakness. But that mask soon morphed into a cold and vicious being of its own. When called upon, its wrath knew no bounds.

May the gods help anyone who stood in my way.

Chapter 12

GRIFFIN

B one crunched from another blow to the cheek. I savored the pain, allowing it to fuel the cruelty within me. It was risky to permit myself to be almost pushed to the point of no return, but I knew I could handle it. A twisted part of me was a masochist, craving punishment for my crimes. But mostly, I fed the darkness more with each hit.

Their blades hadn't been wielded yet, but they were coming. Still, I couldn't use my magic unless I wanted to alert the entire Warrior Guild of my presence. They had specific Kinetics with the ability to track energetic signatures from distances. Mine would light up like a flash bomb if I removed my bracelet.

A booted blow to my ribs had the air forced from my lungs, and a grunt of pain escaped with it. I laughed.

With my vision blackened and outside noise drowned out, I continued to focus my tactile senses on the air's movement around me. Years of training blinded and deafened prepared me for moments like these. So, when a wisp of air brushed my cheek, I knew a knife had finally been pulled. I'd be fucking damned before I succumbed to the poison of a Kinetic blade.

Just as I felt the slice about to land across my face, I jerked to the side while pulling out the knife strategically held up my sleeve. My blade carved across the Kinetic's wrist. He jumped back, and I rolled to the side, still blinded.

The roaring in my head eased as I rose to my knee. And I realized that the screeching in my ears stopped when I cut the Kinetic. As my hearing slowly returned, the cursing of the man I cut registered to my right while I heard boots approach.

Buzzing energy vibrated the air, and I spun again as another blast flew at my head. While keeping my senses open, the fucker's voice in my head resumed his death chant.

Kill. Kill. Kill.

I snapped.

The savagery that swarmed my chest finally won.

Reaching behind me, I slid my double-edged sword from its sheath on my back. The sigils on both blades glowed orange. The familiarity of my sword grounded me, but not enough to control the murderousness singing in my veins. I lunged at them in blind haste. But I was never truly blind as long as I had my other senses.

As I was mid-leap, the sound of two swords sliding free from their sheathes echoed in the alleyway. I knew my strength and body enough to judge how high I'd jumped. Their feet shuffled, indicating they adjusted their stance as I came down on top of them. I kicked one in the chest while crashing on top of the other.

My knees slammed into the rough concrete, sending a searing pain through my bones. I soaked it up, letting it drive me to the peak of my madness. I held my sword above my head, and with a spin, I arced the blade at a downward angle. The glowing weapon sliced through muscle, and cartilage until they no longer resisted my effort, freeing his head from his neck.

In that moment, I hated more than anything that I couldn't witness the crimson pooling on the ground beneath me. Fortunately, the combination of the metallic scent of blood and its warm wetness dripping down my face was enough to appease the beast within for only a fraction of a breath.

A large, solid force struck my body and tackled me to the ground. With my vision still blacked out, I assumed this Kinetic was the culprit. I struggled to free my arms from his hold yet still maintained my grip on my sword.

My right leg was pinned beneath his body weight, but with my left one free, I jabbed him in the side with my knee. The move was enough to loosen his grasp on my arms, allowing me to roll to where we switched positions. I dropped my sword. Its size was ineffective in this position, and I needed at least one hand unburdened to fight the skilled warrior beneath me—especially without my sight.

I punched in the general direction of where I knew his face would be. A sickening crunch brought a savage smirk to my face as I snatched a dagger from my pants leg. The action opened me up for the Kinetic knife sinking into my side.

"Godsdamnit!"

I locked the Kinetic tight between my knees as he struggled underneath me. With my freed hand, I patted the areas of his body that the thick leather of the warrior gear shielded and began to slice in quick, strategic movements across any unprotected surface. I didn't stop. Not when sharp stabs to my thigh, arm, shoulder, and side exploded in pain from his desperate frenzy to escape my hold.

As my vision came into focus from his death, I made out the blurry outlines of a marred and mutilated body. Once it cleared, the shredded face and neck of the warrior were painted a deep ruby. The beast within me jeered at the carnage, but he wasn't satisfied. He wanted *more*.

I had minutes at best before the poison of the Kinetic blade crippled me. I could already feel its effects burning through my veins, scorching a wildfire of hatred through my body. But I shook it off like I had so many times before, forcing myself to climb off the dead Kinetic and then slide the knife back up my sleeve.

Standing, I took in the widened alleyway. Dizziness unsteadied me from the injuries and blood loss of the stab wounds, but a dark viciousness made my heart sing at the sight I left behind. A beheaded corpse sprawled in thick, dark blood lay feet away from me, his unblinking eyes frozen wide with fear.

I bent to retrieve my sword and swiped the bloody blade on my pants before tucking it back in its sheath.

Another blade clanged free, and I snapped my attention to the lone figure slumped against the wall. He groaned as he cupped his neck with one hand. His life force gushed down his neck and soaked into his black uniform. He wielded a Kinetic knife in his fist, preparing to throw it at me.

I cocked my head to the side as I studied him. "Ah," I said, my voice hoarse. "You're still alive, I see." The dying Kinetic scrambled to sit straighter, wincing as he did. I scrunched my face at his predicament. "Well, isn't that little wound just a *dying* pity?"

"Fuck you," the warrior spat, his words garbled. With the redfern from my Elemental blade surging in his veins, his magic was subdued, so it didn't concern me about his blasts.

I took slow measured steps toward him, mainly because I felt myself weakening with each passing second, but at least I was still upright, despite all the injuries. I needed to recoup—and fast. "So, I presume you recognize me."

The warrior's labored breaths wheezed and huffed. And as I neared him, his paling skin made it evident that the single strike across his neck would be fatal. "You're dead." A mixture of fear, hatred, and confusion twisted across his features as he assessed me.

I came to a stop before him and dropped to a squat, ignoring the excruciating pain in my thigh and side. It would soon be healed, anyways. "It would appear that I am, in fact, *not* dead, wouldn't it?" I chuckled. "You, on the other hand, won't be able to say the same in a moment."

With what little strength he had left, he aimed a careless swipe at me with his blade. I dodged it before grabbing his wrist, apprehending the blade for myself. I tsked and held the knife flat in both my palms as I observed its sharp, angular sigils.

"I bet your king doesn't provide any of you with the crushed nickel antidote for the redfern that's poisoning your bloodstream, hm?" I asked, keeping my hazy gaze on the knife in my hands.

"He's gonna kill you," the warrior rasped. I snapped my focus to land on the man inches away from me. Short navy-blue hair blurred in my sight, a jarring contrast to the crimson staining his neck and hands.

"Not if I kill him first."

I adjusted my stance to reach into a well-guarded pocket in my black cargos. After digging with my shaking hand, I sighed in relief when it landed on the last remaining syringe containing the antidote. I shook it in front of him. "Too bad it's not your brand. We could've dueled over it. Now, that would've been quite the sight." I laughed at my own remark as I removed the plastic encasement covering the needle.

"No wonder he's wanted you dead. You're a fucking monster."

"Yes," I said as I thumped the container while watching the air bubbles rise to the surface. "I am. And none of you should ever forget that." I pushed the exposed needle into the major vein protruding in my neck, just as I had done with the princess, and mashed down with my thumb to empty the contents into my bloodstream.

Within seconds, I could feel the sweltering inferno begin to cool while I gasped from the instant relief. The darkness that craved death and suffering still harbored its cold rage within me. Soon enough, though, the heat of the black crystal eased to a simmer, leaving only the welcomed pain from the open wounds behind. I inhaled a dramatic breath. "Godsdamn that feels good. You should try it..."

My sight finally restored to its heightened clarity, and I saw just how ashen the Kinetic had grown. He had minutes left, at best. "Just kill me already," he whispered, his head lolling to the side to rest on his shoulder.

I pretended to ponder the thought because, truly, I wanted nothing more than another excuse to take his life, but I couldn't grant him what he wanted. He needed to suffer.

Or did he?

Ah! The decisions...

After several moments of pondering the difficult choice, I sighed with my final verdict. "I think," I said, shoving the empty syringe into a pocket and pulling out another dagger from my weapons belt, "you caught me on a good day. Don't say I never did anything for you." I shuffled closer until my lips were at his ear, and I murmured, "Send her all my love."

I clenched my jaw as I stabbed my dagger up through his ribcage before pulling it out, only to jam the blade deep into his chest, piercing his heart.

The darkness soaked up the brutality of my acts. It loved every second, savoring every drop of blood spilled, but it wasn't enough. It never would be, no matter how many had to die at my hands. But for now, it was satiated to offer me a slight mental reprieve from the incessant drumbeat of death as it dulled to a low hum.

I braced a hand against the wall to stand, pushing through the pain in my thigh and oblique. Now that the last of my antidote was gone, I had to be careful from here on. I couldn't afford any more wounds from a Kinetic blade.

A deafening crack of a gunshot shattered the darkened silence of the abandoned city. I whipped my head in its direction, remembering Dash. A shock of fear jolted through my chest. With the beast calmed and the adrenaline from the fight waning, the pain from the wounds came to the forefront of my mind, as well as the dizzying blood loss.

I shoved off the wall and staggered out of the alleyway in search of the sixteen-year-old human boy. We'd split up to flank opposite sides of the nearby perimeter of the King's Palace. I needed to get to a place far enough away to remove my bracelet so I could heal faster.

Another shot echoed off the buildings, urging me into a sprint through the street. I weaved between forgotten cars, crunching over broken glass and discarded trash through intersections. After several minutes, I quietly retrieved my sword while seeking cover amongst the buildings toward the sound of the fight ahead. By that point, the adrenaline had returned, but my wounds screamed too loud to ignore. I'd fought in worse conditions before, but I didn't know what lay ahead of me. Stepping into a fight without my magic while severely wounded *and* recovering from black crystal poisoning put me at a major disadvantage.

A pained scream pierced the air. As quickly as the beast had calmed, it just as quickly reared its head at the sound of Dash's struggle. It wasn't so much the darkness coming out in defense of Dash; it was the call of bloodshed that brought it back to life.

I listened to the fight nearby, trying to place how many attackers were present against Dash. No more shots rang out, so I assumed the Kinetics in question used magic to subdue him. And Dash wasn't the untrained human who'd shoot in a wild panic. Ammo was such a rare commodity these days that one didn't waste bullets on hopeful shots. If he wasn't shooting, there must be a solid reason for it.

Based on the sets of moving feet, I gathered that two Kinetics had Dash outnumbered. And with their magic, it wouldn't be a fair fight. Shoving my free hand through my hair, I made a risky decision.

I unclasped the black bracelet that suppressed my Elemental magic. Shoving it into a pocket inside my cloak, I breathed a relieved sigh from the cold affinity of metal as it wafted through my senses. Its strong, unyielding essence grounded me while it fueled my body to begin healing the wounds. My skin transformed from its usual warm tan to its gilded sheen.

I stepped from the alley a bit more balanced as the dizziness fled my mind.

Kill. Kill. Kill.

The pain in my leg ever so slowly faded as I neared the scene transpiring behind an abandoned salon. Voices grew more distinct, and I paused to take stock of the situation.

"We take him back as a prisoner," a deep voice sounded.

A pause. "No," a second male said, "we should kill him. The king hates humans."

"But he's a rebel, part of the militia. King Forest would wanna get information outta him."

"I fucking said *no*. Orders are orders. The kid dies...or we will."

"Godsdamnit. What the fuck was he thinking? He thought he'd hurt us with a gun?" the first voice asked, confusion lacing his tone.

His partner scoffed, "He's a human kid. What do you expect?"

Hearing them speak about humans like they were nothing sent another wave of raging heat coursing through my chest. The grip on my sword tightened, and I had to remind myself it wasn't their fault; they didn't know any better. Forest had everyone's brain completely fucked regarding this world. But they'd earned their death sentences when they hurt my human ally.

"Come on, Russ," the first one said, "let's just get it over with. We need to find the others and spread out. That little cunt is up to something tonight."

That *little cunt* could only mean Princess Gray. And an instinctual part of me snarled at the disrespect, which pissed me off more because I didn't have any fucks to give whether she lived or died after her purpose had been served. She was just as guilty as these two doorknobs I eavesdropped on.

"Wait," the hard-ass named Russ—I assumed was short for Russet—said. "You feel that? That energy?"

"Yeah, who..."

"Fuck," Hard-Ass muttered in a panic. "Go. Grab the boy; we'll finish him off later."

I took that as my opportunity to reveal myself. Listening to these fuck-twats gave my body a chance to heal while riling up the darkness within me. Sliding my shoulder from the salon's brick wall, I slunk around the corner, obscuring myself in the shadows.

The men were busy gathering up the boy and his weapon. As they sensed my presence, they froze their frenzied movements, knowing they hadn't been fast enough to miss my arrival.

"*You're* the king's warriors?" I asked with a raised brow. "I imagine he'd torture you excruciatingly slow if he knew you were running from the chance to kill me." I bit my bottom lip and squinted my eyes as I observed them. "Just think of all the glory you're missing out on."

Both men glanced at each other before removing their blades, a sword and two daggers.

"Leave the boy," I said, my voice hard, dropping all pretenses. "Only cowards murder those that they easily outmatch." Quickly assessing Dash, I noticed he was unconscious. With a swift check with magic, I noted that the iron within his blood still pumped through his bloodstream. Alive.

Hard-Ass apparently decided to grow a pair when he said, "You mean like you?"

The smile that stretched across my face was nothing short of rabid as I fought to keep the madness and rage at bay. "See...I might be the exception to that little rule." Reaching out with my element like an extended limb, I removed four knives from my weapons belt and hovered them in the air in front of me. They spun and rotated to the beat of death's war drum in my mind, the blue glow from their sigils illuminating the dark space.

"It's sad, really, that I must kill the ignorant like yourselves. But that's the world we live in—the one that your master so diligently crafted."

It was dark, and this alley was significantly narrower than the previous one. I couldn't see the shades of their hair, but the currents that glowed on their necks were orange and gold: infrared and light source magics.

"You *are* fucking insane. That was all you, man. You started all this."

I rolled my eyes and sighed, "Godsdamnit, I'm so tired of hearing that." While it's partially true I want King Forest dead out of vengeance for killing my father, King Jonas, there was much more to it than any of them could fathom.

"Put the boy down. *Now*." Two of the knives redirected themselves to point at the two warriors ahead of me.

Hard-Ass scoffed, "No. He goes with us," he said, followed by a warmth spreading throughout my body, starting on my back. *Infrared magic*. It rapidly increased in strength until it became scalding. It sucked, but they didn't know the history of my training, which prepared me for this—no one did.

With time not on my side, I sent the two knives aimed at the men flying like mini-missiles. At the last second, they diverged, one blade targeting

Hard-Ass and the other his sidekick. With a wet *thunk*, one of the knives embedded to the hilt into Hard-Ass's eye, while the other sunk into his companion's carotid. They dropped to the ground, leaving Dash to fall to the concrete in front of them in an unconscious heap.

Hard-Ass died on impact as the blade pierced his brain. To be safe, I sent another knife to his sidekick's throat, gashing it open to ensure he couldn't heal once I retrieved my knives. My darkness sang its victory cry, but as usual, it wanted more.

And it just might get it because more warriors and guards approached, their voices and magic scraping against my senses. I assumed they picked up on my energetic signature after I removed my bracelet.

Fine. I'd kill them all, then.

Using my magic, I removed the knives from the Kinetics' bodies and brought them before me once more. The beast roared for what was to come as I summoned my other blades to encircle me while I slid my sword free, rotating it as my cold power pulsed through me. My element was hungry as it sensed the threats ahead.

My ears perked at the sound of a nocked arrow on the flat rooftop to my right. I sent a dagger upward. Shadows closed in both ends of the alleyway with the varying abilities of the guild, the most elite of them all.

The assassin from the roof plummeted to the ground with the grotesque crunch of bones.

My heart sang to the fierce call of death. Perhaps these offerings would appease the beast long enough to return to the Hollow with the princess in tow without losing myself completely.

Chapter 13

GRAY

Silence greeted me when I exited the elevator to the lobby.

I searched for energies that lay in wait. Only one was nearby, and I knew his aura well.

He hid behind a corner a few paces away. I strode with relaxed indifference toward the exit.

I felt the energy of a weapon slice through the air, aimed at my back. Stepping aside, it whizzed past while I summoned blue electrical magic to my palms. I spun around to find Golden Figgaro's arrogant sneer. His hair gleamed like a polished nugget from the California gold mines.

Cowardly piece of shit.

The reigning Kinetic Tournament champion glared at me with empty eyes. I gazed into the dark depths of a cloudy sea, wondering what Scarlett found attractive about him. Not a kind line marked his face.

"The king sent you as his last hope to stop me." It wasn't a question.

Golden's grin taunted me while orange currents traced his arms and neck, indicating his infrared abilities. "You'll never compare to the likes of Chrome. You didn't even enter the Kinetic Tournament," he said, reminding me of when my father denied me the opportunity this past year. "I'll surpass Chrome's legacy one day, but killing you will be a great start in earning King Forest's confidence. He'll wonder why he ever wasted his time on you."

I cocked an eyebrow. "I wonder the same thing about Scarlett. Surely there are bigger dicks in the bag."

Golden's lip pulled back from his teeth, hurling a red, energetic spear at my chest. I sidestepped again, but this time, into the brawny arms of a warrior. Thick biceps curled around my throat in a tightening chokehold.

It caught me by surprise. However, I remained focused on Golden, launching a compact ball of my magic at him.

Judging by his inferior training, I assumed it was a guard that held me.

I kicked behind me with the heel of my boot, slamming into his shin. He cried out and loosened his grip. I ducked under his arm and spun, grabbing my blue-lit dagger from my weapons belt designed to kill Elementals, not Kinetics. The blade arced across his throat, and his eyes widened in shock. Sheets of blood cascaded down his throat and soaked into his black guardsman uniform.

His body dropped to the floor in a heap of pain. It wouldn't kill him, but he was out of the way, at least.

My victory was short-lived, sensing an incoming attack from behind. I snatched a second dagger from my weapons belt and twisted to block the blow my magic felt coming. Blue blades clashed, clanging out in the palatial lobby. My right dagger collided with Golden's broadsword. He had me at a disadvantage with his strength, so I turned to my agility. I sidestepped and slashed upward diagonally from his stomach to his chest. He retreated two steps, but it was enough for me to take the offensive.

With a flick of my wrist, I shifted the grip I had on my left dagger, angling the tip downward. I stalked toward him, finding his weaknesses.

Golden's nostrils flared with a clenched jaw. Rage seethed within his barren eyes while he took a defensive stance with his broadsword.

I kicked at his kneecap, but he leaped out of the way before my boot heel connected. Golden recovered smoothly and returned to the offensive, swinging his broadsword at my neck. I ducked in time, but he used my unsteadiness to strike my ankles with a swift kick, knocking me off my feet.

My tailbone broke my fall on the marble floor. I cursed at the sharp pain. My magic alerted me to Golden's sword, carving the air aimed at my head. I rolled out of the way as the sword struck the floor.

I needed to regain the upper hand.

Golden swung again, and I rolled once more.

He grunted in pain from the gash on his chest. The dull ache in my tailbone stole my breath, but I ignored it as his sword met the marble for a third time. I dropped a dagger and snagged a throwing knife instead. Driving the heel of my boot into his shin, I threw the knife with precision at his torso. It rotated perfectly through the air before sinking into his gut.

The broadsword clattered to the ground, Golden following close behind. I pulled myself to my feet.

I towered over Golden while he choked on his blood as he squeezed the hilt of my protruding dagger.

Golden looked at me with wide eyes, pleading for his life. Blood dribbled down the corners of his chin, igniting the viciousness within me that clawed to be let loose. I pressed the edge of my dagger against his Adam's apple.

"Put the dagger down, Princess." The firm, gentle tone of Supreme Trainer Smokey Valor echoed in the lobby.

I spun to face him, keeping the dagger in place against Golden's throat. "Come to take me back to my father, Smokey?"

Hair, the color of burnt ash, stood out against skin that resembled the shade of terra-cotta as he stepped into view.

"Princess," he said, coming to stand a few paces away. "You need to let Golden go."

Withdrawing my dagger from Golden's throat, I turned to face the lead trainer. "Why should I?" I asked. "He wouldn't hesitate to kill me."

Smokey gave me a solemn dip of his head and glanced at Golden. "Because," he started. "Killing him when he's already defeated is not something you can easily come back from. He's no longer a threat to you if you go now." He sighed and then straightened his back. "You are every bit as strong as Chrome Freyr was...and it's been an honor to train you, Princess."

I shook my head. "That's bullshit. No one compares to what he was. And even he was defeated in the end." I shrugged.

"True." Smokey cocked his head to the side. His thick, ashy brows leveled me with sadness. "I was there when you were born and have seen you grow into something your father fears. Now, go fly, Princess. Be free from his restraints and see it for yourself."

"Wait," I said, shifting my stance. "How were you there when I was born?"

"You need to leave," he said, glancing at Golden. He would be a problem for Smokey after this.

I narrowed my eyes at him, waiting for the inevitable trap. This was too easy. Of all the outcomes I envisioned playing out, this was not one of them. I couldn't figure out Smokey's motive.

He sighed at my blatant skepticism. "The king ordered an entire garrison stationed out the side and back doors. You're going to need to take an...*unorthodox exit*," Smokey advised with a challenging look.

I knew what he meant by that. "Would this unorthodox exit require your auditory abilities?" I asked with a squinted eye.

The Supreme Trainer offered a knowing smirk. "Be ready to run through the front doors when I give you the signal," he ordered.

Despite his instruction, I remained to observe his magic at work. Golden and the guard groaned and rasped with each breath. The reigning champion of the Kinetic Tournament knelt in a pool of his own blood that soiled his pride. His hatred was palpable.

Trainer Valor opened his mouth to speak, but rather than hearing his voice, my feminine tone left his lips instead. Smokey's energetic magic derived from sound waves, so he could alter them to sound however he desired. I imagined it was a useful skill in battle.

Smokey projected my voice to come from the back hallway leading to the rear emergency exit.

"I have to get out of here," my fake voice said, breathless as if I were muttering to myself. "Fuck this hellhole." Smokey cocked a grin at me, amused at his impersonation. It *was* an accurate depiction.

I remembered the duffel bag I'd dropped by the elevator and backed away to retrieve it, keeping my eyes on him.

"And fuck you, Father!" Trainer Valor made me yell, which I found to be overkill. I cringed before shooting him a deadpanned expression, to which he winked at me in return.

The Supreme Trainer fell silent, waiting for the garrison outside to follow the false trail. The emergency door screeched open and then banged shut. He opened his eyes—so much sadness and loss stuffed within—and gave me a curt nod.

I mouthed a silent thanks to the man who stood to gain nothing by helping me. He bowed at the waist in response. Lowering my head in acknowledgment, I bent to collect my duffle. Freedom couldn't come fast enough.

I sprinted through the double glass doors of the Royal Domain's high-rise. The mid-morning sun beamed down upon me while the briskness of the late October air revived my lungs. Red, orange, and gold painted the abandoned cityscape with displaced beauty in a bleak world.

I was *finally* free. Free from my father's control. Free from the suffocating propriety.

Fifteen minutes into my escape, my legs weakened, and my lungs felt like they'd collapse from the constant sprinting. My chest burned from the exertion, so I stopped to recover. I dropped my bag to the ground, resting my linked hands atop my head while I focused on slowing my breaths. Two abandoned high-end stores stood on either side of me. Moldy moss grew on the light, gray stucco from the humid climate, bringing nature to a once bustling city.

I needed to keep moving.

Trains were off-limits as the Royal Domain ran and monitored them with magic.

Unless...

An idea formed in my mind as I caught my breath and stretched my cramped muscles.

My hand absentmindedly caressed the black crystal that swung from my neck on its leather string. I conjured the image of what I imagined my birth mother and father looked like in my mind. There'd been no photos of either of them, but it never stopped me from envisioning them as a child.

With a jolt, I remembered the magnetic bracelets Scarlett and Cotton had packed for me. The King's Palace was equipped with Kinetics who could trace my magic. I needed to suppress it until I was a safer distance away. And as I clicked the metal band into place, a large part of me wondered...

Would I ever be a safe distance away from King Forest?

Dusk fell while I sat in tall grass, waiting for the next train to pass through. I scratched unreachable places as tiny insects skittered inside my garments. I wasn't ashamed to admit I'd slapped my face in an effort to murder mosquitoes. And ants? Ants were the devil's spawn.

I'd been waiting two hours for the next train's arrival. Impatience ate at me like the insects that gnawed on my skin. Paranoia had me checking the trees at every sound for scouts, anticipating an ambush at any given moment.

Wildlife crunched through the forest behind me while I stared at the bare train tracks. Their sounds served as fuel for my magic reserves. Sitting in nature's purity seemed to cleanse the lingering darkness within me. It was the first chance I'd had to process everything that had unfolded in the past forty-eight hours. Almost dying by Griffin's hands was something I could stomach, but nearly dying by my father's—adopted or not—was something I struggled to cope with. I replayed Hazel's words regarding my father's plans—and Slate's knowledge of it.

A pang of longing mixed with betrayal hit me every time I thought about it.

I wondered what the king's public story would've been had he succeeded in killing me. My chest tightened at the thought.

My introverted nature, combined with Forest's passive-aggressive attitude toward me, did me no favors with the Kinetics who disapproved of me. Now, I no longer needed to worry about the delicate dance of propriety to avoid the smallest of scandals. Despite the shitty situation I was in, I embraced the fact I could breathe for the first time.

I was *free*.

In the distance, steel chugged along the tracks. A horn blasted through the pink and orange sky, startling the wildlife. I jolted upright, snapping me from my hazy exhaustion. I looked around, seeking a spot to obscure myself in the shadows.

The next stop wasn't for another thirty miles south to the next city. The Kinetic conductor couldn't know I would be onboard, leaving me with one option. I would need to jump onto a moving train.

I didn't know where to go. I knew I needed to head south to the more rural areas because north wasn't an option. The Kennesaw Domain had close connections with the Royal Domain, and past Kennesaw, there was Chattanooga. All the smaller domains throughout the continent answered to the Royal. Domains were broken up to reside in larger cities where we had more external energy sources to replenish our magic. Before Devolution Day, highly populated cities made more sense for us due to the booming technology that incessantly fed our magic. For now, rural areas were where I needed to hide until I could figure out my next plan to reduce the risk of getting caught.

I rose to my feet and threw my duffel across my shoulder. The thunderous roar of the train pumped streams of adrenaline through my veins as I waited, revitalizing my lethargic mind.

I fell into a casual jog, warming up my stiff muscles and joints. The deafening cry of the train trudged closer, so I increased my speed. The weight of the duffel wanted to slow me down, but I pushed my legs harder, the cold air burning my throat with each step.

The locomotive pressed on my back as it loomed closer. Its light shined into nature, giving the forest an eerie glow. Tall grass slapped against the leather of my pants as I pushed myself harder.

I glanced over my shoulder and spotted an open car clad in graffiti. I sprinted closer to the tracks, gravel rolling under my feet.

I poured every ounce of strength in my body into making a blind leap. Grasping onto the makeshift handle in the opening, I used my arms to swing myself into the train, then allowed gravity to drop me to the aluminum floor.

My body felt submerged in tar with all my energy spent. I needed sleep, and not the type of sleep redfern poisoning had forced me to endure.

I adjusted my duffel to act as a back cushion against the ridges in the aluminum walls. The repetitive motion of moving down the tracks almost lulled me to sleep, so I tried to spot trees in the darkness through the opening to stay awake despite the burning in my eyes.

To keep my brain ticking, I prepared for unexpected developments that would arise. Pretending to be human would be key. I could join a human militia and hope I wouldn't get recognized. Having an armed group surrounding me would serve as protection. It was the last place the king would think to look, too.

Or I could lay low and remain solitary instead. But then, I'd run the risk of encountering Elementals. And I couldn't forget that there were Endarkened thirsting for an opportunity to deplete a Kinetic like myself.

With a potent sense of resolve fueled by wrath, I promised the gods that if I went down, I'd take the whole fucking lot of Kinetics with me.

Damn the consequences that may follow in its wake.

Chapter 14

GRAY

I skidded and rolled on the sharp rocks. With the impact, air was forced to whoosh from my lungs. Gravel dug into the sleeves of my hooded leather jacket while the cowl protected my face.

Well, that fucking sucked.

The next stop was a few miles away. I couldn't risk being seen by Kinetics, so I'd plunged to the ground as an early exit.

I groaned. Soreness nestled within my bones and muscles, protesting every step to retrieve my bag. My body healed during the train ride, but I was still aching. I hoisted my bag over my shoulder and set off on the next leg of my journey, hoping to find a safe place to truly rest soon.

I didn't know where I was, only that I was near a small town somewhere in the middle of Georgia. However, despite the foggy skies, the moon told me it was about three in the morning.

My stomach grumbled, reminding me it'd been too long since my last meal. I'd have to either hunt or scavenge for food.

Not long after Devolution Day, bartering and trading became the new form of currency, but food was a rare item to trade since most lived underground in fear of the Kinetics and Elementals. The survivalists that came topside to grow or raise food drove steep prices for their product. Foods lower in demand, such as nuts or common vegetables, were more easily bartered.

While on the train, I'd discovered a hidden pocket in the duffel that contained a stash of my jewelry from the palace. Scarlett or Cotton must have raided my drawers while I was with my father and Grim. Depending on the trade, speakeasies sometimes provided meals to nomadic humans and rebels. But it would only get me so far.

I reached into the hidden pocket of the bag, sifting through the gold, silver, and platinum chains and bands. A pair of extravagant diamond earrings snagged against my palm.

That should do. I stuffed the pair into my front pocket with a sigh.

I walked through the trees lining the train tracks, hoping the woods would camouflage me from random passersby. The crickets' cadence to their mating partners told me dawn was bringing an end to their midnight rides. I needed to get out of the open and hole away somewhere.

For five miles, I hugged the inside of the tree line. I was in human territory, even if the majority of them were underground. It didn't lower the risks of running into a rebel. Aside from speakeasies, business was conducted topside, which meant human militias patrolled these rural areas.

After walking for hours, the sun awakened, illuminating the landscape before me. Inside the tree line, I trekked past the outskirts of a town. Abandoned and looted homes sprinkled either side of the quiet road. Former businesses were nothing but crumbling artifacts from a none-too-distant time. I pictured them in their prime when business was flowing.

When life was good. When life was normal.

Abandoned cars rotted in the crumbling road from where the EMP zapped their ability to function. Rust disintegrated the metals into colorful heaps of junk that peeked through the greenery as it devoured them. Vehicles sat on flat tires that would forever kiss the cracked asphalt. Years of the torrid summer heat and moist climate faded the street paint, while the grass I trudged through was tall enough to hide lesser animals on the food chain.

Earth was reclaiming her power, and it left behind the decayed remnants of the humans' brief dominance.

I continued through the town until I reached the antiquated square. An antebellum courthouse was the central point. It stood with southern grit even as vines climbed its structure and holes marred its face.

"Who are you?" a deep voice cut through the silence, breaking my disheartened reverie.

I spun, my right hand landing on a dagger in my weapons belt, and came face to face with a teenage boy. My blade pressed against his windpipe, his tawny skin reminding me of desert sand.

His voice didn't match his age. Unruly, black curls stood untamed on his head, and his clothes hung loose on his thin frame. "Not someone you want to sneak up on, kid."

Through his poker face, his uneven breaths gave away his fear. "I was only asking because we don't see fresh faces around here often."

I didn't respond but pressed the dagger harder against his throat instead.

"If we see newcomers, they usually cause trouble," the kid continued, swallowing against the blade.

"Right." My voice came out flat, unsure whether to remove my weapon. I kept it there, studying the boy.

We both knew I outmatched him, but he remained stalwart, like the courthouse, against my scrutiny. A warmth and softness simmered behind his steadfast and determined gaze.

I dropped the dagger from his throat and backed up two steps. My brows pinched together as I read his rigid posture.

"Where can I barter some food?" I asked, breaking the tension.

A childish smirk played at the edges of his lips. "We don't barter food here. We're pretty stingy folks." He shrugged.

"I'm pretty sure I can be persuasive." I crossed my arms over my chest, cocking a brow.

Tilting his head back, the kid looked at me down the bridge of his nose, "What are we talking here?"

"Enough to make up for the food you sell me, plus some."

"I need to see the evidence," he said, skepticism lacing his voice.

I rolled my eyes. "Seriously?"

"Yeah," his voice cracked, showing his age for the first time.

I suppressed a smile and reached into my pocket, retrieving the diamond earrings.

The boy's eyes widened and his jaw gaped open. "Yeah," he muttered. "That should do."

"Great," I said, shoving the earrings back into my pocket. I glanced at the kid. His eyes were unfocused on an abandoned car on the corner. "Lead the way—"

"Dash." The kid snapped out of his daze with a shake of his head. "The name's Dash."

"Okay, Dash. Take me to your leader."

"Hope you don't need to phone home," Dash said, quoting the movie *E.T.* as he walked ahead of me.

I smiled at the cheesy quip. "Nope. No worries there."

"Good because our ham radio signals are pretty weak here," he said without so much as a glance over his shoulder.

I tucked away that piece of information as my suspicions heightened. Rebel militias used ham radios. Not exclusively, as there were some non-militant humans that could have acquired them prior to Devolution Day.

Was I overlooking this scrawny teen?

"So, Dash," I said, "where exactly are we going?" I looked around as we turned left down an abandoned street. More foregone businesses loomed in our periphery, their ghosts wailing as we passed. Signs were missing letters. Glass doors and windows were shattered from long-ago looters. Dangling from metal frames were scraps of awnings that swayed in the late October breeze.

Dash smirked at me over his shoulder. "You'll see."

We weaved through vehicles that were bound to the road. A Honda Civic sat smashed into the back of a semi-truck. Peeking inside, I spotted a clothed skeleton whose baseball cap was blood-stained. He remained hunched forward with his face pressed into a deflated airbag.

"That's comforting," I retorted in sarcasm as I strolled past.

Dash chuckled. "Relax. It'll be fine," he said with a wave of his hand.

I said nothing as I took in the wreckage that would forever be immortalized until either nature consumed it or it was rebuilt.

We walked in silence. The quiet forced its weight on my shoulders as the ghost town demanded my attention.

A crash shattered the somber atmosphere behind an abandoned farm supply store. We halted our movements, glancing at one another.

I watched as Dash transformed from an innocent kid to a vigilant young man as his back went rigid and shoulders tensed. I raised an eyebrow at his poised hands hovering above his waistband. With keen awareness, his eyes shifted as he scanned the surrounding area.

It was possible that the movement was simply a survival skill that humans had adapted over the past five years. Or...he was part of a human militia that would burn the world down in celebration if they got my head—both concerned me.

A louder crash blasted through the eerie street.

I snatched a pair of regular daggers from my weapons belt designed for human enemies. With my bracelet on, I couldn't detect what we were facing. The chances were high of it being a straggling human who'd gotten separated from a clan.

Dark clouds wiped away the harsh morning sunlight, casting an angry shadow over us. Dash and I glanced at one another in warning before shifting our attention to the blackening sky.

Naturally occurring thunderstorms usually presented warnings upon their onset: looming thunder, the rise or fall of temperature, or breezes. But this impending storm wasn't natural. These clouds seemed to have appeared from nowhere, and complete silence stifled the stagnant air.

My head buzzed from dread as I realized this was the work of an Elemental—or worse, an Endarkened.

With my magic repressed, I felt unprepared, but I couldn't risk revealing myself to Dash.

The sky continued to darken, and footsteps shuffled from around the corner of the farm supply store. With frayed and stained clothing, a woman staggered into view. Upon first glance, matted blonde hair dangled from her patchy scalp. Pallid skin peeked from behind peeling gold flesh. The gold-flecked layer drooped over itself, leaving decomposing skin in its wake. In some spots, the lingering skin was rotten black, where others exposed a graying second layer.

Decaying, dark gray veins dominated her form as they desperately pulsed for the next soul to consume to sustain them.

I stared at the monster before us and realized it *was* worse than an Elemental. We were facing an Endarkened.

Kinetics replenished their magic by absorbing external energy waves from the environment or energy-sharing with other Kinetics. Elementals replenished by absorbing the energetic output from living beings' auras–whether it was Kinetic, Elemental, or human–so long as they didn't drain it. Becoming Endarkened is what happened when Elementals *depleted*. Once an Elemental depleted an aura to the point of death, an addiction unlike anything humans could imagine overtook their rationality.

Once the aura was consumed, they were thrust into the devolution process of becoming Endarkened. The Endarkening process consisted of three phases to make the complete transformation. Each time they depleted, they furthered the process, falling to the frenzy in increments. It was almost impossible to resist the urge to deplete after the first time. By the final stage, they transformed into decaying, mindless creatures with all sense of their former identity lost in the madness, only seeking auras to absorb. Supernatural auras were more potent to feed their heightened elemental magic, making them even more dangerous.

They needed to be put down at all costs.

I debated risking my identity to Dash to fight off the Endarkened. Before I could act, he charged the woman at full speed. A glint of metal flashed from his hand, and I realized he had a gun. I rolled my eyes. A bullet couldn't kill an Elemental, much less an Endarkened. I glanced down at my daggers, realizing I wielded the wrong blades. But activating my Kinetic daggers would expose me to Dash.

The bottom dropped out of the sky, unleashing an onslaught of rain. The Endarkened was a water Elemental who had the ability to control the weather with her increased power. So much for not getting drenched. Water began to pool and rise in front of her, creating a liquid wall that separated her from us.

Dash skidded to a halt before slamming into it, splashing a puddle under his worn boots.

I stood frozen while I thought of a way for us to flee. She wanted our auras. Well, mine, to be exact. So, I did the next best thing.

"Hey!" I yelled to grab her attention. I walked in her direction, giving her a chance to sense my strengthened aura, and stopped at Dash's side.

The wall of water quivered before it collapsed, gushing over our boots. The Endarkened's bloodshot eyes squinted before she took a slow sniff of the air.

I adjusted the cowl that covered my mouth and nose. Her shifty eyes cast down to the wet asphalt beneath her feet. In an unexpected move, she dropped to one knee and bowed her head, her ragged curtain of hair shielding her face.

One of my eyebrows peaked at the strange sight, remembering the Endarkened in the prison who'd done the same. I searched around for anyone else nearby. My magic would've made it much easier to detect.

Dash gaped at the kneeling Endarkened before he recovered from his surprise. Raising the gun, he aimed at the woman. The click of the weapon yanked the Endarkened from her reverent pose, and a guttural growl reverberated from her chest. The deep cadence shook my bones in response.

She moved to lunge at the teen, but the twitch of his finger pulled the trigger.

Dash didn't flinch at the powerful kickback of the gun. The thunderous boom disturbed the unnatural storm.

In mid-stride, the Endarkened froze. A gaping black hole gleamed between her reddened eyes. Dark gray blood cascaded from the wound and the corners of her mouth. She staggered, but the wound wasn't healing. Instead, it seemed to worsen as a range of emotions passed over her features.

Rage, confusion, pain, and fear all morphed across her face. But it was the last one that unsettled me: *relief.*

The Endarkened folded in on herself, crumbling to the black asphalt as she gasped her final breaths.

I stood bewildered by what just unfolded in front of me. None of it was normal. How had she been able to process the emotion of relief? But I realized as I looked at the teenage boy beside me that he was, in fact, a rebel.

The cold-blooded shot he fired with steel repose said it all. He didn't question. He didn't shake. The warmth and kindness in his deep brown eyes had vanished.

With both daggers drawn, I took casual strides to him from behind as he examined the fallen Endarkened. Subtly, I pressed the edge of my dagger against his throat while I dug the tip of the other into his lowest spinal disc. He was much taller, but the arched position I held him in made him compliant.

"Who are you?" I whispered into his ear.

He grunted from the pain in his back, struggling to pull in even breaths. "Why don't you tell me," he said, sounding nothing like the scared kid I'd mistaken him for.

I dug my dagger further into his spine, making him squat a fraction. He growled.

"I'll ask again, Dash. Who are you? And don't think I won't fucking kill you if you lie to me."

Dash chuckled. "You already know the answer."

I pressed the dagger harder into his throat and shifted to kick the back of his knee. As I was about to connect, a bruising grip on my neck stopped me. "Fuck."

I couldn't counter the unknown attack without letting Dash go. So, I maintained my hold on him with my right arm, but they forced my left arm away from his back.

I threw an elbow at my attacker but missed.

And that's all the assailant needed to get the upper hand. A sharp pressure drove into the joints connecting my nape and spine before a cloth covered my nose and mouth.

Darkness swarmed my vision. The world around me turned black, and my body felt incorporeal as strong arms caught my fall.

Chapter 15

GRIFFIN

The princess slackened in my arms from the heavy dose of chloroform.

Carefully, I lay her on the wet asphalt before meeting Dash's earthy brown eyes. "That was fucking stupid of you."

Dash gaped at me, his incredulous expression morphing his severe look into one that matched his age. "Wha—*how*?" he stuttered. "I killed her!"

"Yeah, but that was an Endarkened. You're a human. And as skilled as you are with a gun, she could've had powers that would crumple it, and then she'd rip out your vital organs before you even had the chance to pull the trigger. You got lucky." I bent to pick up the princess's bag and dagger before pocketing it.

Dash huffed, his petulance evident as he pushed the thick-rimmed glasses higher up the bridge of his nose. "But I *had* it!"

"Because you got lucky," I snapped. "Had she not gotten all fucking weird...you'd be dead."

"Well, it's fine now," Dash said, crossing his arms over his chest. "Now what?

I paused, and my lips slid into a grin, despite the nausea threatening to seize me. "Since it's your kill, you have clean-up duty. Leave no evidence behind."

With deflated shoulders, Dash dropped his head. "That is so unfair, dude."

I shrugged. "It's not. We can't leave a trail of bodies for Forest to track us down." I turned to face the unconscious princess at my feet. "You want the glory? Then you gotta take on the shit that comes with it."

"Why didn't you step in sooner if you saw her going all weird?"

Bending, I scooped my arms beneath the Kinetic princess's knees and shoulders, rising with her cradled in my grasp. "Because I wanted to see how the princess would respond. But it seemed she was hesitant to pull out her blades due to your presence." At least she didn't seem eager to kill innocent humans.

Dash flailed his arms at his side. "You're just going to leave me to clean this up on my own? Where are you going?"

I sighed. "I gotta find a place to hide out and sleep tonight. Probably in a nearby house. I'll find you and let you know where once I get her settled in."

Uncertainty crept into the creases of Dash's brows. "What about me? Where do I go?" He might be a fearsome human, but he was still only a kid. A kid who had just encountered his first Endarkened and, not long prior to that, had lost a fight to two Kinetics. The possibility of more lurking around was always a chance. Despite his bravado, he was clearly rattled.

"Like I said, I'll find you when I get in somewhere. Go back to the compound when the sun breaks in the morning. Understood?" I said, shifting Gray in my arms for the trek.

Dash rolled his eyes, but quickly nodded his head in agreement. Wild little sprigs of black hair bounced down over his brow. "Fine."

I tipped my head down in acknowledgement before striding toward the train tracks behind the supply store, carrying the princess. A line of crumbling homes framed the road. I kept going, not wanting to risk detection by the Kinetics on passing trains.

After my run-in with a garrison of Warriors, I re-suppressed my magic and took Dash to hide far enough away from the Royal Domain to prevent detection, yet close enough to Princess Gray's line of escape within the city. We had hopped on the train before she did, and once she rolled off near Macon as predicted, we trailed her at a distance, waiting for the least suspicious time for Dash to make his appearance.

Before Dash had awoken, I'd been about two seconds from flaying the skin from my bones in the desperate hope of removing the evil lurking beneath the surface.

Too much death.

The massacre only fueled the heaviest of temptations built from the darkest parts of me to surrender to its call. To become one with the darkness at long last. I had resisted as much as I could while simultaneously toeing the line of self-destruction. Only killing those who sought to further the King's fucked-up agenda and those who wished to harm the innocent. Those were my boundaries, and I repeated them to myself over and over in a challenge to the wicked voice that sought control.

It took every remaining sliver of self-restraint to not turn on Dash after what I'd done. The more blood I shed, the more it wanted. It wanted complete control of me. Its incessant call to cave to temptation was driving me madder by the day.

Since linking up with the princess, it had waned a bit, but not enough to make a difference. The darkness seemed to blame her for its lack of intense prominence as it began to rage in my chest with a white flame that rivaled the heat of fire Elementals.

After crossing another street, I found a two-story house that stood in shambles.

It had clearly been raided long ago. The lack of upkeep, along with the holes in the siding and windows, allowed the weather to rapidly deteriorate its structure. It didn't matter. Every house was basically the same—nothing remained untouched.

I took measured steps across the debris, and the overwhelming odor of musk assaulted me upon entry. A set of stairs descended into the living room leading to the foyer; I made haste in its direction.

I couldn't wait to drop the princess. My arms burned and shook from carrying her unconscious body so far. It didn't help that my magic reserves were nearly depleted from the events of the past twenty-four hours. I needed sleep, but I knew none would be granted to me anytime soon.

I ascended the unstable stairs to the top floor of the house, convinced that the floor would collapse beneath our weight. Surprisingly, it held firm as I crossed the threshold into the first bedroom available. I picked the top story for logistical purposes in the event the princess awoke while I was absent from the room. It'd be more difficult for her to escape down rickety steps rather than darting out the door on the bottom floor.

A bed pushed askew and stripped of its sheets sat off to one side of the room. I took hurried steps toward it and placed the princess with ease onto its bare and dusty surface. Instant relief flooded my chest. I shook out my arms, but frustration warred through me at my weakened state. That shouldn't have sucked so bad. Wiping the sweat from my forehead, I stretched out my muscles and took a moment to observe the vulnerable little assassin beneath me.

Her restful state smoothed out her typical scowl into a peaceful expression. The cupid's bow of her full lips stood out from the natural pout. She wore the black leathers of the Kinetic Guild uniform for assassins. Hers was form-fitting, highlighting the toned curves. The rise and fall of her chest were slow and melodic, and I had the desire to run my fingers through her glamoured ice-white hair.

The sudden jolt of longing in my heart had me gripping my chest for reasons I didn't understand. I had no reliable memory of her other than our recent encounter at the speakeasy. But the intuitive part, albeit deeply suppressed, begged to differ.

Frustration beat its fists against my skull to recall my lost memories. My breaths picked up in harsh pants as my anger at all I'd lost came slamming into me with renewed vengeance. And as I looked at the sleeping princess,

I blamed her for it all. It was *her* father who ruined my life, corrupting me in the worst ways. She got to live a life of luxury and ease in comparison while innocent lives winked out of existence at her hands. Meanwhile, her sanity was still intact, so in my eyes, she was the enemy.

At least, that's the words that the voice coaxed in my mind.

Kill her. Take what's owed to you.

My hands shook at my sides, the itch to plunge my dagger deep into her chest cavity growing too strong. "No," I gritted out through clenched teeth. "We need her." I needed cocaine, alcohol, my violin...*anything*.

There are other ways, Prince. Take the rightful vengeance that's owed to you.

"Fuck off. No." I shook my head, my eyes sealing shut in my hopeless effort to push him out.

Think of the power—the rush. Think of the satisfaction of seeing her corpse at your feet. She is to blame for it all. Her suffering was nothing in comparison to yours. It's too late for you. Your will to fight this call is weakening with each life you take. You know what you truly need from the deaths. You'll give in. It's inevitable. Stop delaying your suffering.

I tried to block out the alluring words from the inexplicable need to protect her, but the temptation... it was too powerful. He was right; my will to fight it was dissipating with each death. Why not just...take the plunge?

I opened my eyes, and nausea swelled in my gut at the sight of my dagger pressed against Princess Gray's throat. The violent tremors of my hand indicated my intuitive resistance in the background of my psyche. I didn't recall even removing the dagger from my belt.

Do it.

I reeled backward, stumbling over an abandoned shoe on the floor. Dagger still in hand, I spun and launched it at the wall. The deep *thunk* echoed throughout the eerie home. I laced my fingers into the roots of my hair, the long black strands curtaining over the sides. I tugged and tried to force air deep into my lungs where a wall seemed to block its access.

"No, no, no, no." With another look at Gray, blissfully asleep, I took large strides from the room and down the stairs.

I slid into the main bedroom and slunk down the wall. Images of lifeless eyes flashed through my mind, either taunting me with the desire to do it again or with the guilt from killing so joyously.

I hated myself. I hated what I'd been molded into becoming, shaped and sculpted to be savage and merciless. To be the ultimate killing machine until I reached a point where that was all that kept me functioning.

No one knew the real me—not even Orion. What was the point?

I rested my head back against the wall. "Just leave me alone. Please. Just...go away for a bit."

No, boy. You'll come where you belong eventually. Freedom. That's what you're forsaking. Ultimate freedom.

"No," I whispered, my voice breaking, "I'd be a slave."

After composing myself long enough to appear unafflicted, a skill I learned long ago, I set out in search of Dash as promised. I'd been sure to restrain Gray to the bed, even though she lay unconscious, not wanting to take any chances. The Endarkened's body was gone when I arrived, and Dash was in the process of cleaning up the blackened blood from the asphalt. I assessed the area for anything he could've missed that would lead back to us. "Looks good."

Dash's relief was visible in his slumped stance. "Great. I'm never killing another Endarkened again."

My lip twitched. "Come on. Let's find you a place to crash nearby."

With a sigh, he followed without much else to say. After several minutes of nothing but the sounds of our footsteps, his stomach growled in protest.

I glanced at him over my shoulder with a raised brow.

"I'm so fucking hungry. I'm really missing those salted potatoes right about now," Dash grumbled. "Man, what I wouldn't do for a fucking Pop-Tart."

"A Pop-Tart?"

"Hell yes, man. Strawberry. Those were my favorite as a kid before Devolution Day." A pebble skittered past me from the kick of his booted foot as he walked, seeming to aim for every loose stone he saw with each step.

I let out a humph, never having had the experience of eating Pop-Tarts prior to that day. "Well, maybe I can sneak you some of Katia's famous strawberry delight next time I see you."

"I might just kiss you if you do."

"Please don't."

"Afraid you might like it?"

My face contorted in disgust, "Ew. You're like twelve."

"Sixteen!" Dash protested. "This height does not say twelve!"

I shook my head. "Still a kid. Now, come on, this place should suffice until morning," I said as we approached another ramshackle house. This one was only a single story and in worse disrepair than the one Gray and I currently squatted in, but it should do. "I'll check it out and make sure there are no surprises before I leave."

Dash's nostrils flared with a nod, his shoulders stiffening. Another wave of heavy guilt washed through my chest and sank down, down, down into the depths of my gut. He was scared. After the last two encounters, I couldn't blame him. Now, he was to be left to defend himself. I hated having to leave him behind, but I wouldn't be far. And if trouble struck, we had a plan.

We searched the house and declared it clear, with nothing but varmints nesting inside. I passed on a message for him to transfer to Sergeant Hogan, reminded him of the back-up plan if something were to happen, and then bid him goodbye. I couldn't fail him. I'd ensure nothing fucked with him.

With a heavy heart, I exited the small home and made my short trek to the house the Kinetic Princess and I occupied, reminding myself to remove the restraints in a few hours. I tried to sift through the few tangible thoughts I knew were mine. My personal reality became more obscure by the day, warped by the darkness.

Fear iced my veins at the cloudy memory of nearly killing the assassin earlier. I thought of how close I'd come to throwing caution to the wind and losing it all. Without her, any chance of removing Forest from his self-appointed seat of righteousness would vanish.

She was the key. We needed to find the lock next. And without either one, all hope for fixing the mess of this world would be lost.

I only hoped I could hang on long enough to not kill her in her sleep.

Chapter 16

GRAY

I awoke on a soft surface, grogginess and confusion warping my mind.

I didn't know where I was or how I'd gotten here. Ending up in these types of situations was becoming too common. What was left of my pride began to wither away.

The smell of musk and mold overwhelmed my nostrils. In fact, it was too much. My itchy throat forced out a raspy cough, and a heavy pressure weighed on my chest that made breathing a struggle. Sodden and spent, I lay there as I came to full consciousness.

I dared to peek an eye open. A shattered window bared open to my left, filtering in a cool breeze that kissed my cheek and covered my skin in goose bumps.

I shivered and groaned as the aches protested any movement. My body begged me to give it a rest, but I knew I couldn't afford to give in to its desire. A sense of urgency nudged my mind into motion.

All the recent events replayed through my thoughts as I stared at the bright afternoon sunlight streaming through the window. My father wanted me dead. And he had the entire fucking Warrior Guilds hunting me down.

Dash. The Endarkened. Dash killing the Endarkened. Human militia. The kid was no doubt part of the human militia. But where was he?

As the pieces snapped together, I bolted upright. My head spun, and I felt sluggish. So, so sluggish. I pushed through the dizziness and nausea that threatened to take over.

The peeling walls caught my attention first. Chipped paint curled off in large sheets sporadically throughout the room. But it was the dark presence that loomed in the shadowed corner that set my instincts blaring in alarm.

Through the heaviness, I focused on the form. A black cloak draped over their head, obscuring their face, as they clasped their hands together between their knees. I gasped, recognizing it was *him*. Griffin.

What the fuck?

So many questions pummeled my fuzzy mind, but they were irrelevant. What mattered was that I could kill him here and now.

Jumping out of bed, I ignored my body's distress warnings. My feet met the cold wooden floor on tired legs. I didn't have it in me to fight right now. I'd fought in worse conditions before, yet I felt useless against the most dangerous person alive. But I *had* to act. I couldn't just let him go again.

I lunged. The rickety chair he sat in flipped over backward with the force of my collision. A loud crash and thud echoed throughout the room. For half a second, I wondered if the floor would cave in, but I didn't let the thought interfere. I punched his jaw with all my remaining strength, despite my leaden arm. He jerked to the side, but to my surprise, my knuckles still connected with his jaw, rocking his head to the left.

Not even a grunt escaped him as he snapped his head back to face me. Long, black hair whipped across his cheek, the ends playing at the hollow of his throat. A bright blue, glamoured gaze peered at me through the mussed ebony strands. I was plunged into its empty depths, where life was sucked dry. Nothing remained of the mischievous and restless energy he emitted the night we fought topside of the speakeasy. A hollow shell of a man gazed back at me, like he was here, but not really. Like he was already dead.

I reached for his throat and squeezed my fingers around the tattoos covering his skin... and then squeezed more. If I didn't know any better, it seemed like he *allowed* me to choke him, causing something to bristle within me. With a clenched jaw, I grunted. "Fight back, you fucking coward." I punched him again.

At my words, a spark lit his blue eyes back to life. In a swift move, he jolted his hips upward and flipped me onto my back, pinning my arms to the floor as if I was a child. That was way too easy for him. I cursed myself because, once again, I gave him the upper hand.

Me and my damn mouth.

With the roles reversed, he lodged his hips into mine. I grunted, his full weight pressing me into the rotting wood floor.

A curse spat from my lips at the intimate position. I should've capitalized on killing him during his moment of weakness. With my energy spent, my body drained, my magic inhibited, and weapons gone, I was at his mercy—again.

Griffin's face hovered inches above mine as his warm breath huffed out, blanketing my face in waves. He stared down at me, absorbing all my features, his eyes clear of the emptiness that had just resided within them. In fact, a wicked glint began to shine through.

Many small scars marred his smooth, tanned complexion with olive undertones. A deep scar in the shape of a half-moon sat in the corner of his right eye. Thick, dark lashes drew attention to cat-shaped eyes. They held a slight feminine quality to them, which accented the masculine features of his face. I resisted the ridiculous urge to caress the high cheekbones that dipped into a strong jaw. And then I resisted the urge to vomit at the insane thought.

Despite my hatred toward the man, I wasn't above admitting that he was beautiful. Beautiful in the "lure you to your death" type of way. But beautiful, nevertheless.

My lip curled up at him in disgust, the coldness within me begging to bite at him. My breaths came in harshly through my nose as I glared at him with every bit of hatred I harbored for him.

"There she is," Griffin growled. My body reacted to the tenor of his voice before I could do anything about it as heat flushed my skin. He leaned in, brushing the tip of his nose along the shell of my ear. "I always knew there was a little savage in there, waiting to be unleashed." He pulled back and smirked, huffing out a quiet laugh. "Can she come out to play?" he breathed into my ear.

Hearing his taunt sent shivers down my spine, rage flooding my stomach as I clenched my jaw and tossed my head to the side to avoid his touch. Yet, to my horror, my thighs clenched beneath his hips as a slow sensation of lust began to rise in my lower body.

What the *actual fuck?*

"You don't know shit about me," I snapped. "And get your dick off me." I bucked my hips, trying to throw him off, but he remained firmly planted. All the motion accomplished was my dry-humping him. I growled my frustration as this only fueled my need to break free of his hold *immediately.*

"I know more than you think, Princess." He ignored my second statement and remained pressed against me, searing me with his striking gaze in a way that seemed to be an innate gift. "Don't worry, Gray. I don't want you dead—not yet, at least." The corners of his lips curled into a wicked smirk, and I cursed myself as yet another flair of desire shot through my veins.

Stupid fucking hormones can't differentiate friend from foe.

"Good. It'll make killing you a bit easier, then," I seethed. Pushing aside the dark beauty of this man, I called upon the memory of Slate, envisioning his stony gray hair and soft hazel eyes. It was a reminder to not fall for Griffin's charm a second time.

"You still believe I killed your boyfriend." Griffin rolled his eyes. "I believe the humans used to call that 'fake news'." A black eyebrow arched up in amusement.

"You ambushed his squadron."

"Nope. Wasn't me. I wasn't there." A grin formed at the edges of his lips. "I even have witnesses."

Lies. "You expect me to believe anything that comes from your mouth? From any Elemental's mouth for that matter?"

"And yet you believe anything that comes from your king's mouth. Why are you here, anyway?"

Instead of answering him, I countered, "What did you do to me? Where am I?"

"Oh!" Griffin perked up, a manic joy lighting up his eyes. "Chloroform. Sorry 'bout that," he said with an unapologetic shrug. "I couldn't have you fighting me the whole way while I found us this lovely place, could I? It's a bit of a fixer-upper, but—"

"Are you fucking kidding me?" I cut him off as I struggled against him again. Like before, it was futile. His arms were steel, and his weight was relentless. "Fucking chloroform? What do you want with me? To use me as leverage against my father?" If that was the case, he was shit out of luck because he would be doing my father a service.

Griffin snorted, and once again, his breath danced across my skin. "No. Just get up. We need to get moving before we miss the train that's scheduled to hit Macon in a few hours." He sat up and fell back on his heels, releasing the hold he had on me. "And before you think about attacking me again, don't forget who has the advantage. I'll just chloroform you and drag you along if I have to." He said it so nonchalantly that I just gaped at him in horror.

I dropped my head back to the floor in defeat. What did he want with me if not to kill me or hold me hostage? And why did he seem so familiar, aside from our initial meeting at the speakeasy?

I may have lost this battle, but I wasn't giving up on the war. I'd wait until my body healed fully, and then, when he least expected it, I'd make my move. Until then, I'd play along with whatever game this psychopath played.

Bide your time.

"Fine," I said, looking at the drooping ceiling. "Let's go."

"Be ready to run and jump." The infamous Elemental murmured to me, not taking his eyes off the train tracks in the distance.

He'd let me keep my duffel bag but made me hand over my weapons and keep the bracelet intact. And because I had yet to see his gold-covered skin and wild metallic eyes, I knew he was glamoured, too. I almost got away with keeping a small knife, but he hadn't been fooled and made me give it to him as we exited that decrepit home. Well, I might've gotten away with it if I hadn't launched it at his head before he snatched it out of the air, stopping it from lodging between his eyes. He'd laughed. And I'd stood staring with an open mouth—shocked, angry, and deflated.

What was worse was that I was impressed by his reflexes.

With no other options at the moment, I was stuck with Griffin. At least with him close, I stood a chance of killing him. Running would only put me at a disadvantage with the Guilds and militia rebels hunting us down. Sticking with him had somehow turned into the lesser of the other evils in this world. What an ironic twist my life had taken.

I adjusted my duffel on my shoulder when the sound of the train roared in the distance. My body was still weak and aching, but I had to push through. Most importantly, I would show no weakness to this asshole. Well, no more than I already had.

The train announced its arrival, and Griffin ushered me to hide inside the tree line. My heart pulsed, and all lethargy faded away with a spike of adrenaline. I nearly died the last time I pulled this stunt, but I didn't let that unease take root as I focused on staying hidden and making the leap.

As the train hauled past, Griffin launched into a sprint in its direction with me right on his heels. He didn't hesitate to vault through the air at full speed with ease, landing crouched inside. I was right behind him as I made the jump a foot closer. I wasn't nearly as graceful as he was, thanks to my short legs, but I made it inside with a hard thud and a roll.

I plopped onto my back to catch my breath, even with my duffel still strapped to me, and took in the empty metal container. I glanced over to see Griffin squatting by the opening of the train car. A few black strands hung around his lean, defined face. He wasn't even winded.

"Take a nap; you need it. The chloroform is still in your system with your magic suppressed," Griffin said, his head bowed and hands clasped together.

My brows furrowed, trying to figure out his endgame. But he was right. If I was to make this brief journey and kill him at some point, I needed to rest. I was still drained, more so now that the adrenaline had worn off.

I nodded and sat up to take off my duffel to use as a makeshift pillow. It wasn't long before I drifted off to sleep. Exhaustion claimed me before dark thoughts could consume me.

A firm hand jostled me awake. My eyes were heavy and burning as I sat up in a panic and slowly registered my surroundings. Crystal-blue eyes framed by thick, black lashes captured my focus and held me back from leaping to my feet.

His large palm remained on my shoulder. I broke his penetrating stare to look at the tan hand that touched me. It was so tempting to break it. Faint white marks scarred his skin and small, intricate designs inked themselves permanently there. I mentally slapped myself in the face.

"Don't touch me," I snapped and met his gaze again.

He said nothing; he just held my glare in a challenge. As soon as I shifted to remove his hand from my body, he stood and looked out the opening of the moving train car. "Be ready to jump in a few minutes."

I stood up and tossed my bag onto my back again. "Where are we going?"

"You'll see." He turned around and took a step toward the edge of the container. Griffin observed the landscape for a moment before he looked at me over his shoulder. "But I'm gonna need you to be on your best behavior. Think you can manage that, Princess?" A one-sided smirk smeared across his face.

Before I could retort, he jumped.

Moving to the spot Griffin abandoned, I quickly scanned around, gauging the speed and landscape before I followed suit, leaping from the train seconds later.

I bounced off my feet before rolling across the sharp gravel, careful to protect my head with my arms. When I came to a stop, I looked around and spotted Griffin's dark form approaching.

I brushed the dust and stray debris from my clothes as I pulled myself to my feet while fixing my cowl. "Where are we?" I asked as he closed the distance between us.

"In Macon, about thirty miles south of where we just were. We're close to our destination." Griffin's perceptive gaze scanned the area for any threats.

"And where is that destination exactly?"

In response, he turned his back on me and walked away. I reigned in my temper at the blatant dismissal. My jaw ached from grinding my teeth together. But after taking a deep breath, I followed suit, jogging to catch him in stride.

"Speakeasy."

"What's there? Besides the 'shine?" I pushed, trying to pry any information about his plans.

"Why else would I go to a speakeasy if not for the drinks or women?" He looked down at me as we walked. Amusement sparkled in his riveting eyes, hiding secrets that taunted me.

I scoffed, ignoring the comment to press on, "What do you want with me if not to either kill me or hold me as leverage against the king?"

Griffin inhaled deeply and didn't answer right away as he stared at the path ahead of us. "I need your help."

Chapter 17

GRIFFIN

Gray's face twisted in confusion. "Why? With what?"

I kept my senses peaked and my gaze on the approaching thick pines. I wouldn't elaborate yet, no matter how hard she pushed me for answers. I didn't trust her, even if my memories began to return in her presence. And the closer our proximity, the clearer my head became.

The time on the train had been only brief glimpses of...*something*. I wasn't even sure it had been real. The first lucid memory to strike came with the punch she landed on me back at the house, like she'd injected the flashback with her fist and anger. It had been enough to snap me out of the self-deprecating state I'd fallen into, where I had wanted nothing more than for her to end my suffering.

As I had allowed Gray to pin me and unleash her wrath, I felt nothing. I felt hollow. I wanted out, vengeance be damned. That fire had blinked out at some point while I dwelled in my darkness.

I didn't understand why. It didn't make sense, but having been near her for the past several hours had quieted the disturbing force that claimed me as its vessel. However, it came at a cost. The guilt. The pain.

My conscience.

Regret flooded me with all my horrid deeds to where I crumpled under their weight—to the point I had become numb. I remembered all the healing I had worked so hard to achieve several years ago to make peace with my past. The icy grip that restricted my chest came from the realization my efforts had all been for naught. I'd forsaken it all and transgressed so far that the hopelessness of ever recovering from my actions grew deep, complex roots.

Until the Kinetic Princess punched me, and the long-lost memory stolen by madness replayed in my mind's eye...

I hid beneath the fort on the playground, streams of sunlight beaming through the cracks in the wooden slats. Dirt from the other kids' shoes sprinkled down on my hair from their running feet as they passed.

I'd found a little nook the other day to burrow into, away from the others. This wasn't my usual recess time. Second grade had a school play, which moved around our schedules for some dumb reason. So now, fifth grade shared recess with third. I didn't like it. I didn't like change.

It was hard enough being one of few of the magical species hiding amongst the other human kids. We played the role of human, and I hated it. One minor slip-up resulted in the worst of my punishments. To be safe, I hid away, trying to avoid as many beatings as I could.

Leaders of Elementals and Kinetics believed the kids should attend human schools. Blend in, they said. Learn to keep our magic in check in their presence and learn about their cultures, which confused me because I mean, their cultures were basically our cultures, just with magic involved.

Okay, our cultures were a bit different, but not by a lot.

Either way, I hated this stuffy private school. I dealt with the entitled and haughty types enough back home. I guess growing up among royalty naturally subjected me to them. That didn't mean I wanted to be around them more than I needed to.

I twirled my magic-suppressing bracelet around my wrist, fiddling with the engraved sigils on the matte black band. I hadn't had my magic but for a few days, and I already missed the strength and companionship of my element, earth-metal. It was a rare element from my understanding, but I loved its unwavering companionship.

A strong wave of temptation urged me to briefly remove my bracelet. The thought of the cold steel essence of my element almost had me un-clasping it, but jeering cries outside the fort halted me from a promised disaster. Shifting to where I peeked through the thin cracks in the wood, I barely made out a group of kids formed in a ring. Their hollers didn't seem to be in celebration of winning a kickball game.

I crawled out from my space, approaching the crowd, I tried to snag curious glimpses between the gaps of their human wall. A sinking feeling settled in my stomach, urging me forward.

I pushed two third graders aside by their shoulders to make room. Even at ten years old, I towered over the others. A boy I recognized, Jacob-something, stood over a girl. A girl who lay curled in the fetal position in the sand, her arms protectively wrapped around her ribs.

Rage, fiery and hot, ignited through my body. Jacob hauled his leg back and slammed the toe of his boot into the girl's shin. Her spasm allowed me to get a peek of her face, and my heart slammed into my throat.

The princess. The Kinetic Princess. Did the king know his daughter was the victim of bullying in this human school? Despite her obvious pain, she worked hard to hide it, but the kick to her newly unprotected ribs brought out a high-pitched scream, sending a rush of adrenaline and anger through my chest.

Where the hell were the teachers?

My hands shook at my sides as I failed to control my anger. My breaths came in uneven and shallow while my nostrils flared, and my shoulders shook at the force of my magic's wrath. The taste of metal coated my tongue and nose. My element came to the call of my high emotion, every bit as pissed as me. I had no control of my element yet despite my bond to it. But I didn't care.

Unable to hold back any longer, my magic burst from my body. My element latched onto every structure composed of metal: the monkey bars, merry-go-round, swing sets, and slide. In answer to my rage, they buckled in on themselves.

Everyone froze. And for a solid thirty seconds, no one made a sound. Fear permeated the air; I could almost taste it.

At last, everyone spun and took note of their surroundings—of what I did. How I managed to do it with my bracelet intact, I didn't understand, but I couldn't think about that now. I had to help the princess. Jacob was the first to scream, followed by the rest before all the kids took off in a sprint toward the heavy double doors. I couldn't help the twitch of my lips as I watched them pile inside, fighting one another to squeeze through.

The little princess sat up on her elbows, her gaze landing on me in confusion. Her sun-kissed skin clashed with her glamoured, frosty white hair. Wet, dirty tracks streaked down her cheeks, but she looked at me in unity before squinting her eyes to assess me.

"Are you okay?" I asked, my jaw clenched. I skimmed my gaze over her petite frame for visible injuries. With the bullies gone, my magic eased and settled once again. Still, I worked to control the rise and fall of my chest.

"Yeah," the princess said, then glanced around the deserted playground. "Wh...where'd they go?" Her face contorted into one of pain as she struggled to swallow.

"They left," I said and moved to stand at her feet. I squatted down so we were at eye level. "Next time, I'll beat their ass." A vow. To protect the Kinetic Princess.

Princess Gray giggled at my use of bad words. The giggle transformed into a groan, eliciting her to hug her ribcage. On instinct, I reached for her, but she shooed me away. "I'm fine. Not a big deal."

My brows pinched together as I studied the area she nursed on her ribs. Anger rioted inside me at the thought there might be more behind her injuries than the bullies, but I kept my suspicions to myself. I knew all too well how it went.

Her pale blue eyes met my own, and a silent understanding passed between us. A relieved sigh poured from her, and her look of gratitude struck me deeper than expected before she dropped her gaze.

At last, she pushed herself into a sitting position, propping up her legs and resting her forearms on her knees. I averted my eyes because it seemed she was either completely oblivious to the fact she wore a pleated skirt or just didn't care. But I noted the blue and green bruises painting the skin along her legs.

Gray glanced around, startled by the twisted monkey bars. Her mouth gaped wider with each structure her gaze landed on. "How?" she whispered.

I lowered my chin to my chest as the heat wave of shame spread up my neck and face. "I...my magic just awakened a few days ago," I mumbled with a small shrug.

Silence grew, strengthening the tension to the point I couldn't bring myself to meet her eyes in fear of what I'd find. Finally, she said, "But...we're not supposed to awaken it until..."

"We're thirteen. I know," I sighed, daring a glance at her.

Her eyes lit up before her features fell in realization. The only time children awakened their magic sooner than they were supposed to was when they were put under duress. It was their magic's form of protection.

The princess reached toward me, placing a delicate hand on my forearm. "Hey, it's..." At the contact with her skin, an electrifying jolt of energy shot through my body, starting at the point of contact. It felt as if lightning struck from within me, locking me to my spot. My element converged with the foreign force, swelling into something far too powerful for my premature body to contain.

By the look of the Kinetic Princess, she felt the same.

A gust of wind built and built and built until it whipped around the two of us at wild, rapid speeds. Grains of sand bit my flesh in its assault. The familiar flavor of metal overtook my senses while high-voltage lightning charged through every fabric of my being. Through our contact, invisible pulsing waves channeled from her body into mine. It was too much.

The foreign melding of forces felt like I had reconnected with long-lost friends despite its volatile nature. The energies continued to intensify to the point I thought our little hearts would burst.

I remained glued to my squatted position as my heart thumped erratically in my chest, panic seizing me in its grasp as I stared into the princess's terrified eyes. The intensity of the phenomenon soared higher. I couldn't breathe, sparking a fog of vertigo that threatened unconsciousness.

As my eyes began to droop, the powerful forces ripped apart from one another, resulting in a blast that propelled the Kinetic princess and me apart. The expulsion shot me backward, where I wheeled through the air several feet before crashing to my back in the sand. I tried to gasp for breath, but nothing came from the impact. Despite having the air knocked from my lungs, my training kicked in, and I sprung to my feet from my back, scanning the playground for the threat in a defensive stance.

A whimper across the playground snapped my attention to the princess, who struggled to get off the ground. Her sudden lack of bruises gave me pause. Only the power of our magic can heal wounds that quickly. Yet, her magic hadn't awakened. So, how?

The princess stood on shaky legs, wiping the sand from her navy school uniform. She started at the thunderous boom caused by the heavy metal doors slamming into the brick wall at her back. Teachers and the headmistress stepped from the threshold. Panic dripped from their forlorn expressions as they assessed the playground's wreckage before three male faculty members rushed toward us.

I knew what fate had in store for me, so I'd confess to everything to shield the princess from any blame. No doubt, the headmistress had knowledge that a few students weren't human. I'm sure the Elemental and Kinetic leaders pulled some strings and ensured her silence, but I could only imagine that it came with strict conditions—conditions that I undoubtedly just broke.

A heavy, sinking feeling latched onto my chest and seemed to pull it to the depths of my stomach. A vision of my forthcoming punishment had me casting my eyes down to my feet.

I didn't fight as two pairs of hands wrapped around my upper arms. Silver lined the little princess's eyes with unshed tears. Her frightened expression told me she knew what my future held. Holding her gaze, a whispered "Goodbye" tumbled from my lips as the male administrator yanked my arms and roughly guided me to the headmistress's office to face the music.

Gray and I walked in tension-filled silence. She tried to quiet her foot-steps through the leaves, but somehow, she hadn't quite figured out how to mute them altogether. Shouldn't her father have ensured this as part of her training as an assassin? It didn't make sense.

"Walk any louder, and you're going to attract the entire Royal fucking Domain to our location, Princess," I snapped.

A combination of conflicting emotions warred within me at the recent revelation. I was relieved to have a vital memory back, but it only raised more questions. At least I understood *why* she seemed familiar to me. It didn't, however, answer why she didn't appear to remember me, or why I felt this compulsion to protect her...or why her presence seemed to chase away the darkness.

Gray hitched her bag to adjust it higher on her shoulder. "You need to humble yourself...*Prince*."

"Don't call me that, considering the Elemental Kingdom fell at the hands of your father."

Her jaw ticked, "Then maybe you shouldn't go around starting wars you can't fucking finish."

That familiar rush of anger surged through me, but this wasn't incited by my evil companion. This was all me. In the blink of an eye, I stepped in front of her, making her halt to avoid running into my chest. I towered over her and worked to control my anger.

I needed her. Harsh breaths huffed through my nose at her lies.

In a single swift movement, she dropped down and swept my feet from underneath me. I crashed to my back to join the dirt and leaves. Before I could move, she had already pinned my hips between her thighs, had stolen a dagger from my belt, and was now holding it firmly against my throat. "Remind me again why I shouldn't kill you?"

I smiled, craving her violence. "Go ahead, Princess. You'd be doing me a favor."

Her eyes narrowed and shifted back and forth as if she was trying to piece me together. Her high cheekbones and dainty chin contrasted against the fierce little savage who sat on me. A silver scar marred her right cheekbone, catching my eye. Since we healed, we shouldn't have been able to form scars unless it was prevented.

I was beginning to like the way it felt to have her straddle me, but my main thought was maybe she'd grace me with another memory while we were down here.

And damn, she was beautiful as the savage little princess I knew lurked within her. Maybe a part of me that craved my equal wanted her to come out to play. A warmth I hadn't felt in far too long spread through my chest, thawing the ice a fraction that had numbed me many years ago.

Wrinkled skin above her brows appeared as she scrutinized me further. She blew a fallen strand of white-blonde hair from her line of sight before scoffing, "Nah, I'd rather make you suffer."

I hummed, my smile in place. "I'm pretty sure you're doing that right now," I said and cast my eyes downward to where she straddled me.

For a brief second, hunger lit her eyes before her upper lip curled in disgust. A tug on my heart vibrated at the same time a wave of lust struck me in my lower stomach, and I didn't think it belonged to me. "I'd rather fuck an Endarkened," she said, but I got the sense there might've been a slight hesitation in her tone as she climbed off.

I rose to my feet and swiped the debris from my cargos, forgetting about the anger and struggle to maintain just a sliver of my sanity. That brief interaction with the Kinetic princess was the first time I'd felt like my true self since *she* had been alive.

I held hope that Gray remembered me from all those years ago. Because even in my madness, I felt this drive to protect her. I couldn't control it any more than I could control the darkness that made me its bitch.

I held my palm out for her to return my dagger. "You had your fun. Now, give the grown-up toys back to the adults."

Gray's glower affected places in me it shouldn't, but it fueled the masochist in me to bring out her inner beast. "I should've slit your throat," she said.

"I would've let you."

"*Let* me?"

I laughed. "You think you won that round?"

Her nostrils flared, and she looked down at the Elemental blade in her grasp before she sighed in disappointment. "Wouldn't have killed you anyway. Would've been a waste of my energy."

"Hmm. At least you're practical."

Gray slapped the hilt of the dagger in my palm with more force than necessary and then said, "I'm a lot of things, Griffin, but being your personal Angel of Death is at the top of my list." Her fingertips grazed my palm when she pulled her hand back and stormed past me.

Like last time, the contact prompted another memory to surface, reminding me of another person the darkness had attempted to steal. I gasped, more and more pieces of my past falling into place. Sadness gripped my heart at the personal connections I'd been forced to sever.

Moments later, as I watched Gray pointedly tip-toe over a branch and then shot me a scowl, I arrived to the conclusion that my demon—what else do you call it?—chose to take the important people and moments that served as my tethers. Meanwhile, the affliction left behind a plethora of painful memories as motivation to succumb to its manipulation...to take away my hope.

My mouth opened the slightest in awe as I looked at Gray, still not understanding how she was able to do this. But gratitude had me lifting my eyes to the sky as I gazed up into the canopy of trees. She'd never understand. And in her misguided anger, I didn't expect to get the chance to tell her. But my head was clearer than it had been in too long. The call of death and destruction was muted, although I could feel it lurking on the outskirts in the background.

I could *breathe*.

Whatever she was doing to me, I didn't know. But I needed to stay near her in order to come back to myself fully. This mission was more than the king's death. I'd known there had been more, but I couldn't remember why or how until now.

An unusual lightness filled me, and liquid warmth burned my eyes at the foreign feeling I hadn't dared touch since *that* day.

Hope. Just a flicker, but even the tiniest of cinders was all I needed.

Chapter 18

GRAY

An hour of crunching through dead leaves in silence passed. We approached a verdant pasture with an out-of-place wooden cross erected in its center.

Griffin refused to elaborate further on why he needed my help. Even more curious was why he thought I'd be a willing participant in the plan he'd concocted. Plus, what the fuck happened back there? He'd convinced me that he might legitimately be insane, looks be damned.

I hadn't figured out my own plan regarding my father aside from staying alive. And then there were Scarlett, Hazel, and Cotton. Fear for their safety gnawed at my mind. All I could hope was that they'd followed my instructions in order to escape the king's wrath.

I couldn't help but wonder if Griffin planned on slaughtering all the humans in this speakeasy. As excessive as it sounded, that was the image he'd earned himself after the attack on the King's Palace all those years ago. As calm and personable as he appeared with me now...I couldn't forget that fact.

Griffin Silas was a ruthless monster.

I watched as he slid the cross to the side, exposing the wooden hatch door beneath it. He hefted it up with a creak and disappeared below. His black hood peeked over the edge of the ground before submerging to the depths.

Dusk approached. Red, orange, and pink hues painted the sky, pitching a beautiful autumn tint onto the surrounding landscape. I took a deep breath, bracing for the bullshit that, undoubtedly, was to come. I could use a drink—or two.

I tuned my senses into nature, letting the wisps from the breeze caress my face. Birds sang in the distance, and frogs croaked until their voices sounded raw. The sounds eased the tension in my chest, as they always did, bringing a sense of serenity I wished I could hold onto. Since I couldn't remove the bracelet to renew my strength, I took a moment to allow nature to ground me. The damp earth provided steadfast reassurance and comfort in ways I'd never found from anything besides Slate.

I snapped my head toward the woods. A lingering presence in the near distance piqued my attention. They concealed themselves from view, and without my abilities, I couldn't detect the energetic signature. But I could feel their faint energy thrumming with life. My first instinct was to run toward them to see if they were a threat. Suicidal as it may seem, it was second nature for me to eliminate the threat before they had the chance to surprise me. I looked between the speakeasy entrance and the woods, torn about which way to go.

In the end, I convinced myself that it was most likely a random human arriving at the speakeasy. And upon seeing me at the entrance, they must've gotten spooked at the stranger in their territory. I let them go and ignored the sinking feeling in my stomach as I followed Griffin and descended the ladder.

The humans had built this particular ladder from metal pipes rather than wood like the previous one. The chilling temperatures made it cold to the touch. By force of habit, I reached for the black crystal necklace around my chest. I relaxed at the feel of the cool stone and continued my descent into the stifling tunnel.

Griffin waited for me at the bottom, and once my feet thudded to the wooden floor, he set off through the torch-lit passage. Our distorted shadows cast along the walls made us appear like the warped monsters humans believed us to be.

Like the previous speakeasy, a heavy wooden door barricaded at the entrance. Naturally, Griffin flung it open with ease, and I suspected it wasn't as simple as he made it appear.

This speakeasy was larger than the last, but it was still claustrophobic. A staircase constructed of wood and plastic crates led to a second level where more humans congregated. People sat in mismatched, salvaged—or stolen—chairs pushed against wood barrels that had been transformed into tables. Two bars faced each other across opposite sides of the room. I marveled at the lamplights illuminating walls filled with jars of moonshine, casting the room in a colorful glow.

The air was thick with the nauseating mixture of alcohol and dirty sweat, which poured from the unwashed bodies occupying the confined space. I resisted the urge to cover my sensitive ears to the booming and raucous voices, intensifying as the moonshine loosened their vulgar tongues.

I hung behind Griffin, keeping watch on his movements, ready to intervene if he attacked. Scanning the patrons, I checked for rebels, noting the telltale signs of a few in the mix. But overall, it was bedraggled humans that gathered together to make the most of their lackluster reality.

We both kept our hoods intact, as it would be foolish to think my father would not have placed spies in every speakeasy in the region. Our faces were high-profile; therefore, it was likely we would be recognized.

Griffin sauntered to the nearby bar as I trailed behind. He motioned to the runner with a casual wave. Their voices were too low for me to hear, but I caught the hand gesture from Griffin, signaling for two drinks. The runner narrowed his eyes at me, his head tilting slightly before offering Griffin a challenging glare—questioning him about my presence.

The Elemental was silent as he stared down the runner. His posture stiffened as he exuded power, even through the suppression of his magic. "Get the drinks, Jesse. *Now*," he snarled, the maliciousness in his tone raising the hairs on the back of my neck. He looked ready to lunge over the bar.

For several tense moments, I thought I'd be forced to fight a horde of drunken humans. Jesse dropped his shoulders and took a step back. His nostrils flared, and his lip curled as he looked at me again, but he was wordless as he retreated to snag two jars of moonshine.

One glass slid to me across the bar. My hand slapped it to a stop before I removed the lid. Just before it touched my lips, I halted, suspicious whether they had poisoned it with redfern.

"It's fine." Griffin's smooth, deep voice caressed my ear. The vibrations from it sent warmth throughout my body. "See?" He took a long, savoring sip from his own. His tongue slipped out and licked the remaining moisture from his upper lip. It took my brain a moment to catch up with my body, which traitorously began to heat as I leaned in toward Griffin.

Seriously?

I forced my spine to straighten, rolling my shoulders and silently cursing myself for yet another lapse. "You're an Elemental. Your poison is different from mine," I argued, still hesitating to take a swig.

"Mhmm," he agreed, shrugging with a smirk before walking away. He sipped his moonshine with an unnerving grace as he slunk through the clusters of tables stuffed with humans.

I was tempted to follow him, but I took the opportunity to observe him instead. Griffin appeared to be comfortable amongst these humans. These were humans who despised us out of misplaced fear. Surely, they weren't aware of what he was because, if they were, the pitchfork mobs would be swarming him. I waited for a beat while I watched him wade through the crowd, then moved to follow him at a distance.

Eventually, I found an empty table in the corner that allowed a clear view of him standing at the side of the bar. I studied him, leaning against it with a casual arm propped on the edge as he waited for someone.

When several minutes passed, and no one showed, I assumed I'd let my bias get the best of me. Perhaps he wasn't up to anything nefarious. Maybe I was just being too cautious. But as the thought entered my mind, Jesse appeared beside him.

Griffin, who was over six feet tall, towered over Jesse's squat frame. His beady eyes glared up at Griffin, while Griffin penetrated him with an icy look of dismissal—a blatant reminder of the killer he was.

Jesse waved his hands about as he spoke, suggesting there was a dispute of some sort between the two. Griffin stood in menacing silence, boring the weight of his lethal gaze into Jesse, who fell to abrupt stillness.

"Yer kind ain't welcome here." A rough feminine voice laden with a heavy southern accent snatched my attention from the posturing men. The woman who stood at my table was what I'd describe as "scrappy." Her clothes were stained, worn, and had holes that needed patching. Through a particular hole, a bright red bra peeked out from the dingy tee. Her weathered jeans sagged low on her waist, their bagginess almost swallowing her legs. Dark sandy hair sat in a grease-filled mop in a lopsided bun. "This is yer only warnin'. Leave," she said with a sharp glare.

I propped my chin on my fist and graced her with a close-lipped grin. "Afraid I can't do that yet," I said, bored with the situation.

'Scrappy' bared her teeth and shook her head. "The *arr-o*-gance and self-righteousness of yer kind is disgustin'. No regard for anybody but yer damn selves. Git. Out."

"And what *is* my kind exactly, Scrappy?" I raised my eyebrows, curious to hear her colorful response.

"The devil kind. The kind that's an abomination to our god-given planet. The kind that destroyed ev'rything for ev'rybody. Ya don't fuckin' belong here. Now, git." Her sun-baked skin crinkled on her forehead from her hard scowl. When I didn't move to leave, she jerked an arm, pointing to the exit.

"You sure have a lot of balls to talk to someone you believe is the 'devil's kind.'" I was uneasy and outnumbered. And apparently, humans had discovered a way to make bullets to kill us, as I'd learned with Dash. I refused to let her see it, though. Showing weakness was what got you killed in this world.

Heaving unrestrained breaths, she launched herself at me from across the wooden barrel table. I dodged to the side, leaping from my seat, and watched her sail over the top, crashing to the floor in a heap. *Nice.*

I didn't have any weapons on me, which left me vulnerable, nor did I have my magic freed. I could fix that, but it'd open more doors for trouble that I didn't think I'd be able to escape.

Scrappy scrambled to her feet and lunged at me again, this time slinging a fist at my face. I jerked my head to the side and caught her fist, squeezing it in my palm as my eyes locked with hers, filled with rage, hatred, and fear.

I kicked her in the gut, and she stumbled back several feet before her back slammed into the corner wall.

I stalked toward her as she gasped for air. One of her hands braced her weight against the wall, and the other clutched her abdomen. I grabbed her by her oily roots and slammed her head into the wall. She dropped to the floor with a scream.

Suddenly, the loud chatter of the speakeasy muted.

I squatted until I was at eye level with her and said softly, "I wasn't here to hurt anyone." She cradled her head in her palm as I watched her. "*But* you pissed me off," I continued with a shrug. "Can't really blame this on me."

Before I could do anything else, I was snatched by my arm, hauled to my feet, and came face to face with an irate Griffin. His crystalline glare seared into me, burning me to the spot, his grip on my arm bruising.

"Let me go, asshole," I growled through clenched teeth.

He didn't. Instead, he jerked me toward the exit without a word. Angry faces and outraged voices yelled obscenities and death wishes at me as we shoved through the establishment. At some point, a hand snagged on my hood, jerking me backward to a halt. Griffin continued to yank me forward like he was in a game of tug of war.

With limited mobility, I pivoted on one foot and threw a high kick that struck a guy's head. A tall, broad man sailed backward, taking several others out with him as he crashed into a cluster of dirt-stained humans who demanded my death.

Griffin pulled me forward again. Fury poured from his aura in waves, which only fueled my own. Those surrounding him backed up despite their brave words. When we reached the door, he hefted it open and slung me through into the torch-lined tunnel.

"Move," he ordered, latching onto my biceps again while pulling me toward the metal ladder.

"Let go. I'm not a fucking child." I yanked my arm from his grasp. Griffin didn't fight me as he ascended to the ground above. I climbed after him, right on his heels, waiting for the mob to follow us out.

Reaching topside, Griffin whirled on me. Any hints of the kindness he'd displayed up until this point were gone. He was the embodiment of wrath with clenched fists and a coiled posture.

"I could've told you lounging in a speakeasy was a bad idea," I said, shaking my head. I couldn't believe he was mad at *me* for what happened back there. An ice-blonde lock broke free from its loose knot and drifted into my face. It blocked my view of him, so I shoved it aside with a growl of frustration.

"You have no fucking clue what you nearly cost..." Griffin cut himself off and pinched his brow between his fingers. His chest heaved as he worked to calm himself. After several harsh breaths, he finally looked at me. "You nearly fucked up everything and almost got yourself killed in the process," he snarled, throwing his arms wide as if trying to physically expel the rage radiating from his aura.

I opened my mouth in indignation. "*I* didn't do a damn thing except defend myself. And what business do you have with humans, anyway? You looked pretty damn cozy with Jesse in there." I crossed my arms over my chest.

"You couldn't just keep your mouth shut, could you? Can't you at least *pretend* to be nice to the people who are actually suffering? No wonder..." He shook his head. Instead of finishing his sentence, he turned around and began storming back the way we came.

"No wonder what?" I hurried to keep pace with his rushed, long strides.

He said nothing, so we moved in tense silence. I wanted to press him, but I needed to calm down before I reacted out of anger and ended up in another compromising position. I couldn't afford any more slip-ups at this point.

Finally, Griffin spoke. "I need supplies. There's a scorse nearby. Think you can behave?" He didn't so much as spare me a glance.

A scorse?

Scorses were human bartering locations. However, they also sold black market shit, such as drugs, guns, and ammo, as well as prostitutes. The vile trade of human trafficking functioned in networks that made coordinated stops through designated scorses. The stops were random, making it difficult to predict when the trade would pass through one at a given time. The fear of being captured and put into slavery is another element of the world's reality that kept many humans living in groups underground. The leaders of these trafficking rings were ruthless, and they instilled more fear and control into their race than our own. Even the scorse owners had to bow to their whims or risk death—or worse, risk their family's freedom.

"Maybe I'd behave if I knew what the endgame was," I snapped. "But instead, I'm stuck with the psychopath who killed..." I choked on the rest of that statement. "With *you*, going to human hangouts while I'm being hunted by the Royal Domain. My powers are suppressed, and I'm supposed to just tag along with no questions?"

Griffin cleared his throat and seemed to weigh whether to divulge any information. "Why are you being hunted?" If I didn't know better, I would have thought there was a note of softness to his tone.

"Because I failed to kill *you*." I kept my gaze glued to the shadowed line of trees ahead of me, refusing to look at him.

A quiet chuckle escaped him as he shook his head, unamused. "Of course, he'd kill his own daughter. Once you became a liability, you were to be terminated. You're too powerful to keep alive, so that makes you a threat now. Nothing else." He sighed and met my eyes with his icy blues. "So, tell me. Who's *really* the psychopath, Gray?"

I didn't respond. My nose stung, and my face flushed as my eyes threatened tears. All the wounds from my father's mistreatment rose to the surface. I ground my teeth to fight it off.

Never show weakness. Especially in front of Griffin, even if he'd made a point.

Night had fallen, and the nocturnal creatures were out to claim the land. An owl hooted in the distance, calling for its prey as I stared at the abandoned home.

Vines and foliage devoured the structure. The windows were knocked out, and jagged shards of glass formed mini daggers along the sills, daring anyone to enter.

At one time, this was a nice, middle-class home that sat on several acres of property. A pang of sadness stung my chest at the sight of a tire swing hanging on a beautiful oak branch. Moonlight glinted off metal in the corner of my eye. In the tall grass by the porch sat a small, rusted, tricycle abandoned by a child.

I pictured three children of various ages. The parents were probably the doting type, always wanting to capture every moment of their children's childhood—every smile, laugh, and accomplishment.

A heaviness in my heart took root as deep as the oak tree's. It was a fantasy I'd always longed for. I'd always believed that if only I could make my father proud...

"We should be safe here for the night," Griffin said, breaking me from my spiraling thoughts. "At dawn, we'll leave for the scorse." His voice was nearly a whisper, but it still shattered the woeful quietude of what once was.

I nodded and walked up the brick steps before reaching the remnants of the front door, Griffin trailing close behind. The door hung from its hinges awkwardly, indicating the home had been raided. I wrestled it aside to make a large enough gap to squeeze through.

Despite the darkness, we could see overturned couches scattered across the living room alongside the dusty cotton from their innards. Shredded papers, books, and magazines littered the floors, and wooden tables were split in half.

I took careful steps in pursuit of the stairs, avoiding shards of glass or any of the belongings strewn across the floor. It felt disrespectful. I felt somehow responsible, even though this was Griffin's doing.

Perhaps I was guilty by association.

I headed for the room at the end of the upstairs hallway in the hopes that it was the main bedroom. The last thing I wanted was to sleep in a child's room with its ghost haunting me in my sleep, begging for answers.

With a light shove of the door, I froze at the sight that awaited me in the bedroom. Cast in the silver glow of the moon's light, a skeleton lay crumpled on the floor beside the bed. The white carpet around him was stained brown from aged blood. Upon the mattress, another sprawled at a twisted angle. Raided in their sleep. I presumed the husband had tried to protect his family. He'd been too late.

I closed my eyes at the distant horror. I struggled to keep the walls up around my emotions. Too much had happened, and I hadn't had a chance to truly process it all. I was barely keeping it together, but this was the first moment I'd had to myself since I'd encountered Dash, and the cracks in the dam were threatening to unleash the onslaught of my emotional suppression.

I took a deep breath, following it with a shaky exhale. On the farthest side of the room, a large walk-in closet opened into the darkness. I trudged past two shattered glass balcony doors beside the bed. Goosebumps skittered along my flesh at the cool breeze wafting through them. I inhaled again, breathing in the scent of pine and decaying brush that infiltrated the room.

In the spacious closet, the couple's belongings lay ransacked on the floor and shelves. I dropped my duffel and used it as a pillow to curl up on the carpeted floor of the bedroom. At last, I allowed my mind to sift through recent events. The aftermath of everything finally began to settle, which granted me the chance to ponder Griffin's motives—and how I'd kill him.

Because I would kill him, no matter the cost.

Images of all the disheveled humans at the speakeasy crossed my mind. Images of Dash...of Scrappy. What type of lives had they lived before Devolution Day? What all had they lost? *Who* had they lost? More grief for people I'd never known hurt my heart as I lay in the cold, dark closet. I sniffed as hot tears slid down my cheeks before the cool air chilled them, causing me to shiver.

As I drifted into a restless sleep, I wondered how many more innocents would have to die before the world could be set right again.

Chapter 19

GRAY

Muttering voices roused me from sleep. Father frequently had visitors come and go at all hours, so it wasn't unusual to be awoken by strangers. With a groan of annoyance, I rolled over, hoping to slip back into my slumber. But the bed was all wrong. It was stiff and cold instead of lush and warm. A wintry bite chilled the room, which also wasn't right.

Through the sleep-hazed fog, the voices continued to rise, sending a jolt of alarm through my body that had me jumping to my feet. Reality crashed into me as I took in the deserted room with the decaying corpses lying mere feet away.

The voices down the hall startled me into action, and I cursed the fact that Griffin still had my weapons. If there were intruders, I couldn't allow them to catch me off-guard. I contemplated removing my bracelet, but I didn't want to risk drawing Father's attention. As I approached the decomposed skeletons, I chose to make do with what was available, no matter how wrong it felt.

My foot broke through one of the brittle arms, snapping it in half. "Sorry," I whispered to the remains with a grimace. I picked up the jagged bone and crept to the door. It wasn't the ideal weapon, but it would be adequate, I supposed—at least until I could find something better.

Darkness engulfed the empty hallway, and every step screamed with the loudest of creaks. With my back pressed against the wall, I crept along in the direction of the growing voices.

"Just *shut*. *Up*! Shut the fuck up!" It was Griffin's voice disturbing the cryptic silence of the house.

I was hit with the sudden urge to run to him. I couldn't explain it, but I felt pulled to aid him for some reason. It made no sense. I told myself it was for self-preservation and not for his safety. If someone was threatening Griffin, then that could only mean they'd be a threat to me, too.

Upon hearing his voice, I tip-toed to the doorway it came from. Damn, I needed my magic.

Fuck it...

Against my better judgment, I made a decision I hoped I wouldn't regret. I needed to know what I faced before I charged in there with only a bone as a weapon.

Shoving the bone between my knees, I scrambled to remove my bracelet. The latch popped loose, and once it was free from my skin, energy rushed through my veins. A burst of electric blue from my currents illuminated the dark hallway, casting a cool, eerie glow against the ruined walls. The magic bombarded me...overwhelmed me, almost. It felt angry for being shut down for so long. I was fighting to silence my heaving breaths when Griffin's unhinged words had me freezing on the spot.

"You won't *fucking* touch her! No, no, no. Gray is...Gray is *mine*. You can't have her!" Griffin's voice, usually deep and strong, cracked on his last words.

A knot twisted in my stomach. Pushing aside his bullshit claim on me for now, I absorbed the energy waves from his voice into my aura to fuel my magic.

I stuffed the bracelet into my pocket and grabbed the bone from between my knees, shoving off the wall with my shoulder. Peering around the edge of the doorframe, my heart stuttered as I tried to make sense of the scene before me.

A manic Griffin stood in the middle of a little boy's room. Like the rest of the house, it was utterly wrecked.

I scanned the room, but Griffin appeared to be alone. "Enough!" he roared. Griffin's breath came in harsh pants as his hunched shoulders rose and fell. His feline-shaped eyes burned wildly in sheer panic. With his hood pushed back, his obsidian hair hung astray around his jaw. It was a frenzied mess as if he'd been pulling at the roots with his fingers—fingers that shook on unsteady hands. Nothing remained of the composed and calculated killer I'd grown accustomed to seeing.

"Griffin?" At the sound of my voice, he stumbled backward as if I'd struck him. Spinning to face me, he shook his head, his expression twisting in shocked horror.

"No, Gray," he said, breathless in desperate urgency. "Go back to your room. It's not safe in here. *Please*."

I took a slow step forward.

"Listen to me. Just...just go back. I can't..." he begged. His body trembled harder, and his skin's deep tan was so pale that he didn't even look like the same person.

Adrenaline thrummed through my veins as I took another step into the room. "What's going on? Who are you talking to?" I asked, hiding my rising panic with a soft tone. I scanned the moonlit wreckage for the source of the second voice, but I still couldn't find it, even with my magic.

Griffin stood amongst the broken toys and furniture in the darkness. A small skeleton clothed in faded blue pajamas on the bed caught my eye, and my heart squeezed.

Griffin shook his head again before he dropped his chin to his chest in defeat. His voice was soft and defeated when he said, "No one. I...just leave." He lifted his head to peer at me through his dark lashes with the look of a shattered man. "*Please*." His voice broke again, cracking open a part of me that resonated with it.

I took another step, slower this time. "If there's a threat, then you need my help."

"You—you can't help with this threat." Turbulent waves crashed behind his crystal-blue eyes as they pleaded with me to go back to my room.

Something within me softened. I knew it shouldn't, and it was probably the wounds of my traumatic past egging me along, but I couldn't help it as I allowed myself to be pulled toward him. Seeing someone of Griffin's caliber breaking in front of me weakened some of the defenses I'd carefully constructed all these years. Because on the inside, I was broken, too.

"I can try," I offered, my voice coming out softer than intended. I took another step closer to my sworn enemy, the man who'd taken so much from me. What the hell was I doing?

Griffin didn't speak as I took one slow step after another, each step seeming to ease the tension in his body while he watched with trepidation. I approached him as if he was a panicked bird, ready to take flight if I made a sudden move. The closer I got, the more his shaking decreased, and his panting slowed. He was calming down.

What the fuck was happening?

"Tell me you remember. You remember, don't you?" Griffin asked, his tone almost a whisper, laced with pain-filled hope.

I cocked my head to the side with pinched brows. Confusion clouded my mind at his sudden shift. "Remember what, Griffin?"

"The playground. Those kids. Our magic..." He paused. His eyes gleamed with unabashed vulnerability at his prompting. But with his words, a long-suppressed memory broke through. "We touched and...and..."

"Yes," I answered on a breath that vacated my lungs. The image of warped and ruined metal on the playground flashed through my mind.

I had been getting beat up by the other kids when they suddenly stopped. It was before I'd begun training, and I was highly insecure due to my father's abuse. He'd never allowed me to have any meaningful friendships, so I didn't know how to socialize. Because of that, I came off as withdrawn, quiet, awkward, or "weird" as they called me, to the other kids at school.

When I'd dared to open my eyes from the fetal position, I'd come face to face with a blue-eyed boy standing before me. The bullies had vanished. However, it had been the playground's wreckage that had caught my attention. He'd scared them off with magic that he'd been too young to wield. The boy with glamoured blue eyes and short inky hair had threatened to kick their asses if they messed with me again.

He'd said that his magic had recently awakened, and he couldn't control it yet, even though magic for Kinetics and Elementals didn't awaken until the age of thirteen. He was only ten at the time. But it was what followed that exchange that had perplexed me for many years to come. Eventually, I began to believe I'd imagined the entire thing. I had been only eight, so memories could be unreliable at such a young age.

Upon grabbing my hand to help me stand, an incredible blast launched us several feet backward in opposite directions. We had stared at each other in shocked confusion but were soon interrupted by the teachers hauling us to our feet and dragging us away from one another.

I never saw the blue-eyed boy with inky black hair again.

"That was *you*?" I stood frozen at the realization. Stunned. Though it all made sense. Those *eyes*. Those bright blue eyes that saw everything. That boy had been *Griffin Silas*?

A heart-wrenching smile full of unbridled relief graced his sharp features. It brought a light to them that had my stomach doing flips. It was the first true smile he'd graced me, and I surprised myself by wanting to return it.

"I'm so glad they didn't take that from you," Griffin said, sounding almost ecstatic despite his eased demeanor.

"What? Take what from me?" I asked, crossing my arms and frowning.

Griffin's boyish smile dropped. "Never mind that. There's so much you need to know." His voice hitched with an urgency I'd never expected to hear. "But I'm not the one to tell you. I...where we're headed, there's someone who can explain way better than I ever could. But know this: everything you've been taught to think of me...it's all a lie. It's all been a fear tactic deployed by your father and..." He stopped, closing his eyes and squeezing his hands into tight fists at his side to fight whatever battle warred within him.

"You're not making any sense." It was impossible to hold back the tremor of fear from my voice.

Griffin turned to me, his eyes suddenly crystal clear as he stared directly into mine. "Things are more complicated than anyone can imagine. Just know that I didn't kill Slate. That wasn't me. I swear it, Gray," he insisted.

Genuine. His words felt genuine. His tone held no room for malicious intent as he held out his palms, facing me. But my breath hitched as I processed something he said.

"How do you know his name?" I took a step backward and tightened my grip on the bone. I hadn't said Slate's name in Griffin's company, had I? No. It wasn't possible. I didn't think he deserved to know it.

"That's a story for another day. But I didn't kill him, Gray. I need you to trust me when I say that."

I snorted at the audacity. "Excuse me, don't fucking ignore the question. How do you know his name?" My hands began to shake while anger pooled in my stomach; I tried to keep my voice somewhat calm.

Griffin raked his shaking fingers through his hair in frustration, turning from me. "Gray, I'm telling you...*don't.* Don't push this tonight." I wasn't fazed by his sense of urgency. I needed answers. Griffin began to pace, tightening his grip on the dark strands. "Please. Just...wait."

The hot anger that had settled in my stomach lanced through my body. Like a shot of moonshine had mixed with all of my pain, it felt as if someone took a torch to it. "And again, you're telling me that you know the name of the person I was madly in love with. The person I cared for more than anyone else. The person which, by the way, *you killed!*" I shouted. "Did you just conveniently forget that part?"

With a growl, Griffin whipped around and stormed to me, slamming to an immediate halt so our bodies wouldn't touch. Only inches separated our noses as he bore his intensity onto me. His glamoured blue eyes were roiling with dark clouds of rage, and his jaw was clenched tighter than I'd ever seen. "Gray, *enough,*" he snarled, pinning me to where I stood. "Listen to me." His heated breath cascaded over my face. "I will tell you everything. But I want...I need..." Griffin took a deep inhalation, closing his eyes. "Not like this. Not now. It's not safe. *You're* not safe. I need you to be safe. That can't happen if you keep shouting at me and pushing this. So, for fuck's sake, *drop it* for tonight. Got it, Princess?"

I wanted more answers, but it was clear I wasn't getting anything else from him for now. I clenched then unclenched my fists as I steadied my heartbeat and watched as the black clouds of rage slowly dissipated from his eyes. With a steadying breath, I nodded with reluctant acceptance. I wasn't sure I could handle any tonight, anyway.

Seeming satisfied, Griffin let out a long, shaky exhale and stepped away from me. "Okay then," he said, relaxing his shoulders a bit. When he caught my gaze, still focused on his movements, his lips slowly curled into a wicked grin. "That's a good girl," he said in a low, exaggerated drawl.

A heavy, questionable pause lingered before we both erupted into laughter. "Ew, you did *not* just say that to me," I wheezed, clutching my ribs as I tried to catch my breath.

"Yeah, I kinda did." Griffin laughed as he rubbed the back of his neck. "And I'm surprised your smart-ass mouth doesn't have anything to say about it." He grinned at me, daring me to retort.

But for once, I didn't take the bait. Because...*his laugh*. My breathing slowed as our laughter quieted, and I found myself wanting to hear that sound again.

What the hell was happening...

After a few moments of comfortable silence, I cleared my throat. "Thank you...by the way." My fingernails picked against the seams along my pants. "For helping me that day on the playground." I dropped my gaze to study a broken plastic train on the floor. "You were the first person to ever stand up for me." Either in school or at home, but I didn't tell him that.

One side of Griffin's mouth pulled upward in a gentle smile. "It was my pleasure. And I still stand firm on what I said back then." A cold, fierce expression engulfed his features as he added, "Except the only difference is I'll fucking kill anyone who tries to hurt you, now."

My mouth opened the slightest at his words. The intensity behind them. "But...but why? I don't understand..." I shook my head; none of it made sense. He hardly knew me. Then or now. And I struggled to reconcile the fact that Griffin Silas had been the first person to show me kindness. And what did it say about me that I liked the fact that someone would kill for me? The darkness within me purred at the thought. But I didn't need a protector—not anymore. Especially not him, but it sat right with me for some reason.

Pain etched his features before he whirled around, shoving his fingers into the roots of his black hair. I jumped from the sudden movement. A frustrated growl escaped him. The silence stretched on, and neither of us moved. Finally, his shoulders slumped, and his arms fell away at his sides. Griffin angled his head to peer at me over his shoulder, with an obsidian strand draped across his cheekbone. The restless storm had returned to his eyes, and in them, it pleaded with me to understand. "Not tonight. I can't...it won't make sense. Please..."

A surge of irritation bubbled up in my chest. It transformed into anger at the lack of control I seemingly had over everything in my life. My currents glowed brighter in response, and Griffin shifted his focus on them as if he'd just noticed them for the first time.

"Your currents..." Griffin said, lifting his scrutinizing stare back to me. "Put them away. It's not safe for them to be free. Not yet." His tone was demanding, but I heard the underlying hint of fear.

I huffed out a breath at his demand. "I'm weaponless, and I heard voices. There's no one around here. It's fine. I've been suffocating with that damn thing on for too long," I said, referring to my bracelet. My hand absentmindedly rubbed my wrist, dreading the moment I'd have to snap it back in place.

"I get it. Trust me. My magic is drowning, too. But it's only going to attract your father to you. You know he has people with abilities who can trace your energetic signature from miles away, right?"

I nodded. "I know." Sighing, I reached into my pocket for the cold metal bracelet. "You're right," I said as the latch snapped together around my wrist. The familiar, warm buzzing of my magic went cold in my veins, locking away a large part of me again. I was forever a prisoner in some capacity.

"Go get some sleep. We're still leaving at dawn, which is in a few hours."

I looked at him—*really* looked at him—and said nothing as he met my gaze. It was as if I was seeing him for the first time as the grown, hardened version of that little boy from all those years ago. He was beautiful. Darkness seemed to be his only companion. A toxic companion that poisoned any brightness crossing his path if he allowed it too close. Thankfully, he seemed to be able to hold it at arm's length before it consumed him completely. Those eyes spoke a language of their own—and somehow, I knew it on an intuitive level.

"Okay." I nodded, and began backing away to return to the main bedroom. "See you in the morning. Get some rest." I cast a glance over my shoulder one last time before I walked down the hallway. Griffin watched my every step, his crystalline eyes gleamed with a mixture of emotions that I couldn't decipher.

Making my way through the hall, I tried to make sense of everything that had happened. With the bone still clutched in my hand, I realized that I'd never learned who he'd been talking to.

"It should be this building," Griffin said, observing the deserted business in the historic City of Downtown Macon. The property had once housed a tattoo shop. What remained stood looted and empty. Like everything else in this world, it was a ghost begging to be acknowledged and freed from the chains of the past.

The hike from the abandoned house had been relatively short. As promised, we'd left at dawn and walked in a comfortable silence to the scorse location. I'd basked in the fresh morning air while keeping my senses open for any potential threats. Neither one of us mentioned the events from the night before.

Griffin seemed to be shrouded in a dark mood if his permanent scowl had anything to say about it. Probably from the lack of sleep. Despite not having slept much myself, I felt more energized than I had in a few days. I wasn't ready for Griffin's darkness to cloud my first rays of light yet, so I let him brood while I relished nature's grounding abilities.

It wasn't until we were halfway along our hike that I sensed a presence again. It felt similar to the one I'd sensed outside the speakeasy. I contemplated mentioning it to Griffin, but something stopped me. Perhaps it was simply a wild animal, and it knew it was outmatched—as if it knew we weren't prey.

"There's nothing here, Griffin," I said, referring to the tattoo shop. "Are you sure this is the right place?" I peered up at him from the side. Black brows furrowed, and his jaw clenched as he surveyed our surroundings.

Nothing remained of the broken and vulnerable man from the previous night. Aside from the dark circles under his eyes, he looked like his normal glamoured self—healthy, warm, tan skin, straightened posture, and calculated eyes that seemed to see everything. The fearsome warrior my father had taught me to hate.

Acid burned my stomach as questions formed. Had I been lied to about him? If he wasn't the savage killer I thought he was, then what did that mean about Slate? Who really killed him? Was I betraying his memory? What about the attack on the King's Palace that led to Devolution Day? I shoved those thoughts down as I focused on the decrepit tattoo shop in front of us. I noticed Griffin had paused, his body tense. "What is it?"

"Something's wrong. This is where it should be." Ever so slightly, he cocked his head to the side, tuning into the surrounding sounds. I did the same. "It could be one of three things: They gave me the wrong location by accident, the scorse has already moved on, or...." He trailed off for a moment, scanning the environment for any slight movement. "Or...we were set up."

My heart rate spiked, and I instantly reached for the twin daggers that should've been strapped to my weapons belt. They weren't. "I need my weapons. Now." I tried not to allow the panic I felt to fall into my voice, but I felt naked without my weapons.

Without taking his eyes from the rooftop of the antebellum building, Griffin readjusted the weapons bag on his shoulders. "Come on, we're too exposed here. If it *is* a trap, we need to be prepared." His voice was so low it was barely audible, even with my heightened hearing. His long legs hurried to the alleyway separating the close-knit brick buildings. "I feel others nearby. I don't know why they're not attacking yet."

Reaching the alleyway, he swung the bag off his back and we dropped into a crouch, strapping ourselves with weapons. While unease filled my chest with anxiety, I couldn't help the thrill winding through my muscles, anticipating a fight.

Griffin removed his double-edged sword. The Elemental sigils on the blades glowed orange once activated by his magic. That was when I realized I didn't know who we were expecting to fight. I looked at the twin daggers that glowed blue, which were meant to kill an Elemental.

"Are they human?" I asked, hoping that was the case. It would be the easiest option.

"No. Kinetic," he said, and then his eyes landed on the daggers, having the same thought. "Here," he whispered as he rummaged in his duffel and snagged another pair of daggers with the sharp angles of the Elemental sigils etched into the blades.

I shot him a confused expression. "How's this supposed to work for me? I'm not an–" I started, but the whistle of a blue-tipped arrow cut me off. It flew between our heads and bounced off the brick wall behind us.

We leaped apart. "Trust me. Just use those daggers. No powers," Griffin said before he ran off to the end of the alleyway. I ran in the opposite direction, clutching the useless blades. How did he expect me to wield these and inflict any damage upon Kinetics when I'm not an Elemental? I shrugged it off. Any blade was better than none, I supposed.

I sprinted for the alley's opening, back to where we came from. A blue, glowing axe swung at my head the moment I rounded the corner. I skidded and ducked. Dropping to a squat, I spun on the ball of my foot. One hand balanced me as I aimed a well-placed kick at my attacker's ankles and swept him off his feet.

I stalked toward the Kinetic Warrior before he got the chance to stand. I stomped on his chest, pinning him to the concrete. He struggled against me, but before he could throw me off, I plunged one of Griffin's daggers into the side of his neck. I didn't look at his face as I hovered over him, afraid I'd recognize him. Blood squirted from the vicious wound once I removed the dagger, splattering my face. But it wasn't the blood that caught my attention. I'd never shied away from it. I stared, dumbfounded, at the orange sigils that glowed on the blade as they hummed to life with Elemental energy in my hands.

Chapter 20

GRAY

M y pulse quickened as I gaped in shock at the two orange daggers that shouldn't be activated.

The Kinetic gurgled on his blood beneath me, snapping my attention back to him. I still refused to look at his face. But beginning at the stab wound, a web of black veins spread at an alarming speed across his skin. I stared in morbid fascination as the infused redfern poisoned him to his death, consuming his veins and arteries. Crimson coated his hand from grasping his wound in a useless attempt to stop the inevitable. No doubt his body tried and failed to heal itself.

I couldn't move from the grisly scene, too stunned by the sigils glowing on the daggers.

A heavy body barreled into my back, arms wrapping around my waist in an unforgiving tackle. Air whooshed from my lungs as my attacker toppled on me. With my arms locked at my sides, I couldn't break free from the male's grip.

Heat simmered in the air surrounding me. It began as a comfortable warmth protecting me from the crisp air, but the temperature quickly rose. I was sweating within seconds.

I thrashed on the concrete, attempting to stab my assailant's thigh. But it was a futile effort.

My skin burned—blisters ready to form. Unable to hold it in, I screamed. This wasn't the first time I'd suffered from thermal manipulation. A few of the king's favorite warriors had this ability, and it was one of his many methods of conditioning me to withstand pain throughout my childhood and teen years.

The guard Scarlett and I had faced wielded ultraviolet magic like it was the power of the sun, whereas this Kinetic's magic controlled external heat temperatures. The air around me broiled like an oven.

As the heat rose, I grew limp. My heartbeat skyrocketed to a dangerous pace. In that exact moment, over the years, I'd learned to find a place of peace...to force my mind to hollow out from the panic and pain.

I focused on my heart rate and willed it to slow despite the torrid blisters and scalding skin. I squeezed the Elemental dagger in my palm, letting it ground me as I withstood the agony.

The Kinetic Warrior pinned me on my side, wrapping my legs up with his own to where they were immobile. My arms were anchored to my waist, and he held me at an angle that ensured his head was out of striking distance.

My wrists were the only part of my anatomy I could move. And if done right, they could inflict a wound. All I needed was a single cut, just enough to make him loosen his hold on me.

The warrior thought he'd won as he took my stillness as defeat. But just as my father had instilled in the guild's training, he wouldn't yield until I was undoubtedly dead.

I stopped fighting the pain. Instead, I welcomed it, imagining it burning away the trauma of my past and present. With a jerk of my wrist, I jabbed blindly anywhere I could that would penetrate his skin. I stabbed, stabbed, and stabbed, unsure if I was causing any actual damage to him. Finally, after several attempts, I felt him flinch with a grunt.

The Kinetic loosened his grip on my arms, so I threw an elbow behind me. It connected with bone. The heat ceased its wrath, and my body began to heal the burns—slowly. I rolled away, narrowly escaping the warrior's attempt to recapture me.

Crouching, he yanked a knife from his weapon belt. I didn't recognize him, but I recognized the sharp focus of a Kinetic Warrior in his eyes. He rose to his feet, stalking toward me as I struggled to get to my dagger. The blue-lit sigils of a Kinetic blade shouldn't cause me lethal damage, but doubt wiggled in at the memory of nearly dying on the train from the stab wound. A stab wound inflicted by Griffin with *my* knives.

I tried to buy myself some time for my body to heal. Falling into shock was no longer a threat, but I had to act fast—faster than the rate at which my body was healing.

I sat up on one knee, and with a well-placed aim, I launched my dagger at my opponent. It wasn't my best throw, as it wobbled just the slightest through each rotation. But it was enough to sink into the soft flesh of his thigh, cutting through corded muscle. He dropped to a knee and snatched the dagger from his leg. It hit the ground with a clank.

I surged to my feet, pushing myself through the dissipating pain of the burns as I charged him.

The redfern, infused within the dagger, cut off his healing ability while suppressing his thermal magic. I snatched the weapon from the ground and sliced my blade across his throat with cold indifference.

Blood sprayed me again, coating my clothes, but thank the gods it missed my face this time. The warrior collapsed at my feet, an expression of shock forever marred on his face.

I took a moment to observe my surroundings. The sound of weapons clanged on the other side of the building.

Griffin, I thought with a brief sense of panic seizing my chest.

Since when did I care if he lived? I shoved the thought aside, passing it off to the fact he had answers to my endless questions. He couldn't die without giving them to me.

I raced to the end of the alleyway he'd disappeared into when we were first attacked. The scene that unfolded brought me to an abrupt stop. The sight of the insanity I beheld stole my breath.

Holy shit.

An entire garrison of Kinetic Warriors bore the weight of the elite Royal Guilds upon Griffin. He fought in the center of a horde of warriors who attacked him using weapons and energetic magic. The most disconcerting part was how he wasn't even the underdog in this fight.

In a blur of motion, he moved with lethal, beautiful movements—dancing with grace and strength so savage. All I could do was gape at the whirring of his orange blades of his double-edged sword that cut down every Kinetic it touched.

Slice. Stab. Kick. Elbow. Slice. Slice. Block. Slice. He flowed with smooth precision between each blow while he utilized every limb. Each strike resulted in a dropped warrior. He was brutal and unrelenting yet lithe and fluid in a fatal dance. I'd never seen anything like it.

This was the notorious Griffin Silas. *This* was why the king wanted him dead.

Kinetics dropped like flies, but more kept coming in their place. At this rate, Griffin would soon tire, and then they'd be on me. He needed help. And as skilled and powerful as I was, I couldn't do what Griffin was doing.

I raced into the legion of warriors, slicing and jabbing the areas of their gear I knew weren't protected.

Once my presence was detected, Kinetic magic assaulted me. An icy blast slammed into my shoulder, knocking me into a brute on my left. He tried to grab me in a choke hold, but I stabbed him in his thigh first. Then I kicked him to the ground to writhe in pain before retrieving my dagger from his flesh. Sensing someone approaching me from behind, I whirled, carving a ruby line across his throat. His mouth opened, and his face went slack. More blood spilled.

And on I went, relentlessly fighting my way through to the center to aid Griffin. Every time a Kinetic power assaulted me, I hunted down the source. Being short made it easier to duck under their arms. Then, I'd sidestep with a jab to exposed arms, legs, or necks, letting the poison of the Elemental blade take care of the rest as I moved on.

No matter how many warriors we took down, more appeared. We were beyond the point of being overwhelmed. I spotted Griffin fighting in the center as I took down two more on either side of me. He still moved through enemies in his death dance, yet he was dwindling. Fast.

I ran to his side. He glanced at me out of the corner of his eye without slowing his movements.

"Remember how I said, 'no powers?'" He stabbed a man in the eye before shifting to face the next.

"Yeah," I acknowledged. I jammed the heel of my boot into a woman's shin, then a jab to her throat. I repeated the action to an approaching man on her right. There was no room for punches in this fight. It was only dodge, kick, dodge, stab, and move on.

"Go! Get out of here!" Griffin's back was to me as he yelled, "I can't fight like this much longer."

"I'm not leaving!" My pride wouldn't let me. The idea of abandoning a fight ate me to bits.

"Gray, fucking *go*!"

Slice. Stab. Kick.

"Fuck off! I'm not leaving."

Dodge. Stab. Stab.

Griffin yelled a curse as the garrison closed in. "Then, stand beside me. Shoulder to shoulder."

I did, kicking someone in the chest as I moved. My muscles were weakening, and my limbs felt like lead. I wasn't sure how much longer we'd be in this fight.

"Watch my back for a second," he ordered as he drew to a halt.

I fought off the warriors coming at him from his back, unable to do anything for the ones coming at him from every other angle.

But it didn't matter.

Mid-stab, an invisible force snatched my daggers from my hands. They rotated and aimed at the warriors in front of me.

Everyone froze. Not only were my weapons suspended in the air—but every single metal weapon present in the fight. All the sharp points were directed at the legion of elite fighters. Most of the blades glowed blue, but there was orange dotted amongst the electric blue sea of weapons.

I spun to find a rigid Griffin—his palms raised, facing outward, aimed at the remaining garrison.

He twitched his hands. And all at once, every blade—daggers, swords, knives—dove upon the warriors like a vast sentient being. My mouth opened when over half of them crumpled to the ground. But there were so many more still standing. Warriors scrambled to gain control of the weapons that had turned on them.

Griffin squeezed his palms into tight fists, grabbing onto something that no one could see.

Suddenly, coughing fits rang out, and every remaining Kinetic began to choke. I scanned the scene, confused as they clutched their throats, their eyes bulging as they gasped for breath.

I glanced back and forth between Griffin and the warriors, trying to decipher what was happening. The Kinetic nearest to me—a woman with hair the color of fire—dropped to her knees.

Liquid metal dribbled from her mouth and trickled down her chin, a sliver of sunlight glinting off it. I glanced around at the others and witnessed the same thing occurring to them, too.

Griffin still stood with his fists raised, but the harsh tremble in his body was clear.

The ones that remained dropped to the ground, gasping and clutching their throats. The liquified metal began to leak from their eyes, noses, ears, and mouths. And within seconds, they were motionless.

My ears rang from the sudden silence that fell over us. I wiped the blood from my face with the back of my gloved hand and spun in a full circle—all the warriors were dead in what could only be described as a massacre.

I glanced at Griffin and watched as he gave in to his body and collapsed to his knees. He'd overdone it. I'd never seen a show of power on that scale by a single person.

"Griffin."

He sat with his head hung to his chest, his breath haggard. "I'm fine. Just need a recharge," he slurred. The large hood from his cloak blocked his face from view as I rounded him.

I squatted in front of him. The rough stubble on his jaw pricked my exposed fingertips as I lifted his head to focus on me, but he refused to open his eyes. A golden sheen illuminated his skin; the tale-tale sign of an Elemental gleamed in the morning sun.

"How in the actual fuck did you just do that?" I whispered, awestruck by the man in front of me. I never stood a chance against something as extraordinary as that. He had gone easy on me that first night in the speakeasy.

Griffin couldn't hold back the weak chuckle but refused to look at me. "Didn't you know?" His voice carried the weight of a darkness that threatened to pull him permanently to its depths. "I'm a legend," he added with a shrug and a humorless chuckle.

"I wouldn't go that far." I rolled my eyes. Although the Elementals considered him a legend amongst their kind. Now, I could understand why.

"Mhmm..." was all he could manage in response.

"Griffin..." I said, concerned that he'd pass out on me.

"Chrome," he mumbled, barely audible.

"What?" I furrowed my brows, thinking I'd misheard him.

"My name isn't Griffin." He slowly lifted his eyelids, meeting my gaze. But it wasn't the crystal-blue eyes I'd grown used to, and not the glamoured pair I remembered from my childhood. "It's Chrome. Chrome Freyr."

Chapter 21

GRAY

Chrome Freyr might have been a legend amongst our people, but he had always been an obscure and untouchable entity when he'd been alive. He was sixteen when my father announced his death, a little over ten years ago. Most cultures wanted to immortalize their legendary figures, but there were very few photos of him throughout the King's Palace. And the ones that existed never showed his face clearly, almost as if Forest had been trying to hide him, for some reason, which I'd always found odd. The main defining trait he'd had was his short, metallic hair, the color of chrome...a trait Griffin lacked.

My heart lurched. Griffin's knowing gaze locked onto mine. All of his previous humor had completely vanished. They were no longer the rich blue I'd come to appreciate. Now, his eyes were molten metal, swirling like liquid silver paint as they had been the first night at the speakeasy. And a gold-flecked layer of skin illuminated him in the sunlight.

"That's impossible. Chrome is..."

"Dead?" he finished for me. A deep chuckle vibrated his body, but there was no amusement in it. "Nope. As you just witnessed, I'm too dangerous for the king to let live."

"But... but," I began, struggling to wrap my mind around his claim. "Chrome was a Kinetic. You're not."

Griffin or Chrome—I didn't know anymore—offered a sardonic smile. "I'm not? No, I suppose Forest and my mother kept that little secret locked up tight down in the prison with all the rest."

"If you're truly Chrome, and you're a Kinetic," I started, leaning back to rest on the heels of my feet. "Then show me. You'd have currents and..." I focused on his black hair and his chromatic eyes.

Griffin took a deep breath before shifting to pull up the sleeve of his hooded cloak. By exposing the gold skin of his wrist, a silver bracelet with embossed Kinetic sigils stood out against his complexion. I'd never noticed it on him before. With shaking fingers, he unclasped the latch.

The black cloak followed, revealing his inked arms for the first time. More white lines marred the tan flesh beneath the golden sheen, indicating more scars, but I caught the distinct signs of a specific type of mark. Raised welts in the shape of Kinetic symbols were barely perceptible through the tattoos and gilded skin. Brands. So many of them. Dozens of kill marks lined the entirety of both his arms, from shoulders to wrists.

In the stretched silence, I questioned whether I was having a mental breakdown, but the truth was there before my eyes.

Griffin gasped.

I watched as his black hair morphed from pitch-black into metallic, shining chrome. The color was reminiscent of the chrome bumpers on a car. It was unlike any Kinetic I'd ever seen. His golden skin and quicksilver eyes remained, but I stood transfixed as silver currents pulsed from his fingertips and up the sides of his neck. They made the familiar path downward before darting up again.

I tried to wrap my mind around what I was looking at. How could someone encapsulate both Kinetic and Elemental traits and abilities? I backed up a few steps, shaking my head in denial. This wasn't possible. There was no known account of this happening. The cognitive dissonance was real. Not only was Griffin Silas the boy who'd protected me all those years ago, but he was also Chrome Freyr, who was supposed to be dead.

The guy I'd always in some way fangirled over for his accomplishments. Someone I'd always aspired to become.

I wondered if my father knew. Of course, he did. But what was Amethyst's role in this?

"How..."

Chrome shrugged. "It's a long, fucked up story."

"So, I've been committed to killing the most revered legend in our recent history?" My mind was a tangled mess. I didn't even know where to begin processing this revelation, but that seemed like a solid place to start.

"Yeah. Funny, right? You love *and* despise me," Chrome said, one side of his mouth curved upward. "But I'm one and the same. Kinetic and Elemental. Griffin and Chrome." Griffin's—or should I call him Chrome?—gaze burned with an intensity that said he was fighting back another truth, but he held his tongue with a clench of his jaw.

"Those daggers you gave me..." I started, unsure. "They glowed orange for me. Why?" I asked, still curious about that strange anomaly. "Is it because they're yours and are affected by your hybrid nature somehow?"

Griffin... no, *Chrome*... looked away. More secrets he wasn't ready to spill.

"Tell me... *Chrome*." My arms braided across my chest as I waited for an explanation. I suspected what he held back was monumental.

Chrome rose to his feet. Running his fingers through his brilliant hair, he turned away to look at the deserted street behind the building. He shifted his unnerving gaze at me again before slumping his shoulders in defeat. "I shouldn't be telling you, yet. But I guess I can indulge you in the large scope of things."

"Go on..." I encouraged, hugging myself tighter.

"I'm not the only hybrid." Chrome looked up at the sky as if it would give me the answers instead. "There are two, at least, that we're aware of."

I narrowed my eyes. "And?"

"And Forest needed weapons. But not just any weapons." Chrome fell into a pace. "Weapons that would also open a portal to another dimension or realm. At first, we believed he hated Elementals because his fiancé was depleted by an Endarkened many years ago. She was pregnant with their child, and he's blamed the Elementals for their deaths. But there's more to it outside of that..."

"Wait, he's always said that an Elemental killed his fiancé, and then the Endarkened killed my mother. I was spared because she hid me..."

Chrome nodded but cut me off to carry on with his explanation. "Anyway, everything you've been told about Elementals is a lie. He needed a reason to go to war with them, to destabilize the world. Hence the need for his two weapons. He needed Elementals to be hated, while *he* was looked to for hope." He paused to sigh before rubbing the nape of his neck. "He attacked first, not the other way around. But he seized on the opportunity to throw the blame on us. Bet you didn't know there'd been a cordial peace amongst the two races before he rose to power."

"Holy shit." I blew out a breath. This was not the history we'd been taught. A wall of doubt climbed higher and higher in my mind, refusing to believe that everything I'd been taught my entire life was a total lie. I wasn't sure what to believe or who to believe. Did I really want to trust what was coming from Griffin Silas, aka Chrome Freyr's, mouth? Someone who'd hidden his identity through a faked death. There were so many red flags.

"Oh, it gets better," Chrome said with a sarcastic grin before going on. He continued to pace back and forth, the gold shimmering as his skin caught the light with each pass he made. "With the humans out of the way and the Kinetics brainwashed to loathe and kill Elementals, he was left unchecked in his power. No one was watching him. So, he somehow figured out a way to enter another realm. However, it requires a lot."

I held up a hand at the blasé way he just threw that bomb out there. "Wait, hold on. You mean to tell me there is another dimension? Another...world?" I was slow to process all the outlandish claims he continued to make.

"Yes. We live in the human realm. But there are an infinite number of them, all stacked on top of one another within existing planes. Your father wants to reach another one because we think he believes there's a source of great power that resides there. We have an idea of which realm it is, but to create a portal between the two requires immense power. From our general understanding, it needs magic of the two races combined. So, he ordered my conception through Amethyst—"

I cut him off. "Do you realize how fucking delusional you sound right now? Griffin! Or Chrome! Whatever the fuck your name is...this is beyond...it's too much." I massaged my temples to rub out the growing migraine. I paused, glimpsing the macabre scene of massacred Kinetics—having almost forgotten about it.

"I prefer Chrome." He shrugged, unbothered by my fracturing mind.

I shouldn't be showing my weakness, but I was exhausted—physically and mentally. The strength to hold up my walls began to crumble.

Chrome stopped pacing, scraping off the dried blood that marred his golden skin with the sharp edge of an Elemental knife as he waited for me to gather myself. I knew there was more. And I wasn't sure if I was ready for it.

"I need to tell you the rest before we move on. We don't have a lot of time before Forest comes after us. So, do you want to know or not? Because if not, you're free to go." Chrome loosely waved a hand in a gesture that told me he believed I would run right then. "Free to survive on your own, not having any connections with the humans. Not being allies with any Elementals while being hunted down by your own father with little to no information to weaponize yourself with. Your choice, Princess," he said, peeking up through a curtain of metallic hair as he scraped the skin on his thumb.

I stalled, almost giving in to the natural urge to run the fuck away and never look back, rejecting the choice of this defining moment.

But what if he was right? If what Chrome was telling me was true, then no doubt the consequences of Forest's ambition would be devastating. And if there was another Kinetic/Elemental hybrid out there, then we couldn't allow him to have them as a weapon to further his goals.

The Elemental blade that activated for me flashed through my mind. I quickly pushed it aside, refusing to acknowledge its implications.

If I went with Chrome, I knew there would be no turning back from this point. The information I would soon learn would forever change the course of my destiny. I would never be the same, and that scared me.

So much had already happened; could I handle more? I questioned my strength.

The gross feeling of shame sunk in as I realized a significant part of me had still been holding onto the hope that if I could kill Griffin, then it might redeem me in my father's eyes. And then, I could return to my relatively stable life. Leaving with Chrome would obliterate any chance of that. But I wasn't so sure I could kill him now. Not when I knew his identity and the heavy implications it held.

Was my unwavering quest for vengeance worth it? He swore he didn't kill Slate, and I was starting to believe it with each unveiled piece of truth that slapped me, but Griffin's death had become my purpose outside of simply surviving in the King's Palace. My reason for not collapsing in on myself from the grief and loneliness. Where would that leave me without it?

I didn't know where I'd even go if Chrome and I parted ways. If he were somehow masterfully lying to me about all of this, he could be sending me to my death or to some form of imprisonment. I'd killed so many Elementals over the years—twenty-four—so I wouldn't be surprised if he was playing nice in order to get his own form of vengeance. Then, there was the slight chance he wasn't coming from malice. Granted, those chances were low, especially in this harsh world.

But if I could gain some information against my father in order to stand some chance of ending him—of ending his abuse on the world—then I had to take it, right? My string of recent failures had me questioning if I was even worthy or capable of fighting for such a cause. But I needed answers more than anything else.

With my decision made, I took a deep breath, sure I would live to regret this. "I want to know. Tell me more," I said with my shoulders back and my chin held high.

Chrome perked his head up, his metallic waves bouncing as he did. The scraping against his skin stopped, and a sinful smile arched on one side of his mouth. And in a tone that sent heat throughout my entire body, he said, "That's my girl."

We sat inside the ravaged tattoo parlor on the front side of the building. We couldn't continue to talk about these sensitive topics out in the open. I'd suggested having the conversation during the trek to our next location, but Chrome insisted there were ears everywhere. Nowhere could be trusted not to be overheard by the king's spies. And I agreed.

Broken, filthy glass scattered all the surfaces while dusty items littered the floor. Light filtered in the space, casting shadows in corners of the shop where we cloaked ourselves from view.

I sat on an overturned stool. The ruffled dust caused me to sneeze, and every time I shifted my weight, the ripped and warped tattoo chair wobbled. My feet dangled above the ground as if I was a little girl, reminding me of all the times my father sat me down to scold me for hours.

Chrome lounged his back against the red wall in front of me, one foot crossed over the other as he gathered his thoughts.

"Okay. You said my father 'ordered your conception through Amethyst.' What did you mean?" I asked, picking up where he'd left off.

Chrome shrugged. "He captured Elemental King Jonas and forced him to impregnate Amethyst. Amethyst was all too willing for 'the greater purpose'. Clearly, their attempts were a success." Despite the look of abject horror on my face, he said it as if it didn't bother him, but it was clear he didn't care to elaborate. "Then, the king and Amethyst raised me to be their poster boy child soldier. They forced my abilities to awaken when I was only ten through high levels of duress."

I cocked my head to the side. "By 'high levels of duress', do you mean they beat you?"

His molten eyes met mine. So much pain haunted him from their depths, causing my chest to tighten. "Something like that."

I knew exactly what he meant.

Chrome cleared his throat, and the haunted expression in his mercurial eyes dissipated with the action. "So, anyway. They trained me in both my abilities from an early age, eventually forging me into a glorified warrior. On the outside, I was the face of the Kinetic race, but behind closed doors..." Chrome dipped his chin as he trailed off. "But they needed two hybrids. Whereas they trained me and kept me informed of my abilities, they hid everything from the other."

Buzzing resounded in my ears as I sensed where this was going. My breathing came in shorter and harsher breaths, my hands beginning to quiver with anticipation. I wasn't ready for the revelation I *knew* was coming.

"What are you talking about?" My voice betrayed me in its unsteadiness.

Chrome held my gaze, undoing what little resolve I clung to. "At first, Forest didn't trust anyone else with his secret, aside from my mother, to partake in this task. This information was too sensitive to have it leaked. But he later enlisted help and captured an Elemental woman—a powerful one.

"He wasn't pleasant with her. For two years, the king held her captive, torturing and debasing her in the worst of ways. The only time he'd released her from captivity was to force himself on her until she became pregnant. Once she'd successfully conceived the child, Forest eased on the torture...only so that the baby would be viable. When the baby was born, he killed the Elemental woman. And no one outside of his tight circle ever discovered what he'd done."

Regardless of the wobbly chair, I was grateful to be sitting down. I stared at Chrome as he continued unraveling every thread of control I held. I begged the gods for this not to turn out the way I suspected. "What happened to the baby?" My voice was a whisper, the buzzing growing louder in my head.

"Forest raised her to be his own personal assassin."

And there it was. The truth I'd been dreading to hear. The truth that would forever change everything.

I clenched my eyes shut. My head was a whirlwind, and I focused on my breaths until it sunk in.

Chrome continued, despite my despondence. "It's never been a secret that the king wasn't fond of his 'adopted daughter.' I'm sure you've always wondered why. And with you being an heir to his throne, he could never risk the knowledge of your origins becoming public. With his war against the Elementals, people could never know he'd conceived a child with the enemy. The fact you had Elemental blood in your veins disgusted him. Like me, you were merely a weapon to be wielded at his disposal. If or when you proved to be too much of a threat or liability, then he'd scrap the project."

Everything began clicking into place. All the questions I'd secretly held over the years formed logical answers. My head spun, and the world began to drop away, leaving me swaying on the unstable stool.

I'd always known my father was a dick, but Chrome's truth bombs only solidified him to be more monstrous than I'd ever believed possible. A part of me questioned the validity of Chrome's claims. But inside, I felt the weight of the truth. A truth that was suffocating yet liberating.

"So, that's why he made it my mission to kill you. He believed I was the only one capable of doing it," I said, realizing how wrong my father had been. I'd just witnessed the scope of Chrome's power and abilities, and I didn't come close to that. I was one of the best-trained Kinetics, and definitely the most feared. But my power was only a fraction of Chrome's.

It had been a suicide mission from the start. Perhaps he'd hoped we'd kill each other in the process, effectively taking out two birds with one stone. At the least, one of us would kill the other, minimizing his threats.

Chrome nodded slowly, letting me piece together the remaining details on my own.

"He must've known it was a suicide mission for me." My head lowered to my chest, deflated.

"Not necessarily. I'm only as powerful as I am because I've been training both my halves since I was ten years old. You're only at half the power you're capable of because he's suppressed your Elemental side for so long. Which is why I need you. I need to get you trained and ready to kill him," he explained. He took a step closer to me before finishing, "Together."

"How has he been suppressing my...my..." I stumbled over my words, struggling to voice aloud the fact I had the blood of both races running through my veins—something I'd always believed to be genetically impossible. It's what my father had always instilled in us.

Chrome didn't answer. He just simply looked down at the black crystal necklace that hung around my neck. The only sentimental object I'd had of my mother's, or what I'd always *believed* to be my mother's.

On instinct, I reached for it and gripped it in my palm.

"That necklace is black crystal, correct?"

I nodded, squeezing the round, polished stone tighter in my fist to ground me. "My father told me it was my mother's form of protection against Elementals, that she'd have wanted me to have it and to never..." I trailed off as another realization clicked into place. "To never take it off. Not for anything."

"Precisely. It's kept your Elemental magic and traits hidden all these years. But I have reason to believe he didn't rely on that necklace alone. He must've been putting low doses of crushed black crystal in your food as a backup." An eyebrow lifted as he waited to see if I'd confirm that. I had no way of knowing, but...

"The king always had a cook prepare my food," I pondered out loud as I ran my fingers over the single braid on one side of my head. Looking at the glamoured ice-white waves, I wondered what my skin would look like if I was an Elemental, shimmering in gold. "I was never allowed in the kitchen, and I vaguely remember walking in one day to find her crushing something in a bowl. She was terrified to see me standing there, and she tried to usher me out, but my father walked in. And the next day, I had a new cook. She never spoke to me. And I never saw the other one again. I really liked her." I questioned if I'd unknowingly sent a woman to her death. She'd always been kind to me. She was a bright spot in my bleak childhood.

Chrome watched as I analyzed my hair. "It sounds possible."

"How can I trust you're telling me the truth?" I looked at him from beneath my lashes, still pinching my strands between my fingers.

With pursed lips, he cocked his head to the side and pushed off the wall with his shoulder. "Because, Gray, I have no reason to lie to you. I truly do need your help. We all need your help. If Forest opens a portal to the next realm, consequences unlike anything we've ever seen could swallow this world. We don't know for sure what realm he's trying to access or even what would happen if he did, but we can't risk it.

"I don't know how he discovered this information. Everything about our origins has either been hidden or eradicated. I *do* know that we didn't originate in this realm. That's all anyone knows. But we need that information to learn more about what he's planning and how he intends to execute it. We have to kill him before it's too late."

I held Chrome's gaze, seeing him as two different individuals. How long would it take me to see him as one person? How long would it take me to come to terms with the possibility I was an Elemental? All I had to do was remove the necklace.

I was shattering. My head felt foggy, and I didn't know where to begin processing everything I'd just learned or if I should even believe it until I saw it for myself. But for now, I'd do what I needed to get through the day—suppress it.

Chapter 22

Gray

Chrome sat on the squalid floor of the train's metal container. The Kinetic-powered locomotive jostled us. At last, he informed me we were headed to an Elemental Hollow in Perry.

We didn't speak on the ride. Needing to be alone, we sat on the opposite sides of the container. My hood masked my face as I rested my head on my knees with my back to him. Thankfully, Chrome respected my need for solitude and didn't intrude.

I felt insignificant. So small. So disposable. Worthless. A failure. A disappointment. My own father hated me. My only friends were probably dead by now, solely for keeping me alive. The one person who'd ever truly seen me and loved me was dead. And now, I was stuck with someone who was just as hated as myself. If not, more.

It was a depressing turn of events. Chrome, who'd given so much of himself to the Kinetics, was being hunted as if he was a demon stalking the night. We were both premeditated offspring only to be wielded...nothing more. And I'd felt the full brunt of that truth my entire life. Knowing *why* offered me some level of solace, at least.

Given if everything Chrome had said was true.

I still hadn't forgotten about his episode the night before. He'd been nothing like the steel warrior he was known to be. Questions surrounding who he'd been speaking to that night kept circulating in my mind. Or had it been anyone at all? Was it voices in his head? If his upbringing had been anything like mine, it wouldn't surprise me; actually, his was probably much more brutal. And that thought was enough to make me soften toward him just a fraction more. Not because I pitied him, but because he was the one person who I felt genuinely understood.

Hot tears traced a wet path over the bridge of my nose and down my cheek. Thankfully, the train's roar subdued my sniffles. I'd trade physical pain over the constricting grip in my chest any day. It healed much faster. I learned at a young age to suppress it—a necessary skill to survive. Weakness only earned me punishment and more emotional pain.

But some pain couldn't be restrained. It would always come back to claim its due, forcing you to face your demons. I fucking hated it.

After some time, I felt his presence drop down beside me. Chrome didn't speak, and I didn't acknowledge him as we sat together in our shared pain. His strong aura lent its strength, which caught me by surprise with the comfort it brought.

Only twenty-four hours ago, I despised him and wanted his head. I believed Chrome's claim that he wasn't responsible for Slate's death. Now, knowing the truth about my father and his hidden agenda, I wouldn't put it past him to have had him killed. I was brought back to Hazel's confession: what had Slate known about Forest before his death? I had a feeling that mystery was one that would be tough to unravel.

The train screeched to a sudden halt, and Chrome and I sprung to our feet. Chrome had said we weren't due to stop for another thirty minutes. With furrowed brows, I met his matching confused expression.

Our magic inhibitors were back in place, and I wished I could remove mine to sense what was happening. We were blind to any attack.

Without a word, Chrome stalked to the opening of the freight container and pressed his back against its edge. He glimpsed outside, listening for sounds, and I didn't dare move.

Something was *very* wrong.

Chrome's dark brows pinched tight as he listened. His glare alone could've split the aluminum floor in half from his concentration.

He snapped his cutting gaze to me, gutting me where I stood with his intensity. An index finger lifted to touch his lips—soft and slow—in a gesture of silence.

I needed weapons, but I wasn't sure which kind. There was no way for me to know who awaited us outside.

Chrome tensed before pushing himself flat against the aluminum wall as frantic voices approached us. Footsteps stomped, crunching the gravel as they ran past on the tracks.

My forehead creased as the voices drew closer, wondering what had Kinetics panicking.

I joined Chrome pressed against the wall. With my eyes closed and hearing focused, I stretched that sense as far as it could reach.

A deep growl rumbled, and the ground trembled with it. Earthquakes weren't common in this region, at least not of that strength. Another growl followed—louder than the last— shaking the train car.

The shudder flung me from the metal wall, forcing me to crash into Chrome's side. Without looking, he wrapped his arm around my shoulder.

I stood there, steadied against him, studying my hand that pressed against his chest. Hard, tenuous muscle lay underneath the black tee that hugged him. He wasn't beefy, nor was he bony. Tall and streamlined. Deceptively strong. I had no doubt his muscles were made for display.

Another force rocked the train car, and we stumbled apart to catch ourselves.

A bestial roar deafened the landscape. Fear spiked through me, and I lunged for the blades within the duffels. Thankfully, Chrome returned mine.

I sought the swords first. Whatever was wreaking havoc outside required more than daggers to take it down. Grabbing an Elemental and Kinetic sword, I tossed them to Chrome—who easily snatched them from the air with grace—and grabbed two more for myself before making my way to the opening of the train car. Chrome followed and took his place by my side.

There was no way the monstrous roar was from this world as it reverberated in my chest unlike any animal I'd ever heard. Upon setting my sights on the source, my heart skidded to a halt.

"What the fuck?" I braced my hand on the door frame.

Chrome's fierce silence told me he didn't have the answers this time. He embraced the coiled lethality he wore as a second skin while cold violence returned to his ice-blue eyes.

I faced the woods in time to see the foreign creature take out pine trees with a swipe of its paw.

A brown bear, the size of a mid-grade house, wrecked the wilderness surrounding us, but it was the massive black horns gleaming like polished stone atop its head that had me gaping,

I doubted our swords would do the job.

"Take off your bracelet, but leave the necklace on for now. You don't know what to expect from your Elemental magic yet," Chrome instructed. "Might cause more harm than good."

I mumbled an agreement, removing the bracelet. My Kinetic magic I could control. It was one of the few things I had control over in my life, and a sense of calm washed over me at the level of comfort that brought.

The familiar rush of energy electrified my veins. My blue currents raced to life beneath the sleeves of my leather jacket. Closing my eyes, I took half a moment to savor the rush.

The moment I opened my eyes, the monstrous bear obliterated the few Kinetics who'd been running the train. An arm went flying, lodging in a tree limb thirty feet away.

Where in the seven hells did the beast come from? Did it have something to do with Forest's plan to open a portal? Because it was clear this beast didn't hail from this world. How were we supposed to fight this thing?

I stole a look at Chrome and saw he was in his Elemental form. The golden skin shimmered on his face and quicksilver eyes swirled with vicious ferocity. He obscured his Kinetic side as his raven hair hung loose around his face.

"Attack together?" I asked. It was a dumb question I realized after the fact. What other choice did we have?

Chrome nodded, not taking his molten gaze from the bestial creature in the distance, "You come from the back, and I'll keep his attention at the front."

I gave a stiff nod, wanting to have a bigger role in this fight. It was petulant, but the constant need to prove myself was strong.

It stiffened and sniffed the breeze. The beast grunted and then turned glowing red eyes on us.

It had found its next targets.

We leaped from the immobile train car and took off at a sprint into the woods. I swung the blue Kinetic sword, slicing through the branches that threatened to jab me in the eye. Chrome did the same.

The bear moved toward us, ready to clash with its new prey. As it did, Chrome and I split directions, creating a fork around the beast. Its focus was on Chrome, so it turned to follow him—its size slowing it down. It left me free to take up the monster's rear.

I lunged at the beast, testing my swords' effect on it. I sliced at the enormous tendon on its hind leg. Turned out my strike served no purpose other than to piss it off.

It roared, and the trees quaked with the vibrations, which I absorbed. My swords clanged to the ground, falling into a small pile of red and orange leaves as I chose to forgo the weapons in favor of my magic. The energetic waves from the roar fueled me, and I recycled it into a ball of electricity.

I formed a blue electrical orb in my hands, molding it as it grew and grew. Chrome whirled around the bear in his iconic death dance, wielding his swords in an orange and blue blur as he landed well-placed slices across the beast's lower body.

The beast roared at Chrome. A massive paw the size of a compact car swiped at him, but Chrome ducked and slashed his sword across its paw as it sailed over him.

Our weapons had no effect on the bear except to anger it more. I had to do something.

Once the electrical orb was large enough, I shot a blast at its rear. With a yelp, it slammed into the bear's ass. The beast stumbled, shaking the earth with each step. I planted my feet to keep my balance as I swayed from the tremors.

Chrome took the opening to leap at its exposed chest with his sword raised high, aimed for the heart. Putting all his strength into the attack, the sword's tip slammed into the bear's chest. I gasped as it bounced off. Chrome dropped back to the ground, landing in a crouch.

Our weapons were useless.

The bear snapped its gaping jaws at Chrome. Roughly three sets of razor-sharp teeth lined its maw.

I watched Chrome go on the defensive as I absorbed more energy. Sounds, motion, and light all fueled my magic.

I ran to the other side of the bear, launching smaller electrical orbs at its ribs. I didn't stop moving as I ducked and dodged, sending large shocks pummeling into its body. Each one landing in a different spot. Eventually, it began to stumble to and fro, unable to keep up with the blasts I launched in a continuous rhythm.

It stood on its hind legs, black horns gleaming from the sun's rays that streamed through the trees' canopy. Long, piercing claws threatened to impale me when another deafening roar shook my core. I absorbed it.

My blasts grew bigger and bigger with each attack sent into the bear's chest and stomach until I formed the largest one yet. Stepping from the beast's line of fire, I allowed the magic to climb.

"Gray, don't! It's too much!" Chrome shouted from behind the beast as we swapped positions. He stood rigid and taut, but his body trembled. Strands of silver framed his face instead of black inky hair.

I ignored him, continuing to build the incoming blast. Another roar and swipe. And this one landed. The world rushed at me, violently spinning, as my body soared through the air.

A loud crack echoed, followed by a blinding pain in my skull from where it struck a tree trunk. Plummeting to the hard earth on my shoulder, the air was knocked from my lungs as I lay in frozen agony.

Upon impact, my vision blackened, leaving me blind. My magic was coiled too tight, threatening an uncontrolled release. I stifled it, but doing so had my magic compressing on the pain that held my body captive.

I couldn't move.

"Gray!" Chrome shouted in the distance.

I had to get up, or we would both die.

Hot liquid gushed from my side. The deep gouge in my torso from the bear's claws had me in excruciating agony.

All I could do was wait while I healed, listening to the sounds in order to sense what was happening around me. The darkness I'd been thrust into suddenly lit up with differing energy waves. Normally, I could see them with my eyes closed if I chose. The shorter waves revealed soft thuds, whereas the longer waves meant louder noises. I could also see the temperature waves and the movements of people and objects.

It was a complex ability I'd mastered after years of training. The various waves served as a code that I could piece together to form a picture of events in my near vicinity, almost like a second sight.

I could read the differences between the horned bear and Chrome. Chrome seemed to move with a dexterity and speed that kept his waves in short swirling bursts. The bear had the longer and bigger waves, indicating his size and strength.

The pain in my skull began to ease, and the feeling in my limbs slowly returned. I tested my fingers for movement, relieved when I could twitch them a fraction.

If Chrome could occupy the bear long enough to give me time to heal...

I listened to the violence and could bet he was trying to find all the weak points on the bear's body, anywhere his blades or power would allow him to subdue it.

A shout sounded nearby, matching the spike in my second vision. "Shit! Gray..." he said, his breaths labored. "You gotta move!"

I couldn't. My body was healing, but not fast enough. My hands were the only limbs I could do anything with, so I tried to utilize them.

My vision started to come back into focus, but I could only make out the bear's blurred body. He loomed over something, or someone.

Chrome.

I twisted my wrist to aim at the body, planning to launch a massive blast. But before I could unleash it, a harrowing, pained groan reverberated around us. It was deep and mournful, and it struck me in my soul. Through my blurred vision, I spotted the bear-beast hunched on its front legs with its head twisted to the side on the ground. Snorts and grunts vibrated the earth floor, shaking my bones. It was suffering, and despite the carnage it caused, a sting of regret ached in my chest.

I tried and failed to get up to stop Chrome from killing it. My arms were like cinder blocks as I clawed the dirt and leaves to drag my body. The bear groaned, and I met its devastated ruby gaze.

The creature was terrified. Understanding slammed into me that it wasn't from this world, and had only been in survival mode. Similar to myself. And who knew how long it'd been here? But surely, the train spooked it. And when the Kinetics attacked, they put it further on the defensive.

But this? The horned beast—volatile only moments ago—begged for its life.

"Stop! Stop hurting it!" I yelled to Chrome as I heaved my limp lower body through the dirt.

Chrome ignored me, keeping his focus on the foreign animal.

A whimper escaped the massive being, its red eyes begging for help. Liquid silver oozed from its saddened eyes and cavernous nostrils.

"Stop hurting it!" Just a few more feet.

Chrome didn't budge.

I didn't know why I had a sudden shift toward the creature, but I couldn't stand the thought of allowing it to die. I had to save it.

The more I dragged myself across the ground, the more feeling returned to my limbs. I pulled myself into a crawl before standing up. I stumbled toward Chrome, his back propped against the trunk of a pine tree.

Once again, he trembled from the exertion his magic required to take down this massive creature. I didn't know what Elemental power Chrome wielded, but it was obvious he was a master at it, judging by his previous show.

My foot snagged on a root buried in leaves, and I caught myself before I face-planted. My heart lurched as I glimpsed the light fading from the bear's scarlet eyes. It was resigned to its fate.

As the bear exhaled with a final grunt, my body collided with Chrome's, my hands clasping his. My only desperate thought was for the bear to return to its home, away from this cruel and twisted world.

It was a truth in my soul; I knew the horned bear wasn't a malevolent being. It didn't ask to be here.

A loud clap, like a strike of lightning, split the air, followed by a white flash of light that blinded us. I tried to shield my eyes, but my palms were glued to Chrome's.

I risked a glance down between us and saw the light encompassing our hold; our contact was its source.

Feet away from us, the brightness dimmed to a shimmering glow. Its hazy iridescence encircled us and the horned bear.

The bear huffed a hard breath, its gaze landing on the flowing, iridescent curtain. Recognition lit in its eyes, and it clambered to its paws. It took a step toward the magic as if it knew it was the answer to its salvation. Stopping, it turned its attention toward me, black horns aglow from the radiance. Our eyes met for a moment before it dipped its head in...*respect*?

All I could do was stare in wonderment as my mouth parted. With a gentle calmness, it walked through the shimmering curtain, disappearing from this world.

Whatever power kept our palms bound dissipated, allowing me to snatch my hands free from Chrome's. The beautiful curtain dissolved, leaving me straddling the top of Chrome's torso, our breaths ragged.

"What the fuck was that? And what the fuck just happened?" I asked, attempting to not-so-subtlety remove myself from him while trying not to notice the hardness of his body between my thighs.

"First of all, I'm going to have to ask you to *never* interfere with me like that again," Chrome said, pushing up onto his elbows. His hood had fallen, exposing that stunning gold skin and the chromatic hair and eyes.

"Excuse me, but..." I argued.

"No, my power could've latched onto you, pulling the iron from your blood. I'm a metal wielder with my Elemental magic. I gotta go into a trance when I do that particular skill. It's not always easy to decipher who to target. So, when you interfere like that, you're asking for me to latch onto you," he explained, peeved.

"Well," I scoffed and rolled my eyes. "I tried to yell for you to stop, but that clearly didn't work."

"Like I said," he retorted, "I go into a trance."

"Well, I couldn't let you kill it. It clearly wasn't from here and it was scared. I don't think it was a predatory animal."

"No, I suppose not." He said nothing else, but he shifted his attention to a group of trees nearby, seeming to be lost in his thoughts for a moment.

"Any theories on what that—that *thing* was, it just walked through?" I asked, having an idea but needing him to confirm it. I felt insane to even entertain the thought.

Chrome pushed himself to his feet. With a deft hand, he brushed the dirt and debris from his clothes before running his fingers through his hair. He took his time digging a hand into his pocket to pull out his bracelets. Snapping the black one in place, the gold skin and fluid silver eyes shifted to tan skin and those familiar sapphire eyes. He did the same with the silver bracelet, subduing his silver currents and unique metallic hair.

Finally, he pinned me in place with his gaze before responding, making my heart jump at its intensity. "I think we just opened a portal to the next realm."

Chapter 23

CHROME

*M*y cheek pressed against the cold cement floor of the interrogation room. Every orifice and pore in my body screamed from my punishment while I lay sprawled in broken silence. My stunt on the playground had earned me a more severe punishment than I ever anticipated.

As it turned out, I awakened my Kinetic half when I touched the princess today. The king and my mother shared mixed feelings about it. My mother was all too jubilant now that I could wield an unbelievable amount of magic at their disposal; the king, however, was irritated because it awakened the princess's powers—which wasn't on his terms.

The king unleashed his unrestrained fury on me for exposing my magic at the human school. He didn't hold back with either fists or magic, whether it was his own or commanding someone else's.

And then, he introduced another form of torture.

Grim.

Not only did Grim hold the ability to cancel out magic, depravity seeped from his breath, but in ways no one else knew about. My stepfather had no limits when it came to torture. And his task was not only to break me mentally, but to physically break me in a way no one should ever be ruined.

Hot, angry tears leaked from my eyes. My body ached in places I didn't know could hurt in such a way. Violated wasn't even the word to completely describe how I felt as an icy numbness latched its claws into my heart, similar to the phantom feeling of Grim's grip as he pinned me down.

I lay broken and twisted at odd angles. My mind shattered as I tried to comprehend what I had just experienced. The black band on my wrist mocked me, knowing I couldn't move to remove it. Why couldn't my magic have stepped in to help me now? Why did it want to break past the bracelet's suppressant to protect the princess?

I needed it now. But it failed me.

I wouldn't give Grim the satisfaction of seeing me suffer. Never once did I make a sound during his assault. Instead, I found myself in a world I didn't believe existed, with a little Kinetic Princess whose fire in her eyes spoke more than her actual words.

After he had finished, Grim stood up and adjusted his clothes, his belt buckle snapping into place with a sickening click. His last words, before leaving me alone and destroyed on the interrogation room floor, echoed in my ears. "Since you're so fucking powerful, figure out how to heal yourself from this with the bracelets on...you little half-breed shit." Spitting at my broken body, Grim turned and strode out of the room as if this was just another day and it was just another regular beating.

"Well? Did you do it?" I heard my mother's hardened voice on the opposite side of the metal door seconds after he left the room.

Grim scoffed. "Of course, I did. He submitted. His will to fight is gone, and he is ours to control." Hearing the pride oozing from his voice had a bout of nausea slamming into me so hard. I vomited onto the stone floor beneath me, still unable to move.

"Good," she said. "Now, hurry up and remove his bracelets so he can heal. Otherwise, he's useless to us." The clicking of her heels disappeared down the corridor, and seconds later, Grim returned.

With his sneering scowl in place, he squatted beside me. "Act out of line again, and this will be your punishment from now on. You are ours. We made you. We can just as easily end your existence. Don't forget it."

I knew all too well what he meant a la the history of my conception. My body wasn't mine to control. My mind wasn't mine to control. My emotions weren't mine either. I was their weapon. Theirs to be wielded at their disposal.

I wasn't sure how much time had passed since Grim had left the interrogation room after having removed the bracelets so my body could heal. It could've been hours, or it could've been minutes. I didn't care.

I didn't even feel like a person—more like a ghost—as the real me had died hours ago at Grim's hands.

The door squeaked open, breaking the silence of the cold room. "Chrome?" Peri. "Go away."

"Chrome, are you okay?" Her frantic voice came closer, as did her running feet slapping against the floor.

My baby sister wasn't supposed to see me like this. I was her protector. A warrior. "Just go back, Peri," I answered in a dead tone, keeping my eyes glued to a spot on the wall ahead.

"Chrome. You gotta get up. King Forest is coming down here soon. He can't see you here like this." Peri grabbed my hand and tried to pull my weight.

"It's fine, Peri. Just go. You shouldn't be here."

"Chrome. You're not getting it. He's coming down here with someone else," she said, which made me finally meet her hazel eyes.

"Who?"

"I can't tell you. I shouldn't even know. I overheard Momma tell Dad. And when I realized you still weren't back yet..." Her eyes scanned me, concern wrapped in her eyes. "What happened to you?"

"Don't worry about it. I'm getting up," I said, pulling my hand from hers and pushing myself to my feet on shaky arms. The pain was gone, but I winced anyway.

"Come on," Peri said, tugging me after her. We ran past the prisoners in the cells, ignoring them as we went, then stepped into the elevator. Looking at each other, we breathed a sigh of relief that we hadn't run into anyone yet.

We reached the second to top floor of the King's Palace, where our suite encapsulated the entire area. Once inside our home, Peri and I scanned the space for any sign of my mother and stepfather's presence. They seemed to be absent, so she tugged me after her into her room where she closed the door and leaned against it. "Are you okay?" she asked again.

"I'll be fine, Peri. Promise." I offered a weak smile in an attempt to convince her, but she didn't buy it given the deadpan expression she shot me.

"What happened today?" she pushed further.

I pressed my palms into my eyeballs in some sort of effort to rid the day's events. "I don't want to talk about it. The less you know the better. You're only eight." I released a sigh.

She stomped her foot, garnering my attention. A fierce little scowl planted on her face and arms crossed over her chest. "And you're only ten! Not much of a difference, Chrome!"

I rolled my eyes. I wasn't really ten, and she knew it. At least, based on my experiences. Thankfully, she hadn't been forced to grow up as fast as me. Unfortunately, regardless of how much I tried to protect her, she still witnessed and knew things she shouldn't. And she was sharp in piecing stuff together at times. But she had my mother and Grim fooled, as they saw only a sweet, innocent, and naïve little angel. "I—"

My words were cut off by a tug on my heart, vibrating like a violin string just before I was slammed with a fear so intense it knocked me back a few steps. Panic. I gripped a hand to my chest, my heart pounding in a riot as I looked at Peri for answers that she had no way of knowing.

Peri's big honey-colored eyes widened further as she rushed to me. "What's happening?"

My lungs felt restricted. No air. My hands shook as I searched for a way out of the room. From what? I didn't know. I only knew that I was in danger. As quickly as the fear struck me, a sense of deflation chased it away, leaving behind a hopelessness I was well-acquainted with.

Yet, there was still a tiny fire burning within. A small flame that flickered out during Grim's assault. That's when I realized, these weren't my emotions. How could they be? Everything was numb now. Frozen and accepting of the life that lay ahead of me.

So, if they weren't mine, then to whom did they belong?

A slow simmer of power rose from the depths of my belly. It built and built until it consumed the desolation and fear. It blew through my veins like hurricane winds combined with high-voltage energetic waves, ready to explode.

As had happened on the playground, my feet remained planted to the carpeted floor. A vengeful, protective power was being forced to the surface. Just as it had been for me only a few days ago. This time, I experienced it as though it was second-hand, like an echo of the real thing but still potent all the same.

I could only think of the princess, and the pieces clicked into place.

Princess Gray was a hybrid like me. The king and my mother basically told me as much. They never told me who exactly was the other hybrid, only that they existed in the Royal Domain. Today proved everything that had transpired was due to both of our hybrid natures.

And the king was currently forcing her magic to awaken prematurely—like they had with me.

And if the princess was as powerful as me, then what was stopping her father from sending Grim to control her as well?

I had to protect her at all costs. It was an instinctual drive that I couldn't explain...I just had to.

The memory looped in my head as Gray and I pushed deeper into the woods. Neither one of us had said much as we both needed to process everything that had happened back there with the bear.

Every touch of Gray's presented me with a new vital memory. Sometimes, it didn't involve her, but the ones that did had me reeling. The twisted nature of it all was that I had no way of knowing whether she knew of these events or not. The king did have ways of erasing memories, so it wouldn't surprise me.

"When did you say your magic awakened?" I asked, breaking the silence.

Gray's brows pinched together in confusion. "When I was thirteen. Why?"

I shook my head and sighed. "No reason. Just double-checking."

The familiar vibrating tug on my heart jolted again as a strong wave of suspicion washed over me. Confusion, too? Gray's lips were pushed out as her eyes narrowed ahead while stepping over sticks and limbs in the woods.

Her emotions. I *still* felt her emotions.

With my returning memories, I remembered that I'd always felt them. Parts of my past were still murky, just out of my reach in a dark fog. I recalled all the times since I was ten years old where I would be struck with her intense feelings out of the blue—but only if I was in her vicinity.

Especially when it came to Slate's death.

How much of the anger I felt during my mental spiraling belonged to me? The darkness? Or was it Gray's? The night of her escape and my fight with the Guild crossed my mind. I'd been close enough to the Palace to sense it. Savage rage gripped me after she had just discovered her father's attempt to kill her. That begged the question, did that rage ever truly belong to the darkness to begin with?

My thoughts went into a tailspin as we continued to walk through the woods. More pieces of my past clicked into place. I tried not to dwell much on the trauma, as I'd already healed those wounds years ago after my escape. It took many dark years to deconstruct everything I'd experienced as a child and teen. Had it not been for Orion and the Elementals, I would've succumbed to the affliction long ago. Besides, the madness left the traumatizing memories for me to dwell in while leaving none of the beautiful connections or moments for me to hold onto.

My mind latched onto the most pressing concern. Should I tell Gray that I had always felt her emotions when nearby since that day on the playground? She was only beginning to trust me. To reveal something that could be perceived as a personal violation could undo that. Too much was at risk. And now, it seemed my sanity depended on her nearness, which threw in another factor.

That thought alone made me nauseous. I didn't *want* to be dependent on her for my sanity. How fair was it to *her* to have that responsibility on her shoulders? On top of our realm's fate resting in her palms.

It wasn't.

I couldn't do that to her. Not now. She already had too much to process. In the meantime, I'd work to block out her emotions to preserve her privacy.

"We need food." I scanned the woods, listening for any disturbances in the nearby wildlife.

Gray's stomach grumbled in agreement, causing a small smirk to twitch on one side of my mouth. "So, we hunt," she said.

"I'll hunt. You rest," I said without thinking.

"Excuse me?"

Gray stood to my left, her notable scowl casting an icy glare at me, the one that always sent a thrill racing through me. "Problem?"

"I can hunt just fine." Her words were clipped through her clenched jaw.

I raised my brows, my smirk growing. "Oh, you think this is because you're a woman that I automatically assume you can't hunt, hm?"

Gray continued to glare at me.

"Well, I'd hate to burst the horrible image you have concocted of me in that brain of yours, but you need rest. You haven't had a chance to recover since the redfern poisoning."

It wasn't a complete lie, but it wasn't the entire truth, either.

Gray scoffed and relaxed her stance. "I'm fine."

"Are you? Because the dark circles under your eyes beg to differ," I quipped, raising a brow. With each encounter, I watched exhaustion wear her down further and further.

"I'm not too tired to kill an animal." A visible wince on her face said it all. She didn't want to kill an animal—even for food.

My face fell from the softening in my heart at the realization. She was trying to prove herself to me, even though she had already far surpassed any expectations I'd ever held for her.

In a tone softer than I typically used, I said, "I know you could if you needed, but I'm offering to take the load off you. So, let me."

Gray wrapped her arms around her midsection as she probably fought an inner battle of wills with herself on whether she ought to push the issue with me or not. But at last, she dropped her shoulders with a nod, "Okay," she muttered, and the weight of the exhaustion pressed her down in defeat.

After Gray and I set up a temporary, makeshift campsite in the small clearing, I set off deeper into the woods, creating markers to find my way back. I knew where we were—as I chose it strategically—to be close enough to the rendezvous point, but it couldn't hurt to be careful.

If all went well, Onyx should be waiting for my arrival. We weren't far from the Hollow, only another half-day trek on foot before reaching the town of Perry. The plan was routine.

When we left for separate missions, we usually met up at specific checkpoints at designated times, to ensure both of us remained alive, while also gathering any new information that could be useful along the way. I missed the last checkpoint due to Gray tailing me, so I could imagine Onyx's relief upon seeing me at this particular one.

Approaching the deadened pine tree marked with two pieces of metal pinned into the trunk in the shape of an X, I spotted my friend leaning against the bark, his back facing me.

With intention, I stepped on a stick, causing the snap and rustle of leaves to sound beneath my boots. Onyx spun around, his dagger out and aglow. "Holy shit." As expected, his shoulders sagged in relief, and a smile pulled at the edges. "Thank fuck."

Suddenly, big arms snatched me into a hug, patting my back, to which I returned. I was genuinely happy to see him, especially now that I remembered the valuable friendship we shared. A brotherly love for my friend swarmed my chest as a grin broke free. Relief washed through me, realizing I no longer ran on autopilot. I could actually *feel*.

"Dude, where were you back in Covington?" Onyx released me and took a step back to examine my state.

"I got caught up. Had the princess tailing me for three weeks in preparation to kill me on the king's orders. I couldn't lead her to you," I explained.

Onyx cocked his head to the side. "And where is she now? Do you have her? Is she alive?" Uncertainty laced with an edge of fear crept into his voice with each word.

"She's alive," I assured, then chuckled at his hysterics. "She's back at the campsite resting. It's been an ordeal for her, so I insisted on hunting down dinner for the night."

Onyx nodded in understanding and relief. "Good. It's been years since I saw her last. It'll be cool to have another familiar face around the Hollow."

I shared that sentiment with him. "Anything new happening with the militia?"

Onyx's cheeks puffed up before he blew out a breath. "Not really. I ran some food supplies to them—as well as some clothes. Hogan said it should last for a bit."

"Good," I said and pulled out a buck knife. "You up for a hunt?"

Excitement and challenge lit Onyx's amber eyes with mischief. "Fuck yes."

Chapter 24

GRAY

My ass hurt. Actually, it was beginning to go numb from the hard ground, adding to the growing ball of tension in my chest. While Chrome had been off hunting, I'd built a small fire, its warmth now almost singing the hairs on my head.

My mind was a maelstrom of discombobulated thoughts, unable to land on a particular one. What the fuck happened to my life? How did I end up here? Was I destined for misery from birth?

It was getting harder and harder to breathe, and the declining temperature wasn't helping. A crisp breeze slithered down the back of my hoodie. Heavy footsteps sounded from the edge of the woods of our little clearing, and Chrome's tall figure came tromping through, dragging a dead animal at his heels.

I sat up straighter, locking away my emotions for a later date. I couldn't break in front of anyone—especially him.

He approached me, beginning to pluck feathers from a dead turkey's body. The sight of the raw food ignited what little restraint I held onto. I was so fucking hungry. To try to distract myself from my warring thoughts and starvation, I asked, "So you think my father is responsible for that creature we just dealt with?" I tried to make sense of everything.

"Obviously," Chrome scoffed, annoyance showing in his eye roll.

My eyebrows rose at the sudden attitude. "You can drop the sass."

He sighed and ran a hand through his black hair and sighed, deflating. "Sorry. This little trip has turned out to be more difficult than I anticipated."

I jerked my head in his direction and seared him with a look that spoke of all the emotions I'd been suppressing over the past few days: hot anger, betrayal, childhood neglect, and abuse all rising to the surface since I left the Royal Domain. "I'm at my fucking limit, Chrome," I snapped, barely keeping my voice below a scream. He stared at me, a twinge of shock racing across his face before his head cocked. He raised an eyebrow. "Within days, I went from being an assassin princess to being nearly killed by you, and then being nearly killed by my father. Only to find out the man I've been taught to hate with every fiber of my being is actually the legendary Chrome Freyr! You're supposed to be dead." Chrome dipped his head in mock acknowledgment as I continued, "Then, I learn you're also a formulated hybrid who talks to himself in the middle of the night. Because *that* makes total sense.

"Oh! And let's not forget, the man who raised me is *not* my adopted father. He is, in fact, my biological father, who kidnapped and tortured my unknown biological mother and raped her to produce me. Then killed her. I've discovered that I, too, am a formulated fucked-up hybrid who's been lied to her entire life. I've even had my godsdamn food poisoned since I was a small child! My psychopathic king of a father is trying to open a portal to another world with the delusional hopes of finding some source of great power, whatever the hell that means. Or so we think, at least. Actually, so *you* think—you still haven't told me who *we are* because all I see is you in the chaos." I paused to catch my breath, my chest heaving. "But the most sickening part of it all? I've killed for him. Killed so many..." I trailed off on that last thought and looked into the trees, feeling tears threatening to fall.

My chest tightened with the determination to keep them from spilling over. My hands shook, so I dug my nails into the palms of my hands, allowing the sting of the pain to ground me. I took a steadying breath. "Did I forget anything?" I aimed a look of contempt at what appeared to be the only ally I had left—the most unlikely one at that.

Without missing a beat, Chrome lifted a finger and said, "You left out that I saved your ass as a small child and continue to save your ass as a grown woman." He flashed an exaggerated smile that crinkled the corners of his cat eyes.

Ugh, he was sexy.

"So, you're welcome for that." A second finger ticked up. "Also, I did *not* kill Slate. Still want my name cleared on that accusation." A third finger met the others. "And we just fought a little beastie-bear while accidentally opening a portal to another world to send it back." Amusement danced in those ice-blue eyes.

"I hate you," I said, my voice flat and with a deadpan expression. "You have *not* saved my ass," I snorted, crossing my arms over my chest. "I don't get saved. Ever."

A smirk teased the corners of his lips. "Oh, but you do, little savage. By me. And only me."

Dammit, why did his voice have to sound sensual when he talked like that?

I narrowed my eyes. "I don't want, nor need, to be saved, especially by someone whose ego is the size of that bear back there."

The smile grew, melting his stark features and my resolve. "Oh really? What else of mine do you think is big?"

His eyes sparkled with amusement and...*lust?* No, I must have imagined it. But then why did my heart start to race and my cheeks heat from a torturous blush?

I bit the inside of my cheek, fighting the urge to smile. I walked into that one. "Nothing. You're small. Just a small man. With a little peen." I locked eyes with him and tried to remain stoic, though I knew I wouldn't last long.

Loud, belly-deep laughter erupted from him. I'd never heard anything so... *infectious*. I couldn't help but to chuckle with him.

"Peen?" Chrome exclaimed, when he came up for air. "How old are you?"

I chuckled. "Old enough to know I can spot an arrogant dick when he presents himself."

He rose, and took two long strides toward me until we stood mere inches apart. A dark smile and a promise danced in those blue eyes of his. I held my chin up as he dipped lower, meeting my determined gaze with his own. "You know I'm anything but small, Princess. You try to pretend like you don't feel what's between us, or maybe you're just in denial with yourself. But it's there." Chrome's smooth voice caressed me with dark sensuality, pulling tight at something in my core. Like a chord tugging me toward him. "It's always been there. Since that day on the playground."

The passion burned in his eyes, pinning me to the spot. The force of his presence, his energy, or perhaps it was some weird hybrid connection buzzing between us, robbed me of my breath.

Damn, he was so beautiful.

Warmth spread through my body, starting from my chest. My breaths became a little more ragged as I studied his tense body, seeming to fight the urge to close the short distance between us.

I really needed to get laid. Even just a meaningless roll in the sack. Nothing else. Too much tension had built up, causing me to feel things that weren't wanted.

But were they really unwanted? The thought of his lips pressed to mine, his fingers gripping my waist...

It was obvious his close proximity affected me. I knew it; he knew it. But I couldn't give him the satisfaction of vocally acknowledging it. With every last ounce of willpower, I shrugged, feigning indifference. "All I feel is exhaustion. So, let's just fucking eat."

Chrome paused, his eyes flaming with desire as his gaze raked over my body. I shivered, a heat burning deep in my stomach. "Don't tempt me, little savage," he growled, his eyes meeting mine as he bit his bottom lip. "I don't think you can handle my appetite."

It was as if the campfire had sucked all the oxygen from my lungs. My neck and face heated, my palms were sweating. But I enacted the stoic expression I'd trained my entire life to perfect. I rolled my eyes, "Please, get over yourself. I'm sure it's nothing special." I shoulder-checked him as I passed by, hoping I succeeded in hiding my overactive hormones. I was anything but calm on the inside, but he couldn't know that.

To settle myself, I conjured the fading memory of Slate's loving hands, and sensual mouth on my body. He'd always made me feel loved, wanted—something I doubted anyone else could ever make me feel.

I moved to work on plucking the turkey, giving Chrome a second to breathe from his little adventure in the woods. It gave me the space I needed to allow the feelings of guilt to settle in my heart. I shouldn't, but I felt like I was betraying Slate, even a year and a half after his death.

Ugh. Fuck this.

Heat warmed my face, thawing my frozen insides. The flames from the campfire flicked through the air, holding me in a trance. I wondered if fire would be my element as an Elemental. It didn't call to me, but at the moment, I cherished its life force.

Mixed hues of blue and purple painted the sky, casting a calm over our makeshift campsite as sunset approached. I kept my senses open for any intruders, but all was clear, at least for now.

Chrome was preparing the turkey he'd killed. He'd been at it for over an hour. I'd offered to help, but he'd refused, insisting I get the fire ready to roast it.

I was painfully starved. It'd been nearly three days since I'd last eaten. But I didn't want to be in the way, so I sat huddled on the ground near the fire.

I learned long ago that I was different from others. My father's outward treatment of me did me no favors. I supposed that was his goal: to keep me isolated.

Then Slate came along. We'd done everything we could to keep our relationship hidden from the king. I knew he wouldn't allow it. And in the end, my father had gotten his way.

Slate had come into my life when I'd thought about crushing redfern into my coffee before school one morning. I'd hated myself and my entire existence. Everyone considered me too quiet, too unnerving. A burden. Too much. If someone was nice to me, it was because they wanted favor with my father, as if I held any sway with him.

Add in the daily beatings and the public humiliation, and it was no shocker that I believed everything my father had told me. I was nothing, just a placeholder. He'd tell me that since he was stuck with me, the least I could do was be a decent assassin so he could get something useful out of me. I'd always wanted to join the warriors, but he said that was for those worthy of it. Forest would tell me that I'd already disgraced his family name, he couldn't have me disgracing the esteemed Guilds, too. So, I was to remain hidden away and monitored at all times—unless he needed me to make a public appearance for his own motives.

The crunch of Chrome's steps on the dead leaves signaled his return, pulling me from my past reflected in the flames. A heavy thud punched the hard earth, making me jump. I glanced around and spotted a severed tree trunk sitting at my side.

"Sit." Chrome gestured to the stump as he placed the pile of sliced, raw turkey meat onto one of his shirts that rested on the ground. "There are some sticks that I debarked and soaked in water that we can use as skewers."

"Thanks," I murmured, my stomach giving a painful rumble. When I saw he had two stumps, I stood and went to sit on the one he'd gestured toward.

Chrome nodded in acknowledgement, his hood draped over his head, blocking my view of his eyes. "There's also turkey legs, of course."

I nodded. "I could've helped."

"I know, but you're tired." Chrome shrugged.

"And so are you," I said, knowing he was brushing me off.

"Yeah, but working with my hands and using a blade is therapeutic for me," he said, grabbing a stick and a raw piece of meat, and then piercing the stick through it. He repeated the action to the other one.

I watched, annoyance rising in me as he did it for me, too. "I'm capable of doing things on my own, you know. You don't have to do everything."

He raised his striking gaze to peer up through his thick, dark lashes. It held a gentleness to it that made me squirm and look away. "I didn't do this because I thought you couldn't help me. You're very capable. I just know you have a lot to process and probably needed some time by yourself." His voice was unnervingly soothing.

I frowned. The thought never occurred to me that his actions came from a selfless place. My chest tightened, and then guilt squeezed it harder. "Oh, I didn't think you'd..." I said, cutting myself off, realizing how harsh I was about to sound. I looked at him. "Sorry. I didn't realize."

"I get it." Was all he said before he returned to the stringent task of impaling pieces of turkey onto sticks.

I didn't say anything as he worked. I just watched his calloused hands as his long fingers delicately picked up raw meat and skewered the thick slices in a smooth rhythm.

As I watched him work, I felt the weight of his past pressing on him, too. Whatever I'd gone through, he'd probably endured much worse.

It wasn't until recent events I'd even allowed my daddy issues to affect me. It'd been my way of life that I'd accepted long ago. I never believed I'd experience anything different. It was always my belief he did it to make me an unstoppable assassin, to make me tough. And I thought if I did everything he asked, I'd eventually make him proud. It'd been my primary goal.

Oh, how I'd failed so epically.

But Chrome? He seemed to have demons that ravaged his soul at all hours. I wasn't sure if I was prepared to know what he'd endured during his time at the King's Palace.

"So," I started, breaking the hypnotic sound of the crackling fire as my curiosity got the better of me. "What happened? Why did you flee Atlanta, and how did you manage to do it?"

Chrome's body went rigid as he stared at the ground. I quickly got the sense that this was a dark demon he didn't want to acknowledge. I regretted asking as soon as I saw his physical reaction, the coiled tension making me want to claw out of my skin.

I opened my mouth to tell him to forget about it when he said, "It's a long story. The details aren't that important, but essentially..." he trailed off, trying to find the right words. "Essentially, I'd reached my breaking point, and Forest's own weapon became too unstable to control."

My eyebrows rose to my hairline. "What do you mean, 'you reached your breaking point'?" I couldn't help but ask.

"It wasn't just your father who 'trained' me," he spit the word "train" like it was a curse as he continued spearing the turkey. "My mother was just as involved. As well as Grim." My skin crawled at the mention of him. His presence had always made me want to flee in the opposite direction. "They put me in intense conditions and forced me to overcome them. It wasn't until they used my sister as a form of...*motivation* that things took a turn for the worse."

Peri, as everyone had called her—short for Periwinkle. She was the daughter of Amethyst and Grim. I'd never met her, but I'd seen her in passing. Everyone treated her as if she had been the beloved princess. I'd always admired her from afar, wishing I could be more like her with her outgoing and gentle nature, always known for her beaming smile and kindness.

The rumor was that Griffin Silas had broken into the Palace and attacked, killing several Kinetics—including Peri and Chrome. It was the event that had rallied our kind into backing my father's decision to wage war against the Elementals. We were under the belief that the son of the deceased Elemental King blamed us for his father's death, therefore wanting revenge.

Kinetics had been terrified. If one could breach our security and kill Chrome Freyr, then what else was this man capable of? He became the face of the Elementals and public enemy number one. But now, knowing Griffin and Chrome were one and the same, I begged to know the truth of this world-altering event.

My heart plummeted at the implications.

"What really happened that day, Chrome?"

He stood, holding onto the skewered turkey slices—one in each hand. His jaw worked as he stared off into the distant woods before responding, "Like I said, it's a long story. But it's a day that will haunt me forever." He cleared his throat before taking a few steps toward me, handing me a stick.

I scooted the tree stump closer to the fire before hovering the piece of turkey over it. In my peripheral, I saw Chrome do the same. His brows were drawn together, as if lost in memories of his own. I didn't want to pry, but I knew he was withholding more game-changing information.

Whatever it was, it seemed the truth was too horrid for him to speak.

We sat in silence, roasting our turkey meat until it was thoroughly cooked. It was flavorless, except for the smokiness seeped into it, but it was food. I didn't care what it tasted like at that point.

"So," Chrome spoke up, swallowing a piece of meat, "what happened with you? How'd you escape?"

I cleared my throat and stared at the naked stick in my hand, twisting it around in circles. "Well, after I returned from my failed mission," I began and gave him a pointed look. "Thanks for the mortal wound, by the way." An amused smirk grew on one side of his mouth, to which I rolled my eyes. "It was my birthday. So, there was the customary revel in my 'honor'." I said it with another eye roll and looked to the ground between my feet.

"I've always hated those things. Knew it would be a farce from the beginning. And it turned out I was right. My father ordered a bartender to poison my drink with redfern. If it wasn't for Hazel, Scarlett, and Cotton…" Dread for their fates rose to the surface again and squeezed my throat. "I'd be dead. Hazel stole the antidote from your mother's office. They packed my bag for me and held off the guards. It wasn't pretty. I had to fight Grim…and confront my father," I said, thinking of how I'd stabbed him in the spine. "And some warriors. But…I made it out."

"Scarlett Kittle?" He angled his head to the side. "Daughter of the Guilds' Supreme Commander Cammo? Sister of Granite and Cardinal?"

I nodded. "Mhm," I hummed, swallowing a mouthful of turkey. "Yeah, she's the emissary for the king."

"Cammo was my primary trainer. Total asshole, but a good man. But he's loyal to Forest. I'm surprised she went against him." He chuckled. "She was always a fiery little shit."

I laughed, imagining Scarlett's fierce nature and her boldness, something I'd always admired about her. I could pretend to be fearless, but she wore it like the saucy dresses she loved. "She still is," I said, remembering our exchange at the revel, missing her wit.

"Her brothers..." Chrome trailed off, grabbing more raw meat and impaling it on the stick before he continued, "Granite, is he still the Supreme Guards Commander?"

"Yes," I said with a snort, reaching for more meat. "And these days, he's got a stick ten times bigger than this one stuck up his ass because of it." I waved the stick of turkey for effect.

Chrome chuckled. "We trained together a bit. He used to be such a cocky asshole, but I saw the pressure he was under. He never veered from his orders, always playing exactly by the book. The perfect soldier."

I nodded, never having thought of it like that before. I wondered if Scarlett had.

"Cardinal, though," Chrome said as he cracked a smile. "He's my age, so I spent more time around him during my teen years. He was a bit more rebellious," he explained, his grin wistful. "But with flattery and innocent denials, he could pretty much get away with anything."

That sounded similar to Scarlett, but she didn't even try hiding her rebelliousness. I struggled to imagine Cardinal the way Chrome described him, almost like they were friends. Perhaps they were. "He's changed a lot." I never realized he'd been anything besides the stoic statue he was now. "I've worked with him before on occasion. He's an assassin like me, but he's never struck me as having much of a personality."

Chrome's brows furrowed, and his shoulders dropped more. He finished cooking the piece of meat, then held it over his lap to cool. "Well, I guess, like the rest of us, that rebelliousness caught up to him."

I swallowed and looked back at the fire that bathed the piece of turkey I held. "I suppose so."

A heavy silence filled with the weight of our pasts sank over us. We sat in the pitch dark with only the light of our campfire illuminating the surrounding space.

I thought about the version of Cardinal I knew. To learn he'd once been a vibrant and youthful kid, that sounded so similar to Scarlett, disheartened me. I wondered what had changed for him. What had stolen his light?

I thought of Scarlett's give-no-fucks attitude. Surely by now, my father had discovered her and Cotton's involvement in my escape. And that meant one of two things: they were dead, or they were being tortured into submission. I prayed to the gods that neither was the case, and they'd listened to me. But we lived in a world orchestrated by a madman, and I no longer believed they'd get out of there alive.

Chapter 25

CHROME

The night sky blanketed me overhead as the stars peeked through the trees' canopy. I lay with my fingers laced together at the back of my head, breathing in the dying scent of fall. The temperature chilled me, but it was nothing compared to the icy numbness I'd been living with for the past year.

The moment Gray drifted off into a deep slumber, I rose from the cold, hard tundra, sneaking back into the thicket to meet with my contact regarding the information surrounding Forest and his plans. They also needed to be informed about the portal and the beastie-bear.

Afterward, I found a small clearing in the woods, and sprawled on the leaf covered dirt, basking in nature. Serenity nestled deep within as I meditated, feeling whole and content. Gratitude expanded my chest as I felt the best I had in years.

Time seemed to suspend as I lay in solitude, unsure how long I'd been there. I took this time to just...*be*. To be myself again with my own thoughts and emotions. I knew it could be ripped away at any moment, and I wanted to cherish the moments of lucidity I had been graced with.

I felt her before I heard her.

"You make it a habit to lie in the woods alone?"

I didn't say anything as I patted the spot beside me in a gesture for her to join me.

Gray's steps were careful as she sat down on my left before reclining onto her back. For several minutes, neither of us spoke. I rolled my head to the side and caught the silhouette of her side profile. Her glamoured white hair glowed from the moonlight, and for once, she bore a relaxed expression.

"What woke you?" I asked.

A long pause strung out the silence, leaving only the crickets and frogs to respond in her wake. Finally, she said, "Nightmare."

An ache in my heart had me almost lifting my hand to cup the side of her face, but I refrained. "They don't ever really go away."

A nod. "I figured."

"I know where we're going goes against everything you've been taught about Elementals, but you won't be alone anymore. You've never truly been alone."

Gray shifted to meet my eyes, then rumpled her brows with a slight pinch. "What do you mean?"

I offered the smallest of smiles, wishing I could tell her the whole truth about everything. She deserved to know, but I couldn't bring myself to flip her world over again just yet. "You'll see."

"You're so fucking cryptic," Gray retorted with an eye roll. "Do you have any guesses as to how that beastie-bear came here? Or where it came from?"

"Beastie-bear?" A chuckle slipped out at the nickname I bestowed upon that thing.

"Yeah, that's what you called it, right?"

I mulled over her question, then nodded. "I'll claim that as the official term. It's settled."

"Well?"

I hesitated. Unsure what to reveal just yet. "We'll figure it out. You'll get your answers soon enough, Princess."

I prayed we returned to the Hollow before the Tempest could expedite Forest's plans. I needed to get Gray trained in both her Kinetic and El-

emental abilities and fast while also figuring out this connection that
we seemed to share.

Perhaps together, we could put a stop to it all.

Gray had no idea how much power lay at her disposal. I felt it myself
all those years ago. The king had taken the opposite approach with
her as he had with me, probably because I was male. He'd kept her
suppressed—mentally and magically—in his attempt to control her
and her power.

I decided we needed a subject change. "Tell me about him."

"Who?"

"Slate."

A long pause followed. I didn't think she'd respond until she said,
"He was my light. Always trying to protect me when I didn't even
need it." Gray chuckled, "He's the one who gave me the backbone to
earn respect, even if it was misguided in the way of fear. But that's the
Kinetic way. Respect by fear."

A lump formed in my throat, making it hard to swallow. "I'm sorry
he's gone. I remember him. He was a good guy." I heard Gray sniffle
beside me, and I felt her heartache as if it were my own, felt her longing.
"I believe it was a set-up by Forest in an attempt to have full control
over you." It was the only bit of information I could give her at that
point, despite my yearning to divulge it all.

"I'm not even surprised to hear that anymore. That was my theory
back at the tattoo shop when you told me about...everything."

I nodded, keeping my gaze fixed on the shadowed leaves blanketing
us from above. "He took someone special to me, too."

Gray sucked in a sharp breath. "Peri," she whispered.

That lump formed in my throat again, just thinking about the periwinkle hair and beaming smile. Her big hazel eyes always filled with
warmth and acuity that she hid from my mother and Grim so well.

My silence dragged on, and neither of us spoke as we sat in the pain
of our losses at the king's hands.

"So, the Elementals," Gray said, breaking the quietude. I angled my head to meet her icy gaze filled with anxiety. "What's to stop them from locking me up upon our arrival? Why would they trust me?"

I understood her concern. "You're valid in that fear. I would know because I experienced the same thing when I arrived there a few years ago." Treading the line on what to reveal to her, I chose my words carefully. "Like you, I was brought there. After I fled the King's Palace five years ago, I was lost. Living amongst the humans and doing everything in my power to chase away the pain. The Chrome of legend no longer existed. I was a fallen hero. Because how could I have been a hero if I had been serving the wrong side all along? I hated myself, and I wanted to be rid of that version of me, even if it meant my own self-destruction."

I sighed, allowing those memories to surface for a brief moment. "As we all know, I held the record for killing the most Elementals. So why would they take me in?"

"And?" Gray asked, her voice hoarse with emotion and barely above a whisper.

I smiled to myself, remembering how Orion had given me little choice in the matter at the time. "They believe that we're the best they have to fight against Forest. The best chance to stop him from his plans and to restore a sense of peace to this world. In doing so, it would stop the persecution of their people, and we could live freely once again with the hope we could coexist with the Kinetics and humans alike."

Another tug on my heart, followed by a spike of doubt, struck me. The emotion wasn't mine, so I looked at Gray. "I know. It's all so much. And you won't be alone anymore, so it's not all on your shoulders."

"But why would they *trust* me?" The way she asked reminded me of the little girl on the playground—scared, broken.

"Because they know that if I'm bringing you in, then it's for a good reason," I explained. But her doubt, flickering as it was, still coursed through me, so I said in a firmer voice, "They also know that everyone who serves the king is brainwashed by his lies. While you may have served him proudly, they understand that you didn't do so without your own wounds to show for it. That if you're seeking asylum with us, then you truly have nowhere to go. They aren't hardened like Kinetics; you'll see that for yourself soon enough. They've been waiting for the day you come to us."

"Really?" Surprise lit her darkened expression.

"Yeah, they look to you for hope, Gray. They've just been waiting for you to break free of his control." Before it's too late.

"That's..." she mused aloud. "Really fucking weird. And perhaps a little misguided."

I chuckled. "No," I murmured, the muscles in my face softening. "They believe in you, even when you don't believe in yourself."

Another gentle tug that hummed moved through me. I felt a warmth ignite in my chest, and I couldn't tell if it was mine or hers. Maybe both. For the first time since I met her, she seemed shy, and it was endearing.

"What? Weren't expecting big, bad Griffin Silas to have...a *heart*?" I joked.

Gray scoffed. "I wasn't expecting Griffin Silas to be Chrome Freyr, for starters. So, the identity change has been quite an adjustment, to say the least."

I held her gaze, which softened from playfully annoyed into something more tender. Her lips parted, and her eyes dilated. My chest constricted as I fought to pull air into my lungs. I needed to touch her, hold her close to me. Kiss her. The way the glamoured iced-blonde strands draped across her face gave her a wildly seductive pull that fed the inner beast within me.

Before I knew what I was doing, I sat up on my elbows and rolled to one side, bringing my mouth inches from her jaw. The scent of lavender and vanilla rushed my senses, making me want to take what I felt in my tattered soul was mine, even if she wasn't aware of it yet.

Gray didn't breathe as she lay locked in a frozen state as if she were my prey, waiting me out.

The tips of my fingers caressed the column of her throat before they wrapped around just the slightest, applying a little pressure. Pulling my bottom lip between my teeth, I let out a husky chuckle in her ear. "I fucking love it when you say my name. My *real* name." Sliding my palm from her throat to cup her jaw, I said, "You always say it like it means something to you."

I pulled back and met her eyes that burned with so much fire, a fire that had me hardening against her hip. "It's always meant something to me," she said, her voice raw and unstable as her gaze dropped to my lips.

If I didn't return to my previous spot beside her, then I was going to fuck up everything. Pulling in a deep breath, I sat up, dropping down in my place on the hard earth. A silence enveloped us as we tried to process whatever the fuck that was between us.

"Were you one of my fangirls? *Please* tell me you were one of my fangirls," I broke the silence at last with an attempt at humor.

Gray scoffed, her voice still shaken. "I most definitely was *not* one of your fangirls. I wanted to *be* you."

If only she knew the truth of what I had to endure and was forced to be. "I hate to tell you this, but the persona I put on was all a lie."

"What do you mean?"

I cleared my throat. "The valiant Chrome Freyr that everyone knew, was only a mask concocted by my endearing mother and stepfather. This is the real me."

"Well, I assumed as much. I mean, I created my own. But no, I wanted to be powerful and skilled like you. Untouchable."

A bitter laugh escaped me before I realized it happened. "I wouldn't say untouchable." The stars glittered through the swaying shadowed leaves as she seemed to process that statement. Their whispers to one another were carried by the cool, crisp breeze.

It was Gray who broke our comfortable silence. "What brought you out here anyway?"

"Just..." I said. "Just felt called to this spot for some reason. Perhaps it's the Elemental in me." Guilt settled in at the lie, knowing my real purpose had been to meet up with my contact.

Gray hesitated, thinking over the possibility.

I hated the acidic feeling sinking in my stomach, twisting at my dishonesty. She hadn't earned that trust yet, seeing as only a few days ago, she wanted me dead at her hands. Some things would take time.

Gray didn't speak her thoughts, but I could basically hear the gears turning in her mind at a high speed. Her fierce scowl was back in place, but it looked more like she was deep in thought, not murderous. I couldn't tell if I liked that fact or not, sending my mind spinning at a high speed of its own in a direction it had no business going.

We continued to lay side by side in our separate bubbles. For how long, I couldn't say. We were simply sharing the space together and just being—nothing more, nothing less. Lost to our thoughts and everything they could possibly mean, it surprised me how easy the companionship felt.

I reflected back on my time with Onyx earlier: how, for the first time in a very long time, I could be around him and not force a smile or a laugh. It all came naturally because I could *feel* again. I remembered our meaningful times. I remembered *me*.

The more time I'd spent around Gray, the more distant and silent the affliction's voice grew. At last, I was granted a true sense of peace. And that alone was attributed to the girl beside me, the one I'd been saving since she was eight years old, whether she knew it or not.

The notion didn't escape me that it was her turn now.

Her turn to save *me*.

Chapter 26

GRAY

"I think you'll find you might actually like it here," Chrome said as we trudged the final steps toward the long-abandoned drive of the Elemental Hollow. It'd been a stressful journey, and I was ready to settle somewhere at last. But as we reached our destination, anxiety seized me at the idea of being surrounded by people I'd been trained to kill. They'd surely know who I was, so I worried about their reception of the Kinetic King's assassin daughter.

Chrome insisted otherwise. "They knew who I was when I first arrived. And now, they're my family."

I swallowed the lump in my throat. The sound of our feet crunching down the long gravel drive echoed off the tree boughs. Hidden deep in the woods, the Georgia pines hugged us along the pathway. "Please forgive me for not trusting your word on this. There're plenty of reasons why they'd want me to suffer."

Chrome glanced at me as we walked side by side. "Gray, there's more information you need to know. One person, specifically, has the answers." He paused and returned his gaze to the path ahead, combing his fingers through his black hair. "He saved me. I owe him everything."

A weight settled between us as he seemed to fall back into the clutches of his demons. I tried to imagine the horrors Chrome endured at the King's Palace. The public abuse I had been subjected to couldn't compare to what he must've gone through in private. Many of the punishments I experienced still haunted me, but gaining the notoriety that Chrome had achieved couldn't have come without a heavy cost.

"The lodge and cabins are hidden from sight unless you're granted permission. You're safe here," Chrome informed me. I wondered what Elemental magic allowed for that to be possible.

"It's not the Elemental power that provides that glamour," he added, as if he read my thoughts. "It's my Kinetic ability. It prevents us from being detected so we don't have to wear our bracelets all the time."

"What *are* your abilities, by the way? I don't think we've covered that. I keep meaning to ask." My nails dug into my palms the closer we got to the Hollow, my anxiety climbing higher and higher.

"I'm an earth-metal Elemental." I recalled our first meeting when he'd stolen my blades off my person, and how he wielded them against the Kinetics. Then, the liquid metal that had seeped from the Kinetics and beastie-bear's orifices. "My Kinetic ability—it's a lot more complex. I rarely use it because it can be volatile and...*unstable*," he hesitated, straightening his shoulders. Unstable—I noted how he used that word again. "But I can control electromagnetic energy. It's what gives the Hollow electricity."

My brows rose, and I almost stumbled at the admission. "That's..." I started, unsure how to react. "An extremely rare ability." Not only was that ability few and far between, but for someone to power an entire building on their own at all times required an enormous amount of power. At the King's Palace, it took an entire team of Kinetics with varying abilities to run all the electricity.

Chrome nodded. "Yeah, I know. Imagine trying to train with it..."

I fell silent, wondering how one would train such a rare ability. "So, how do you replenish your reserves?"

"I can absorb electromagnetic energy, as well as the others on the spectrum." Like me, but my power was much different than his.

"How do you fight offensively with it?" I asked, curious about this unknown power.

"The most effective and controllable way to wield that energy is through pressurized pulses," he explained as we neared a towering, intricate gate made of iron. "But it requires a lot."

Something niggled in my mind at his words, but he stopped me from pressing further.

"We're here." Chrome twisted his hand into a fist, unlocking the gate. It seemed to recognize him and his magic, which granted us entry. "Brace yourself," he warned. "Some are very excited to meet you."

We stepped through the gate, and before us, a beautiful, dark oak lodge demanded our attention. Sitting atop the peak of a hill like a beacon of hope, stood an enormous lodge that resembled something from a dream. The lawn surrounding it was perfectly manicured, untouched by the world beyond. A large lake sparkled in the distance off the edge of the property.

Behind the expansive and lavish lodge, dotted smaller, but equally luxurious cabins framing the lodge on either side. They stretched around and bordered the lake along the tree line.

It was absolutely stunning.

Once I'd gotten the first glimpse of the Hollow, Chrome urged me along. "Come on."

We walked up the black pavement leading to the front steps of the lodge. Beginning at the front, a large wrap-around porch encircled the majestic oak structure. A stacked wall of windows lined the tall, bottom floor.

"This is the main lodge where we eat, celebrate, meet, and train. Only a few of us have our sleeping quarters here."

"I assume you're one of them?" I asked with an arched brow.

Chrome shrugged. "You assume correct, Princess." The hint of a smile twinkled in his blue eyes, and I swallowed past the knot in my throat at the memory of him the night before, the tension between us searing me alive. Had he kissed me, I doubted I would've pushed him away.

His shoulders relaxed as he made his way to the front steps. However, anxiety warred inside me the closer we approached the towering, ornate double doors.

The second we stepped inside, a force almost knocked me aside, plowing into Chrome.

"Welcome back," a deep voice said, arms wrapping Chrome in a full-body hug.

Chrome returned it, patting him on the back. "It's good to see you, too, Onyx."

I narrowed my eyes at the cropped, inky hair darker than Chrome's. When Onyx stepped back, I noticed it swept to the side. Silver flecks dotted the pitch black throughout, reminding me of a clear night sky.

"Everything good?" Onyx asked, his brow furrowed. He still hadn't acknowledged my existence yet, which was fine. I preferred to stay out of the spotlight. It usually didn't end well for me otherwise.

Chrome snorted. "We're fine. We had a late start this morning." A smirk played on his sharp features, a light entering his eyes that hadn't previously been there. "Where's Orion? An urgent meeting needs to be called."

A silence fell between them. Onyx narrowed his light amber eyes at Chrome. Then, as if realizing not one but *two* people walked through the front door, he snapped his attention to me.

A beaming smile, full of perfect teeth, slowly lit up his handsome face that was a warm russet-brown. "Holy shit, brother," he whispered in awe. "She's here."

I wanted to hide. The staring made me feel exposed, but years of practice at the King's Palace had me holding my chin high and meeting the bright eyes that stood out against his complexion.

Onyx's face was familiar. I couldn't place where I'd seen it before. I knew I had. "Onyx," I began, "that's a Kinetic name. And your hair seems to agree." The black cloak he wore didn't allow me to see if he had currents.

With a dip of his head, he said, "Yep. Onyx Valor. Son of Supreme Trainer Smokey Valor."

I gaped in shock as recognition came to the surface. "*You're* his missing son that we all presumed to be dead?" I asked.

His face fell, and Chrome stiffened beside me. "Yeah. Things happened." Onyx cast a quick glance at Chrome. Chrome said nothing. "It wasn't safe for me to stay."

I wondered if he knew how hard it affected his father, Smokey. What could've possibly happened to make it unsafe for him—to the point he disappeared in the middle of the night? How did he end up at an Elemental stronghold?

Onyx's broad shoulders dropped, and his gaze fell with them to stare at the dark, walnut floor.

Chrome placed a hand on his friend's shoulder. "Where's Orion? Can you call a meeting?"

Shaking off the heaviness that plagued him, Onyx nodded. "Yeah, I'm on it, brother." He dipped his head to me. "Pleasure to meet you, Princess Gray. It's my honor." Then, he dropped at the waist to give me a proper bow before he spun on his heel and disappeared through the expansive living area and up a set of spiraling wooden stairs.

Chrome said to me in a low voice, "Like us, Onyx had no choice but to disappear. He worries about his father every day."

Guilt gnawed at me at his words. Were any Kinetics truly happy under my father's rule? Or were they all stifled and controlled with threats hanging over their heads daily, like it had been for me? I used to envy others for the freedom they must've possessed, not having been royalty. But perhaps no one there was truly free.

One thing was certain: my father was equal parts loved and feared by his people.

"Follow me," Chrome instructed, following Onyx's path. Striding toward the stairs, I took in more of the lodge's interior. Dark logs were stacked atop one another to form the walls. Large, stained tree trunks acted as rafters high above. But it was the stunning oak tree standing as the focal point in the common area that caught my attention. The second-story landing was open, visible from either floor. The oak tree crested higher, its leaves draping over the balcony. And on the far wall to my left, sat a stone fireplace made of gray river rock, stretching to the peak of the lodge.

This place embraced me with its comfort. I imagined curling up with a book or a sketchpad and pencils in one of the many cushioned chairs for hours.

Tree branches formed massive chandeliers, hanging at differing lengths throughout the main floor's common area. Warm light lit the space in a welcoming fashion as the aroma of cinnamon melted me from within. If I hadn't been on edge, I would've savored the space more.

I followed Chrome up the stairs and along the open landing at the top. When I glanced down, I didn't see any other Elementals striding about.

We entered a long hallway lined with rooms. Natural light streaming in through tall windows exposed the beautiful scenic view outside.

We walked in silence, apprehension once again rising in my chest.

I adjusted my duffel across my shoulder and stopped as we approached a door at the end of the hall. Chrome opened it, waiting for me to walk in first before he strode inside. The door shut with a soft click behind us.

A long table constructed from walnut sat in the center of the room.

Chrome dropped his bag against the wall, gesturing for me to do the same. "I'd take that one," he said, pointing to the head chair at the end of the table before sitting down on the opposite side.

I took my seat in the wooden chair he'd instructed. My feet and legs screamed with relief after the long journey we'd made that morning. I took a deep breath, trying to keep the rising nervousness at bay.

Voices sounded down the hallway, and my heart rate spiked at the thought of being exposed to new people. I'd never really had the best experiences with them.

Chrome straightened his shoulders at the sound, a mask of strength washing over his tired features. He was looking pale again, and I grew concerned at the memory of the night he'd been in the throes of what I'd deemed a traumatic panic attack.

The door flew open. A man with light blond hair and gleaming gold skin swept into the room. He beamed in relief as he spotted Chrome, who rose from his seat and greeted him with a hug. "So good to have you back, nephew," the man said into Chrome's shoulder.

Chrome nodded and pulled his face into the tight mask of control again. "It's good to be back."

I watched as others filed inside the doorway, but before I got the chance to observe them, Chrome turned and gestured toward me at the far end of the table. The man standing beside him turned his attention to me, and pure emotion overcame his handsome face.

"Aeran?" the man nearly whispered. I looked around, confused. I didn't speak.

"She doesn't know that name, Orion," Chrome explained. "She goes by Gray, her Kinetic name."

The man—Orion—took hurried steps to close the distance between us. Everyone in the room was silent, staring...at me.

I wanted to claw out of my skin. I hated this attention.

"Gray," Orion said as he stood next to me. I looked up, meeting eyes the color of warm tropical seas. He was an attractive man—with a scruffy jaw and sharp cheekbones—appearing to be in his early thirties.

I nodded, focusing on the sting of my nails as they dug into my palms.

"I've waited so many years to meet you," Orion said.

The mood in the room turned solemn, and I didn't know why. What didn't I know? I hated feeling like I was being kept out of the loop.

"Nice to meet you," I said and cleared my throat. "Thanks for allowing me refuge in your Hollow."

"It's not my Hollow, dear one." The beige skin underlying the gold-flecks on Orion's forehead wrinkled, like the ripples in light, beachy sand. He shifted his confused expression to Chrome. "It's Chrome's."

My eyebrows rose to my hairline. "Oh." My cheeks flushed red from embarrassment. "That... *knowledge*," I said, shooting daggers at Chrome with a glare, "was conveniently withheld."

Orion gave me a compassionate smile despite my tight one. "No worries, dear," he said, and placed a gentle hand on my shoulder. "After this meeting is adjourned, and you're settled in, I'd like to discuss many things with you. If that's okay? I'm sure you have a great deal of questions."

With a snort, I mumbled, "No shit."

"Colorful, I see." Orion smirked.

I looked away, his scrutiny overwhelming me.

Chrome tried to hide his smile before he cleared his throat. "Okay, everyone. Please sit. There's much to discuss."

Roughly ten people filed in, but a few stood out. I caught Onyx's star-speckled hair. His tall, broad body sauntered to the chair on Chrome's left while Orion took the right.

A beautiful, petite woman with rich, deep-brown skin beneath a radiating layer of gold flecks entered the room. Textured curls of her long, black hair bounced with each movement. She moved with fluid strides to a seat beside Orion. Her posture exuded a quiet confidence and the promise to inflict pain upon any threat. She wore a mask of steel, but her eyes....

Baby-blue irises laced around white pupils landed on me, almost appearing to glow.

A hulking man scraped a chair across the hardwood floor before plopping into it. His physique was in the shape of an inverted triangle, with muscles birthing more muscles. He folded his beefy hands together, resting his elbows on the table. He focused his astute attention on Chrome. Shining, gold-flecked skin layered atop a sun-bronzed complexion complimented his short brown hair.

In fact, everyone, minus Chrome and Onyx, had their gold skin and unusual eyes unglamoured. I wondered what my eyes would look like.

Both magic inhibitors were still in place, but was I ready to test out my possible Elemental side? Not seeing the physical proof still allowed me to believe all of this was some sort of mistake. That maybe I *wasn't* some fucked-up hybrid my father was hell-bent on using and destroying.

Deep down, I knew that was a lie.

"As you can see," Chrome started as all the seats in the room filled. He glanced around the table once he had everyone's undivided attention. "I have brought Princess Gray Monroe before you all."

I cocked my head to the side, narrowing my eyes. I didn't like the way he began this meeting.

Chrome ignored my expression and continued on. The powerful energy of a leader pulsed from his aura. "King Forest has decided that her usefulness ran out when she failed to kill me. On the journey back, however, several developments took place."

The Elementals surrounding the table listened to every word as he recounted all the... *developments*. Some of it was new to me, as he explained the interaction with Jesse at the speakeasy. He'd noticed him acting dodgy, and it hadn't sat right with Chrome. He was sure that the attack outside of the abandoned tattoo shop was by his design. When he reached the part about the beastie-bear, everyone fell still. Tension rolled across the table in such thick waves that it nearly suffocated me. But the dense layer of tension pivoted to me when he told them about the portal we'd somehow opened and sent the horned bear back to its realm.

I shifted in my seat, but straightened my back, refusing to show fear or discomfort to this room full of strangers.

Someone cleared their throat. "Has she removed her glamour yet?" It was the petite woman who'd caught my eye. She glanced at me before returning her focus to Chrome, speaking about me as if I wasn't sitting at the same table as everyone else.

"No," Chrome responded. The power within his feline-shaped eyes held me in place, like he sensed my desire to quip a smart-ass remark and dared me to keep my mouth shut. "It's been quite a shitshow. Untested powers in an uncontrolled environment would surely take that shitshow and turn it into an absolute nightmare. Didn't wanna risk it." His mouth opened, then shut again.

I squinted my eyes, wondering what was on the tip of his tongue.

Everyone at the table nodded in agreement.

"I assume you and Orion will train her magic?" a voice heavy with bass asked. The owner belonged to a man whose skin was deeper than the woman's. Thick locs twisted neatly to rest against his broad chest. He held himself carefully composed with his hands in his lap. He sat pin straight so his back didn't touch the chair.

"Yes," Chrome said, still speaking about me as if I wasn't present, yet he never broke eye contact. "But you'll take part in her combat training."

I lifted my hand to halt the conversation. "Hold on," I said. "Combat training? You realize I'm..."

"Yes, but there's more you could learn. Void has a particular skill-set that will prove advantageous for you in the future," Chrome explained. "Seeing as you have so many enemies now, you might want to jump on the offer."

I slumped back into my seat. "Fine."

"Well, isn't she just full of rainbows?" someone chimed in. A younger male sitting a few spots down from Void. He looked at me with bright eyes that danced with amusement. Those eyes glowed orange like an Elemental blade. They contrasted with the Native-brown skin gleaming beneath the gold, and the silken black hair pulled into a loose bun. The mischievous grin he wore promised this wouldn't be our last interaction.

Chrome snorted a chuckle. Everyone looked around the table, eyes shifting in confusion at his reaction as if it were an unusual thing for him. "You have no idea."

Chapter 27

GRAY

"Wait. So, ya'll work with humans? What about the militia?" The concept that humans willingly worked with one of our kind weaved even more of a tangled web of questions in my mind.

Orion nodded. "We've established cordial relations with some of the human militia in the surrounding areas," he said, rubbing the stubble on his jaw absentmindedly.

I leaned forward with my forearms resting on the table, fingers interlaced together.

"The humans blame us all for Devolution Day. For losing their loved ones and their entire way of life. As you know, Forest revealed our kind and blamed Elementals for the attacks leading up to that day. Humans turned on us, while they viewed Kinetics as the more benevolent race."

Before my escape, that was my truth. I'd never doubted Elementals had been responsible. But everything I'd ever believed was a lie. So, what was the *actual* truth?

"In actuality, it was the *Kinetics* making attacks on *us*. Forest ordered false-flags upon us in order to manipulate everyone to support his planned declaration of war. He needed a reason to escalate a conflict. It would cause turmoil if he didn't. Not only with the humans coming at him with weapons of mass destruction, but also with us, too. Between our numbers and the humans', he didn't stand a chance. So, he created a reason for the public to back him. He knew the humans would be scared and would turn on the people they were told were responsible. They'd never really made it a habit to think for themselves with those types of things. So, it wasn't hard for Forest to accomplish.

"What he didn't expect was that Chrome, or Griffin, would survive his escape. He didn't expect Chrome to join forces with the Elementals and become their leader. And he didn't expect Chrome to have built silent networks amongst the human militia in order to fight back."

I closed my eyes as acidic guilt ate my insides. All those Elemental lives I'd taken... Was it for nothing? I was no better than the humans who'd blindly taken my father at his word. I'd been too wrapped up in trying to make him proud that I never stopped to think, to ask questions.

Orion's eyes softened, sensing where my thoughts were leading. Everyone at the table slid their attention toward me, assessing me. I didn't like the feeling...at all. "It's okay. The situation you were under is understandable. No one wholly blames you for your actions while under your father's manipulation. Had you not complied with his orders, you would have been killed."

My throat felt like sandpaper as I took a deep breath and then nodded, urging him to continue.

"We work with the humans in the sense that we help them fight back against Kinetics and Endarkened. In turn, they lend their information on Forest's movements and aid us with supplies we might need."

I tilted my head to the side. "You mean you aren't self-sufficient here?" I asked, confused. They used magic to grow their own food and functioned as if the world had never collapsed. Why would they need supplies from humans?

Orion's blond hair wisped back and forth with a shake of his head. "No, no, you misunderstand, dear. We don't get food supplies and weapons from them. At least, not for the Hollow. When we're out on missions, we might require someplace to stay, food to eat, and the likes of that. But it's the information they provide us that's the most valuable. They give us the times and routes of the trains, the locations of scorses where there might be an important drop, and the intelligence their spies are able to obtain."

And that's when it clicked why Chrome was talking to Jesse at the speakeasy and why he insisted on getting to the nearest scorse. But when we arrived, the Guild ambushed us.

I looked at Chrome. "If you are working with the rebel militia, then why were we attacked when we arrived at that tattoo parlor?"

He shrugged. "Someone in that network turned against us, probably Jesse. He either gave us the wrong scorse location, or it was all a lie to begin with, knowing the king's forces would be waiting."

"That kid, Ash..."

"Dash," Chrome corrected.

I rolled my eyes with an added huff. "Dash. So, you know him? He's militia, then?"

Chrome's intense gaze fought off laughter. "Yep."

I *fucking* knew it.

"So that's how he could take down that Endarkened? You told them about black crystal's lethality to an Elemental, which also kills Endarkened?" I asked, feeling slightly betrayed. The Elementals must've been helping humans forge their bullets with black crystal. Which meant they probably had bullets forged with redfern, too.

These were well-hidden secrets from humans and for a damn good reason. They were *way* too trigger-happy, especially with people and things they didn't understand.

If my father knew this, he'd find a way to disintegrate the rest of the surviving world as it stood. It saddened me I couldn't be a fly on a wall to witness him learn of this discovery.

Something else from that encounter popped into my mind. Something I'd forgotten about amongst the events that followed. "That Endarkened woman..." I said, bringing his attention to that topic. "When she was dying, did you notice how she... she seemed at peace? It was as if her lucidity returned in those last moments."

Another staunch silence reigned oppressively in the room. Everyone shifted in their seats before once again looking to Chrome for answers.

At first, he didn't speak. He seemed to replay the memory in his mind as he stared at the wall behind me. For a moment, his stark expression flickered with a hint of something that was dangerous in our world. It was so faint, I doubted anyone else caught it. Like a fleeting butterfly, it was gone before it had the chance to settle.

But it bore the question: *why?*

He didn't deign to answer me. Before I could protest, he spoke, "Meeting adjourned."

That look vanished. In its place sat the composed, hardened mask of the living ghost of our past. But I couldn't erase that glint of emotion from my mind.

The first time I'd seen him don—well, *hope.*

The room they gave me was within the oak lodge, not one of the cabins lining it. I stood wrapped in a fluffy towel at the edge of the queen-sized bed. The thick mattress perched on top of a stacked-stone frame, a mixture of light and dark grays.

I rifled through the clothes Scarlett and Cotton had packed for me. The cool breeze from the balcony chilled my skin from the scalding shower. I'd never appreciated that luxury until I'd scrubbed away recent events.

The scented soaps soothed my mind and lavished my skin like the silkiest of creams. I felt like a new woman. And in a sense, I was. The Gray Monroe from four days ago was left behind on the cold marble floor of the King's Palace ballroom.

I thought of the name that Orion had first called me: Aeran. Was that my Elemental name? Given to me by whom?

After Chrome's dismissal of the debriefing, I was escorted to my sleeping quarters. I was grateful to be allowed to clean up and change before my meeting with Orion.

I chose a worn pair of black cargo pants that hugged my shins, one of my favorite pairs. Scarlett really pulled through for me. Another pang shot through my chest at the thought of my dear friend and what befell her after my disappearance.

I sifted through the jumble of clothes. I layered a matching hooded sweater over a tight white tee. I was finally out of the leather gear I wore on missions and into my casual attire that was more comfortable.

I found my combat boots and laced them up, steeling my warring emotions with each eyelet I tightened. Everything had happened so fast since my return from the failed mission to kill Griffin...or Chrome. It was all a whirlwind of events and revelations that threw everything I thought was true for a loop.

And the most shameful part of all was I still craved my father's approval. I still held out just the slightest bit of hope that he might change his mind about me, seeing as I was his only child. But the voice of reason—anger—always shut it down before that hopeful voice rose too loud.

There wasn't much a brush could do for my knotted waves. The braids on either side were tangled, and I simply didn't have the energy to battle it.

The bathroom didn't disappoint. A jacuzzi that could easily fit three adults was off to the side against the wall. Whereas the room was made of wood, the bathroom was nothing but beautiful shades of gray riverbed stone.

The shower wasn't exempt. Greenery draped down the stone walls, bringing a more serene sense of nature to the experience.

The Hollow was nothing like the cold, gaudy beauty of the King's Palace. It was a luxurious beauty of peace and comfort. I felt like I could finally breathe.

In the mirror in my bathroom, my blue eyes looked haunted—empty—behind shades of gray. Angry, I couldn't stand the reflection. Such a disappointment. A failure. A burden. A waste of valuable resources.

I closed my eyes and pulled on the mask of Princess Gray, the one who faced down her people's opposition daily and made them cower with only the cut of her gaze. The mask that declared I feared no one, even though I was familiar enough with the emotion that it had become a companion. I may harbor fear like a host of an oversized parasite, but I'd be sure to instill more into others around me.

A knock came on my door an hour later as I perused the built-in bookshelves. I placed the book I'd been skimming back in its place and moved to open the door.

I was greeted with white pupils lined with baby-blue irises. Her lip pulled upward just the slightest as she assessed me. Suspicion bathed her unnerving eyes as she peered down her nose at me.

Despite her distrust toward me, she gave off a soothing energy.

"I'm here to take you to Orion's office." She spoke in a stiff tone not compatible with her delicate persona.

I gave a brief nod and followed her out, clicking my door shut behind me. I studied her movements for any potential weaknesses as we strolled through the hallways. She was all grace with her silent steps and fluid motions. Every action reminded me of a whisper, so quiet and smooth that it would be easy to underestimate her in combat.

She never looked over her shoulder as we walked in the echoes of our footsteps. It wasn't a complicated layout—with a few long hallways that branched off every so often.

Like the rest of the lodge, the interior consisted of oak logs and thick trunks that served as rafters. Sconces lined the hallways, providing a warm glow of comfort. Various sizes of framed photos and paintings lined the walls. All were candid shots or group photos of a happy community prior to Devolution Day.

The young woman reached a door in the center of the hallway, rapping it lightly with her knuckles without hesitation. She tossed another skeptical glance at me before the door swung open.

Orion stood on the threshold with his forearm braced on the doorframe with an amiable smile. "Princess Gray." The calm seas in his gaze brought a fraction of ease. "Thank you for meeting with me."

I gave a brief nod and moved to step past the young woman who escorted me.

"And thank you, Aella. As always, your generosity is appreciated, my dear," he said, turning his soft gaze to the lithe Elemental.

Aella's lips pulled up into a tight smile, her eyes shifting to me. "Of course, Orion," she said, her voluminous black hair bouncing with the nod. She adjusted her white, loose-fitting sweater before turning on her heels and drifting down the hall.

Orion stepped aside and swept his arm in a welcoming gesture into his office. Organized chaos best described the cluttered room.

"Please, have a seat," Orion said and moved behind his broad desk, scattered with open books and two picture frames. It was a brief glimpse, but in one, there were three individuals all huddled together—one of them being a younger Orion. Smiles painted their golden-flecked faces.

Following Orion's lead, I took a seat in the dark leather chair opposite him and fought to maintain eye contact with the gentle man facing me.

"You must have so many questions, dear." Orion's brows pulled downward as his focus trained on me with compassion.

"I do," I said, nodding, my features tight. Glancing away from him, I scanned the walls lined with packed bookshelves.

"Once Chrome arrives," Orion said with an endearing smile, "I'll be able to give you your answers."

My head tilted in question.

"It was at his insistence. He made it very clear he wanted to be present."

"Why?"

The door opened behind us, and Chrome strode inside with tight restraint. There was an empty chair next to mine, but he remained standing by Orion's side. "Are you settling in all right, Princess?" he asked me, all glamours removed from him. His golden skin, chromatic hair, swirling molten eyes, and silver currents all dominated the space, somehow making this room his just by stepping into it.

Fucking hell. Why did he have to be sexy?

"Yeah, as much as I can," I said with a disinterested shrug. Seeing him in this environment changed him, somehow. Or, at least, it changed how I saw him.

Chrome was no longer just a survival partner; he was a respected leader. He carried himself with a distinct air—approachable yet unapproachable at the same time. It was clear this was *his* Hollow. *His* people. *His* war against my father.

Chrome pinned me to my chair with his molten stare. My chest tightened from the emotion that poured from them. It was a silent promise that I wouldn't be alone during this meeting.

Orion beamed, "Great! We're all here. So, let's begin, shall we?" I wasn't sure if he noticed the silent exchange between Chrome and me or if he'd simply ignored it.

I shifted my eyes from Chrome to tune into Orion. "I'm still not sure if I even believe I'm part Elemental," I confessed to Orion.

Orion nodded. "Of course. I'm sure you're dying to remove that necklace to test the theory." A pained expression entered his shiny blue eyes at the black crystal hanging over my chest.

I gave him a tight smile. In truth, I was, but I was also terrified. It would make everything more real and concrete, effectively changing everything about me.

Chrome seemed to sense this. "You're not alone in this, Gray."

I waved a dismissive hand at him and returned my attention back to Orion.

"When an Elemental comes into their magic for the first time," he began. "Powers tend to be quite...*volatile*. With no way of knowing which Elements you possess, you could level the lodge unintentionally. We suspect that, like Chrome, your power is immense. So, we must take precautions and plan accordingly." Orion laced his fingers together on top of the desk as he gazed at me softly.

"Well, shit..." I said, still doubtful of whether to believe the claims of my potential strength or not. "Why do you believe I'll be so powerful? My Kinetic side shouldn't influence the strength of my Elemental, right?" I asked, shifting my eyes back and forth between the two men. My eyes lingered on Chrome's overwhelming gaze longer than I intended as his quicksilver eyes drew me in.

Orion swallowed and looked down at his clasped hands perched atop the desk. He sighed, letting the tension linger. When he glanced up at me, his eyes were heavy with grief. "Your mother was an extremely powerful Elemental."

I narrowed my eyes. "You know who my mother is? Was?"

Orion cleared his throat and sat back in the seat, as if the weight of the truth exhausted him. "Your mother was a very dear friend of mine. She was extraordinary. A powerful, fierce warrior with a heart as gold as our skin. She was grace, beauty, and kindness. And that's how she ruled our people."

My heart slammed to a stop. "Ruled?"

Orion nodded with his eyes closed. "She was the Elemental Queen, Lilliana Willow. And her husband, King Jonas..." he said and looked up at Chrome standing by his side. "King Jonas was Chrome's father and my older brother."

Chapter 28

GRAY

"Holy shit." It was the only thought that kept repeating in my mind. The implications of such a monumental claim were unthinkable.

"Wait. Hold on..." I held up my hand, having the most disturbing thought. "Does that make me and Chrome siblings?" I'm sure my expression was horrified.

Orion shook his head. "Oh, no. While they *were* married, you do not share the same blood."

I visibly sighed in relief. How horrible would it be if I was turned on by a surprise hidden brother that I never knew existed?

Chrome worked to bite back a smile, and I narrowed my eyes at him for thinking this was funny. It most definitely was not fucking funny after this weird chemistry.

"How is that possible?" I asked, returning my focus back to the main point at hand. "They were killed when they..."

"When they were supposedly attacked by Endarkened?" Orion finished for me and then scoffed. A hard edge entered his voice. "No, they were deceived. Weakened and captured in the middle of the night by Kinetics under your father's orders. He reduced them to mere breeding animals for him and Amethyst to torture at their disposal."

I felt sick. My stomach churned as heavy chains squeezed my chest. "How...how do you know this?"

"Your mother, Lilly, as we called her, wrote me a letter detailing everything that had happened in the two years she'd been held there and everything your father had planned. I'm still not sure how she got the letter out, but I suspect there was someone who sympathized with her and worked closely with Forest. She appointed me the King of the Elementals in their wake until I found the two of you." Orion looked back at Chrome. "She said you two are the only way to stop Forest and to restore our races to our peaceful ways."

I heard everything he said. But it'd have to wait until later when I was alone to digest it. So, instead, I said, "What do you mean 'restore' to our peaceful ways? Has there ever been a time when we were truly at peace?"

"Yes," Orion and Chrome both said in unison.

"Tell me how," I said to Orion. He sat up straighter in his desk chair, bronze undertones in his ash-blond hair catching in the warm light of the room.

"My brother and Lilly worked to attain their vision of establishing true peace between Elementals and Kinetics. They wanted to end all conflict between our races. Forest's father, King Brick, had been a rather benevolent leader for the Kinetics. He'd encouraged positive relations and worked with Jonas and Lilly to achieve it.

"The main issues at that time were the Endarkened. They were attacking humans and even a few of our kind. Because Endarkened were once Elementals, we used to always get blamed for their attacks. As if we actively wielded them as a fighting force, which is just absurd because they can't be controlled. Brick was sympathetic to this. So, he allowed the Elementals to handle the Endarkened. He said it wasn't his place to inject Kinetics into our internal issues. He agreed to capture any Endarkened that were causing trouble and hand them over, but that was as far as he would go.

"When he died, Forest rose to power. He was young. We'd all met him many times in the past. Each time, he'd grown more cunning, more arrogant. They knew right away he craved power." Orion sighed. "As a teenager, he'd met and fallen in love with a beautiful Kinetic named Coral. She was common, but it'd never mattered to him. She'd became pregnant when he was just shy of his twentieth birthday. One night, she was out in the city walking back to the palace and was attacked by Endarkened—killing her and their unborn child. Forest only grew worse after that.

"Your mother and Jonas grew more concerned once he took the throne within a year after her death. They hoped they'd be able to work with him, that they'd be able to maintain the growing peace between our people." Orion's chin drooped lower to his chest, tightening his hold on the armrests of his chair as he recounted the history that had been hidden from Kinetics. He lifted his gaze to settle on me, reflections of his past rippling on teal seas.

He took a deep breath before he carried on, focusing on an oak log bracing the wall. With an absent-minded wave, a soft breeze swept around the desk before washing over his face and rustling his light blond hair. His element seemed to bring him some comfort as he shook his head.

"Jonas and Lilly hosted some delegates from the King's Palace. Our kingdoms were close together in the northern region of the state. Ours was remote, in the mountainous landscape where we could be closer to nature and far from the dense human population.

"Several members of Forest's court arrived, having led Lilly and Jonas to believe they came to work out a treaty that would bring absolute peace between our races once and for all. They remained for several days, playing the role of respectful guests. Little did we know, they were poisoning our food and drink with small amounts of crushed black crystal, weakening our power. It wasn't until that final night..."

"Who was it?" I asked, cutting him off. "Who were the delegate members?"

Orion closed his mouth and cleared his throat. "There were many," he said with hesitance. "But Amethyst and Grim, for starters. Smokey, Onyx's father, was there as the Supreme Leader of the Guard..."

"*Smokey* was there?" I asked, dumbfounded. I glanced at Chrome, whose jaw was clenched tight. "But he's the reason I made it out of the palace alive. I don't understand..."

Orion cocked his head and looked up to meet Chrome's calculating gaze. A silent conversation passed as they pieced together the snippet I'd offered. "That's...an interesting development. I believe Onyx will be pleased to learn about."

My mind worked over the facts, trying to make sense of everything. I grounded myself as I dug my nails into my palms.

Orion leaned forward on his desk, his forearms perched on the lacquered wood to finish the story that'd been withheld from me. "We knew something was terribly wrong that final night. Jonas and Lilly were pale, weak, and shaking. I, too, was in no better shape. The poisoning had taken its root and was at its peak by the time we'd realized. It was too late." Shadows of regret shrouded his handsome features.

Orion reached for a crystal glass of amber liquid that smelled of strong bourbon. "They killed our guards and many soldiers in the middle of the night. Some were brutally tortured before they were slain, while others were silently killed with Kinetic magic." He swirled the dark bourbon in his glass. "I was meant to die that night, but they underestimated the amount of poison required to kill me." He took a large swig of his drink, not flinching from the taste or burn.

"Once everyone was incapacitated, including our king and queen, they took them. And they never came home. I became the new king, even though I never wanted the position. It was always meant for Jonas. He was made for it, and it was natural for him. I've never been one to make the hard decisions that came with the title. My strengths were in seeing the unseen, the hidden facets, and easing burdens when I could. Taking on all of it was...too much. I couldn't rule an entire race spanning the entire continent. So, I did what I believed would ensure the survival of our people." Orion took a more substantial sip of bourbon.

"I disbanded the monarchy and broke us up into smaller factions. I allowed all the Hollows throughout the country to rule themselves, but we all remained within a network with one another while going into hiding. I believe that move saved our kind from complete eradication."

Chrome nodded in agreement. A mixture of wrath and anguish sharpened his features, the molten silver in his eyes swirling with fervor.

"Forest had too many resources. You know your father mingled in the human business world prior to Devolution Day, but he also secretly worked with the human government. They'd offered their help with their military weapons designed to kill both races. We stood no chance. Having us out in the open would've ensured extinction."

I was speechless hearing the amount of carnage my father caused in the tale Orion weaved. Cinder blocks continued to pile on my chest, the weight almost too much to bear, making it hard to breathe. I stared at my hands laced in my lap, remorse burrowing deep in my soul for the lives I'd taken, all for the sense of gaining his approval and pride. "I'm so sorry," I whispered, unable to meet their eyes. "I didn't know."

Orion sat up, and Chrome straightened. Orion opened his mouth to speak, but Chrome beat him to it. "Stop it. What's important at this moment is you're free from his control and you know the truth. All we can do is move forward at this point to help atone for our actions of the past."

The hard conviction in his tone forced me to meet his fierce gaze. He knew what I felt. He, too, had been a weapon for my father against Elementals, more so than I. And here he stood as their leader. I nodded and dropped my gaze to my lap again as shame swallowed me in its maw.

"You had no way of knowing any of this," Orion said. His tone was much gentler than Chrome's—calming even. "Your father kept this knowledge tight-lipped. Only a select few in his inner circle know the truth. And they were a part of that delegation."

How could I never have realized the extent of my father's depravity? He was the keeper of information for the Kinetics, so it made sense. He'd always been an utter prick—but this?

I realized I could never have made him proud. I didn't think he was capable of feeling such an emotion for anyone, or anything, except himself.

I peeked upward through my lashes. "What happened on Devolution Day? Was he responsible for the EMP, too?" I asked.

A faraway look blanketed Chrome's rigid exterior. I frowned, but kept further questions to myself.

"We don't know for sure," Orion answered. "We suspect he played a hand in it, perhaps with the human government. But honestly? That part remains a mystery, I'm afraid."

I cut my gaze to Chrome again, who'd regained his confident air. Harried secrets—harbored in darkness—taunted me behind his mercurial eyes. They begged to be released from their burdening depths as if their weight grew suffocating.

The memory of Chrome's vulnerable state in that abandoned house flashed through my mind. His washed-out complexion and trembling body had stricken me to the derelict floor. The wide eyes and mussed hair, the unsteady voice...his plea. *"You remember, don't you? Please tell me you remember."* It made my heart ache.

As I held his gaze, that plea still echoed through the silence. I remembered, but I couldn't get rid of the niggling feeling that there were more secrets yet to be unearthed.

"You get a personal tour of the Hollow from yours truly. Many ladies would consider you lucky," Chrome said from beside me, a smile peeking through. His hood was lowered and silver hair kissed his face as he led me along a maintained gravel path surrounded by falling leaves. The air felt cleaner, fresher—detoxed from the negativity that contaminated the outside world.

I rolled my eyes, but a smile peaked at the corners of my lips. "So, you're the leader here. You conveniently left out that *minor* fact." We strolled at a leisurely pace, and I scanned the beautiful shrubbery that lined the pathway. Floral aromas imbued my nose, lightening the weight on my chest a bit.

Chrome ran his fingers through his hair. "It's not something I feel the need to boast about. It's a duty and honor that was entrusted to me by a good man," he said with a shrug.

My heart squeezed. Nodding, I asked, "So, my role here is to what? Help you piece together the Elementals again and rule?" The possibility of one day becoming a ruler had always been there—just not of the Elementals. Yet the idea felt so foreign.

Chrome tilted his head and stuffed his hands in his front pockets, watching crows take flight from a nearby tree as dusk fell. "In a sense, yeah. But mostly, we need both the hybrids to take down your father if we want our world to survive."

I wasn't sure what to say. The confidence and hope he and Orion held in me was unsettling. The fear of failing in such a monumental task bared its weight on my chest and sank. I shifted directions instead. "My father has hunted for this place for years. Every mission he sent me on held the hope that I'd come across it. You did well keeping it hidden."

Chrome glanced down his shoulder at me. "I know," he said, a slight grin playing at the edges of his mouth. "Although, I thoroughly enjoyed our little game of cat and mouse. I don't know what I'll do to pass the time now."

My shoulder bumped his. "How do you know I'm not still planning to kill you and sell this place out to my father?" I raised my brows with a smirk.

"You won't," Chrome said, his tone not leaving any room for doubt.

"Oh? What makes you think that?"

Those molten eyes swirled slowly, sending my pulse spiking. His voice was husky with emotion when he said, "Because you're finally home, Princess."

Something twinged in my chest at that word. *Home.* The place I'd called home for twenty-four years had always been cold, distant. Hurtful, even. Would this place be any better?

I pulled away from the gaze that had me softening. I didn't like it. It had only been a year and a half since Slate's death. How could I look at another man yet? And Chrome was already starting to get to me. I told myself it was because I was in a vulnerable state, and I was seeking the comfort Slate had always provided. That wasn't healthy. Especially when this man seemed to have his own demons to contend with.

A heavy silence fell between us, the sky emitting autumn colors in the sunset that draped over us. Chrome gently grabbed my elbow and directed me to turn off the path to the right. We walked through vibrant grass that belonged to summer and stopped about thirty feet away.

Chrome pointed to the vast, abundant fields full of crops before us. "These are the fields where we grow our foods and materials for our necessities."

The endless sprawling fields stole my breath. Rows upon rows lined the land that stretched for miles. "You guys don't share any of it with the human population?" My breath fogged as I spoke, the chilling air wrapping around me.

Chrome looked at me as if I'd insulted his Hollow. "Of course, we share. But we ensure our people are provided for first. We trade with the rebel militia. But sometimes, we'll place a haul in a known haunt for civilians to find."

I looked at him. "That must've been Orion's idea. He seems so...gentle like that."

"It was both of ours." He shrugged, facing the fields again. Before I could respond, he said, "Come on. We're headed to the training grounds, seeing as you start first thing in the morning."

I couldn't help the small hit of excitement that rose at the idea of train-ing. It was the only time I'd ever felt free back at the King's Palace. "Great."

My step faltered. The familiar energetic presence that lingered outside the speakeasy, and then at the scorse, tickled my suppressed awareness again. I was tempted to remove my bracelet to pinpoint the source, but I needed these people to trust me. No doubt they'd think I was walking around, planning to attack them if I removed my bracelet. And at the moment, it was nice knowing I had a comfortable bed to lie in.

The presence lurked—watching—rippling up my spine and into the hairline of my scalp, and it wasn't from the chilling fall air. It was curious, biding its time. Chrome didn't seem affected as he strode away in the direction of the lodge.

Shaking off the uneasiness that settled in my chest, I jogged after him.

Chapter 29

CHROME

I stood in Orion's office with Onyx sitting beside me. This time, Gray was in her room waiting for dinner. Her nervous anxiety thrummed through my body, making me wish I could ease her mind. I hadn't been successful in blocking her emotions yet.

I couldn't help her, though. There were things I needed to discuss with Orion and Onyx in private. Things we weren't ready to talk to the others about yet.

Orion breezed in, sandy hair sweeping across his forehead. The door closed with a click. He flashed us a smile before moving to round his desk, dropping into his large leather chair. I took the seat Gray had occupied only two hours prior.

"I'm so glad you're both back," Orion said with a sigh, shoulders slumping.

I dipped my head. "As am I, Uncle."

"Fuck. I'm glad to have a warm shower and Katia's delicious food again. If I had to eat goopy slop that they try to call oatmeal *one* more time, I'd have vomited," Onyx muttered next to me.

I chuckled. "Your entitlement is showing, Onyx."

Onyx rolled his eyes dramatically.

Orion's bemused grin said he missed our banter. "What is it you need to discuss, Chrome?"

I released a long sigh. "I met with my contact last night while Gray slept—"

"Still don't want to give up this 'contact' of yours, hmm?" Onyx piped in, cutting me off.

"I've already told you, I can't—not yet."

"Continue, Chrome," Orion encouraged. "What did you learn?"

"Well," I started, trying to organize my thoughts. Another wave of gratitude washed over me that I was able to think lucidly now that the urge to viciously kill wasn't taunting me. "My contact said that Arcadia is weakening, decaying more with each sunrise. It's due to the Tempests, who are basically dark sorcerers and sorceresses. They practice blood magic that depletes the magic from the realm—including the wildlife—and in its wake, death and blackness are left behind."

Orion's eyes widened, "Like...the Endarkened?"

"Very similar, it appears."

"So, what does this have to do with Forest and his plans *here*?" Onyx asked.

I cleared my throat and sat up straight to deliver this next part. "It seems that the noble King Forest has been working with the Tempests since before Gray and I were born. Apparently, there's something of great power, and he wants it."

"I'm assuming he's been promised that power if he helps them somehow?"

I nodded. "Weakening the veil."

"How?" Onyx questioned, his voice pitching a little high.

I hesitated, trying to piece it together myself. "I don't know. But I have a feeling it has a whole lot to do with Gray and me. It's not a coincidence we were able to open a portal for the beastie-bear."

"Beastie-bear?" Onyx said. And after pondering it over, he added with an approving nod, "I'll allow it."

"Anyway," I said, steering the topic back to the importance at hand. "The first time we met, our magic...*reacted*."

"Reacted *how*?" Onyx pressed, while Orion narrowed his eyes, wondering why I'd never spoken of this before, I presumed.

I blew out a breath, running a hand through my metallic strands, glad to have them back. "Like an explosion." I relaxed into my chair, bracing for the barrage of questions that was to come as I recounted the story.

Orion's face had gone sheet white, while Onyx gaped at me like I'd committed the ultimate crime against him. The Kinetic beside me asked, "Why haven't you *ever* told us this before?"

"Because I didn't think it really mattered," I lied. "I thought it was a freak thing."

Orion didn't buy it, judging by his raised brows. "Well, that information is quite helpful. Apparently, due to your hybrid natures, your powers are intertwined, perhaps?" he mused.

"Maybe. But that's not the only weird thing that happened that day," I continued to confess, and went on to divulge the secret about feeling her emotions.

It typically took a lot to shock Orion, but it seemed this did it. Silence fell. "Chrome, you do realize what you're saying has never been accounted for before, right?"

"I do realize that. Why do you think I haven't said anything until now, Uncle?" I snapped, annoyed that they didn't believe me.

Orion exhaled, poured a pinch of bourbon, and then tossed it back. "Okay, I believe you," he conceded. "Does she know?"

I shook my head. "Not yet. I can't bring myself to tell her, with everything she's learned and has been through. She'll likely feel like it's an invasion. And it is. Which is why I'm bringing it up now, to learn how to control it."

"What did your contact say?" Onyx inquired.

"He said he'd look into it, but it was new to him, so he didn't have anything for me."

Orion leaned back in his seat, head falling back on the chair. "Anything else?"

"Just that this magic-draining dark magic is killing off Arcadia. The beastie-bear is apparently considered a regal and honored animal there," I explained. "But we do think there is a link between the Endarkened and the magic that the Tempests are wielding."

"And if we fail in stopping Forest from opening the portal? Then what?" Orion pushed to get to the crux of it all.

"That's the thing," I said. "The magic they're working with won't just be opening a portal. The power is designed to obliterate the entire veil altogether, plopping Arcadia down right on top of this world. Our worlds would be merged. Tempests will attempt to drain what magic exists here. The poisonous residue left from their magic will infect this world, and the humans wouldn't stand a chance."

"Wonderful," Onyx hummed sarcastically, sinking into his seat.

Aella and River waited on me outside my room after my meeting with Onyx and Orion. Aella stood with her long, dark tresses full of voluminous tight curls resting on her waist. Her arms hung relaxed at her sides, but a hint of anxiety glinted in her eyes. River Oakland propped her shoulder against the doorframe, arms crossed over her chest, wearing her usual spearing expression that rivaled Gray's.

"Ladies," I greeted, my tone languid as I expected their pushback.

"We need to talk," River demanded, while Aella nodded in agreement before casting her eyes to the floor.

I sighed, running my fingers through my hair. Not out of annoyance by their arrival, as it was expected, but I had hoped to grab a few minutes alone with my violin before showing Gray to the dining hall for dinner. "Of course," I said, and used my magic to unlock the metal mechanism that composed the lock on my door. "After you."

River didn't hesitate to stride through the doorway and make a beeline to my bed, where she jumped and plopped on top of the mattress. Aella moved like a wispy shadow, easing inside and sitting in a chair in front of my desk.

"What's up?" I asked, glancing between the two before sitting on the sofa in the living area.

It didn't surprise me that River spoke up first, her bright red lipstick vibrant against her brown skin and sleek black hair. "I know most of us here are happy about the princess's arrival, but let's not forget there are a few that are rightfully skeptical." At the tilt of my head, River rolled her eyes. "Not me, I think I'll actually like her. But some of the quieter ones here feel their opinion matters, too," she explained before casting an encouraging look to Aella.

Aella nodded but refused to meet my eyes. "I don't trust her. I mean, she's...an *assassin* and the king's daughter. She is known for killing our kind and wanting your head. What's to say she's not putting on an act to destroy us from within? Like the Kinetic delegates did all those years ago."

I leaned forward, my forearms braced on my knees, and offered her a soft smile. "I hear you, Aella. And I understand where your worries stem from. You're validated in that," I assured her. I'd always made an effort to allow those here to feel like they could come to me with concerns, to be heard, and to have a voice in their home, to be the opposite of Forest's ironfist rule.

A small breeze swept around Aella, lifting her long, textured hair in its wake, offering comfort to her in its embrace. "It's just...are you sure that this is wise? To let the enemy inside our home?" she asked. She may be a fierce and a formidable warrior, but Aella didn't like opposing me about decisions made regarding the Hollow.

I thought on my words carefully before answering. "The king tried to have her killed when she failed to kill me." River looked taken aback, while Aella stared at me with a stoicism that matched my own. "I don't know all the details, only that he had her drink poisoned with redfern at her birthday revel. He concealed the truth about her hybrid nature her entire life, and I think it's safe to assume he was less than warm as a father to her growing up." I took a deep breath to calm the surge of anger that shot through my body at the thought, only fueling my desire to kill him.

"She only learned of her origins two hours ago. And the remorse she feels for..." I trailed off, remembering the rush of overbearing guilt that sat heavy on her heart when she realized she had been killing pointlessly this entire time. It wasn't much different than what I'd experienced when I learned the entire truth myself. "She feels duped by her father. He's been lying to her and their people, using and controlling her for her entire life. Not only that, but he killed someone close to her and blamed me for it. You can bet she has redirected her rage at this point."

Aella exhaled and looked away with a clenched jaw, an internal battle going on within her. The breeze picked up around her as her element responded to her conflicting emotions. The look in River's eyes hardened, her hands balling into fists at her sides.

"I don't expect you to trust her right away, Aella. You have every right to feel the way you do. But at this point, Gray has nowhere else to go. The Warrior Guild is hunting her now, and without connections to the militia, the black market won't hesitate to capture her and throw her into slavery."

"What if she throws off the balance here? This is our home, our refuge." Aella's hands fiddled in her lap as she worked to remain poised in the desk chair.

I offered her another gentle smile. "I don't have the answer for that right now. All I know is we need to give her a chance to breathe for the first time. I'm sure she's having a hard time coming to grips with everything she's learned and experienced in recent days. Give her time to adjust to her new reality, and then we'll play it by ear. But know that your opinions and feelings matter here. Everyone's do. If she ever became a problem, I'd handle her myself. I may be the leader, but I'll never be a dictator."

Aella exhaled and then nodded. "Okay. Thank you, Chrome," she said, her voice gentle and tinted with relief. "I'll try to give her a chance, but she is going to have to work for my trust."

"Noted. We'll see if she lives up to the challenge."

River met my gaze in solidarity, silently conveying her confidence in me. I dipped my head in acknowledgement, to which she returned.

"Is there anything else I can help you two with?" I asked them.

River chewed on the inside of her lip, highlighting the sharp features of her face. "Nope. See you in the dining hall. Is the princess coming?"

"Yes, I'll be escorting her there shortly."

River nodded. "Sweet. See you, then."

Chapter 30

GRAY

T he dining hall led outside to a glittering swimming pool, reminding me of liquified black crystal and tempting me with the call of comfort and relaxation. The surrounding landscape was a combination of greenery and autumn shades. Climbing vines created a stunning oasis with sprawling hills and forestry in the background.

I'd grown used to the silence that accompanied me on my journey from the King's Palace, so the loud chatter and abundance of people overwhelmed me. Despite the noise, a waterfall cascading against boulders into a pool of water acted as a balm to ease my nerves.

"Come," Chrome said without room for argument.

I planted my feet in place, and my eyebrows rose to my hairline at his clipped and demanding tone. "Excuse me, but I'm not a dog you can bark orders at."

Chrome looked over his shoulder, meeting my eyes. His lip angled upward in amusement. "Good." He walked away toward an expansive table lining the wall to my right.

I scoffed, shaking my head. At the sight of so many people, my chest constricted, my palms becoming sweaty. So many unfamiliar faces who probably hated my existence more than the Kinetics did looked back at me.

I slipped on my mask of indifference—my armor—feeling the stares and sensing the whispers as I weaved through tables to join Chrome.

Gazes burned into my back as my eyes widened at the amount of food displayed on the table. Savory, seasoned dishes of all types triggered an angry growl from my stomach, reminding me how hungry I was despite the turkey we'd cooked the night before.

"Do I need to be concerned the food is laced with redfern?" I asked. Chrome stood to my left, hunched over the table as he piled his plate.

My eyes and nose were bigger than my stomach. I scooped a massive heap of buttery mashed potatoes, carrots, corn, roast beef, and any other colorful veggie that was within my arm's reach.

A dimple I hadn't noticed before outlined the smirk that crept up his face. A shadow coated his jaw from the lack of shaving while on our journey. But it was a good look on him. He kept his eyes on the food as he said, "Come now, little savage. I'm insulted you think I'd resort to trickery to kill you. If I wanted you dead, I'd have a blade in your chest while staring into those fake blue eyes of yours."

I angled my head at Chrome, my heart racing at the sight of his dimpled, crooked smile. I definitely hated myself for that. My only response was a mumbled, "I don't have fake eyes." I mindlessly plopped more food onto my plate, feeling the heat rise to my cheeks. Why in the actual fuck was I blushing? Since when did I blush? "Asshole."

"Oh, but you do," Chrome said, that face growing ever cockier—like he *knew*. "The necklace?"

The Elemental glamour. I paused mid-scoop. "Right." There was way too much food on my plate. I felt guilty knowing I would waste a portion when most people outside the Hollow killed each other for a small fraction of what I would leave behind.

Finally, Chrome straightened, holding his packed dish in front of him, and angled his head toward me. "Sit anywhere you like. We don't bite. Unless..." He slanted his brow in a suggestion of how he was going to finish that sentence.

"I swear on everything alive on this godsforsaken planet, Chrome. If you finish by saying, 'unless you want me to...' I *will* change my mind and gut you where you stand."

He barked a laugh, "You can try...*again*." And then he disappeared into the midst of the tables.

Fuck him.

I took a deep breath and scanned the dining area for an available spot to sit, preferably alone.

The uneasiness coiled a path from my heart to my stomach, cinching tight at the curious stares that averted once I met them. Since Chrome was the only person I knew, I searched the sea of people for his chromatic hair. It didn't take long to spot him at a table in front of the glass door overlooking the pool.

He wasn't sitting alone. I ignored the familiar hands of anxiety threatening to trip me in front of the foreign crowd. If they didn't already, they no doubt searched for a reason to hate me.

I stayed alert and held my posture straight, ignoring the desperate need to look at the floor. I weaved through the tables as if it were an obstacle course, careful to avoid corners and chair legs that poked out.

Finding an empty spot on the end I set my plate down and quietly took my seat. The chatter ceased, but I pretended to ignore it as I dug into the food that called to my soul.

Someone cleared their throat. I peered up from my plate, scanning the golden faces and extraordinary eyes. Chrome was smug, enjoying the sight of me flailing outside of my comfort zone. Asshole.

With my mouth full of buttery potatoes, I looked around, seeking the throat-clearer. I recognized the petite beauty from earlier—Aella. My faux confidence snuffed out like a dying flame. I'd always found other women to be judgmental, scrutinizing even. At least toward me. And I'd felt her discernment—distrust—from the moment she'd laid eyes on me.

The deep male voice from earlier broke through my scattered thoughts. "I'm so fucking happy you're finally here, Princess."

I spotted Onyx sitting across from Chrome, a few chairs down from me. His orange currents raced up his arms as he propped his chin on his fists. The excited smile he beamed at me was genuine. I didn't know how to respond.

"Seriously," Onyx said, glancing at Chrome, "we've been waiting years to get you both here. Can't wait for training tomorrow. Which reminds me," he paused, lowering his forearms to bear on the table, leaning forward. "Did you ever surpass Golden? Please tell me you kicked his ass." His amber gaze pleaded with me to confirm.

The smallest of smiles betrayed me. "Yes." The memory of plunging my dagger hilt-deep into his gut flitted through my mind. "I should've killed him, but..." Smokey, Onyx's father, had stopped me.

"At least you knocked down his bloated ego a bit," he responded with a quick nod.

I returned to spearing the juicy, tender asparagus. It melted in my mouth. I'd never known it could be so savory. The food at the palace was good, but there was no extra effort put into it. At least, not mine. There'd never been any...*heart* in it.

"Gray," Chrome said, gentle authority lacing his voice. I pulled my enamored gaze from my plate to peer at him. "I want you to meet everyone here. You've already met Onyx."

Onyx waggled his fingers in a wave as he grinned.

I scanned the table and recognized many of the same faces from the meeting upon my arrival. Setting my fork down, I sat up straight in my chair and met their gazes.

"I am Kodiak Vines. It's a pleasure to finally meet you, Princess." The bronzed, beefy man from the meeting greeted. Appearing no younger than his mid-twenties, he offered a gentle smile. "I am the Hollow's Warrior General and cartographer. So, I'll be a part of your combat training. I'm at your service, just as I am for Chrome." He dipped his head in a solemn bow.

The man sitting next to him spoke next. Underneath that golden sheen, his skin was the deepest of umber. His irises were solid black, void of any light or color, rimmed with twin silver rings. "I'm Void Halcyon, Top Advisor and Elemental warrior. I'll be leading your training. Welcome." Void's baritone voice was clipped as he spoke. A thick loc fell over his muscular shoulder as he squinted at me for a beat—as if he saw me but didn't at the same time—before silently returning to his food.

"I'm River. Emissary." My eyes met the bright violet, assessing stare piercing me from across the table. "Welcome, Princess. I think we'll get along just fine." She wore her black hair pulled back into a sleek ponytail at the nape. Her prominent jawline highlighted the severe expression on her Native features.

I recognized her from the meeting, but there, she'd remained silent and observant. She shared physical traits with the mischievous, fire-eyed boy with the wicked grin but lacked any of his playfulness. Siblings, perhaps?

I gave her a tight smile and a nod. She swallowed and returned to her plate, picking at her vegetables with a fork.

"I'm Aella Wisp, the Hollow's Warrior Captain," Aella guided a springy curl behind her ear. I wondered if it was out of habit. "Welcome," she said in a stiff tone, offering a tight smile.

Silence reigned over the table while they waited for me to say something. The soothing sound of the water crashing to the boulders put me in a temporary trance. I wasn't great at public speaking, so I said, "Thanks for having me in your home. Your secrets are safe with me." And I meant it.

Chrome's quicksilver eyes appraised me. The barest hint of a smile ghosted his sharp features. He dipped his head the slightest fraction. No one else noticed his silent exchange that read, "Well done. Welcome home."

My chest ached with homesickness. Homesick only for the bright spots of my former life. Would I ever find a place to truly call my home? Where I could be accepted and not ostracized? The few friends I held dear were most likely dead or imprisoned. Labeling Cotton as a friend was a stretch, at least prior to my revel. The way he came through for me in my escape not only surprised me, but warmed me toward him, regardless of his motivations.

Conversation resumed at the table, so I focused on the food a divine being must've created, getting sucked into the memories of my past.

I hated the unknown. The past might've been painful, but at least it was constant. I knew what to expect. My longing for Slate grew stifling as I tried to bury it with mouthfuls of buttery bread and potatoes. Since I was fourteen, he'd been my safe space, my comfort. I needed him more than ever as I sat and dined in what I'd once considered enemy territory.

Spearing a forkful of green beans, I allowed myself to be swept away in the memory of Slate's comfort, imagining he was beside me now.

Tears slid down my cheeks in the shadows of the school gymnasium, wondering what was wrong with me. I hugged my knees to my chest. Why did my father hate me? Why did I struggle so hard to make friends? I glamoured my currents and hair color from the human kids, so what was it that had always made me a target? Weren't princesses supposed to be loved and considered popular? At least, that's what the fairytales made you believe.

"Princesses aren't supposed to cry."

I popped my head up, adrenaline surging through my veins at the unexpected visitor. I jumped to my feet and turned to see the handsome, boyish face of Slate Helair, a well-known and well-liked Kinetic—even among the human students. I swiped my cheeks with the palms of my hands in haste to hide the evidence of my weakness. "I wasn't crying." My stuffed-up nose betrayed my lie.

A soft expression crossed his features. "You were. And it's okay that you were. You're entitled to that—everyone is. It's just that..." Slate's shoulders relaxed as he reached out a hand to me. "You deserve to have a shoulder to lean on when you do." His natural hair was the hue of a wet stone, but it was now glamoured a dark brown, and his sun-kissed skin bore no gold currents on his arms.

"Why would I do that? Like you said, princesses aren't supposed to cry. It's weak."

Slate moved to take the seat beside the one I'd abandoned, patting the spot with his hand. "I never said it was weak."

I lowered into the seat beside him, adjusting the navy, pleated uniform skirt. I looked down at my feet, and fought the urge to hide the bruises on my legs from my father's frustration that morning that were slow to heal due to the bracelet. My face heated as I glanced up and caught Slate pulling his attention to my eyes, away from my legs. He didn't mention them.

"I hear how the commoners treat you. And the human kids here," he said, shaking his head, "they're fucking ignorant. The girls are jealous of you, and the guys are afraid to show interest because of it. But no one deserves to be treated the way you are. Please know that not everyone dislikes you. We're just...hesitant to show it. Your dad wouldn't approve because it would be considered to be undermining his authority in his eyes."

I shrugged, sniffling. "It doesn't matter."

Slate cupped my cheeks, making me face his genuine determination. "It does matter, Princess Gray. Your light is too bright to be dimmed."

My heart fractured. For once, I felt seen. My jaw trembled as I fought the onslaught of ugly tears that threatened to fall.

Slate's hazel stare held mine, seeing all my broken shards laid bare. "Let me lend you some of my strength."

The dam burst in my chest, unleashing my pent-up pain at the first sign of empathy from someone. I didn't fight him as he wrapped an arm around my shoulder and tucked me into his side while I sobbed.

"After you get this out, let's go set everyone straight, shall we? Nobody will fuck with you after today," Slate said in a firm, yet gentle tone. "If you ever feel alone, know that I'll always be there as your friend, my princess."

I kept my head down as Onyx burst into loud laughter at some quip from River.

My chest constricted at the first memory of Slate, and how much I missed his warm magic powered by light energy. I missed his beaming smile whenever I walked into a room, his grounding hugs, undying support, and love. No matter how skilled a fighter I became, he'd always remained protective.

After that day, Slate worked to build me up—giving me the confidence that had always been absent. He taught me even though my father worked to turn our people against me, I could still make them respect me. And most importantly, he taught me what unconditional love was.

The day my father coldly broke the news of Slate's death to me, I went into denial. Once the reality set in that he wasn't coming home, I crumbled, becoming lost and directionless. Broken. Alone. I hardened my heart and constructed walls of steel to keep everyone out. And I vowed to kill the man who took him from me.

When he died, the wolves in the King's Palace tried to circle again, but I wasn't the weak girl I'd once been. They quickly learned I didn't need Slate as a guardian.

And with Slate came his younger sister, Hazel. Not long after we got together, I met her, and she became like a sister of my own. Her meek nature complemented Slate's outgoing one. She helped ground me when facing my father, Amethyst, and those who didn't want me as their future queen.

I missed the constant bickering between those two. Hazel always had a remark that had me clutching my stomach with laughter.

I glanced up, noting Chrome leaning back in his seat. He sat detached from the conversations as he observed the waterfall with scrunched brows, lost in the trance of his own thoughts.

As if he felt my stare, he swiveled his head to look at me. The smallest of somber smiles inched up the corners before he turned his attention back to his plate.

Chapter 31

CHROME

I sat in the heated pool with a strained smile. It hadn't been three hours since being out of close proximity to the Kinetic Princess before the whispers of my affliction began to call. It started with an itch beneath the skin, a restless yearning for oblivion. At first, I panicked, but I did my best to enjoy the company of my friends as they celebrated my return to the Hollow.

Princess Gray chose to stay in her room, which was on the opposite end of the vast lodge. I couldn't blame her for it. She had a lot to process, and socializing had never really been her thing—much less with people she'd been raised to kill at all costs. It would take her time to deconstruct her father's programming about the world and herself. She especially needed to come to terms with the many hard truths she'd just faced.

My eyes landed on an Elemental man on the opposite side of the pool. His eyes were haunted, but a lightness spread in my chest at the sight of the slave I'd freed from the scorse the night I'd fought in the cage. A small smile pulled at the edges of my mouth, knowing Dash had followed through and helped guide him home.

Onyx's loud laughter rang out as he jumped out of the hot tub and began scaling the backside of the lodge to the roof. He was already drunk and determined to prove himself with River's dare.

"Triple backflip! Off the roof! And into the pool! Watch me, River. One of these days you'll stop betting against me," he said with a grunt as he pulled himself upright on the edge of the roof, turning his back to us.

As much as I wanted to stick around and watch Onyx eat shit, I needed to get the fuck out of here. The claws of madness brought on the echoes of that dreaded cackle. I didn't need to be around the others for that. Just as Onyx counted to three, I bolted out of the hot tub while all eyes were on him, making a quick escape back inside the lodge. I sought out the bar that had once been a vacated basement, grabbed two bottles of rum, then rushed to my room, where I strove for solace in my violin.

My bow glided across the strings of my violin in seamless, sharp strokes. I didn't have to think. The notes were second nature to me, allowing me to fall into the melody and get lost in the haunting and riveting tune that mirrored my emotions.

I downed several shots of rum in fast succession, hoping to get ahead of the impending decline of my mental state. By the time I was halfway through the first song, my panic morphed into hopelessness that transferred into the music.

I'd foolishly tricked myself into thinking I'd escaped the darkness that ravaged me. I'd dealt with it for years now, but after healing when I arrived at the Hollow, it seemed to settle, allowing me to build real relationships and trust with those around me for the first time in my life. But in recent months, the affliction decided that enough was enough and began to expedite my fall into madness. It wanted me wholly in its grasp, and it was tired of waiting around.

Then came Gray, and her nearness seemed to lock the entity away, freeing me from my internal suffering. I didn't realize I needed to remain in close proximity to her as I had when we had been traveling. Like a dumbass, I'd hoped that just having her here at the Hollow and on the premises would be enough to keep the affliction at bay. However, on my first night back and on the opposite side of the lodge as her, the darkness crept back into my periphery, offering taunts of my impending downfall.

It would be easy to go to Gray's room with any excuse to be near her, but I refused. This wasn't her battle nor her responsibility, so I rejected the idea of thrusting this burden onto her shoulders on top of everything else. No, I'd find a way to handle my shit. At least until we stopped Forest—ideally with his death.

High notes soared with an ever-present quiver that sounded as if it were seconds away from breaking apart altogether. It paralleled my high moments during my mania, living off the thirst for violence. And just when it seemed the notes would falter and give way, they dropped to the lowest of lows, flowing into the minor notes that captured the sense of my depressive state that trailed closely behind my unhinged madness.

A distant knock sounded at my door, but I didn't dare pull myself from the music's embrace. My despair poured into the room with a forlorn heart, exposing my pain for all to see if they looked close enough. I wouldn't hide that. Not that I would offer it up unprompted, but my room was my safe space, and I wasn't apologetic for my very mortal emotions—regardless of the fact I was a leader.

The knock sounded again, this time harder than the last. Without missing a note, I unlocked the door with my element, allowing whoever was on the other side entrance. In my peripheral, the door opened slowly as if whoever entered approached with caution.

I expected to see dark hair flecked with stars. Instead of Onyx, I was greeted by Kodiak's hulking frame. I glanced at him, not stopping the song until it fell from its crescendo to its finish. I rested the violin and bow in my lap, already feeling the itch return. I ignored it and offered a forced smile to my friend. My head swam for a moment from the rum, so I closed my eyes for a moment to adjust.

"Kodiak," I greeted in a tone chippier than I felt. "To what do I owe you, my friend?"

Kodiak's size made my expansive suite feel cramped. All muscle and height, he was huge. But his heart was just as big as his brain. Out of all of us, he was the softest and most caring.

"Just came by to check on you," Kodiak said, his voice a deep timber. "Did something happen in the pool?"

I waved him off with false assurance. He always was one to note the small things in others. "No, nothing at all. Just craved the quietude and my violin after that shitty mission. Nothing to worry about."

Kodiak noted the bottle of rum that was a quarter low with a head dip. "Mind if I get a shot? Despite the fact it's not vodka," he asked with a wry grin.

I poured us each a shot, handing one to him. "To your safe return. Good to have you back, Prince." We tapped our glasses and downed them, the warmth spreading across my chest like a blanket.

I cleared my throat. "Tell me why you're really here, Kodiak. Did Orion send you? Or Onyx?"

Kodiak frowned, looking perplexed. "No," he responded. "I don't know what bothers you; that is your business. But I figured you didn't need to suffer alone." He wore a genuine expression of empathy, his eyes matching the warmth of his deep bronze skin beneath the gold layer. "I'm just here as your friend."

I wasn't sure if it was from the alcohol consumption or the fact that I wasn't sure how much longer I'd be able to share these moments with those closest to me in this way, but my throat tightened, and tears threatened to fill my eyes. I clenched my jaw to fight it. "Thank you," I whispered, dropping my head.

Kodiak rested a hand on my shoulder, offering his support. "So, the princess..." he hedged, prompting me to elaborate.

My shoulders shook from my chuckle. "What do *you* think of her?"

My friend removed his hand. Moving the desk chair in front of my bed, he took a seat. "She's...interesting. But I believe she'll be a great asset and, one day, a strong leader."

Relief flooded my chest at his approval because, at some point, she'd be the sole leader of my people. It was important she had their support, considering she fled from a kingdom of those who sought her demise. "I think she will, too."

"I've looked forward to the day we had both of you here since I was a child. Many of us have. Our stolen heirs. Finally home. I just hate the damage that's been done in the meantime."

I nodded. "As do I. But your support means the world. She'll need your kindness to get acclimated so we can build a foundation of trust between her and our people."

Kodiak smiled, the dark beard lining his jaw highlighting his white teeth. "It'll be my honor." Scrunching his face, he reached for the bottle of rum, but his distaste didn't hinder him from pouring another shot. "I don't know how you drink this," he muttered as he threw back the light amber liquid, then shook his head.

"Vodka might as well be rubbing alcohol," I said, wincing.

"You never tasted the kind that came from my lineage. It was refined and smooth. What I'd do to get my hands on it again," he said wistfully. After a second, he nodded to the violin still perched in my lap. "Don't let me stop you. I can sit, drink, and enjoy your music."

I ran my fingertips over the neck of my instrument, appreciating the smooth texture that always helped ground me. With a nod, I picked it and the bow back up, beginning another mournful melody. This one represented my acceptance of the losses I was doomed to suffer after finally finding true acceptance and love.

Chapter 32

GRAY

The next morning, I arrived heavy-eyed in the combat training arena. Pink hues peeked on the horizon, and the cold air seeped into my bones. I desperately craved the warm comfort of the jacuzzi in my bathroom oasis. The leggings and long-sleeved tee I wore provided little protection from the chill.

The arena was yet another wooden structure built by the Elementals. Chrome explained this to me yesterday during our tour of the property. It wasn't designed like the lodge, where it breathed comfort and home. This place smelled of musk and vengeance.

Like the lodge, beautiful log beams lined the high, vaulted ceilings, but that's where the similarities ended. There were no wall windows, decorative staircases, or natural oasis embracing its comforting arms around the building. Windows were kept to a minimum and installed near the ceiling. It was an open arena split up into designated sections for training. This place was designed for war prep.

Dummies bordered the oak walls. White lines marked the entire floor with sparring circles. A hallway led to the entry of the training room, where all the weapons were stored and cleaned.

Rows upon rows of built-in nooks stored a cache of various small blades near the dummies. Sorted by their blade styles and sizes, I selected an array to test—three knives, two daggers, and five throwing stars—and slid them into my weapons belt. I backed up to the marker line on the floor to stand near the opposite wall.

I hadn't stretched, but it didn't matter. In real-world situations, I never got the chance to warm up before a fight. I wielded the knife in my hand, growing familiar with its hilt in my palm. Its blade had a slight curve to it, making it different from what I was accustomed to. The throwing blades Kinetics used are shaped similarly to the kunai. Its blade weight was heavier, whereas the one I held was lighter and more balanced.

I closed my eyes and breathed in deeply, imagining the knife's tip piercing my target between the eyes. I shifted my body into the proper stance, holding the hilt in the correct grip. When I opened my eyes, I released my breath. On the exhale, I launched the knife with power and ease. It cleaved the air apart while it sailed and rotated into the target. It didn't hit the perfect mark, but it was close. The curve and the weight difference in the blade threw me off.

Void's baritone voice vibrated through the weapons' area. "Not bad for changing blade styles."

Elementals strolled in as others prepped their blades and stretched their muscles to begin their training for the day.

Void stood off to the side of the blades' cache with his dark, corded arms crossed over his chest. His vacant stare assessed me, and I squirmed under his scrutiny. He'd pulled his locs back into a low ponytail that draped down his back.

I shrugged. "Throwing blades have always been my favorite."

He maintained his vacant stare. "You are too unaware of your surroundings," he finally said after several quiet beats.

I raised an eyebrow and shifted my stance to square my shoulders. "That is not true."

"I have to disagree, Princess. You were trained in the art of combat and to wield your Kinetic powers, but they absolutely failed you in the art of awareness. You have enough to get by, but it would be most beneficial for you to improve those skills."

"My ability allows me to sense any movement, sound—" I began.

"Yes," Void cut in, "but that's the problem. When rendered without your abilities, you're left vulnerable. You depend on your abilities too much. From Chrome's account, every situation you found yourself in, you were caught unaware without your abilities. It's almost as if your father designed that little programming flaw as a failsafe for him to exploit. It's your weakness. So, let's fix it."

My stony mask fell into place as I combed through his words, reflecting on all the events that led me here. I'd been unaware when Chrome—posing as Griffin—got the best of me. I'd been unaware of the redfern in my drink at the revel. I'd been unaware when ambushed outside of the tattoo parlor, while Chrome had already picked up on it.

Was it possible I could've avoided the beastie-bear's paralyzing blow if I'd been more aware?

I shoved my bruised pride aside as I studied Void. He emitted an unsaid strength. I wondered why he was so qualified for this sort of thing. "So, what makes your training any different from a master trainer?" The question wasn't meant to be snarky; I was genuinely curious.

Void took a step forward, then another. Each step, meticulous, until he stood inches in front of me. He breathed in a slow, deep breath. "Look into my eyes. What do you see?" he asked.

It was uncomfortable, staring into a stranger's eyes with intensity. Aside from the black eyes ringed in silver, his gaze remained vacant, devoid of life. I gasped. "Nothing. I don't...see... anything." I searched between each of his eyes, trying to figure out what I was missing.

He gave a curt nod. "Exactly. It is because I can't see. I'm blind."

"That's impossible," I said, shaking my head. But he knew I'd almost hit my mark... "How? Elementals can heal..."

"It was a Kinetic ability that eradicated my vision." His expression was flat. "But it is why I'm able to help you with this skill set."

Understanding slammed into me as I overcame the shock of a blind Elemental. I'd never heard of a case where either race was robbed of their senses since we could heal. It shouldn't be possible.

"What kind of power caused it?" I asked, curiosity getting the best of me.

Void angled his head to the side, his lips pursed as if he debated whether to share that information. It was clearly a sensitive topic for him, and I didn't have that right. But I needed to know what my people were capable of.

After several silent moments, he finally responded, "Ultraviolet."

I nodded, thinking back to the blistering burns on my back at the palace in my escape. The Kinetic responsible for Void's vision must've wielded it in light form. "I'm sorry that happened to you. It never occurred to me we couldn't heal those kinds of injuries."

Void cleared his throat. "Perhaps it was the black crystal-laced arrow that sliced into my arm that didn't allow me to heal."

I released a shuddering breath, unsure of what to say, so I scanned the training area around us. Elementals sparred in pairs, some even in groups of three or four, using different blades and various styles of fighting. It was familiar from my run-ins with them in the past, but I couldn't replicate it.

The fighting styles were very fluid, graceful, and swift. It involved a lot of quick hits that tired the opponent while they spent their energy on heavy blows. It's been rumored that Ancient Asian cultures learned and adapted the Elemental fighting styles centuries ago. While the Ancient Romans learned and adapted from the Kinetics. And the more I observed their sparring styles, the more I wanted to believe the stories.

"Before we start, I want to assess where you are," Void said, drawing my attention from the sparring groups around the arena. "Close your eyes."

I hesitated for a moment, the instinct to mistrust his intentions stiffening my posture. I twisted my chest away from him and narrowed my eyes.

"Relax." Void's voice was deep and calm, soothing the rushing waves of the rising tide of fear. "I need to see what level of awareness you hold."

I exhaled and nodded. "Okay." Ever so slowly, I closed my eyes, leaving me with only the sounds of the combat echoing around me.

Before he could even finish, a thick arm locked around my throat from behind, putting me in a chokehold. On instinct, my eyes flew open, and I jabbed an elbow behind me, aimed at his ribs. He didn't flinch. I braced my arm for another jab, but Void released me.

I whirled on him, trying to gasp for air with subtlety. "What the fuck was that?" I refused to touch my throat, not wanting to show that the sneak attack shook me.

"A test," Void said, shrugging his broad, corded shoulders.

"That was some bullshit test," I hissed.

"Your father purposefully left out awareness training. There is no other excuse for you to be so ungodly ill-prepared," Void said.

My breaths came in ragged and fast, seething at being humiliated and beaten with ease. "The joke's on me, right? I'm so glad you got a good laugh at my expense."

Void stood there in his quiet stoicism. His vacant gaze pierced right through me, his jaw clenching. "Listen, *Princess*," he snapped. His deep tone dropped a few more octaves with the quiet anger that rolled through his body. "I'm not doing this for my amusement. Training an already highly skilled enemy assassin isn't something that I'd do for fucking laughs. I'm doing this because it was an order. I'm doing this with the small hope that you have a heart inside that cold-ass exterior of yours. Chrome and Orion may blindly trust you, but I don't. I have a hard time believing that someone who has been brainwashed by a psychopath her entire life has suddenly seen the light and wants to throw us a bone.

"However," Void's voice grew sharper, "since I'm not in charge around here, I'm to follow orders even if I disagree with them. Perhaps you can learn something if you get your head out of your ass. And let's pray I don't live to regret it."

My mouth formed a slight O, and I angled my head to the side. "That..." I began, "is the most I've ever heard you speak," I quipped. It was my only thought. The image I'd conjured of him being this calm, stout man of very few words conflicted with his emotional rant. It didn't fit. I was too stunned to be angry.

"And it'll likely remain that way. Now," he said, blowing out a breath. "Let's go again. Close your eyes and stop me."

I didn't stop Void. Not once. He proved to me time and time again that my sense of awareness outside of my magic was next to none. To say I was beyond frustrated was a vast understatement. How had I allowed this to happen?

Hours later, my body and mind ached from the training session. Every time, he had me pinned on my back with the breath knocked out of me before I could focus my senses.

Void insisted I feel for the air's movements, which I did. He embodied stealth and silence to the point the air never alerted me. When I failed, he told me to use my nose to track which direction his scent moved. But he was too swift. By the time I caught it, he'd already slammed me on my back, my arms pinned above my head. Finally, he told me to use my hearing. But he was silent as well.

Void ensured that with practice, I'd be able to tune into my senses much quicker. Until then, I decided I needed to break his holds.

I left the training arena, taking fast strides to the dining hall. My stomach danced in excitement as I bypassed the liquid black pool and strolled inside. Once again, savory aromas flooded my nose. The other Elementals stared at me as I walked to the arranged food. Loud chatter died as I passed by tables. I pretended not to notice or care, being sure to carry myself with a little extra swagger instead.

Once I filled my plate, I searched for an empty table. This time, there was one available. Achievement rang through my chest as I claimed that golden spot and slid into my chair. Solitude. It's what I did best. I could eat in peace. I could...

Another plate clunked on the spot across from me. I looked up to find Onyx with his inky black hair, glittering like the clearest summer night, plop in the seat with casual indifference. My heart sank. I *really* wanted to eat alone.

"So glad I caught you on your lunch break," Onyx said, flashing a quick, beaming smile that'd made all the Kinetic girls swoon. He dug into his mac and cheese like a man starved. His orange currents illuminated his forearms, causing a pang of longing in my chest.

I looked around. The rest of the seats were empty. It was just me. "Why would you want to catch me on my lunch break?"

Onyx looked up from his loaded plate, looking like a chipmunk with puffy cheeks. An eyebrow quirked at my question. "B'cos..." he dragged out, the food hindering his speech. He waved his fork around in dramatic effect. "We're friends?"

I fell back in my seat. "Whoa, slow down, big guy. We hardly qualify as friends, don't you think?" Fuck, why couldn't I just eat by myself? Awkward situations drained me.

Without a second's hesitation, he said, "Oh, but we will be, Gray. We will. Just wait and see." He wagged and pointed his fork at me with utter seriousness.

I rolled my lips inward, my brows raised to my forehead. "Right. Because we're both Kinetics who've flipped over to the dark side?"

"I'm a Kinetic. You..." Onyx said, swallowing his food. "You are a hybrid. But yeah, I won't lie. It's cool having someone else here who gets it." He shrugged.

"I feel like my experience was different from most Kinetics," I said, picking at the food, pushing it around on my plate. "Being owned by the king didn't make for a very pleasant childhood."

Onyx nodded, his eyes softening. He looked back down at his food. "Yeah, I remember."

My chest tightened, hoping he hadn't ever witnessed any of my father's punishments, but I knew better.

Another chair squeaked against the floor on my right, followed by a plate landing on the tabletop. A feminine body slid into the seat with care. Surprise filled me to find River sitting there looking like an heiress. She was so striking it made me want to sit up straight in my seat.

Frustration clawed at my chest. My plan to sit in peace without the stress of others around to assess me, ogle me—like I was a damn new pet that needed to be trained—got flushed down the toilet.

I was no longer hungry. Which sucked because I was to meet Chrome afterward to work on my Elemental abilities. Any black crystal residue that my father had ordered into my food should be passed by now, allowing for that side to manifest. It became hard to breathe as I recalled that reality.

"Calm down. We won't kill you unless you give us a reason to," River drawled, eyeing her plate. Unlike Onyx's, hers wasn't piled with every food option available. Instead, she only had four small portions that were evenly dispersed. The vegetables didn't touch each other—not even close.

I watched her delicately drive her fork into a few green beans as if she would break the plate were she to add just the slightest pressure. Her jet-black hair was once again pulled into a sleek, low bun at the base of her neck. The part down the middle could cut a diamond it was so sharp.

"I'm not worried about that." I was fifty percent sure of that fact.

"If he's bothering you," she said, lifting her fork in Onyx's direction, who snapped his head to attention, "just ignore him. He's like a puppy that won't stop nipping at your heels until you give it attention. And once you do, it's game over."

I chuckled. Onyx's mouth opened wide at the insult. He looked positively affronted. He clutched his chest. "How *could* you? See if I smuggle anymore of that hair plaster you are so fond of, River."

River simply rolled her eyes. Thick black lashes nearly touched her perfectly-shaped brows. "Oh, please. You enjoy the thrill of procuring that gel as much as I love organizing the weapons cache."

Onyx threw his fork down. I assumed it was for dramatic effect, but River didn't seem phased in the least. "I enjoy it because I value our friendship. A friendship you clearly exploit for your own gain."

"Has anyone ever told you to stop whining?" She gave him a tight smile.

"You love me." Onyx shifted his light amber gaze toward me. He smiled and shook his head. "Don't let her fool you. She adores me. Probably is secretly in love with me, but she doesn't want the world to know she has one of those things called a heart." He shrugged and returned to his oversized meal.

Oh shit.

I volleyed my eyes back and forth between the two, expecting things to turn ugly. River just cracked another smile to herself but didn't respond.

That left me wanting to shift uncomfortably in my seat. To avoid that, I pretended to be interested in our surroundings. My eyes landed on the black pool outside.

"Does anyone actually swim in that pool?"

Onyx looked up at me. His throat bobbed as he swallowed his food. "Yeah. All the time. Mainly at night."

"Why at night?"

"It's just better," he said with a shrug, a smile hiding some inside humor underneath.

"It's also heated. So, it feels great after a long day. There are also healing properties within it that soothe a sore body after a hard day of training, or a mission to the Earthen hellhole," River explained further. "Some people like to get unabashedly drunk and perform childish acts all in the name of being *valiant*." Her searing violet eyes rolled again at the last word.

"Hey!" Onyx said, his hand slapping the table with a sudden bang. I jumped. "I'll have you know," his forefinger pointed fiercely at River, who wore an expression of boredom like she invented the emotion, "doing a triple backflip into the pool from the top of the lodge could prove life-saving one day. Just you wait and see." He shook his head in disgust.

I bit my bottom lip as I tried not to smile at their antics. I searched around the dining hall, looking for a clock somewhere. There wasn't one, so I pushed away from the table and reached for my plate.

Onyx's hand halted me, his orange currents contrasting against his black sleeve. "Where are you off to in such a hurry?" His dark brows furrowed.

"I gotta meet up with Chrome." I tried to snag the plate back, but Onyx held firm.

Understanding chimed in his eyes. "Ah. Well," he started, looking down at the table. He still wouldn't release me. "Would you mind leaving me your leftovers?"

I gaped. His plate was nearly clean. The gargantuan midday meal he had? Gone. And he wanted more. "That can't be healthy."

Onyx shrugged. "I have a fast metabolism."

I snorted and let go of the dish. "Fine." I moved to walk away.

"See ya around, Gray," River called out, her tone slightly lighter.

I paused, assessing her as she maintained eye contact with her food. "Sure," I said, leaving the dining hall more at ease than I'd felt in a long time just by witnessing such a jovial interaction. It reminded me so much of the others I'd left behind.

An ache replaced that lightness in my chest at the thought of my friends. Then, the heaviness returned in full force at the thought of my next stop—meeting up with Chrome and Orion to test my Elemental abilities. I didn't know what to expect if anything at all. I only knew permanent changes would alter everything within me.

Chapter 33

GRAY

"Take off the necklace."

In the training fields, Chrome stood poised several feet in front of me as if bracing for an attack. His Kinetic and Elemental forms were on display, ready to be unleashed if needed.

We'd decided that keeping my Kinetic magic contained while I discovered my Elemental powers would be the wisest choice. It was safer not knowing how I'd react or how my suppressed Elemental magic would respond to being freed at last. It could be quite destructive.

The afternoon sun warmed the skin on the back of my neck as a soft breeze weaved through my glamoured ice-blonde waves. I'd let them loose after the training session I'd had with Void. The smell of pine needles lifted my spirit enough to give me the courage to push through my fear of discovering an unknown part of myself. Or perhaps it was the fear there was nothing new after all. That this was all for nothing.

Chrome's impenetrable steel gaze saw it all. He relaxed his shoulders, closing the distance between us. His quicksilver gaze never left mine.

With deft and gentle hands, he reached around the back of my neck, brushing my hair to one side. My breath faltered at the touch. Ever so slowly, he skimmed his fingers along the sensitive skin until he found the leather string holding the black stone in place. He fiddled with the knot and gave it a tug until the necklace fell loose. He caught it with one hand, while the other shifted to brace my neck, forcing me to hold his gaze.

Warmth buzzed through my chest, causing my heart rate to spike. His grip loosened, brushing sensuous circles on my nape, studying my eyes as if they held his soul within them. A shiver danced down my spine while my skin heated all over.

Chrome cleared his throat and finally broke our gaze. With visible effort, he forced himself to take a step back. Then another, followed by two more until he was a safe distance away. He remembered he still held the black crystal necklace by the leather strap and quickly stuffed it in his pocket.

"It might take a few minutes before you feel anything," Chrome said.

I nodded and then hugged myself as I waited, feeling colder now that he'd put distance between us again. Guilt clawed at my chest as Slate's bright smile crossed my mind.

Chrome lowered his brows in confusion at the same moment his metallic eyes sharpened on me.

I was about to question him when, without warning, a sudden gust of wind stormed me from within, making me gasp for air. I staggered back a few steps at the force of a wild gale. It built and built, snuffing out my air.

The wind was neither hot nor cold; it was the right temperature my body craved. But it continued to build, the pressure forcing me to my knees. I groaned and looked from beneath my lashes at Chrome. He watched me with untethered eyes, waiting to intervene.

The wind grew to a torrential whirlwind that moved to my chest. It was like sticking my head out the window of a moving car while trying to breathe.

I panicked, clawing at my chest and clutching my throat.

"Gray," Chrome said with forced calm lacing his tone, "you can't panic. Settle your emotions. Your power is in control of you right now. You gotta take it back."

I shook my head at him, pleading for help. In a guttural voice, I asked, "H...how?"

"Close your eyes," Chrome demanded. I didn't, gasping for tiny sips of air instead. "*Now!* Do it, Gray! Close your *goddamn* eyes." Power and authority poured from his entire aura.

I closed my eyes.

"Imagine forcing it to stop," Chrome instructed in a calmer voice. A whimper escaped me. Fear overrode every sense I held. "You got this, Gray. Make it fucking bow to you."

I didn't know how, but I was willing to try if it meant being able to take a breath again. Dizziness swarmed my mind. I braced myself on the yellowing grass, squeezing the brittle blades between my fingers—focusing on the feel of its coarseness. Giving it a tug, I released it before snapping the plants free from the ground. I repeated the action, rocking my body back and forth softly with the movement. Pull, then rock back. Release and lean forward.

"Good. That's good. Ground yourself to the earth; let it anchor you," Chrome encouraged in a gentle tone that surprised me, like he genuinely believed in me.

I continued this movement several times, taking my mind away from the panic and suffocation.

"You're a queen. Make it *fucking* bow." I could feel echoes of Chrome's intensity carried to me by the roaring wind inside.

It didn't want to bow.

But I needed it to. I *wanted* it to. Chrome was right; I *was* a queen. And I was tired of being ruled by others.

In the recesses of my mind, almost as if I were on another plane, I rose to my feet, seeing a gust of wind in the form of a devastating tsunami towering over me from behind—threatening to obliterate me into sand. Everything was white, and no sound existed. I turned around and faced it down—daring it to move another inch toward me. It did, so I threw my arms in front of me, palms facing outward, toward the air-tsunami. I finally managed a breath, deep and reviving.

"You will bow. You are bound to me, *not* the other way around," I said, my voice deeper, rawer than I'd realized—imbued with command.

The wind-wave crashed to a halt inches from me. I didn't flinch. "I know you're angry. We've been locked away for so long. But you need me to harness you. *I'm* your justice. We are one and the same." Its iridescence hovered, my hair flowing in my face. "Now, bow."

The air-tsunami inched forward as if it contemplated wrestling the oxygen from my lungs again.

I held my ground, refusing it—either in my head or on another plane, I wasn't sure. I didn't understand where this power originated, but I had felt its strength in my words.

As if my element did, too, the wall of air began to retreat like a tide returning to the sea. The swell at the top of the air-wave got smaller and smaller until it deflated, drifting above the ground. The shimmering veil hovered, stretching far and wide, swirling around my feet.

"I'm honored to be one with you," I said to my element, realizing that despite having not been awakened to my Elemental side, I'd always felt a kinship with air all my life. "I've always sensed you try to comfort me when I needed it most. I just never knew I needed to accept our bond. So, I thank you for never giving up on me. We will make those who kept us separated pay. You have my word." The flat veil of wind rippled at the mention of vengeance.

The air drifted toward me. And like a dog with its tail tucked, it crept forward to caress my ankles. I relaxed at the soothing gesture. I took it as a positive sign as it gently coiled itself around my body in a comforting and protective manner until it embraced me completely.

I sank into it, the feeling of comfort and protection foreign to me. Knowing I now had the ultimate loyal ally had my eyes burning against the tears I fought. I eased out a shaky breath as it cooled my scalp, combing invisible fingers through my hair.

A long-forgotten part of me snapped into place. Over the years, a slow wound had woven itself into the fabric of my being. Like some vital part of me I'd never known was missing until now. And now, I felt whole...well, almost. I hadn't expected my element to be a force of its own in addition to being my loyal companion filled with love, compassion, and protection.

It was strange, but for once, I allowed myself to feel at peace. I opened my eyes, my consciousness returning to the training fields, still squeezing the grass strands between my fingers. I gasped. My hands were no longer the light bronze I'd known all my life. No.

Gold. They were fucking gold. My skin glinted with a sheen of gilded luminance.

I jolted, scrambling to my knees—the hardened earth dug and scraped as I did. I shoved the sleeves up my arms to observe my new golden skin.

Well, fuck.

Speechless, I rotated my hands back and forth in front of me, my mouth open, eyes wide.

"It's beautiful, isn't it?"

I snatched my gaze from my gilded fingers to the forgotten presence. Chrome stood there with a slight smile and softened look. It was strange to know I shared something with him and everyone else at the Hollow. That maybe I could belong somewhere.

"It's..." I trailed off, looking at my hands again. "It's so surreal. I didn't fully believe I was an Elemental."

"You are," Chrome said. He took two long strides in my direction, dropping to his knees only inches from me. "And it's regal on you."

My breath faltered. The wind remained with me, but it was subdued— a light breeze constantly stirring. But the lack of air this time had nothing to do with my element.

"Thanks," I mumbled. It felt like such a lame response, so I cast a sheepish smile, glad that my gold skin could hide the blush that arose. Well, hopefully.

Chrome rocked back on his heels as his swirling metal eyes met mine. His jaw slackened, a subtle gasp hitching his breath. His lean, muscled shoulders relaxed. Dazed. *He* was dazed! "Your eyes..." he whispered.

On instinct, I brushed my fingertips against the corners of my eyes. "What do they look like?"

He shook his head. "This is something you have to see for yourself."

Without lifting a hand, Chrome conjured a dagger from his weapons belt. It hovered from behind him, the point facing downward, floating to me. Once it was inches away from my face, it rotated sideways, serving as a mirror.

Icy, blue-gray eyes had always been my color. Now, I mirrored Chrome's reaction at first glance. I lifted a hand to cover my mouth, leaning forward to get a better view.

The first thing that caught my attention was the shimmering gold skin on my face. It was as if someone had glazed the most vibrant and saturated shade of metallic paint on top of my skin, then sprinkled shimmering gold flakes over the top. I looked and felt ethereal. Otherworldly.

I glided my fingertips from my temples down my cheeks. It felt like skin, not like dried flakes that would peel off. But once I settled from the shock...

My irises drew my attention next. Instead of the subdued blue-gray hues, they now displayed every color of the rainbow as if they served as a color wheelchart. They were so vibrant—not a word typically used to describe me. "They're..."

"A rainbow. All the colors on the spectrum. They're light and dark, and everything in between," Chrome said in a tender tone, still kneeling beside me. "They're perfect."

Warmth spread through my chest, heating my cheeks and neck. He looked at me as if...no. I would not go there. The air within me—or, at least, it felt like it was within me—answered my call to chase away the telling flush with soothing wisps. I gave him a slight smile before looking back at my eyes in the dagger's reflection.

"I can't believe this is real. That my father went to such lengths to hide this from me. How did I never suspect it? I mean, there must've been times when this side of me peeked through somehow. There's no way it's been able to remain hidden this long, right?" I inspected the girl in the reflection. A version of me that was old but new. A version I'd never known existed. Who was I really? Who could I be if I wasn't so fucked up from the trauma of my past?

Chrome nodded in my peripheral. "That's been a debate between Orion and me for years. He believes you had to have noticed something at some point. But I know what Forest is capable of. And there's no way he'd ever allow you to know the truth. He'd do whatever was necessary to prevent that from happening."

I squinted. "What are you saying?"

Chrome paused and looked away, focusing on the leaves drifting from the autumnal branches. His lips pursed as he chewed his cheek in contemplation. "I think..." he finally said. "He awakened your Elemental side the day we met on the playground." He turned his head to look at me, his steel eyes showing me the conviction in his words.

I lifted an eyebrow. "I think I would remember something like that happening. Especially that day." That day was forever entrenched in my mind. It was something I'd never understood.

When we'd touched, a powerful force collided, exploding between us. Skittish teachers had snatched Chrome away, whereas they'd guided me to the vice-principal's office. Father had been immediately called and informed of the events.

Of course, he hadn't been too pleased when I came home from school that day. I must've repressed the punishment that ensued because, for the life of me, I could never recall it.

"I think he had your memory wiped," Chrome said. The floating dagger backed away and tucked itself into Chrome's weapons belt.

I shook my head, running my fingers through my hair, still trying to remember what happened after I'd returned from school that day. "How is that possible? I don't know any ability capable of doing that."

Chrome snorted. "Oh, it's possible, Rainbow."

I gave him a deadpan expression. "Don't call me that."

"I've seen him do it. Not with his power, of course, but those with magnetic and electrical abilities. They can go into the brain, target the impulses of neural pathways in certain memory centers, and just...short-circuit them."

The world around me seemed to slow, my heart rate picking up in speed in contrast. I dug my nails into the palms of my hands. "Oh god. How did this never occur to me?"

The liquid metal in his eyes seemed to swirl faster, fueled with an emotion he worked hard to hide from the world. His jaw clenched so tight I thought his teeth would shatter. "It's one of his well-guarded secrets." He closed his eyes and forced a deep breath into his lungs. When he opened them, the quicksilver eyes might as well have glowed red. "I'm going to kill that motherfucker, Gray. For every ounce of pain he's ever inflicted on you. His life is on loan because I will fucking own his fate when I get him in my hands. And he's known it for years."

With a humming sharp tug, a blazing rage suddenly scorched my heart. I was *livid*. And as much as it pissed me off about everything my father had done and lied about, this unyielding fury didn't feel like it belonged to me. My breaths came in short, my nostrils flaring. I couldn't think past the turmoil.

The air stirred around us, lifting the colorful leaves from the ground and tossing them haphazardly about in changing directions. Chrome crinkled his brows as he shifted his eyes from the accelerating wind back to me. "Gray?" he asked, caution lacing his tone.

The anger was hot. It threatened to incinerate me into a black pile of ash left for my wind to carry away. My breaths became raspy. I didn't know from where this wrath derived, but it consumed me.

"Gray," Chrome said, his voice commanding with authority. "Look at me."

I did. The wind whipped through his metallic hair, leaving it mussed. Concern threaded knots in his eyes as he reached out to rest his palms on my shoulders. His head dipped, and like a receding tide, the anger went with it, leaving me drained.

"What the fuck just happened?" I asked, breathless. I searched around, the wind dying away as it returned the leaves to the earth to decay.

Chrome looked up at me. Guilt pressed on his beautiful features as they dropped in resignation. "I'm sorry," he whispered.

I frowned, confused. "Why? What did you do?"

"I didn't do it intentionally. I should've realized..." he said, scooting backward using his hands and feet.

"I don't understand. Out with it, Chrome," I demanded, scrutinizing him with a shrewd glare.

Chrome blew out a breath and dropped his head in his hands, elbows propped on his knees. "That was my anger you felt, not yours."

"What do you mean? How are you able to do that?" Once again, I wrapped my arms around my torso.

"Like I said," Chrome said, his voice muffled between his knees. "It wasn't intentional. I didn't realize you'd be able to feel it."

"Okay, you're going to have to give me more than that."

Chrome lifted his head, and so many emotions fought to reach the surface. They begged to be freed, but he closed his eyes. And when he opened them, they hid once again behind that steel wall he'd constructed so well. Another breath left him. "Since the day we first met, when our magic collided, I've been able to feel your emotions. I didn't know if you could feel mine, too. But when we met again, all I felt from you was pain, anger, and revenge...and I knew that wasn't the case. You didn't even remember me, or so I thought.

"I thought this emotional tie to you was one-sided. That it was a specific gift of my own that came with being a hybrid. A gift I didn't want. It made little sense because I couldn't feel others' emotions around me. Just yours. Only from a close distance, though." He paused, barely lifting his head over his arm to see me. "I've felt your pain and your anger. Your fear. Your determination. Your shame. Your love. Your...*everything* over the years. I've felt what that motherfucker has made you feel. And it just added to my anger for what he's done to me.

"And now that you've accessed and formed a bond with your Elemental side, it seems to have awakened your ability to feel mine. It never occurred to me you couldn't feel mine because half of your being had been subdued for so long. And I didn't think to prepare for that today." Chrome's eyes were drenched in regret and swam in guilt. "I'm so sorry." He dropped his head again.

I sat there, stunned for several moments at his admission. But once the initial surprise wore off, another thought crossed my mind. "You mean to tell me," I said, my tone dropping lower and lower with each word, "you have felt my every emotion this entire time? And you never once thought you should fucking tell me?" Rage, my own this time, reared its ugly head again, this time directed at Chrome. "Do you feel *that*?" I asked, hands shaking.

Chrome clenched his jaw, his eyes squeezed shut. He took ragged, deep breaths, but he didn't respond.

"You've been basically spying on me for the majority of my life as a godsdamn stranger! Who does that shit?" I sprung to my feet. Chrome didn't; he just sat there resigned. "You're no different from my father, you prick," I said, my lip curling at the edge. "You disgust me," I said, my voice barely audible.

Again, something tugged on my heart, like a thin cord pulled taut. Shame washed through my chest, but I was too pissed off to care about *his* emotions right now.

I whirled around and stormed back to the lodge. Back to my room, where I *thought* I'd had some privacy. Turned out I'd been monitored here, too. Just as I was at the palace.

Chapter 34

GRAY

Tears threatened to fall as the weight of betrayal crushed me. I felt so stupid for believing our friendship had been genuine—a rare treasure for me. Was all of it borne from pity because he felt my fear and anxiety?

What I hated the most was the fact that everything I'd worked hard to keep hidden—my truths and emotions—had never been a secret, after all. He'd known everything. He saw what lay beneath my mask of indifference. And I had never given him permission to have such access. Only one person had that, and he was dead.

I felt violated. Actually, that word wasn't quite strong enough.

I stalked back to the lodge with the hope of sulking in my room alone. Would I ever have that freedom? Or would he feel how broken and pathetic I was inside, only for him to mock me with a smirk?

The wind lashed through my ice-blonde hair, whipping it into my face. I didn't care. Maybe it would block my tears from the others.

Everyone stopped and stared as I neared the entrance.

Realization struck that Chrome still held the black crystal necklace in his pocket. I was now on full display, like a foreign animal in the zoo.

I was tempted to breeze past them, but I stopped instead. Something within forced me to face them. I felt the steady hand of my element imparting its strength to me.

Scowling, I shoved my hair out of my face, exposing my gold skin and rainbow eyes for all to see. I met their stares—one by one—daring them to say anything. They didn't. Their thoughts scrawled across their features like a scorse code. I met each set of wide eyes and open mouths, all of which quickly cast to the ground in submission.

I blew out a breath and continued inside, heading to my room. More stares from those in the foyer and the open living space followed as I passed. I didn't stop this time. Word would soon spread from those outside.

The winding stairs to the top floor didn't slow me down. I took them as fast as I could without running. A few people milled about on the landing, but as I had downstairs, I didn't acknowledge them.

Almost there.

The hallway opened up on the right. As I rounded it, I slammed into a hard chest with my cheek. "Fuck!"

"Oh, Gray!" Orion's soothing voice caught me. His hands braced my shoulders so I wouldn't fall on my ass. "I'm so sorry, my dear. I didn't see you..."

The mess of my hair fell into my face. Annoyed, I shoved it back with my fingers. It got tangled and snagged on the roots. I growled, moving to push past Orion.

"Wait," he called out. "I want to see."

I stopped. Slowly, I turned my head to meet his kind, teal eyes. A warm smile spread, emitting a sense of comfort. Pride—that was pride on his face. "Beautiful. Just like her."

I shifted my gaze around the wooden hallway, hoping to make a quick escape. "Are you all right?" he asked, brows dipping low in concern, wiping away that beaming smile of a proud father.

I shrugged. "Doesn't really matter, does it?"

"Of course, it does."

I snorted and ran my fingers through my hair, trying hard to find anything else to look at but him.

"Walk with me, Gray. There's still much I want to discuss with you."

It wasn't a request.

I debated telling him to fuck off, but something in those gentle eyes told me it was worth putting off my escapism for a bit longer. I sighed, dropping my shoulders. They ached from the tension. The betrayal in my heart didn't recede, though. "Okay."

Orion offered a small smile and a nod of his head. "I just have to make a quick stop by my office to grab something. Follow me?"

Orion led me to the bank of the glistening blue lake that bordered the left side of the Hollow. Deep blue, calm water reflected the sun's dying light. The temperature dipped as evening approached.

How long had I been in the training fields with Chrome? It had felt like maybe half an hour at the most. Perhaps I'd been bonding—as Chrome called it—with my element longer than I realized.

Orion swept a hand toward the grass. "Sit with me," he said with an inviting smile. How someone who could look so young and feel so wise confused me.

He hitched his knee-length, black cloak before sitting cross-legged on the grass. He gazed out at the lake with a peaceful smile, resting his forearms gently on his knees.

I followed him and sank beside him in the grass. Silence sat between us for several moments as we took in the beauty and peace before us. It wasn't uncomfortable. It was nice not needing to fill the space with awkward words just for the sake of doing so.

"I come here to meditate often. It's such a great place to ground myself and be with my element," Orion said. He shuttered his eyes as a kiss of wind breezed between us softly.

I nodded. The scenery was indeed peaceful. Trees draped around the edges of the lake, serving as a small canopy.

"Your mother was the most beautiful woman I'd known. Not just on the outside but truly on the inside. She was light and strength embodied in a single person," Orion said softly. A glazed look encompassed his distant gaze. "She was my closest friend." He dropped his head with a heavy sigh, his chin resting on his chest.

"I wish I could've met her." I found a stick and began digging the dirt from under my nails. "She sounds like she would've been a wonderful mother."

"Indeed. She loved you long before you were born despite how you were conceived. She told me as much in the letter she'd snuck out while in captivity." Orion looked at me, grief burrowed in his eyes.

I looked over the water, watching the small swells as they lapped over one another. "What was her element?" I asked, feeling the answer before he gave it.

Orion joined me in my lake gazing. "Water," he said, smiling at the body before us as if it contained my birth mother herself. "Such a perfect fit for her."

I tried to imagine a world where I grew up with this woman as my mother. A life where I hadn't been raised by Forest Monroe. How different would I be? Would I be happy?

"I assume you discovered your element today?" Orion asked, casting a sideways glance at me over his shoulder.

I nodded, and a genuine—albeit small—smile crept up my cheeks. "Air," I whispered.

Orion perked up. "Yeah? Well, you know...." he said, dragging out the last word and giving me an innocent shrug. "I happen to be a very skilled air-wielder myself. If you'd like some help mastering it..."

"Yes," I said quickly. For multiple reasons, but the main one being... "You think you could replace Chrome with those sessions?"

Orion frowned in confusion. "I mean, I *could*, I suppose. Although, only he can help you master the use of both your forms simultaneously. But I'd be happy to join your sessions."

I blew out a breath, deflated by his answer. But I'd settle for having him there as a buffer.

"What happened today? You seemed quite upset when you ran into me." It was genuine concern, and something about Orion made me feel safe, comfortable. There was no judgment.

I cleared my throat before I launched into explaining the session between Chrome and me. I told him about how I'd bonded with the air element, followed by the shared emotional connection between Chrome and me. How he'd been hiding that fact since we'd met.

"I feel violated. Betrayed. Which is so dumb because I barely know him, but I..." I began and shook my head. "I just know he's holding so many secrets, which I respect. But when they pertain to me, I thought he'd respect *me* enough to disclose that sort of information."

Orion nodded. "You are entitled to your emotions, Gray. I don't know what you've endured, but I can imagine if you were raised by Forest, then discovering a secret like that would feel like a betrayal. I'd like to think I know Chrome. He is my nephew, after all, so I know he probably hates himself for hiding something like that from you. Truly. He bears so much responsibility, carrying the world on his shoulders when he shouldn't. And whatever this bond that links the two of you is, I know you're probably the last person he wishes to bring harm upon," Orion explained gently.

"I'm not telling you this to make any excuses for him withholding this truth from you. You are justified in your anger. But sometimes, our trauma makes us react before we can rationally respond. So perhaps take some time to think deeply about this issue before confronting him."

I nodded, mulling over his words. It was nice to have someone to talk to about these types of conflicts. I'd never had that someone wise and kind to listen. Slate had always been there for me, but this support was different.

A knot formed in my throat, threatening to spill pent-up emotions. I swallowed it down instead.

Orion shifted next to me, reaching into his back pocket and retrieving a pink envelope. He ran a finger over it. "This is for you. From Lilly. She sent this to me along with the other letters she sent all those years ago."

I hesitated. My hand itched to snatch it from him, but my mind paused in fear. Fear of becoming attached to a woman I'd never meet, hug, or receive the motherly affection I'd craved my entire life. And once I read it, that'd be it. There'd be nothing else left of her.

Ever so slowly, I reached out a hand, my heart so heavy from the exchange. More loss. I'd be losing someone I'd never truly had.

I stared down at the pale pink envelope scrawled with elegant calligraphy, indicating it derived from a royal. She was every bit the queen Orion made her out to be. Instead of the Kinetic name I was used to, *Aeran* was written in its place.

Orion must've seen my confused expression because he said, "That was her name for you—Aeran. It's your Elemental name. Like Griffin is Chrome's."

I met his eyes once again. He was parting with one of the last things he had left of his dearest friend. I said, "Thank you. I can't wait to learn more about her."

Orion dipped his chin in acknowledgment. "Nothing would make me happier. You're a piece of her, so I'm here for you anytime."

A rare emotion filled my chest, clenching my throat: gratitude. I reached for his hand that rested on a black-clad knee and pulled it into my own. "Thank you, Orion. Your kindness...it's not something I'm used to. I'll always be grateful for it."

He gave my hand a small squeeze, followed by an empathetic smile. "Sometimes, that's all we need. Just one kind person to show us things differently. To perhaps give a perspective shift, even if it's a small one."

That night, I grabbed a meal from the dining hall and brought it to my room to eat in seclusion.

The jacuzzi in the bathroom oasis sang to me like a siren's song. So, after I ate, I slid into its warm depths. Varying salts soaked into the water, sending wafting aromas around the chamber.

The gilded layer on my skin stunned me whenever I caught a glance of my bare body. Before climbing into the bath, I studied my rainbow irises. My true eye color. It was jarring after becoming so accustomed to a particular appearance all my life, but I liked it.

A new version of me, I told myself.

I mulled over Orion's advice as it pertained to Chrome. He might not have intended to hurt me, but he did. Perhaps I reacted a bit too harshly. Maybe calling him "disgusting" was a tad excessive. Guilt clenched my stomach at the memory of his crestfallen face, and the abject shame from his emotions that had assaulted me.

I shifted my thoughts to my mother, who was the polar opposite of my father in every way. My heart broke for the woman Orion described. The final years of her life were spent in terror, making the man I'd been raised by more of a monster than I'd ever realized.

That triggered more questions: what did that say about the person I was? Did that make me a monster, too? I'd killed twenty-four Elementals who had just been defending themselves and their families—all for the sake of earning his acceptance and pride.

I'd been so engrossed in my own issues that the bigger picture never occurred to me. I'd been fed these "truths" about Elementals since I could form memories, and I never thought to question them.

It felt *gross*. Chrome wasn't the one who was disgusting. I was. Which is maybe why I struggled with meeting other Elementals eye to eye. I wasn't worthy of their respect, loyalty, or kindness. Not that I'd ever expected it. I'd never received it from the people that I'd actually been born to lead, but somewhere hidden inside, I'd secretly hoped things could be different here. A fresh start. New people.

But in actuality, did I deserve it?

I inhaled deeply, breathing in the calming lavender before sliding beneath the water's surface. If only I could stay hidden under the water's warmth indefinitely.

Water. My mother's element. I imagined her guiding the water to soothe, protect, and cleanse me. I emptied all the air from my lungs, feeling myself grow weightier until I lay flat on the bottom of the tub. The rippling water's surface blurred the view of the warm light from the ceiling above.

Just when my lungs began to spasm, I pushed myself to the surface. I gulped in air, guiding my drenched hair from my face.

The lights refracted off the silver bracelet on my wrist. My Kinetic magic had been repressed for too long. But the shame from my past made it to where I didn't want it anymore.

With that thought, my chest tightened, effectively bringing my relaxation to an end.

Once dried off, I stared at the pink envelope Orion had given me. It felt like a bomb ready to ignite in my hands, imploding what remained of my identity.

As long as I didn't open it, I had something *new* from her. After I opened and read it, there would be nothing else from her again. It'd be like she never existed...again. And I wasn't ready to face that yet. I wasn't ready to face any more truths regarding my past.

I ventured to one of the built-in shelves on the wall and plucked out a thick novel. It was an aging fantasy I'd never heard of. So, I flipped to a random page and wedged the envelope in the crease. Once it was snug, I snapped the book closed and placed the novel back in its home.

Scanning the shelves, a book caught my eye. It was titled, *A Guide to Meditation and Finding Inner Peace for Beginners*. My forefinger caressed the spine as I debated whether to pick it up. Something about it called to me, so I gave in to the urge.

Orion had mentioned meditating by the lake earlier, and something about that caused a sense of longing in my heart. Maybe it could be beneficial for me. We all knew I lacked any sort of inner peace.

Curling a leg under me on the bed, I scanned through the pages. I saw topics discussing breathing techniques. Words like "grounding" that even Chrome had used earlier when I was losing myself to the will of my element. Visualization was another huge topic.

When I came across the empowering effects that came with finding inner peace, I was sold. Because if there was one thing I was most tired of, it was feeling powerless. No matter how strong or physically powerful I was, I still felt like a mental or emotional slave to those around me.

Chapter 35

CHROME

"I'll be back soon," I muttered, stuffing blades everywhere on my person I could fit them.

Onyx held his arms out to the side. "Dude, you just got back three days ago. What do you need to do now?"

"Leave," I said, refusing to meet his eyes. "I need to talk with the militia."

"About what?" Onyx challenged.

I blew out a harsh breath, beginning to lose my patience. "Things."

Onyx's chuckle held no humor. "Wrong answer, Prince. Talk."

"Fuck, Onyx." Dropping my arms at my sides, I turned to face him. "I need to see if their intel has anything new on the king's plans." I couldn't confess that I needed to distance myself from Gray. It would only solidify the fact that I was a coward for running again.

Onyx narrowed his eyes. "But don't we have people for that job? We need you here."

"No, you don't. You're here, and so is Orion. It'll only be a day or two at the most."

Onyx palmed his hands over his face, frustrated at the losing battle. "What can I do?"

"Just help Gray get acclimated. Keep an eye on her."

"In what way?" "In the way that her element is new to her, and she might lose control of it. I don't know, Onyx. Just watch out for her, okay?"

Just thinking about how stunning she looked in her full form stole my breath. Her marbled hair, golden Elemental skin, and shocking rainbow eyes that appeared after bonding with her element, rocked me in a way I hadn't been expecting. She was every bit the fierce warrior I knew her to be. I resisted the intense desire to drop to my knees and worship her right there.

Gray's words kept repeating in my mind since she'd said them. She had every right to be mad and feel violated by my emotional eavesdropping, even if it was unintentional. But it was her words, *"You're no different than my father. You disgust me,"* that I couldn't seem to silence, triggering old trauma from my youth that I'd thought had been healed since my escape from the Royal Domain. Apparently not. Some wounds never truly healed.

Onyx narrowed his amber eyes at me in suspicion. "What's got you so worked up that you're up and leaving out of nowhere?"

I snapped on my black and silver bracelets, shutting down my magic. It only seemed to heighten the growing frenzy in my body. At Gray's words, painful memories were dredged to the forefront again. Once I put a stark distance between Gray and me after the training session, the madness found a foothold to latch onto. I couldn't seek her out now, and I didn't want anyone at the lodge to witness me like this.

I needed a release.

"Nothing. Just...I need to check on some things." I flipped the hood over my head and looked at him again, ignoring the clawing darkness within me, already announcing its unwelcome arrival. Its distant excitement grew with each passing moment. "Inform Orion and the others. Keep it discreet. A small mission—nothing more or less."

I hated asking him, but I couldn't afford their questions right now.

Onyx relaxed his shoulders and rubbed the back of his neck. I could see his discomfort, but he nodded anyway. "Fine. Just come back in one piece, yeah?"

"Always do." After grabbing a final knife and sliding it up the inside of my sleeve, I strode toward Onyx, pulling him into a hug. "It'll be fine. Just keep her occupied and help train her in her combat deficiencies."

With a pat on my back, my friend agreed. "Okay. Will do."

The itch began to grow into an internal squirming, and the voice—Grim's voice—grew more distinct in my mind, taunting me with things like, *You thought you could get rid of me for good, did you? That's cute. I've missed you; I'm so glad to be reunited again. I'm going to have so much fun with you.*

Stepping back, I gave my dearest friend a final parting nod before leaving my bedroom suite altogether to rush through the lodge's natural luxury to the back exit, slipping out into the dusk. I removed the glamoured wards long enough for me to exit the premises, and headed for the outside world once again—feeling the distance grow between Gray and me with every step.

Grim's oily voice wouldn't shut the fuck up. Since this affliction began, the darkness chose my abuser's voice to haunt and torture me.

If he wasn't laughing at my backslide, he was ratcheting up the craving to spill blood. Repeated words from all those years ago continued to echo in my mind like a loop, reminding me how helpless I'd been at his mercy. Some things could never fully heal; you just learned to live with the pain, but you also figured out how to move forward in your life without allowing that pain to dictate your path or choices. He threatened to unravel it all again.

Sitting in the nearest speakeasy, I downed another glass of moonshine. Its potency made me woozy, but I didn't care. I needed to numb the craving. Withdrawal symptoms weren't helping. Sweat beaded down the side of my face as I felt hot and stifled on the outside while I fought to stop my shivering teeth caused by the iciness within me.

I needed Gray. But I didn't *want* to need her. She hated me anyway. I disgusted her, and rightfully so.

Who was I to think I could ever be redeemable?

Glad you finally came to your senses, boy. We're gonna have so much fun together.

My stomach lurched, and I almost lost its contents.

"Holy shit." A whispered voice filled with awe snatched me from my thoughts. I jerked my head to the side to find a dark-haired human woman. Her worn and holey clothes told me she was not militia.

I cocked an eyebrow, not in the mood to socialize.

"You're..." she said with her brown eyes wide, dirt smudged on her cheeks and forehead. "You're one of those Elemental creatures."

I gave her an unimpressed stare. "And? What gave me away?"

"The skin," she answered, not picking up on my sarcasm. She touched her cheek. "And the eyes." The woman leaned an inch closer to me as if to inspect them.

I glanced down at my wrists, noticing the missing black bracelet that was supposed to adorn it. With a sigh, I remembered that I'd forgotten to put it back in place after my Kinetic run-in earlier. Thankfully, the black clothing covered the bloodstains.

"Well, it appears that would do it. Can I help you?" I drawled, uninterested.

Just kill her already.

I rolled my eyes at Grim's bullshit.

"Is it true you're an angel?" she asked, hope brimming in her eyes with unshed tears. "Here to save humanity?"

While most humans who weren't part of the militia feared us, there were a few highly religious ones who theorized that Kinetics and Elementals were either angels or an alien race here to save humanity. "It depends on how you define angels." I took another swig of 'shine. My sanity wasn't on the fringes like it had been when playing my game of cat and mouse with Gray. The memories of my time as a Kinetic were beginning to fade, but I had enough memories to remember the important shit.

"Can you heal others?" Desperation cracked her voice.

My expression softened, ignoring Grim in my mind. "No, I can't heal others. I'm sorry."

"Oh," she conceded. Her head and shoulders dropped as the loss of hope deflated the light in her eyes.

"You have more questions," I stated. I gestured to the seat at the table. "Sit. Let's see if I can answer any." If there was one thing I understood, it was the misery of living in the unknown. Of not being equipped with knowledge that could help me better defend myself against the world. As endearing as their beliefs toward us were, they were dangerous for them. Forest would have her and her entire family killed in an instant without a second thought.

The woman's demeanor picked back up again, and she smiled. "Thank you." She climbed onto the steel stool across from the wooden barrel that served as a table.

The hot and cold sweats were returning, as well as my heart rate, beating in uneven patterns. My skin began to itch, but I resisted the urge to scratch, knowing it wouldn't do any good but drive me further insane. Hopefully, I could use this conversation as a nice distraction.

"So," the woman started, "where did you come from? What are y'all able to do?" The rapid-fire questions were full of excitement, and I struggled to keep up with them. But I signed myself up for it.

"We've been here for many millennia. We don't know our exact origins, but we suspect we came from another realm or world. However, we are not considered angels."

"Why are there rumors that you are healers?" she asked, face pinched in confusion.

"Because we can heal ourselves, but not others."

"Oo-kay. What happened on Devolution Day?"

The question slammed into me like a brick wall. I should've expected it, but given my current state, I wasn't prepared to answer through my foggy mind. "Uhm," I said, running a hand through my raven waves. Answering this question was risky when it pertained to unknown humans. It could go either way. "Well, I'm going to give you the story not many humans know," I said, settling on my resolve. "The truth."

Excitement lit her eyes again, a hint of a smile playing on the edges of her mouth. I bet she'd been a reporter—no doubt. Good, she could go back and spread it to the others. I'd take my chances.

As I delved into the story, the brunette remained riveted as she leaned across the table with her forearms pressed to the surface. I withheld a few details, things that no one else knew. But she got the idea. The narrative that had been spread all those years ago had been a complete lie. The Elementals were just as much the victims as the humans. Yet, we were fighting alongside them to help give them their world back.

"What's your name?" she asked. And again, my words got caught in my throat. Both the names, Griffin and Chrome, were well-known to every group. I couldn't give that away.

A hand clamped on my shoulder, making me whirl around to face the newcomer, immediately reaching for the knife in my sleeve. "How odd it is to find you here."

Observing the man, I couldn't place him. I knew him, and we'd interacted many times. He was a Kinetic, which meant my older memories from that time in my life were lost to me at the moment. His bracelet was intact, which masked his true hair color and currents, making it more difficult for me to place. The only thing I knew was that he was my contact.

He smiled wide, exposing bright teeth beneath a dark beard. "Mind if I steal you away from your new friend?" he asked me.

The woman's expression fell, but she caught it quickly, trying to hide her disappointment. "Oh, sure. Thank you for your time..." she trailed off, still unsure of my name.

"Silas," I finished for her.

"As in Griffin Silas?" she asked.

"No, Silas is my first name."

"Oh," she responded in what sounded and looked like relief.

After saying parting words, I rose from the table and faced my contact. I couldn't bring myself to ask his name. It would raise alarms, and people had trust in me. Regardless, I would see to Forest's bloody death before I succumbed to my affliction. "Follow me," he muttered loud enough for me to hear before doing a quick scan of the speakeasy.

I trailed closely behind him through the tunnel door leading to the steps above ground. As per usual, the air in the speakeasy was muggy and stifled, making the first breath of fresh air a relief once reaching topside.

My contact didn't stop; instead, he walked in silence across the expansive field to an abandoned home. Thunder rumbled in the distance, and the night air felt dense with moisture building from the impending storm. Lightning lit up the sky, faint yet beautiful, nonetheless.

Lost to my personal torture, I didn't hear the whistling of an arrow. "Chrome! Snatch it," my contact ordered.

Out of pure instinct, I struck my right arm out, feeling the air's movements, and snatched the arrow from its trajectory.

Observing the blue-tipped arrow, I pushed my awareness outward to sense the energies. Judging by the quieted steps, there were several Kinetic warriors hiding in the trees at the edge of the woods nearby. It dawned on me that my unrepressed Elemental energy made it easy for Forest to find me. I couldn't be too mad, it offered me an excuse to bring hell on earth.

Excitement zipped through my veins, ready to bathe in the carnage. "I hope our little chat can wait. I've got a fuck ton of pent-up anxiety I need to release. You in?"

My Kinetic contact grinned, mischief lighting up his eyes. Pulling two daggers from his belt, we bolted toward the direction of the Kinetics as the beast inside me roared to life.

Chapter 36

GRAY

"You're actually an Elemental, I see," Void said, none too impressed.

I gave him a smirk. "Sorry to disappoint."

My muscles were sore from training yesterday, so I made a point to stretch before today's session.

Void stood in his cool indifference, his blank stare tracking me as if he could see my movements.

"How can you tell I'm an Elemental if you can't see?" I lifted my head from the bent position that stretched my hamstrings.

Void narrowed his eyes, his thick arms banding across his muscular chest, which was partially exposed in the gray tank he wore. Black ink marred the skin, but I couldn't discern the designs. "Just because I can't see doesn't mean I'm deaf to the gossip of this Hollow."

I rolled my eyes. "Right." I shouldn't have been surprised.

Void shifted and reached into his back pocket. "I brought something. Figured it would make you a bit more trustworthy during our sessions."

I cocked my head, ignoring the jab at my character. He pulled out a black cotton cloth from his pocket—a handkerchief.

"If you wanted to get kinky and level the playing field, Void, all you had to do was ask." There was a part of me that needed to crack his apathetic front.

Void dropped his arms, and the handkerchief fluttered at his side. He deadpanned his features even more. "Could you not?"

I chuckled. "Whatever. Lay it on me, big guy."

Void answered with silence and moved to stand behind me. How did he move so damn silently? He wrapped the cloth around my eyes, binding it at the back of my head, with a jerk.

"Okay, I can't see. Let's get down and..." My back slammed to the floor, stealing the end of my smartass retort. A heavy body pressed down on my torso.

"Okay," I wheezed. "I see you like it rough. I can adjust."

A sigh of exasperation reached me as the weight lifted from my body. "You talk too much."

"Actually, I don't. You just bring out the best in me," I said, wiggling my shoulders.

"Focus."

I sighed dramatically. "Fine," I grumbled, tuning my senses into my surroundings.

This time, before he wrapped me in a chokehold, I heard it. The slightest movement to my right. It wasn't enough, however, to prevent the inevitable whoosh of air that left my lungs. I was too slow.

"I heard you," I said, grunting as I stood up.

"But you still failed. Try again," Void instructed.

And on it went. Each time I sensed him, either I felt the air brush against me or heard its whisper, or even caught a whiff of his scent. But I was never quick enough to deflect him. It was a start. And I was a fast learner.

Lunch in the dining hall was the same as the day prior. Onyx and River accompanied me for the first half of my meal. Kodiak—the kind, beefy warrior—joined us for the second half.

I couldn't help myself as I found my eyes subconsciously searching the room for Chrome. He never came by.

"So," Onyx said, "how does being an Elemental feel?" He propped his elbows on the table and waited for my reply. My expression must've been bland because his eyes widened, shaking his head. "What? You just discovered a new part of yourself. You gotta feel different, right?"

I huffed out a breath before shoveling another spoonful of potatoes and stuffing it into my mouth. "I mean, aside from the new element that I always feel stirring inside me, I feel like myself." If one defined their identity to be completely lost, then I suppose that could be true.

"What is your element, anyway?" River asked, her sharp, violet gaze piercing me to my seat. I wasn't sure if it was socially acceptable to be asking such things, if they considered their elements personal information or not. River gave me a cunning, burgundy smile. "I'll tell you mine if you tell me yours." A wicked smile, indeed.

I gave her a pointed look. "Fine," I said, stabbing the juicy slab of roast beef on my plate. "Air."

"Shit," Onyx hissed and dug into back pocket, retrieving a knife and sliding it across the table to River. "You may take my blades, but you will *not* take my pride, woman!"

"Water," River snipped as she snatched the knife with fluid grace and analyzed it. Her gaze devoured it the way Onyx devoured the mounted food on his plate.

I looked between the two of them before settling on Kodiak. The mountainous man sat with a bemused expression and then shook his head to himself before returning to his food.

"Uh, am I missing something?" I asked, confused. Feeling like, yet again, the butt end of a joke.

Kodiak looked at me with rich emerald eyes that reminded me of a spring field. "They made a bet on what your element would be." He took a sip of water. The glass clanked on the table with a soft thud before he went on. "River won. And in the process, she won the coveted knife she's been hounding Onyx about for years now. It's a rare blade that completes an entire set of its kind."

I snorted, relieved that it was something innocent this time around. "Serves you right, Onyx."

Onyx reeled in his seat, his head shaking so fast one would've thought he'd earned a blindsided punch. "What the fuck? Why?"

I smiled. "For holding out on River's collection."

His jaw gaped wide. "Wait a minute," he said, recovering enough to hold up a glowing orange hand. "She *stole* that priceless collection. I figured it'd only be right if the entire set was stolen, too. It'd make it even more rare and special, ya know? If you start something, you gotta see it all the way through. Don't get lazy at the end."

Kodiak rumbled a deep laugh between the two of us. "You're a piece of work; you know that, O?"

"What? You can't tell me you don't see the value," Onyx said. "Come on."

River cleared her throat. After having inspected, cleaned, and stashed away the blade, she returned her attention to the conversation. She pushed her plate aside, then clasped her hands together delicately. "Onyx, the point is..." She flattened her severe features. "You're a shithead." Then she turned her intense stare on me. "Now you know."

I bit my lip to keep from laughing and looked down at my plate, spearing some fresh and seasoned green beans.

"Who cooks the food here?" I asked anyone willing to answer. This food was fucking divine.

"My mother," Kodiak said from beside me. "Like me, she's an earth Elemental."

"Your mom cooks this *food of the gods*? No wonder you're fucking built like that."

Onyx choked on his food while River chuckled. Kodiak fought to hide his smile but wasn't successful. "Yes," he said, wiping his mouth with a cloth napkin. "She runs the Elemental's farming operations."

"Why doesn't she get others to cook, then? Surely that would be less work for her?"

Kodiak offered a wistful grin. "She loves it. Cooking is her passion. She always says she wants everyone to experience some sliver of happiness in this shitty situation we're all in. That if she can contribute by providing delicious food, then she is happy."

"She sounds lovely," I said, averting my eyes back to the food in front of me. A deep sense of longing nestled deep in my heart, wishing I'd been raised here rather than at the King's Palace.

My heart dropped to my stomach, remembering that I had a session with Chrome. But then I cursed the flutter that quickly followed.

I cleared my eating area, trying to hide the mounting nerves. "I gotta go train with Chrome."

"Uh," Onyx piped in. When I looked at him, he was glancing between Kodiak and River.

"Out with it," I sighed, deflating the tension I'd worked myself into.

But it was Kodiak who answered. "Chrome isn't able to work with you today. He didn't get the chance to tell you himself, but he went out on a small mission."

My brows pinched. How come I didn't know about this? Was he purposefully ignoring me after yesterday? Would he not be training me at all anymore? I couldn't blame him if that were the case.

"Oh," I said, relaxing back into my seat, embarrassed. "Thanks for telling me."

"We're headed to the training arena to squeeze in a sparring session. You wanna join?" River asked, surprising me.

I didn't want to intrude or interfere with their plans, so I scanned their faces. Onyx looked hopeful, while Kodiak gave an encouraging soft smile. "You're welcome to join us. I'm supposed to be training with you in physical combat, anyhow," he said with a nod.

"I don't want to interfere..."

"You're not. Swear it, Gray. It'll be fun to train with a Kinetic again. Keep me on my toes," Onyx said, assuring me.

"You think you can keep up?" I taunted, surprised at how natural it felt.

Onyx gave a devious grin, a challenge written all over it. His pitch-black hair glinted from the sunlight filtering through the glass doors. "You're on, Princess."

The four of us paired up into teams of two in the training arena: guys versus girls. It was River's idea. She'd said the men around here were weak compared to the females.

Kodiak also wanted to sense my skill level—like Void had—so he could better train me.

I stood beside River in a sparring stance, shoulders squared, knees bent, and hands facing outward. We stood against the two men before us. One happened to be a giant in his own right.

I felt confident in my chances of taking out Onyx. We'd trained in the same place, likely by the same people—his father being one of them. But Onyx had earned himself an esteemed reputation within the Guilds as a guard back at the Kinetic stronghold. Well, not just at the Palace, but amongst the Kinetics all over the world.

Our abilities weren't to be used. They never were in the training arena. It was strictly for sparring and weapons only. No holds barred.

We all circled each other, sizing one another up. I wanted to match with Onyx, but I could tell the plan was for Kodiak to spar with me one-on-one.

It was Onyx who made the first move on River, all traces of the earlier humor and light-hearted nature gone. He became the fighter I'd always heard about. He feigned as if he were going to tackle her, and when she deflected, he struck her with his shin in her thigh, using a diagonal kick. She almost fell but stumbled to catch herself, which allowed Onyx the slight window of opportunity to exploit her momentary weakness.

That was all I could witness before I caught Kodiak's advance. I honed in on my target. He braced his hands in front of him, mirroring my own, but with lightning-quick speed, he threw a jab at my ribs. Because I wasn't expecting his swiftness, I wasn't able to defend against it in time.

I felt a bone crack, followed by a sharp pain that reverberated in my lungs, robbing me of my breath. I grunted but refused to nurse the injury.

I managed to land several blows before Kodiak started anticipating them. After he blocked my strikes, I aimed for the sensitive spot on the side of his knee. I thought I had him when he stumbled, but once again his agility took me by surprise.

In a blur, he landed three consecutive jabs—my cheek, ribs, and waist. In the half moment when I reeled from the confusion, he had me pinned on my back with two of my limbs locked in a bear hold. I gasped for air. A sharp pain seared my ribs with each breath as I waited for the healing process to begin.

"Fuck," I grunted, tapping out on the floor. "*That* was unexpected."

Kodiak released my limbs and rolled his crushing weight off my body. A deep chuckle rumbled through his chest, and he held out a palm to me to help me to my feet. "You're really good, Princess. But you have room to improve."

I nodded. "Do your worst."

"You're a fucking cheat!" River yelled, her sharp voice echoing throughout the training arena.

I looked over as I heard a deafening crack. Onyx lay on his back, a hand clutching his cheekbone. He released a long string of curses. "I didn't cheat, you cruel woman."

River stood over him, arms crossed over her chest. "I know."

I cocked an eyebrow at the two, confused by their antics. River stepped over him without a second glance. Then she settled those laser-focused eyes on me. "Go again?"

Three hours of sparring went by. Kodiak bested me several more times before I swapped with Onyx, where we each got several wins in. It took some time for me to maneuver around the Elemental's fighting style, but I adjusted and had Onyx on his ass a few times.

Kodiak would observe me while he and River took a break, offering tips and suggesting new techniques once the round between us was over.

It was a lighthearted session. Back at the King's Palace, that didn't exist. The Kinetic culture was so cutthroat that they considered anything less a weakness. I preferred the Elemental way.

"Well, that was fun," Onyx said as we walked out of the training arena. It was unusually warm outside, considering it was the beginning of November. It was Georgia, however, which meant the weather changed its mind every other week. The pleasant reprieve from the chilly air allowed me to spend more time outdoors.

"So, it's different from back at the King's Palace, isn't it?" Onyx asked. The late afternoon sun blinded us as we rounded the corner of the building, spotting a copse of oak trees to my right.

"It's the attitude here that has surprised me the most," I said. "People are actually *happy*."

"Yeah. We are. We don't have a dictator threatening our livelihoods at every turn. There's a freedom here that doesn't exist back there."

Freedom. The word rang around in my mind and struck me with longing. It was what I'd always craved. I'd never expected it to happen, but could I possibly be free here?

Onyx stopped walking. He combed his fingers through his star-flecked hair. His bright currents were stark against the deep reddish-brown hue of his complexion. He glanced around, awkwardness taking over. "I just want to say," he said, averting his gaze. "How the Kinetics treated you was total shit. The propaganda your father spread was..." Onyx shook his head and cleared his throat, meeting my eyes again. "I never bought into it. I always felt a king who publicly humiliated his own daughter—adopted or not—shouldn't be trusted. Turns out my intuition was right. I'm glad you're free and are here with us now...where you're wanted."

Tears stung my eyes as a knot formed in my throat. Why was everyone being so nice to me? I didn't feel like I deserved it.

I tried to swallow the knot, offering him a grateful smile. "Thank you for telling me that." My hand went to my chest. "Until now, I never realized how much I needed to hear it."

Onyx dipped his head. "You're a badass and our future queen. I gotta get on your good side from the start, ya know?"

A chuckle escaped me, followed by a sniffle. "Ass-kisser," I muttered.

Onyx threw a hand to his chest. "An ass-kisser I may be, but at least you know I'll have your back."

Without warning, Onyx wrapped his arms around me and pulled me into a tight hug. I tensed beneath his grip. I wasn't a hugger.

"I'm your new bestie. Get used to it," Onyx whispered into the top of my hair. "Come on, G. Just relax. I'm not gonna take you hostage."

"Are you sure about that?" another male voice piped in from behind Onyx, saving me from the assault.

The kid with flaming orange eyes that sparkled with mischief stood with a smirk on his face. "Well," he said. "Looks like you are, in fact, full of rainbows." He looked way too pleased with himself.

I recalled the remark he'd made in the meeting, "*Well, isn't she just full of rainbows?*" I remained silent, observing the younger male, who oddly resembled River.

Onyx looked at my eyes and barked a laugh as it registered. "Blaize, meet the ever-cheerful Princess Gray. Gray, this is Blaize, the Hollow's resident nuisance."

Blaize punched Onyx in the arm. "I take offense to that." He picked off the invisible lint on his white shirt before settling those fiery eyes on me. "I'm the bringer of joy, but it comes with the drawback of attracting joy killers. One must overlook such deviants and keep the spirits high."

Who was this kid? He had a naturally easy aura about him, making it difficult not to smile.

Onyx rolled his eyes. "That's a little excessive..."

"'Tis not!" Blaize declared with conviction. "The likes of you and those of your kind are what's excessive. You with your..." He crinkled his button nose, scrunching up his high cheekbones. "Your rabble-rousing and childish antics."

"I think you're confusing me with yourself, Blaize," Onyx said, shaking his head.

Blaize whipped his head to face me. A black strand of hair fell loose from the top knot on his head. "Is he bothering you, my lady? I can *easily* get rid of him."

"Oh, for fuck's sake, Blaize. Do I need to get River to personally remove your obnoxious ass?" Onyx said, clearly exasperated with this conversation.

"Joy killer," Blaize muttered with an eye roll. He stuffed his hands in his pockets, exposing the tattoos adorning his native skin, shimmering in gold.

A smug smile painted Onyx's attractive features. "Works every time."

"Well," I said, turning my attention to Blaize. "Thanks for the introduction. It was...uh *nice*...to meet you." The word "nice" felt like a flat word to describe that exchange.

"Seriously, if he bothers you," Blaize said, jabbing a thumb toward Onyx. "Let me know. I'll take care of him."

"You're like the little brother nobody asked for."

I chuckled, and both males lit up from the simple act. "I'll see you guys around. Thanks for the sparring session, Onyx. Nice to meet you, Blaize." I offered a small wave as I backed away, dipping my head before turning around.

I wasn't sure where I was heading, but I needed solitude. Social interaction drained me after so long.

I meandered around the Hollow's property, finding trails where the sun streams drifted through the trees, giving the place an ethereal glow. A cozy copse was nestled off to the side, surrounded by verdant grass where Elementals lazed around, enjoying the warmer weather.

I drifted back toward the lake Orion had shown me the previous day. He was right. The beauty and quiet brought a majestic feel to the space. The water lapped against the bank hypnotically, silencing my thoughts.

I found a large boulder perched under an oak tree. I climbed on top, hugging my knees to my chest as I stared ahead and absorbed the pure energy—not for my Kinetic magic but to restore my soul.

My entire life had flipped upside down. Had someone told me a few weeks ago that this is where I'd end up, I'd have questioned their sanity.

A soft breeze caressed my cheek, tickling my scalp. Ripples in the water waltzed over the sparkling surface. The new power within me stirred, itching to flow freely.

I closed my eyes and listened to the power's gentle pleas. Holding out a hand, I released a stream of air from my palm.

My eyelids drifted open, and I tested my limits by swaying my hand from side to side. Air zig-zagged back and forth before I pushed it outward toward a pile of fallen leaves. A swirl of red, orange, and yellow shot upward, scattering sporadically. But I made them remain, levitating on a wall of air.

I smiled. Peace. This was a peace that I'd never known I could have.

"Beautiful, isn't it?"

I jumped, losing concentration of my control of my element. I spun around on the boulder.

Chrome hunched in shadow near the lake's clearing, looking like an avenging angel ready to toy with his mark.

Chapter 37

GRAY

Chrome looked like shit. His golden skin lacked its normal vibrancy and luster, while his tousled chromatic hair appeared unwashed.

"How'd you find me?" I narrowed my eyes at him, willing my heartbeat to slow to a normal pace. I hugged my knees to my chest again.

He stepped closer until he stood only a foot before me. "I have my ways," he mumbled. Something was wrong.

Upon closer inspection, I noted how his eyes were bloodshot and heavy-lidded, bruised below with blueish-purple circles. He reeked of the strong tang of whiskey as if it leaked from his pores. "What's wrong?"

I didn't feel any foreign emotions like I had in the training field. All was empty and quiet on his end, which confused me. How did this phenomenon work?

Chrome snorted and then slurred, "What isn't wrong, little savage? Everything is wrong." I caught him wringing his fingers with one another, twisting, twining, and squeezing until they were nearly white.

Why was he wearing a ripped hoodie? And was that blood splotching the black fabric? A sheen of sweat washed out his golden complexion. "If you're hot, you can just take off the hoodie."

He gave a half-hearted, hoarse laugh, being vigilant to not look me in the eye. "Oh, you'd like that, wouldn't you?"

"Fuck off." The air within me stirred to attention, ready to protect if needed.

"Mhm..." He swayed on his feet. "Oh, don't get all feisty with me now, Princess. I only came by to return your necklace."

I arched my brows as he fumbled through each of the many pockets of his black cargo pants that had seen better days.

"Day drinking's your thing?" I asked as he continued to search his pockets.

He peeked through the curtain of his reflective hair. "Careful. It sounds like you give a shit."

"I'm pretty sure your people might. Can't have a drunken leader promising to free them from my father's tyrannical bullshit, can they?"

"I've never made such promises. I'm going to kill the motherfucker...probably die in the process. *Then*, they can do with the world as they please." Chrome shrugged and nearly fell forward, only barely catching himself at the last second.

Realization dawned on me. "That's why you brought me here: to become their leader. You don't expect to be around after all is said and done."

Chrome stood up straight and continued his search for my necklace. This time in his back pockets. A dark, crooked smile taunted me. "Well, look who thinks she has it all figured out. You know nothing of the gravity of this situation."

Anger burned a fiery path through my veins at his condescension. I'd been talked down to enough throughout my life. I had to put up with it from my father, but I didn't have to deal with it anymore. "Well, how about you do me a solid and fucking tell me?"

Chrome retrieved the necklace from a pocket on his pants leg at last. He looked at me with empty, reddened eyes that said he had nothing to lose. Those were eyes that spoke more than his words ever would.

"Why would you listen to someone who *disgusts* you?"

I felt the verbal slap as if he'd physically done it himself. The guilt from yesterday came thrashing to the surface, and my anger dissipated faster than my little nature show had upon his arrival.

"I...I'm..." I stuttered, searching for the right words but falling short. My heart clenched with shame. "I'm sorry I said that. I shouldn't..."

"Forget it. Here's your necklace." He tossed the heavy black stone to me. "We have a session tomorrow. Lucky for you, Orion will be there."

I sat there with my mouth hanging open, squeezing my knees tighter to my chest. He swallowed, the knot in his throat bobbing with the motion, pinning me in place with his lifeless gaze for several silent moments before he turned and stumbled away, back through the clearing.

Chrome left me staring after him, yet I couldn't bring myself to stop him.

I held the black crystal necklace in my palm, already feeling my Elemental magic weakening. I set it down beside me on the boulder, wondering what use I even had for the thing now. Like Kinetics, Elementals used bracelets to mask their natures if they needed to.

Sentimentality be damned as it never belonged to my mother. The necklace had only been a tool for Forest to manipulate me.

Fuck him.

I picked the necklace up again, rearing my arm back. Allowing my turmoil to fuel me, I launched the stone into the lake. It sailed thirty feet before landing with a heavy *thunk* in the water.

That was liberating.

After basking in my minor victory for a few minutes, my thoughts returned to Chrome. What was going on with him? Surely he couldn't be that drunk because of me? He'd said there was more that I didn't understand. What more could there possibly be?

I didn't know how long I'd remained on that large boulder. A couple of hours passed, judging by the sun. Along with my mood, it sank beneath the horizon, stealing the day's warmth with it. I pulled my hoodie back on.

A weight sat on my chest, crushing me, as I recalled Chrome's lifeless stare that said so much while he'd said so little. I had to make this right. I wasn't sure how, but I'd do it because no one deserved that level of pain.

It was dark when I approached the front porch of the lodge. That didn't mean it was abandoned. Elementals loitered about in conversation and laughter. Now and then, I'd see a shadow floating in the air, and after closer inspection, I'd see it was a piece of wood or stone being lazily guided by the wielder, as if it was their companion.

It grew more difficult to keep my Kinetic form hidden. The need to set my currents free and my magic flowing set me on edge. Onyx and Chrome liberated their Kinetic forms. Perhaps it would be accepted if I did, too. More than likely, I was overthinking the idea I'd step on toes too soon. I wasn't willing to risk upsetting the kindness they'd granted me in providing a place to stay.

My boots clunked up the sturdy wooden steps of the vast front porch. Lights illuminated it in sconces, creating a cozy atmosphere. I rushed through the hulking double doors with plans to isolate in the privacy of my room.

"Gray!" A sharp voice caught my attention to my right.

My steps hitched, and I scanned the area for the voice.

River. And beside her sat Aella and Onyx.

I internally groaned. It wasn't that I didn't like them; I simply needed solitude. Especially after my encounter with Chrome. "Hey, I was just headed..." I cast my eyes toward the ornate, spiraling staircase.

"Over here," River said. Onyx held his usual smug smile. Aella was stiff and looked at me with a wary gaze.

"I'm tired. I need to..."

"Come here." River crossed her arms over her chest. Her severe expression left no room for argument.

Resigned, I sulked over to the three Elementals sitting within a group of lofty cushioned chairs. Glasses of brown and clear liquor sat atop the oak coffee table in the middle of their group.

I approached the trio. River sat stiff-backed in the chair with one leg draped perfectly over the other. Onyx propped his ass on the arm of Aella's chair. Her elbow perched on the other arm, resting her jaw on her fist as she assessed me.

I raised my brows, my hands going to my waist as I faced them. "Is it important?"

River gave me a slow smile. It was Onyx, however, who answered, "Of course it's important. You're hanging out with us tonight."

I sighed, noting the acoustic guitar leaning against the chair. "I'm tired and just wanna shower and go to bed."

"Dude!" Onyx said. "Can I call you that? Or do you prefer your highness? Or lady? Or—"

"Shut up, O," River piped in with a sharp eye roll.

"As I was saying..." Onyx cut in again. "It's only seven. You can't go to bed that early," he said, appalled at the idea.

"If she wants to go, let her. Clearly she doesn't want to be around us." Aella narrowed her blue-and-white eyes as she addressed me for the first time. She had opinions, and it was obvious she didn't trust me. I didn't fault her for that.

I dropped my arms. "It's not that I don't want to be around you. I'm just tired, overwhelmed even. There's so much I'm still processing." I held out my golden palms as if that explained everything.

Onyx nodded in understanding and dropped his eyes. River's violet gaze seared through me. "You need to decompress, Gray. Look, I'm not the social type either. Ask anyone. But even I need to be around others. Come chill with us."

I dropped my shoulders in defeat with a sigh. "Fine. But I'm gonna need a drink."

Aella cracked the smallest of smiles as if I'd passed some test I was unaware of. Onyx jumped to his feet. "I'll go! We need refills, anyway."

If Chrome could get blasted drunk in the middle of the day, then I could have a few. I think I was entitled to it after the past week.

Aella turned out to be fun. It was a pleasant surprise, considering her distant behavior toward me from day one.

After having consumed a few glasses of 'shine, I loosened up around the trio. I found them rather easy to converse and joke with.

Aella had a rather loose tongue due to the drinks. She sat sprawled in the large black chair where full springy curls bunched up around her reclined head. "Ya know..." she said in a high-pitched voice. "I like you. I mean...I *actually* like you, Gray. Didn't think I would...with you being that asshole's daughter and all." She gave a dainty shrug.

I laughed. It felt so good to laugh again. "How did you miss my outgoing nature?"

River and Onyx joined in on our laughter.

"You guys should've seen it," Onyx said, slouched in a man-spread in his own chair. "You would've thought Chrome dragged her in by the roots of her hair when she first arrived." He gripped his gut, laughing at the memory.

I kept laughing with them. "Oh, shut up. Had you witnessed the beastie-bear, you would've looked like that, too."

Everyone's mirth suddenly died. I looked around, lacing my fingers together in my lap. "What?"

They looked at each other, silently questioning who would ask. It was Aella. "Did you and Chrome really open a portal and send it back?"

I studied my hands in my lap. "So it seems..."

River sat rigid in her chair, still looking regal. "What happened? Chrome gave us the brief rundown, as you heard, but we want the full play-by-play. Spill it."

My wide grin reached my eyes. I was all in for it. I *needed* to tell this story. So, I did, starting from the train.

Their eyes were wide as I told the tale. Onyx's mouth hung slack, riveted as he remained slumped in his seat. Aella sat up, focusing her eyes on me. Not once did she cast a distrustful look. And River, even drunk, was clear-eyed and sharp, not missing a detail.

When I finished, it was Aella who asked, "Can we see them?" And when I cocked my head in confusion at her question, she clarified, "Your currents? We've obviously seen Onyx's and Chrome's, but everyone is curious to see yours. I bet they're pretty."

I couldn't help the blush that crept up my neck at the attention. It wasn't the type of attention I was used to. No one had ever taken an interest in me like that before. "Sure. I've been hesitant to free my Kinetic form around here—"

"What?" Onyx cut me off, scrambling to sit up straight. "Are you fucking serious? Gray, it's been how long?"

I opened and closed my mouth. Was he *scolding* me? Shifting in my seat and looking away, I said, "Uhm...since the beastie bear?"

"What the hell? Take the damn thing off. Let us see it all," Onyx demanded—damn, so stern. I wanted to laugh but held it in.

"He doesn't mean literally *everything*," Aella said with a shake of her head.

I chuckled and looked around the lodge, scanning for other Elementals nearby.

River caught me. "It's fine. Everyone knows what you are, Princess. We all accept that like we did with Chrome. It's actually weird to us that you *haven't* exposed your Kinetic form yet."

I took a deep breath and nodded. "Okay, but I don't know how it will feel now that my Elemental form isn't suppressed anymore. Maybe we should go outside..." I said, not wanting to risk bringing down the lodge.

"Sounds great," said Onyx with a clap of his hands. "Bring the 'shine."

We stood outside in the training field Chrome had taken me to yesterday. I shook out my arms as they all stood in front of me. Onyx's orange currents gave him an eerie glow in the darkness. He looked relaxed, but I could tell he was ready to act in defense if something went wrong.

My Kinetic magic pulsed within me, sensing it was about to be freed. I closed my eyes and took a calming breath, letting the air settle in my chest. The alcohol made me feel lighter, but I was still anxious about combining the two forces untested...while drunk. Was it the best idea? Probably not.

"You guys ready?" I asked, looking each of them in the eyes.

"Fuck, yes!" Onyx said way too emphatically.

I cocked an eyebrow at him, and he shrugged. "What? I've been dying to see another set of currents around this place for a while. Chrome's always wearing that beaten up cloak or something."

I understood that. It must feel isolating to be the only pure Kinetic in an Elemental stronghold, no matter how loyal you were to their cause.

"Okay," I said. I blew out a breath. "Here it goes." I snapped off the metal clasp of my suppressing bracelet.

The air element within me stirred at the presence of the energetic waves pulsing in my veins. It was as if they greeted one another while they twined around the other in a sensitive dance. They never got too close, but it was *euphoric.*

I dropped my head back. The electric blue currents glowed to life on my forearms and raced up my neck. I couldn't feel it, but I knew my glamoured, ice-blonde hair had morphed into its unusual dual-toned medley of white and black that resembled marble.

"Wow," I heard Aella say in awe. "We have a beautiful princess, you guys!"

"And powerful." That was River.

On instinct, I absorbed the energy waves around me. The sounds, the movement, and even the faint light coming from the lodge fed my Kinetic power.

Once I felt sated, I lowered my head and looked at the others. They stared at me in awe. "The king is a fucking idiot for creating two weapons that will be responsible for his death." Onyx's amber eyes gleamed with hope and determination.

A smile crept up the sides of my cheek, relishing no longer feeling powerless.

Aella wanted to see my ability in action next. We shared the same element, but Kinetic powers were foreign to them aside from Onyx and Chrome's.

So, I showed them while also stretching my magic's legs for the first time in several days. I would mold the energy waves into tiny balls of compact energy and release it straight up into the air, causing little blue, electrical explosions.

Aella was fascinated. Onyx was accustomed to our range of abilities. River, however, watched with a studious air. She stood with her lips tight and her arms crossed, as if she were breaking it down in ways her brain could understand best.

"Maybe we should head back now," I said reluctantly, feeling wholly free for the first time.

Everyone nodded, and we all soon trekked our way to the lodge.

Once we reached the staircase, we decided to part ways and turn in for the night.

"It was great hanging with you tonight, Gray. Thanks for sharing your Kinetic form with us," Aella said, gripping my hands in her dainty ebony ones laced in gold. She offered a kind smile, softening those baby-blue-and-milky-white eyes.

I dipped my head and returned a one-sided smile. "Thank you for accepting me. I'm so grateful."

Onyx opened his mouth to say something, but I felt it before I heard it. I felt the sound waves slamming into me from a distance. Energy waves that told me someone was pounding the ground in a full sprint toward us.

I stiffened and snapped my attention in the direction it came from. "Wait," I said, holding up a blue-lit hand. "Someone's coming."

They all frowned, not understanding why I seemed bothered by this. "Okay? There's a bunch of people here, Gray..." Onyx said.

"No," I said. "Something's wrong."

About that time, the front doors of the lodge slammed open, ushering in Blaize. "River!"

River stiffened. She moved with perfect posture to meet him. "What is it?"

Blaize, whose black top knot fell loose around his face, was breathless. His fiery eyes burned with fear. "There's someone here," he said between breaths. "A Kinetic."

We all glanced between each other in question. River and Aella flitted their unearthly eyes back and forth between Onyx and me. We were all thinking the same thing; maybe Blaize saw my power display outside, probably from a distance, and freaked.

"No," Blaize said, shaking his head hard enough to knock the bun lower on his head. "Not *them*," he said, glancing between Onyx and me. "Another one."

"There's no way," Onyx said, shaking his head. "I checked the wards earlier. They were firmly intact." He closed his eyes. After several silent beats he opened them with a shrug. "Still are."

I mentally kicked myself for numbing my awareness with alcohol. We all had. Onyx more than the rest.

Fear gripped my chest like a vice grip. I knew they'd find me. How could I be so fucking stupid to think my father wouldn't track me down? Now, he knew where the Elementals' main Hollow was hidden.

Fuck. Fuck. Fuck.

"Did you see them?" I asked Blaize.

Blaize shook his head again. "No, they were shrouded in darkness, but not before I saw the glow of currents. And they weren't any of theirs." He motioned a hand at Onyx and me.

"Have you informed Orion? Chrome?" River asked. She should be the one with the fire element as fierce as her gaze bored into Blaize, threatening to incinerate him on the spot.

"No, I came straight in, and you guys are the first I ran across," he rushed out in his defense.

River turned to Onyx. "You're his Second. Find him. Now."

Onyx disappeared before she finished her command. He took the stairs two at a time, somehow not tripping during his ascent.

Chapter 38

GRAY

"Let's find Orion," River said, heading for the stairs. "But we need Chrome to secure the wards."

The alcohol still buzzed through my system, but thankfully, none of us had drank to the point of no return. With a fuzzy yet clear enough mind, River, Blaize, and I followed Onyx up the stairs to seek Orion.

Once we hit the landing, I felt it. The presence Blaize had mentioned. It was distant—too distant to detect it specifically—yet I could sense the familiar Kinetic aura.

"What is it?" River asked when I stopped abruptly. I scanned the area as if the intruder would pop out at any moment despite knowing they were too far away.

I stretched my awareness to locate and detect the source. It was like a word on the tip of my tongue. I knew it, but their identity wouldn't come to my mortal brain.

Shoving my fingers through my hair, I growled, "I know who it is, but I..." I trailed off, still trying to place them. "They're just too far away." I ran my palm over my face. "*Fuck.*"

River's violet eyes zeroed in on me before casting her keen stare out into the darkness beyond the wall windows on the top floor.

"I'm going to find them. You go find Orion," I said and turned to head back down the steps.

River latched a tight grip on my wrist, snatching me to a halt. "No. You can't go alone."

"I'm fine. I can handle Kinetics," I said because I could. I may not be Chrome Freyr, but they feared me for a reason.

Blaize shifted his weight back and forth, casting his flaming irises between his sister and me.

I shook my head. "Just go. Let me find them before they get too far." I spun around, taking off down the stairs without looking back.

The night grew significantly quieter, as if nature knew there was an unwelcome guest in its midst.

The chill in the breeze bit my cheeks. I pulled my hood over my head and held my arms steady by my sides, ready to attack. The leaves crunched beneath my boots despite my best efforts to silence them. Closing my eyes, I scanned the area with my magic.

The energy waves of the intruding Kinetic retreated into the woods. I still couldn't detect them, but the familiar essence clawed at my mind. Taunting me.

"You should be inside." A deep, raw voice broke through the evening's eerie calm.

I spun, summoning an electric ball ready in my palms. I relaxed upon seeing the feline-shaped eyes illuminated by the glow of my magic. "Holy shit. Don't sneak up on me like that."

"You really need to be more aware of your surroundings, little savage," Chrome said. His tone was flat, deep, and unnervingly quiet. I could barely make out his words.

I lowered my hands and relaxed my stance. "Where've you been? There was a Kinetic here."

"I know. I sensed them." Chills trickled down my spine at the deadness in his tone, whereas his eyes were wild—manic.

"So," I asked, with widened eyes. "We gotta do something. We can't just—"

"I already handled it." Chrome's breaths were harsh as he cut me off. "They're gone."

"Gone?" I asked, skeptical.

"Yeah. They won't be coming back."

I tilted my head as I studied him in the faint light between us. Both of us exposed our full hybrid forms, mirror images of one another. But all I could see was his shaking shoulders. His teeth chattered while glistening beads of sweat trailed down his temples.

"What's going on with you, Chrome?" I asked. The ominous feeling ratcheted up at the sight of him, reminding me of the night I discovered him spiraling in the abandoned house.

Still shaking, his frenzied gaze pleaded to me. "I need your help."

I frowned. The longer I remained there, the more my gut twisted. "What can I do?"

"I...I...just..." He chattered through gritted teeth. "Just...be...be near me. It helps."

I nodded. "Okay," I whispered and sat on the prickly grass, patting the spot next to me.

He hesitated for a moment, jerking his head around in paranoia. He took a few shaky steps and settled beside me, shoulder brushing against shoulder.

He held out his hand. "Touch," he said through gritted teeth. "I need it."

I bit my lower lip, my frown deepening. None of this made sense, but if he thought it would help him, I'd oblige. To see someone of his strength and caliber crumbling before me cleaved my soul.

So, I placed my golden palm, alight with my currents, in his. His silver currents complimented mine, but I shut down the thought before I could let it gain any traction. "Talk to me. About anything," I said, noting his clammy hand.

Chrome squeezed my fingers like it was a lifeline, sending a tingle up my arm that spread to my chest at the feel of his calloused skin on mine. "I...I'll try." That tone, so hopeless, twisted my heart.

"I'll go first," I said, wracking my brain for something remotely interesting. But then it hit me. I looked sideways at his profile, noticing the gauntness. "I'm sorry for what I said yesterday. I didn't mean it."

His chin dropped to his chest—his head seemed too heavy to hold upright any longer. He chuckled with no sign of amusement. "No, you were right. If...if only you...you knew...you'd see how disgusting I truly am."

I shook my head. "No," I said, my voice growing sharp. "Don't. Don't do that to yourself. You're struggling with...something, but look at what you've done. At what you're doing. You're far from that." I focused on the lodge ahead of us, illuminated by the moonlight on the hilltop. "I said that because I've never had any control over my life. Every action I've ever made has been monitored by my father or someone he appointed. Hearing that...struck a nerve. And I didn't handle it well."

Chrome shook his head. "No," he said, his voice growing even more hoarse. "You don't understand," he said. "I wish I could tell you, but...it could...ruin everything." A hard shiver wracked his body, and he groaned a pain-filled noise, fraying a thread on my heart.

"Then, tell me. You said I could help, right?" He didn't respond. His head hung low, resigned to whatever fate he'd convinced himself awaited him. "Look, I trusted you enough to not lock me up, torture, and kill me when you brought me here. Everything inside me screamed I was walking into a trap, that I was a fucking idiot for entertaining the thought you weren't the heartless killer I believed you were." I released his hand and cupped his jaw, stubble poking the skin on my palms, and forced him to meet my eyes.

Empty shells hollowed out those fierce eyes I knew. Broken. "I trusted you enough when I shouldn't have. You can trust me, Chrome." I held his gaze, willing him to start somewhere, anywhere.

Several beats of silence passed. He gave nothing away—not even a blink. I was about to accept defeat and withdraw my palms from his face. He wrapped his long fingers around the tops of my hands to stop me, shifting them to rest between us without letting go.

Chrome faced forward again, gazing at the back side of the lodge. He took a shuddering breath to steady himself for what he was about to confess. I was scared to breathe—afraid any sound or movement would make him change his mind.

"You know how I was conceived. Amethyst...she's twisted on a level few are aware of. Not even you," he said and shook his head, his metallic hair catching in the moon's rays like a halo. "She and your father knew how powerful I'd become. They had bred me, after all. But they needed to control me. I needed to be *broken*...from a young age."

My gut sank, preparing for the horrific tale I knew was coming.

"Amethyst and Grim got together right after I was born. They formed a sick type of bond that centered on depravity. By the time I turned one, they were married. Then, Peri was born the next year. Amethyst never loved me. Hell, she never even liked me. She hated me for who my biological father was. But Peri, she was *theirs*." Chrome took a deep breath before he continued, squeezing my hand again. "I loved Peri, too. She was my baby sister, and I felt this intense need to protect her. She was just...the embodiment of light. A joy. They doted on her and luckily spared her from their twisted shit. But me? No, I was the abomination, but one they'd use to their advantage.

"They beat me—a lot. But after a while, I'd grown desensitized. I'd manifested my Elemental powers way before the natural age. And then, a few days later, my Kinetic magic awakened with you on the playground. Orion and I believe it's because the abuse fueled it, but also, there was something about you and me that sparked it into manifestation," he explained. He'd regained color to his pallor since holding my hand. Steadiness returned to his voice, and the shivering was receding. But his hand never wavered from mine. Now, he was only a touch of gold and madness, instead of a full blown assault.

"I was ten years old. And that day, they realized my strength. They *knew*. They knew I could easily overpower them and feared I'd one day retaliate for all their abuse. But instead of changing course, they doubled down. Grim...he," he whispered, looking too ashamed to say it out loud.

I felt sick. The alcohol burned my stomach, threatening to retch at where this was headed. But I stayed still, willing myself not to react, to allow him this safety.

"He violated me. *Owned* me." His voice broke.

My free hand covered my mouth, tears blurring my vision as I choked down emotion. "Chrome..."

Chrome shook his head, forcing himself to push forward. "They needed me to know they were my masters, no matter how powerful I was. They needed me broken—spiritually and mentally. So, I went on to become the person every Kinetic reveres. But the people only knew the persona they'd crafted as the face of our kind. It was a role. And I played it well while becoming what they wanted. I had no will to fight them, even when I became their personal lab rat.

"They would take me down to the interrogation room and push me to the brink of death. They'd torture me, starve me from replenishing my reserves from either form. All so they'd see what I was capable of and what they were dealing with. But they fucked up." He paused and bit the inside of his cheek.

This horror story was about to worsen.

"The worst happened when I was sixteen. Weeks went by, and I hadn't replenished either form. My Elemental form was going insane. It was such a hell that I couldn't think straight. I needed to feed from an aura. It didn't matter whose it was or how much I'd take. I didn't care whether I depleted them, even knowing the risk. Add to that, I was starved from my Kinetic energy, too. It was the worst form of torture anyone could imagine.

"So, when they brought someone in the room, I was mindless. Their orders, however, were for me to restrain myself. They wanted me to have self-control while in a depraved state. And they assumed since they brought the one person I cared about the most, the one person I'd do anything to protect, I'd be able to achieve it."

Tears slid down his cheeks, the wetness darkening the gold skin on his profile. "Peri didn't stand a chance. I fed from her aura...and...and I couldn't stop. Gray, I couldn't fucking *stop*." He shoved his free hand into his hair as he wept, his shoulders shaking with silent sobs.

My heart splintered, slicing my soul. Hot tears streamed down my cheeks alongside him. This was beyond sadistic. How was he even still going?

"I depleted her," he whispered. "I killed my baby sister, the only person who had ever shown me any love. My best friend."

I wrapped my arms around his shoulders, pulling him into me. Words wouldn't suffice for something like this. Hell, I wasn't good with words, to begin with. So, I remained silent, holding him in his pain.

I felt it again, the humming tug on my heart chakra. Then, a soul-splintering ache erupted in my chest as if it were my own. I knew it was his emotions again, like I'd felt his anger the day before. I took it in silence and grieved with him. The least I could do was give him the chance to finally not bear this loss alone.

"It wasn't your fault, Chrome," I said through choked sobs.

Chrome buried his face in the crook of my shoulder. "I killed her. I should've stopped."

His emotions were like a torrential storm finally being set free into the night. Even the soothing comfort of air within me couldn't appease the pain. I wanted to scream at the pale beacon in the sky to do something. To bring her back. None of this was fair. How did no one know about this?

"No one could've withstood that temptation," I said. My tears soaked through the black fabric of his hoodie.

"I was supposed to, and I failed. So, I deserve to suffer for it."

I sucked in a breath and pulled away, forcing him to meet my eyes again. I'd never seen such a broken look on a man before. Bracing his face in my hands, I said, "No. No, you don't. They do. And they will. We will take their heads, but first, they will pay for what they've done."

The liquid metal in his irises twitched again, wanting to stir at my words. Chrome's jaw tightened. His beauty was drenched in his tears. Slowly, without breaking eye contact, he regained control of himself with a harsh sniffle. I could sense the strength rebuilding—see it hardening in the steel of his eyes.

"Yes, we will, my little savage," he said, his voice but a mere rumble in his chest. His warm breath washed over my own tears. Lifting a hand, he slowly—oh so slowly—combed his fingers through my marbled locks. "They have so much to answer for."

His gravelly voice, hoarse from the turbulent emotions, brought a heat to my chest that had nothing to do with anger. It spread, warming me against the crisp night air. My lungs constricted at the intensity of his gaze that pinned me in place. That gaze that said he saw it all, *felt* it all. The look that's unnerved me since the moment I held my knife to his throat in the speakeasy.

I nodded, unable to form any coherent thoughts between the shift in his stare—now shining vibrant with life—and the large hand that cradled the back of my head with renewed strength.

"You look so fucking beautiful in your full form," Chrome whispered. "You're my rainbow. My beam of hope."

My cheeks flushed hot. I sat there, too captivated by him to do anything but hold his gaze. Something kept tickling the back of my mind. Something that kept begging me to speak on it, but I couldn't bring myself to focus. I was lost, drowning in whatever thrall he seemed to have me in.

"Thank you, Gray," Chrome murmured.

For what?

But after a moment, I shook my head, forcing myself to regain my senses again. I squeezed my eyes shut, willing myself back to reality, to the present.

I cleared my throat. His hand remained fixed on the back of my head as if he was afraid to let go. "No, thank you for trusting me with such..." I trailed off. That niggling thought persisted.

The pieces clicked together. If he...

"Wait..." I froze. My eyes widened, heart racing. "If you depleted her, that means..." I whispered, scared to voice it aloud.

Chrome's eyes fell away from mine. As did his hand, leaving an icy shiver in its wake.

"Yeah," Chrome said, shame filling his tone once again. He squared his shoulders. "When I depleted Peri, it thrust me into devolution. I'm becoming Endarkened."

Chapter 39

GRAY

Someone took a serrated dagger to my heart. Or so it felt.

How was I supposed to react to that kind of news? Becoming Endarkened was a fate far worse than death.

I immediately thought of the woman we'd faced back in the deserted small town. How her skin was gray—peeling—while blackish blood oozed from her decaying flesh. How mindless she had been.

The image of Chrome morphing into that rabid being, seeking only the next aura to consume...

Everything about him would be gone.

The thought wrung my insides more than I'd ever expected it to. There was clearly some type of connection between us that grew with each meeting, starting with our first encounter as children. I'd been resisting it because of my devotion to Slate.

A hand covered my mouth as I scanned the hopeless expression on his crestfallen face. *This* was the weight on his shoulders he carried with dignity and strength. The weight he hid from the world. Tears welled up in my eyes again. "No," I whispered. "There has to be some other way..."

Chrome cupped my cheek, severing my hope with an apology sitting heavy in his eyes. "No, Rainbow. There's not. I've been fighting it off, but I don't know for how much longer."

"How bad is it? Where are you in the process?" I dared to ask, not really wanting to know the answer.

Chrome pursed his lips and closed his eyes, struggling to swallow. "I'm in the second phase. I only have one more time before I'm gone."

I exhaled a suffocating, shaky breath, as if all oxygen was being devoured in a vacuum. "Fuck," I said. "How have you held out this long? It's unheard of."

Chrome shrugged. "I had a lot to live for. But I'm not going anywhere until those three are dead and the Elementals are in good hands."

"Is that what the drinking is about?" I asked, ignoring the possibility of him not being around after we achieved our goals.

Chrome nodded, his thumb rubbing gently against my cheekbone. "Yeah, that...and other extreme recreational activities help numb the craving enough to where I can have some clarity to my thoughts. The *cravings*..." He shuddered. "God, Gray. It's unbearable. The withdrawals, too. You saw what they do."

I recalled the sweaty, clammy skin, the shaking, chattering, fidgeting, and, of course, his paranoia that night. "Is it like that all the time? Or does it just come in waves?"

"The cravings are always there. The thought of depleting someone and becoming powerful enough to wipe out the Kinetic kingdom alone is so fucking enticing. I have this voice, *Grim's* voice, always taunting me to succumb to the call. Always telling me shit that makes me feel like I'd be better off Endarkened. He threatens and..." he stopped.

The warmth of his hand left my cheek, replaced by the chilled bite from a breeze. "That's what happened that night? Back at that house?"

Chrome nodded again. "Yeah, I was having a pretty bad episode that night until you walked in..."

I frowned and shook my head. "I don't understand. How do *I* help?" My ass was going numb from the hard ground, so I adjusted to where I perched on my knees. Only an inch separated us.

Chrome offered a resigned smile. "I don't know, but your presence eases the withdrawals. Touching you takes it away somehow while also bringing back memories that the devolution process steals from you. I don't know. Perhaps it's a hybrid thing..."

I pondered over his outward thoughts. He'd never fallen prey to these fits around me during our journey to the Perry Hollow. However, every time I found him in that state, it wasn't long before his condition improved.

"Well, perhaps if we stick together, we can find a way to beat this?" I asked, a tiny spark of hope igniting in my chest. It was a dangerous emotion I didn't indulge in often, but I'd already lost Slate. I didn't want to lose something with potential before it even began.

A devious smile tilted upward. "I knew you couldn't get enough of me, little savage. I guess all I needed was a sob story to keep you around."

I punched him in the arm, not holding back. He laughed, deep and throaty, with his head tipped toward the moon. A hand nursed the biceps I'd struck.

"Not funny, asshole," I said, pointing an accusing finger at him with a sharp glare.

After he regained himself, he zeroed in on me again. "I know. But I won't object to spending more time with you."

My heartbeat faltered at his words and the emotions emanating from him. I gulped. "Who else knows about this?"

"No one. Only those who witnessed me..." Chrome squeezed his eyes shut to ward off the memories. "Just you, Princess."

"I won't tell anyone." In the meantime, I'd search for a way to fix this. "If you start experiencing the physical withdrawal symptoms, you have my permission to touch me."

Shit. I bit my lip and winced at my insinuating delivery.

Someone fucking come get me. Now.

Chrome's quicksilver eyes swirled with a tempestuous heat, like molten lava. His nostrils flared. In a tone that came from his chest, he said, "I'm going to need you to clarify what you mean by *'touch you.'* Because I'm going to be honest, Gray. There's a million ways I want to touch you. And none of them are innocent."

Oh.

My core bottomed out. I shook my head, trying to gain control of my libido. How long had it been? Too long now. I wasn't a virgin, and I'd be damned if I was going to act like one.

I tilted my head to the side, pretending to scrutinize him. When, in actuality, I was trying to slow my heart rate and shut down my raging hormones. The images of Chrome touching me, kissing me, pinning me to a bed...a wall...a *godsdamn* tree...would not go away, no matter how much I willed it.

"What are my emotions telling you?" My voice dipped lower. I knew he could feel them still. I could feel his, but mine were much louder.

Chrome smirked. "That you want more than just innocent touches." He narrowed in on my lips. "If you keep biting your lip like that..."

I popped my lip from between my teeth, unaware I'd been doing that. His lips were only a breath away from mine. My heart sped up in anticipation, waiting for the brush of his lips and whatever else would follow.

I didn't breathe as he leaned in, fingers weaving through my hair and gripping it with a gentle firmness. He angled my head, making me look into those eyes that said everything. It hit every emotional chord that sat dangling from fringed strings.

It was too much. As much as I wanted to give in to the moment with Chrome, I couldn't. I wasn't ready. I still felt like I'd be betraying Slate.

I dropped my gaze and let out the breath I'd been holding. Our knees were now touching, and I was unsure when that had happened, too.

Chrome understood. He loosened his grip on my hair and pulled away, giving me space. I was ashamed to look at him. "I'm sorry," I said, finding a blade of grass on the ground and focusing on it.

"No," he said. The authority he held as the leader of Elementals rang deep in his voice. "Gray, look at me."

I did.

Understanding and empathy cascaded in smooth waves in the metallic irises. "Don't ever, and I mean *never*, apologize for that. I would never guilt you for owning your body." He understood what it meant to not have control over his. "I feel your emotions. You wouldn't be betraying him for being...intimate...with someone else, but I understand if you're not ready. I will never fault you for that."

My heart squeezed at the pure compassion and understanding in his expression and emotions. Underlying guilt echoed through the connection, which intensified my own for turning him down. My eyes welled up with warm tears. "It's just that..." I trailed off and stared into the shadowed tree line in the distance. "It's not that I haven't been with anyone since he died. Because I have—several times—but they were never more than that. There were no emotional ties," I explained. I shuddered a breath. "But to sleep with someone I might actually care about? That feels like a betrayal. It feels like I'm forgetting about him. Like I'm saying he was never here."

I wrapped my arms around my torso, hugging myself. "Plus, all of this has just been so much, so fast. Just a few days ago, I wanted you dead. Like...dead, *dead*. As dead as you want my father."

Chrome grinned. "Oh, I know. I felt that in the speakeasy. Your rage is such a turn-on."

I huffed out a laugh. "Everything is flipped upside down, and I'm trying to go with the changes. I think I just need to adjust to my new reality." I lifted an eyebrow. "At least I don't hate you anymore. That's saying a lot."

Chrome puffed his chest out with pride. "What can I say? I'm quite the catch."

I couldn't help but giggle. "You're not too bad," I said with a shrug. "But I meant what I said. I'm going to help you discover a way out of the Endarkening process. You don't deserve to suffer this fate, Chrome."

Chrome sighed and ran his fingers through his hair. A chill breezed between us, and he tossed his hood up. The leaves rustled, and trees swayed, surrounding the field with giant dancing shadows. "There's no one who's ever escaped the Endarkening process. I'm lucky to have made it this far. I've accepted it, Gray. But if I'm going down, those motherfuckers are going down with me."

Did I really have time to sit around and wait? No, I refused to accept that he wouldn't be around. I changed direction. "So, do you really think this connection between us relates to being hybrids?"

Chrome hesitated before answering me. He chewed his lip as he stared into the darkness surrounding us. "It's my best guess," he said. "What I do know is that we share a bond. It's called the Twin Soul Bond. I don't know everything about it, just that we share two halves of the same soul that go back for lifetimes." He scratched his stubbled jaw before taking a deep breath. "I've always been able to feel it because my Elemental side hasn't been suppressed like yours. Both sides of our natures needed to be awakened and active in order to feel it. That day on the playground changed everything for both of us. I think our bond awakened at our contact that day, which manifested your magic and my Kinetic powers."

I froze. "What do you mean? I awakened my magic when I was thirteen."

Chrome snorted. "No, Princess. You didn't."

"Explain."

Chrome took a deep breath. "Later that day, when we'd been sent home from school, I had my consequences to deal with. But I felt something tug on my heart like a chord was attached to it, and whatever was on the other end jerked it taut. Then, I was hit with another set of emotions that were foreign, distant, feminine." He pivoted his gaze back onto me again before continuing, "It was this intense fear that didn't belong to me. Then, suddenly, the fear morphed into empowerment, into complete confidence and control. Then, anger, which led to this powerful explosion of air magic I felt in a secondhand way. Immediately, the fear returned, followed by confusion," he explained. His dark brows pulled together as he revisited the memory.

Something within me told me it was true, even if I couldn't remember it.

Perhaps it was my element confirming it as it stirred excitedly. Chrome had mentioned he believed someone had wiped my memories of what happened to me that day. So, I supposed it was possible.

"I wish I could remember," I said, pinching the bridge of my nose as if I could squeeze the memories back into my brain.

Those molten eyes swirled viciously. "We'll figure something out. I just know that after that day, if I was in your near vicinity, I've always felt your emotions. I've felt everything."

"Oh, god." I buried my face in my palm. "That's awkward."

Chrome chuckled. "No, not at all."

"So, after freeing my Elemental form yesterday, I'm now able to feel your emotions, it seems."

"Looks that way. But I think when I go into my episodes, that it blocks it off from you. Like I'm losing my connection to the soul bond because of those parts of myself that are declining into devolution. My memories begin to fade, the good ones, because memories are attached to emotions that are engraved in our essence. Losing those alters me in the worst ways," Chrome said, sadness creeping into his voice.

"We'll figure it out," I repeated.

He nodded. "We need to figure out what this bond is capable of. Clearly, it affects our magic. We opened a fucking portal, Gray. Orion and I suspected they existed, but what happened with the beastie-bear caught me off-guard. If we can do that," he said, pondering out loud. "Then, I wonder what we can do to put an end to Forest."

I sat up straighter, observing the wheels turning in his mind. "My father fucked up when he created us. His ultimate ambition will be his downfall," I said, balling my hands into tight fists by my side. "How fucking poetic."

We arrived back at the lodge to a group of warriors ready to spread out and assess, but they relaxed upon seeing us enter through the front doors. Orion and River made a beeline for us without hesitation.

I remembered the whole reason I left to begin with. Fuck.

"Where the hell have you two been? We've been searching everywhere. We were about to go on a battle-ready search party," River scolded, chastising us with her intensity and sharp glare.

Chrome quirked an eyebrow at her, and she backed down a fraction, remembering who she was talking to. "They left. Gone. It's safe. I secured the wards."

I looked up at him from my side, wondering when he might've done that, but I wouldn't question him in front of everyone.

River flitted her scrutinizing stare back and forth between us. "Good. I'll pass word along to Onyx for them to stand down." She turned and stalked back to the group of awaiting men and women as she sought out the starlight-haired Kinetic.

I spotted Kodiak and Void among the group. Void gazed straight through me. His thick locs were pulled half up while knives, daggers, and throwing stars adorned his waist and chest. He'd strapped a hefty bow to his back, joined by a quiver of arrows.

Orion remained before us in River's wake, trying to assess what had transpired. "Everything okay?" His turquoise gaze questioned Chrome.

Chrome smiled reassuringly before peering down his shoulder at me. "Yeah," he said. I nodded to him before he proceeded, "I think all is going to be okay, Uncle."

Orion beamed at me. His sandy blond hair was sticking up on the sides. Onyx must've roused him from bed. Oops. "Great. I'm relieved to hear it." He flashed me a subtle wink, no doubt referring to our conversation by the lake.

I offered an awkward smile and glanced away to study the expansive oak tree protruding from the floor in the common area.

"Harlow returned earlier, and she has some news regarding Sergeant Hogan," Orion began, referring to Kodiak's sister who served as the emissary for the Hollow. Apparently, she had just returned with information about the human militia leader. "Her source says he's in possession of something vital to stopping Forest from ascending to the next realm," Orion explained, mainly looking at Chrome, but he cast pointed glances at me as well.

Chrome stiffened and then scanned the dispersing crowd of warriors. He nodded. "Let's meet in your office."

Orion dipped his head before turning on his heel and striding toward the stairs.

I leaned into Chrome. "Am I welcome at this meeting?"

He made a face, suggesting I'd asked an absurd question. "Obviously." Then he placed a gentle hand between my shoulder blades, urging me to follow Orion.

We weaved through the crowd of Elementals. I kept my chin high and dared a glance at the others as we passed. I assumed they'd be shooting me distrustful looks. So, surprise filled me when I was met with awestruck expressions instead.

I angled my head toward Chrome in question. He smiled in understanding. Leaning down, he murmured in my ear, "You're not just my Rainbow. You're theirs, too."

I wasn't sure what to make of that. In my experience, people at large weren't fond of me, much less looked to me for hope. It was overwhelming knowing so many believed I could be the saving grace of our world.

Back in Orion's office, Chrome sat beside me in the empty seat to my right rather than insisting on standing the entire time.

Orion offered us a drink, and we both declined. I'd had my share earlier. As for Chrome, I think he enjoyed not needing to be drunk in order to be functional.

I was exhausted—mentally and emotionally drained, to be exact. I pushed through the fog to learn what Orion had gleaned in recent hours.

"So, what did Harlow learn?" Chrome asked. He sat alert and poised to take in the news.

Orion gulped down the brown liquor, the glass *thunking* against the oak desk. "Through her close contact, Jensen, she was able to get Sergeant Hogan's location at last."

The name Jensen sounded oddly familiar. I racked my brain trying to place it. It hit me, "Jensen? That's the runner at the—"

"The speakeasy where you tried to slit my throat? Yes, little savage, that's the one," Chrome cut in, drawling with an amused grin.

I snorted, shaking my head but otherwise keeping silent, ignoring the heated reaction my body had to his seductive tone.

Orion bit his cheeks to hide his smile, but the twinkle in his sea-green eyes gave him away. "Anyway," he said. "She met him at his current scorse location. His scouts and spies reported that Forest plans to make a move—and fast. He's desperately searching for the location of this Hollow. He knows you run it, Chrome." Orion trained a pointed look at Chrome and then swiveled that gaze to me. "Gray, he's searching for you, too. He suspects you've met up with Chrome. It seems he doesn't want either of you dead, after all. Now that he's expediting his plans, he will stop at nothing to have you both brought to him alive."

Orion sighed and leaned back in his seat. "Harlow also mentioned there's a book. A book about both Elementals and Kinetics origins. It's been lost to our kind for millennia. No one in our recent generations knows it even exists because it fell into the humans' hands long ago for protection. Now, Hogan and his clan are charged with its safekeeping. Harlow's source didn't say how they retrieved it, only that it was a top-priority mission of theirs."

Chrome leaned forward and narrowed his eyes at Orion, listening intently. I combed through my memories for any mention of a book that matched Orion's description. Nothing was there. This was brand-new information to me. And by the looks of it, it was for Chrome, too.

"Roughly translated, it's titled *The Book of the Arcane*," Orion said, falling into a teacher mode that seemed so natural for him. "According to Hogan, it holds the key to stopping Forest's plans. It has all the knowledge our kind has sought for so long regarding our origins, our purpose, the Endarkened, and many other secrets. If it fell into the wrong hands, then..." He didn't need to finish.

My head snapped up at the mention of the Endarkened. I dared a sideways glance at Chrome. He sat motionless. I wondered if he was even breathing.

"So, we retrieve the book from Hogan in the morning," Chrome said, leaving no room for debate.

Orion leaned forward, propping his weight on his forearms on the desk. "We would, but Sergeant Hogan insisted we wait a few months. He's moving his militia to their underground compound. And since our emissary was recently at his current location, it isn't safe to visit the same location twice. It increases the risk of exposure to scouts, which could blow everything."

Chrome closed his eyes and dropped his neck to the side. Loud pops rippled down it before he repeated the same motion on the other side. "A few months? That's asking a lot." He sighed. "But we leave as soon as it's safe."

Orion cleared his throat. "He also said he'd come to us. Figures the travel will be more discreet that way. He can bring the tome and only a handful of his most trusted confidants," he explained. "There's one more thing. The militia's intel gathered more information on Forest." He poured another glass of liquor, the pungent smell wafting to my nose.

The knuckles on Chrome's fingers were white as he squeezed the wooden armchair. "And?"

Orion took a casual sip. "And he's received an ancient book of his own. Apparently, he's been developing a backup plan in the event you two died before he could use you. We still don't know precisely what he seeks. But it's believed that it's detailed in the *Book of the Arcane*." He raised his brows and glanced between us. His gaze lingered on Chrome, a disapproving expression crossing his face.

I studied them, trying to figure out what wasn't being said and what I was missing. "What? What are you not telling me?"

Chrome sighed, rubbing his palms over his face. Orion looked at him expectantly, crossing his arms. "Yes, Chrome. Do share with the princess the vital information you've been withholding."

"Excuse me?" I turned to face Chrome. How much more new information was he going to reveal to me in one night? How much more was he hiding?

Chrome shot an accusing glare at Orion before sitting back and facing me head-on. "The realm that Forest seeks to enter is called Arcadia. What he may or may not know is that if he opens the veil separating the two worlds, it won't just be a portal. It'll collapse the veil between here and Arcadia. Seeing as Arcadia is the dimension that sits right above ours, separated only by the thin veil, that would mean that without it, our worlds would be combined, with Arcadia plopping right on top of us."

I gave Chrome a blank expression. "And you're just now telling me this because..."

"Because there's more that ties into it."

"For fuck's sake." I looked up at the ceiling, my chest tight.

"Arcadia is a magical realm, but not a pure one anymore. It's full of dark magic, cast by these sorceresses and sorcerers called Tempests. They practice blood magic, and their power feeds off the magic of other beings, leaving behind a poison on everything it depletes, including wildlife and nature. The realm is decaying from the lack of magic. If Arcadia merges with our world, that would leave us vulnerable for the Tempests to deplete from." "That sounds like the—"

"The Endarkened. We think there's a connection," Chrome finished for me.

"Who is 'we'?"

Chrome's shoulders tensed, hesitating. "I have a confidential source. I can't reveal who they are. But they are relaying me information about Arcadia."

"How?"

With another sigh, he said, "I can't go into that. But they have connections with your father."

"Do I know them?"

Orion cleared his throat. "There's more you should know, Gray," he interrupted, dipping his head at Chrome, indicating for him to continue.

I bet I knew his contact. The question was, *who was it?* "What?"

"Forest has been involved with the Tempests since before we were born. Our births were orchestrated in order to open this portal. I only have very limited information on the Twin Soul Bond, but I'm positive he knows more. And I bet he's been allowing us to use our bond to unknowingly weaken the veil for him like we did with the beastie-bear." When I didn't answer, he continued, "It makes sense that he went to great lengths to keep us apart when I lived at the palace. Perhaps his plan wasn't ready, so he manipulated us until the time was right."

I felt numb. What the hell had my life become?

Orion spoke again, "While we will soon have the *Book of the Arcane* that will provide us with more answers and clarity, it should be known that Harlow informed me that Forest also has a book. I presume it came from these Tempests. It's a dark tome. According to Hogan, their intel gathered that, through the tome, it'd be easier to open the portal if he had one of you, but it'd be more efficient to have you both. A higher success rate. However, it can be done without you altogether. It would simply take longer and be much harder to achieve."

I could no longer focus on all the lies and secrets regarding me and my origins. All I could do was focus on what could be controlled. "This three-month wait will allow us to test what this bond of ours is capable of. We can learn to control it and prepare for the worst. Use it to our advantage."

Orion nodded. "That sounds like an excellent idea, Gray."

"I'll talk to the others. We'll increase training for everyone in the Hollow and stock up on the antidote while we wait for Hogan's arrival. We need to be prepared for an attack since it seems Forest suspects Gray and I have linked up," Chrome added.

I felt Chrome's piercing stare willing me to look at him. I refused. I wasn't sure how I felt toward him at the moment after the rollercoaster of emotions tonight. A simmering hint of vengeance belied his exterior. His internal emotions, however, were a raging inferno, threatening to burn the world to the ground. He wasn't fucking around. And I'd be lying if I said the anticipation of mass bloodshed didn't thrill me, too.

Chapter 40

CHROME

"Great, so we're fucked," River said.

I stood before my core crew in the war room to fill them in on the extent of Forest's plans, my full knowledge of Arcadia, and the bond I shared with Gray. It was time everyone knew. Just because I feared it would lead to my own secrets being revealed didn't mean that I had the right to withhold important information.

"What does it mean if Forest gets ahold of you and Gray together? Can he force you two to open another portal for him?" Void asked, sitting beside River at the long meeting table.

I moved to sit at one end, while Gray headed the other. Onyx and Orion flanked either side of me, as Aella and River flanked Gray's.

"Don't know," I said. "There's a lot to our bond that has yet to be discovered."

"But if we can explore it, learn some control over it, then we'll know better how to protect ourselves from Forest," Gray added, holding my gaze in solidarity.

"What do you need?" Kodiak sat straight in his seat, his beard looking just a tad longer than usual.

"Since Forest is looking for us, we need to be prepared for an attack. From now on, everyone at this Hollow is to be armed at all times. No bracelets either. We also need to build up a reserve on antidotes because everyone will need to always have a syringe on them, too."

Kodiak nodded. "I'll talk to my mother about the antidote. I'll also schedule ways to increase training for the warriors."

"Everyone, warrior or not, will need to be included in training."

Onyx leaned forward on his forearms, lacing his fingers together. "I'll coordinate with Orion and Kodiak to organize that."

"I'll handle hand-to-hand sparring," Void said, and everyone nodded in agreement. "I don't know if I'll have time to be present for weapons, as well, if everyone in the Hollow is to be trained. But I can put the Rambo triplets in charge of weapons."

I looked to Orion. "You'll take magic combat?"

"Yes, of course. I'll organize the schedules and delegate the trainings to those most experienced in their element." He turned his gaze to Aella. "So that means you'll take the lead with air elementals, yes?"

Aella offered a gentle smile and a dip of her head. "Thank you, Orion."

"No, thank you. You have a way of working with others."

River and Kodiak agreed to take up the combat training for the earth and water elementals while we couldn't choose the right fire elemental just yet.

When all that was settled, we ventured to the topic of preparing for Sergeant Hogan's arrival. He was said to be bringing at least two others with him, so it wouldn't require much. But we wanted to provide comfort for the humans. Especially since it had been far too long since they'd experienced any sort of luxury.

"I'll make sure two cabins are cleaned and prepared," Orion offered.

"I'll continue to work with Gray on mastering her Kinetic and Elemental abilities. And, Void, whenever you get the chance, it would much be appreciated if you continued to work with her in sensory awareness?" I asked.

Void shifted in his seat and turned his silver-rimmed gaze onto Gray. He didn't answer right away, clearly pondering his response. "As difficult as the princess can be, I'll accept. Only because I don't want her ignorance to get us all killed."

"Don't," I said through clenched teeth. "Don't speak to her like that." My magic thrummed through my body, both parts, electrifying me and wanting to burst. I shook trying to hold in.

Void slowly turned his head toward me, cocking a brow. The silence was heavy as everyone waited with bated breath to see how this would turn out. With a quirk of his lip, he said, "I knew it."

"What?" I snapped.

"I guess this bond between you two is real, after all." Void laughed deeply before turning his attention back to Gray. It was rare to hear his laugh. But when he did, it meant something. "I hate to admit it, Princess, but you're growing on me. Just a little. If there's anyone with bigger pride issues than you, it's him," he quipped, nodding his head in my direction. Void rubbed his bottom lip with his forefinger and thumb. "I'm still going to give you shit on a daily basis. Don't think otherwise."

The bond told me that Gray was confused by his acceptance of her, but I understood he could tell a difference in me since her arrival.

Gray bit her bottom lip, trying not to smile. "Sure. And I'm gonna continue to show off my charming personality until you officially crack. It's my main goal here."

"Your main goal?" I asked with a tilt of my head. What the hell went on in those sessions?

"Yes, Oh, Mighty Chrome, it is. I do not wish to elaborate, so if you have an issue with it, please...take the floor." Gray swept an arm in front of her to elaborate her point.

Onyx leaned over to whisper to River, "What the fuck just happened?"

River shook her head, meeting Aella's knowing expression as they communicated something silently to one another. "You wouldn't understand, dumbass."

I sighed and leaned back in my seat. "Onyx," I said, grabbing his attention. "You and I need to fortify the wards over the Hollow to ensure Forest can't find it and sneak attack us."

"Absolutely."

"How does your magic work for that?" Gray asked, looking between Onyx and me.

"The energy that auras put off are electromagnetic, so I'm able to suppress that output while Onyx's infrared magic can suppress all of our heat signatures. It's not perfect, but it's enough to keep us off Forest's radar to keep other Kinetic's from digging further."

Gray smiled. "Nothing like using Kinetic magic against the Kinetic king to hinder his goals. I'm here for it. Let me know if I can help."

My heart swelled with pride to see her stepping into acceptance. I never doubted that she would.

"Shield!"

Gray struggled to wield her element as a weapon, either of the offensive or defensive variety. I launched daggers and knives at her without the use of my hands. It might've been a bit unfair as she wasn't allowed weapons of her own to ward off my attacks. But she needed to gain control and mastery of her element.

Gray cursed, ducked, and dodged the blades that kept flying at her. And once I ran out of blades, I stole Orion's. "You know you could've just used your fallen blades from the ground, right?" he asked from beside me, arms crossed over his chest as he watched the tragedy that was Gray unfold.

"Yeah, I know," I responded as I slid another dagger from his belt with my element. He tried to grab it but wasn't fast enough. "But this is more fun."

"I'm gonna fucking kill you, Chrome!" Gray shouted at me as she leaped over a flying blade and rolled across the grass with surprising grace.

"Then you might wanna shield from me so that you can, Princess," I retorted, a wry grin on my face. "Maybe one day, you'll follow through on your empty threats." Somehow, she managed to toss up the middle finger in the midst of a dodge.

"Should we stop? I feel like we should stop at this point," Orion muttered.

"Nah, it's good for her cardio."

Orion just shook his head and tried to hide his laughter through his rolled-in lips.

Once all the blades were gone—Orion's and mine included—and I'd recycled them from the ground for another round, I finally called it quits, letting Gray breathe.

"Why can't you build a shield?" I approached her heaving form, hunched over and leaning her weight on her knees.

If looks could kill, she might have actually succeeded in my murder at that point. "Fuck off."

"Wrong." I inched closer, breathing the same air as her, reveling in the viciousness that thrived in her soul. I needed it to come out; I needed her to be prepared for it. "I'll ask again, why can't you build," I paused, dropping my voice deep and quiet, holding her glaring rainbow eyes, "a *fucking* shield?"

Orion had been working with her, but she hadn't managed it yet. If she couldn't build a shield, then she wouldn't be able to use her element as a weapon.

Gray didn't respond. She simply fumed, bearing the weight of her anger and frustration in her glare at me. I soaked it up and closed the distance between our faces, our noses almost touching.

The world around us disappeared, seeming only to capture the two of us in our own bubble. My voice lowered to a whisper, "You're overthinking it, Princess. Release your need to control everything. You and your element are a team. Don't forget that." Unable to stop myself, I cupped the side of her face and rested my forehead against hers. Air soothed my lungs as if they'd been starved of oxygen for too long. "You can do this. I believe in you."

The tension in Gray's body relaxed at my touch. I breathed her in, the longing to make her mine consuming my chest in a vice grip. "Come on out, little savage. I wanna play."

The princess snapped her gaze up to meet mine. A burning hunger ignited in her eyes, making it extremely difficult for me to not take her on the spot and claim her as mine. The hardening in my pants had me clenching my jaw and pulling away. We were supposed to remain friends, that's it. And I respected her too much to breach that line.

"Remember what Orion and Aella have taught you. Let it flow." Orion's eyebrows basically touched his hairline as I returned to my previous spot beside him.

"Well, that was..." he mused, rubbing the stubble on his jaw.

"Shut the fuck up."

He laughed and raised his hands in surrender. "My apologies."

Gray returned to her spot in the field, seeming unaffected by our heated moment, but I knew better.

All the discarded blades levitated and drifted to me, where I snagged a couple for one hand to have on deck.

Without warning, I sent a knife sailing at Gray. She did as before, ducking before rolling to avoid the next one. And the next. I didn't stop. "Stop overthinking, Gray." The blades flew for several minutes, whizzing dangerously close by her head a few times.

These daggers were average metal blades, so she wasn't at risk of dying from the poisons, but if not healed fast enough in a vital spot, she could be permanently altered. She needed to fucking shield.

Another masculine presence stepped up to my left as I continued to launch blade after blade at our princess. "I see she still hasn't managed an air shield," Void's deep timber rumbled.

"No," I responded, keeping my focus on all the metal weapons. "But it's coming."

"She is a fast learner. I'm surprised she hasn't mastered it yet." Void couldn't see, but it didn't stop him from knowing everything going on around him. His immensely heightened senses allowed him to form images of what transpired. In my opinion, Void was our greatest asset. No one would ever compare to him.

"Was that...a *compliment*, Void?" I joked.

He snorted. "Never. Just an observation."

"Right."

"How is she progressing in your training?" Orion asked Void from my left.

Gray leaped in the air a breath before a knife almost impaled her stomach. She had been dodging a dagger coming from a different direction, so she hadn't seen it coming; rather, she must've felt or heard it. "It seems her lessons with me are paying off. Otherwise, she would've been dead by now," he answered, his voice deadpan.

Somehow, my little savage had managed to skirt around every weapon thrown her way and avoided being struck. Until I got creative with a knife. Instead of launching one directly at her, I tricked her, making her think it would sail on past her dodge. When she turned her back to avoid another, I made the knife follow her from behind while she was warding off the others and sliced her arm from the back.

She froze. A smile threatened to break loose on my face, but I held it back.

"What is she doing?" Orion whispered from my side.

"Hopefully building a godsdamn shield."

But that is not what she did. An unseen force took hold of the weapons' hilts, making them halt midair from their trajectories. I battled for control of the metal, trying to mentally snatch them back as I was caught by surprise. But once I realized it was Gray, using her air element to grab them, I let go, taking this opportunity to let her learn.

Gray resembled an avenging angel who'd finally had enough. Her blended dual-toned tresses floated up and down under the pillow of air that surrounded her. The scowl she graced me with said what she had planned with the levitating weapons now under her control.

"Now, what are you gonna do with them? Wait for me to steal them back?" I taunted, ready to see her wrath.

With an imperceptible twitch of her lip, the weapons went on attack, flying at Orion, Void, and me like a flock of birds. I grabbed the metal, essentially pushing Gray's air control aside just before the blades struck, but I felt Orion's air shield go up in front of us at the last second.

"Not quite a shield, but that works," I said, pride filling my chest.

"What about this?" she asked.

I felt the air's movement and heard the slight whistle just before the sharp sting of a blade sliced across my chest. Invisible.

I looked down at the bleeding wound and then met the eyes of its creator. "Did you just make an air weapon and cut me with it?"

Gray couldn't hide the smug smile that was followed by a shrug. "I did."

"Before a shield?" Orion asked, doubt evident in his tone and raised an eyebrow.

Gray nodded once.

I held her gaze, unspoken words passing between us. The pride continued to swell in my heart, loving the savagery within her. "Perfect," I said. "Again."

My fists pummeled the leather punching bag full of rice from our fields.

I struck the bag with my shin before beating it in quick succession with precise jabs. Tension released with each strike, as well as the intensity of trying to keep my distance from Gray for the past two weeks. The madness started to return in small waves. But the anger and hunger continued to build. My withdrawals and need to replenish my reserves began to grow unbearable as Grim's haunting laugh echoed in the depths of my mind.

Salt dripped into my mouth from the sweat. I hadn't stopped, even as I released my tension and irrational anger in the best way I knew how: through violence. Images of bloodshed and ruined bodies splayed about flashed in my mind, tempting me to inflict pain and take their auras for myself. The potent memory of the euphoria the act fed me lived rent-free in my mind and soul. I couldn't forget it, tempting me every day to cave just one more time.

The all-encompassing craving began to ease little by little two hours into my workout. Grim's voice trailed off, quieting in the recesses of my mind. I still didn't stop, focused on the punching bag. The faces I imagined shifted from Forest to Grim to my mother. The ever-present pain and betrayal of Amethyst stung me. What kind of mother did that shit?

"Hey."

I spun and swung. Very rarely did I get caught by surprise by someone. Gray blocked my punch and landed one of her own in my ribs. "Fuck," I wheezed, rubbing the spot she assaulted. "Sorry."

The princess stepped forward with a concerned expression and placed her hand on my arm to make skin-on-skin contact. "You okay?"

I nodded and inhaled a deep breath from the reprieve her touch offered me. The hug I pulled her into was instinctual, tucking her head under my chin, emotion clogging my throat at how close I was to slipping away again, yet I was beyond grateful I was granted the chance to free myself from it. "Thank you," I whispered, my chin resting on the crown of her head and breathing in her warm vanilla scent.

"Where have you been the past two weeks?" she asked, her voice muffled. "You've barely been around lately."

I cleared my throat. "Trying to give you space."

Gray straightened and pulled back to look up at me. Her face twisted in confusion. "What? Why?"

"Because you don't need me clinging onto you while you're figuring things out and getting acclimated here. You need to make your own path while healing your trauma. I'm not trying to add stress to you while you do that. Plus, this is *my* issue, and I won't put that responsibility on you."

I fought the urge to run my fingers through her hair to brush it away from her face.

"And I've told you," Gray insisted. "I want to help."

I smiled. "I know, Rainbow," I said, studying her multicolored eyes. "Beneath that steel exterior of yours, you have a heart of gold."

Gray rolled her eyes dramatically. "Not cringey at all."

I laughed and then took her palm in mine. "Come on," I said and gave it a tug, gesturing for her to follow me.

"Where?" she asked but trailed after me anyway.

I glanced over my shoulder, flashing her a wide grin. "You'll see."

"Seriously? Hide and seek?"

"Let's see if you can actually catch me this time, little savage."

Gray narrowed her rainbow irises at me and pursed her lips. "What are the rules, oh legendary one?"

I leaned my shoulder against the oak tree and crossed my feet, holding out my palm. "No weapons. No magic."

Gray sighed. "Fine." She removed her weapons belt, placing all her blades on the grass in a nook of two tree roots. I did the same.

Balling my fist, I placed it on the flat of my other palm. "Ready?"

Gray looked at my hands like they'd grown a fungus. "What is this?"

"Rock, paper, scissors. It's the only way to decide who hides first."

"Oh."

"You ever done it before?"

Gray bit her bottom lip, her cheeks flushing pink as shame filled those expressive eyes of hers.

"You haven't, have you?" And when her silence sang louder than the birds, I grabbed the sides of her face and made her look at me. "It's okay. No big deal. I'll show you."

Gray listened intently as I detailed how to play the childhood-decision-making game of all other games passed onto me by Peri. Once finished, she positioned her hands as I had and straightened her shoulders.

"On the count of three. Loser hides first." I studied the excited anticipation building in her features, wanting to soak up the fact that I was the one bringing it out of her. "One. Two. Three," I counted, dragging out each number to allow the anticipation to grow. I chose paper while Gray maintained her hand in a fist to demonstrate rock. I closed my hand over the top of hers and gave it a squeeze. I didn't move it away, and she didn't retreat. "Paper beats rock, Princess."

Her nostrils flared, and a strong hit of desire slammed into me with the familiar tug on my heart. Instead of commenting on it, I growled, "*Run.*"

Chapter 41

GRAY

I ran, unable to stop the ache in my cheeks because of the wide grin plastered across my face.

We weren't far from the lodge or the other cabins surrounding it, but these woods were unfamiliar, so I felt like Chrome's prey. And oddly, I wasn't objecting. It was only a game, but I felt like there was an underlying meaning behind it: that he'd always find me, no matter the mind state he rested in.

We couldn't use our magic, and we couldn't use weapons, but pretending we were mere mortals was unrealistic.

I kept my senses wide open, focusing on my surroundings in the ways I'd been trained by Void. It was November in the South, where it didn't snow, but the temperature became bitter cold. The gusts of wind stole my breath and brought tears to my eyes while making me sniffle nonstop.

I came to a stop at the edge of a small creek. The shallow water washed over rocks and sticks buried in the bed. Heart racing, I scanned the surrounding area, totally unaware of my location, but I had no doubt that Chrome knew.

A large, coiled tree arched over the creek, leading to the other side of the bank. The trunk wasn't dead, so I scaled it and tight-walked to the other side, all the while feeling the adrenaline from being hunted down pumping through my veins. I loved the thrill.

I couldn't remember the last time I'd done something fun and childlike. My best guess was when Slate was still alive, but even then, we were limited in our quests and activities due to the king's oppressive hold on me. I needed this.

I sprinted through the woods, not bothering to quiet my footsteps as I tried to find a concealed spot to hide. The smile never wavered.

At last, I found a large animal den of some type—probably vacated by coyotes—burrowed into the ground under a leaning tree. The entrance was large enough for me to squeeze through. Barely.

I probably should've inspected whether the den was truly abandoned before making the executive decision to enter, but I had to hide somewhere, and time was running out. Chrome would be upon me any minute.

The protection from the den spared me from the brisk wind that chilled my bones, but I still only wore a cloak that wasn't quite warm enough.

Roughly five minutes passed, and my fingertips had already begun losing feeling. It was times like these when I questioned why I preferred the cold to the brutal heat. But I'd take it over the humidity any day. Hypothermia for the win.

Another five minutes went by, and I started to question if I had hidden too well. How long was I supposed to hide? Wasn't there supposed to be a base I needed to beat him back to? Or was that another game? I couldn't remember because I'd never been invited to play with the other kids either at school or at the palace. I decided to just sit and wait him out.

If anything, my chattering teeth would give me away.

The softest crunch of leaves sounded from the ground above me. I did my best to still my shivering.

The light footfalls moved past me. A mixture of glee and frustration warred within me that he hadn't found me. Until he stopped and turned around.

I tried to silence my breaths, but it was hard to mute them completely.

Finally, his face framed with chrome hair came into view through the hole in the ground, surrounding his head with a halo of waning light. A wicked grin and a hungry glint in his eyes, marked him as the most dangerous being alive—an apex predator.

"I found you," he murmured, his voice husky.

A puff of fog huffed from my mouth and nostrils. "About time. I was about to become hypothermic," I quipped, fighting my smile.

Chrome held out his hand to help me exit the den. I accepted his aid because I was cramped and could barely move. With an easy tug, he guided me from the coyote hole, dusting the dirt that clung to my clothes.

"Sounds like you wanted me to catch you, little savage."

I hadn't realized how close we stood to one another as I lifted my head to come a breath away from his chest. Chrome's molten eyes swirled with a heat that had me warming up from within. "Maybe I did."

He took another step, closing the non-existent space between us, encircling an arm around my waist and pulling me against him. "You need to get warm."

I couldn't breathe, and the fogginess in my mind clouded any thoughts. I tilted my head to meet his heated eyes. And those *lips*. He held me in an invisible chokehold solely by his overpowering gaze alone.

As if to put action to his words, he wrapped his other arm around me. One palm began a slow ascent up my back, followed by the slow trace of his calloused fingertips that grazed underneath my hair, his touch leaving a flaming path on my neck.

Tremors ran down my spine, which seemed to encourage him further. He brushed his fingers through the hair at the base of my head, where he latched onto a handful before giving it a gentle tug, forcing my eyes to stay locked on his. His thumb glided along my lower lip.

"I will always find you, Gray," Chrome whispered. Somehow, we'd gravitated to the point where our lips nearly touched when he said, "No matter the realm. No matter if I'm Endarkened. I will *always* find you."

Ever so tenderly, he captured my lips between his full ones. Sliding his hand to cradle the underside of my chin, he glided his tongue along my bottom lip before dipping inside to twine with mine at a languid and torturous pace.

I whimpered as he held me upright against his lean muscles. I melted for him, wholly his to command as he wished.

I needed to be closer to him. I needed *more*. Rising to the tips of my toes, I cupped the back of his neck, closing any space between our bodies as he deepened the kiss.

The world seemed to spin around me, lost to the intensity of him. I bit his bottom lip, which elicited a growl. My legs weakened more, and my core tightened at the delicious sound.

Without breaking the kiss, he spun us around and pushed my back against the tree I'd been hiding under only a minute prior.

Our breaths clouded the surrounding air as we worked to breathe. "It's been killing me to not be able to do this," he said, his voice rough with need. He broke away from my mouth only to trail heated kisses from my jaw and down the column of my neck. His scent of sage and peppermint overwhelmed my senses, jumbling my thoughts.

Holy shit, *that feels good.*

Chrome pulled a moan from my throat by scraping his teeth against sensitive skin, teasing me.

I needed him inside me. Now.

His large palm caressed from my waist up to my ribcage, not stopping until my breast fit in his hand. "I bet you taste divine. Like my salvation." His tongue whipped out, lapping up the front of my throat and then my chin, to where he took my lips in his mouth again. "I'm so fucking starved for you. I imagine once I start, I won't stop until you're trembling on my tongue."

A roaring flame ignited my chest, overtaking my core. The timber in his voice delivering his erotic words had me squeezing my thighs, ready to bare it all.

The bitter cold air on my throat hit the moisture his tongue left behind, acting like frigid water dousing me from above. The sensation jolted me out of my body and back into my fucked-up brain.

"Wait. I can't..." I said breathlessly, angling my head to the side as Slate's face came swimming into my mind. The familiar twist of guilt crashed into me.

Chrome froze. Slowly, he stepped back, chest heaving and eyes burning with a desire that almost had me regretting drawing us to a halt. "Okay," he managed, and the knot in his throat bobbed. "I'm sorry." He took a step back. His warmth that had thawed me fled like heat in a poorly insulated house.

I wrapped my arms around my torso and looked down. "No, it's not you. But—"

Chrome laid a tentative hand on my shoulder. A safe touch. "It's okay, Gray. I understand."

I let out a shaky breath. "I'm sorry."

"What did I tell you about apologizing for that? You owe me nothing."

I nodded, conceding to him, and beyond grateful for his respect and compassion. "Thank you."

"Always." Chrome offered me a reassuring smile. "Let's head back and get you warmed up."

"Yes, that sounds like a dream," I groaned as I pushed off the tree and straightened my ruffled clothing, trying and failing to wipe the kiss from my brain.

That kiss was fire and ice, burning me from the inside to the point I thought I'd combust into the ether. I couldn't imagine a kiss with anyone else ever being so world-altering. Like the broken pieces that constructed my essence just found their way back together again. And that scared me. Because wasn't it supposed to have been like that with Slate?

Another two weeks went by after the kiss in the woods with Chrome, and the memory of his lips pressed against mine haunted my waking hours and dreams. I tried to block it out, replacing the memories with that of Slate.

Every time, Slate's bare jaw morphed into Chrome's short scruff beneath my fingertips, and the feeling of comfort and safety was replaced with a crushing passion that starved me of air.

I hated it. I didn't want to move on. Because then it'd be like he never existed at all.

I needed to replenish my Elemental magic soon. Since my arrival, I'd only done it a handful of times, with the help of Chrome and Orion. It made my stomach twist just thinking about it. How it could go so wrong, but I was beginning to feel the connection to my element weaken.

Cozied in a chair in the lodge's living area, my view of the fireplace's flames blurred as I absorbed its warmth. If only replenishing my elemental magic was as effortless. A book sat in my lap, but I was unable to focus on fictional characters battling evil. My mind wandered to the feel of Chrome's hands buried in my hair, tasting sage and peppermint on his tongue. Instead, I redirected my attention on the calming scent of burning wood, but the log's crackles snatched me out of my traitorous daydreams.

"Mind if I sit with you?"

I snapped my attention to find Aella standing before a chair, looking at me hesitantly before she sat. I straightened in the seat and faced her. "Of course not. Go ahead," I said, gesturing to the empty chair.

"You've been pretty spacey lately. Is everything okay?" Aella asked, getting right to the point as she nestled in the chair across from me.

I sighed. "I haven't been spacey."

Aella raised a black eyebrow. "No? How's that air shield coming?"

She had me there. I averted my gaze back to the fire.

"Did something happen with Chrome?"

"No. Yes. I don't know." I dropped my head back against the chair. "It's...complicated."

A knowing smile lit Aella's dainty features. "You bring out a side of him that many of us didn't believe existed." As if suddenly aware of her prying, she began to nervously fidget her fingers in her lap. "I only say that because I saw him when he first arrived and how he's progressed since. Months leading up to his departure to find you, he became more and more distant.

He was here, but not really. Something was off, and no one could put their finger on it and we didn't want to say anything. We trusted that if it were something important, he'd come to us. Once he returned with you, he's been different. He's back to his normal self."

Alarm bells went off at how perceptive the others had been of Chrome's behavior. I snorted. "He's not who I originally thought he was, that's for sure."

Aella's giggle was light and feminine. "I can only imagine how surprised you were when you discovered the villainous Griffin Silas was actually your precious Chrome Freyr."

I rolled my eyes at the memory. "He had just slaughtered over fifty Kinetic Warriors at once. So, I was already in shock. Leave it to him to be fucking dramatic about the big reveal."

A comfortable silence blanketed us for a beat, only the sound of the popping wood breaking it. Until Aella finally said, "So about that shield. What's going on?"

I honestly didn't know. "I can't do it for some reason. Whenever something comes at me, my instinct is to take control of it, not defend against it."

Aella nodded. "That's what I anticipated. The element air is bonded to you, which means it responds to your emotions and personality. You're apparently an offensive fighter. And that's fine. We just gotta get you trusting in your element more and accept its control to defend you."

"How do I do that?"

"Have you been meditating?"

I hesitated. "I'm learning..."

"Well, learning to surrender control is key to building your shield. Meditation is a great way to practice that. It helps in other ways, too."

"So, I need to be good at meditating before I can build a shield?"

"Not necessarily. It's just a helpful tool. Remember when you bonded with your element, and it submitted to you?"

I nodded.

"Well, it's your turn to submit to it."

A breath of fear locked in my chest at the memory. "But it took over...and was too much."

"That's because Forest suppressed your power for so long. It was angry for not being able to serve you all those years," Aella explained gently, empathy shining in her eyes.

"Oh," I whispered, breathing out my worries. "That makes sense."

"Now that things have settled, you can surrender to it. The energy isn't as volatile now. It wants to work *with* you. Not *for* you."

"Why hasn't anyone else told me this yet? Orion is an air elemental, right?"

"Well, the bonding is a bit different for air elementals. It's similar for water elementals, but air is fluid and exists for every living thing in order to function. It's more sentient than the others. Orion probably assumed you surrendered your control when you bonded because that's normally how the process works. We're taught these things growing up. You weren't, so it makes sense that you wouldn't know."

I blew out a breath. "Okay. I want to try."

Aella beamed a perfect smile. "You can do it right here if you like."I glanced around the lodge, noting a few Elementals lounging around or ambling past. "Is that safe?"

Her gold-tinted hand covered her mouth to mute the giggle. "It's fine. It won't be like before. You just need to return to that place you went before when you bonded with it the first time. We call it the In-Between."

Breathing in deeply, I adjusted in my seat again, preparing for insanity to erupt, like it did before. I envisioned the same setting I'd experienced the last time: a place of blissful nothingness consisting of a rejuvenating white fog.

Everything happened in a panic before, meaning I couldn't process the experience. Now that I stood there on my own terms and not under duress, the In-Between felt ethereal. The air was thin and soothing like the aroma of bath salts.

A breeze embraced me, reassuring me with its presence in a hug. I wasn't sure when the opportune time would be to surrender. Would the air somehow signal it? Would I just *know*?

The breeze picked up in speed, my hair whipping across my face. I realized I was overthinking, and that was the point of this exercise: to stop thinking and trust my element. I released a breath. "Okay," I said, closing my eyes and releasing the need to control. "I'm surrendering."

It occurred to me that I felt this need to have control over everything because all my life, I was never afforded the opportunity to make my own decisions, be my own person, or choose my own path. I hadn't had many trustworthy people, only a select few, but even then, they had been at my father's whims. I never wholly trusted my friends in the ways I should've. And being bonded with a force as wild, independent, and powerful as air, scared me to release that control when it could crush me instantly.

I relaxed my shoulders, focusing on the sensation in my chest that craved latching onto control. I loosened my grip inch by inch until, at last, I surrendered my trust in my element. "I hold faith in my element to protect me, serve me, and fight with me in times of need. I trust it will always have my well-being at its forefront and will be a formidable foe against anyone who wishes me harm. It is an honor to have you by my side."

I dropped to my knees, allowing the elemental force to surge through me and soothe the roiling emotions that plagued me. Swiftly and gently, it breathed fresh life into me, and I felt the element's gratitude for my acceptance and trust. A heaviness sat in my chest as I realized that it had been long awaited.

I opened my eyes, finding Aella watching expectantly. "Well?"

The smile that overcame my face couldn't be helped at the special moment. I regretted I hadn't done it sooner. "I'm fully bonded. I surrendered."

Aella clapped with childlike excitement, bouncing in her seat, a little squeal leaving her body. "Okay, let's test for the shield."

My smile faltered as self-doubt attacked. "Uhm..."

"Let's try it. What's the worst that could happen in here? You fail to toss up a shield?"

"Or I get stabbed? Or we cause a tornado inside the lodge. Pretty sure Orion would be peeved about the cleanup efforts..."

Aella shook her head. "I'm the one that needs to be concerned. If your shield fails, you'll just attack me offensively. That's been the case, I hear. And if you do, I'll just put up my shield."

I squinted at her confident shrug. "Okay, let's try then. But this is on you if disaster strikes inside the lodge."

"Well, construct that shield, and we won't have anything to worry about, right?" she asked. A predatory gleam lit her blue and white eyes, morphing her from her sweet, gentle self to her fierce warrior side.

With a wave of her hand, an air whip lashed out, blowing back my hair and aiming for my throat. It was so quick I never had time to react. It loped around my neck before giving a tight squeeze. I gasped for breath, unable to think of a counter-response in less than a second.

When Aella realized I wasn't responding, she immediately let the air whip fall free, and oxygen flooded my lungs. "Again," she said.

This time, I would be ready. With the same strike, she struck again, but I felt my element rise to the surface. I lifted my palm in a halting motion, allowing my element to flow from my arm to construct a barrier to block the attack.

The flames in the hearth flickered from the wind created by two air Elementals, but I remained unscathed, and I didn't try to overpower her. "I did it." I beamed. "I fucking did it."

"You did it, Princess," Aella returned my excitement and rushed over to hug me.

"Thank you," I whispered into her textured curls.

"That was all you. I just helped you unlock that final piece that was holding you back."

Chapter 42

GRAY

An invisible rope coiled around my ankles, returning me to the present as it snatched my feet from under me. My butt caught my fall with a sharp thud, causing an acute pain to radiate through my hip bone. I groaned and tried to roll over, but the chord of air wouldn't relent from my ankles.

"Wield your air, Gray," Orion coaxed, guiding me through the pain. "Breathe."

Gathering my element within me, I unleashed it in small, powerful bursts at Orion's chest. He stumbled backward with each hit that slammed into him like rapid gunfire. Once he broke the concentration, I wrapped my own conduit of air around the invisible chord and melded it to make it my own, taking control of his power. With an outward swish of my wrist, the ropes flew free from my feet in little gusts of wind.

"There you go, Rainbow," Chrome encouraged as I rose to my feet, ignoring the pain spreading from my tailbone around my hips.

Air blasted from my palm at Orion. It squeezed through his mouth and down his throat. He gripped the column of his neck, his teal eyes wide as he gasped for air. I tightened my hand into a fist, and he dropped to his knees.

Chrome's voice was faint as he called my name. I was too focused on the unyielding control I had on the enemy. He was close. I could end this now and save myself. The powers raged within me, begging it of me.

More.

More power. More of his life force. I *needed* it. My magic urged me to keep taking until there was nothing left.

My enemy's eyes drooped, and his face became beet-red beneath the gold layer. He was only a gasp away from the end.

An unseen force shoved me away from the control I had of my element, like someone slid into the driver's seat and booted me out before slamming the door shut.

What the fuck?

I was still tethered to my magic, but it was faint. My air untwined itself from the steel grip it had on my enemy—no, *not* my enemy. *Orion.* The horror of what I almost did slammed into me as I watched him gasp for breath. He caught his body weight on his palms, heaving.

A shaking hand covered my mouth, guilt and confusion already consuming me as I stared, dazed.

What the hell just happened?

"Gray."

Chrome grasped me by the shoulders, forcing me to look at him. I averted my gaze, unable to meet his eyes.

"Look at me." His voice was firm and direct, striking something alive within me. "Are you okay?"

I said nothing, just stared wide-eyed at him in shock.

"*That* is what happens when you lose control while replenishing. You began feeding from him without even realizing it," Chrome explained.

A heavy weight sank low in my stomach. I took a shaky breath. The dangers of replenishing rocked me. For the thousandth time, I hated my father for hiding this part of myself for so long, leaving me so ill-equipped to handle the most basic aspect of being an Elemental.

"Is...is he okay?" I whispered and glanced around Chrome to check on Orion. He stood, looking a little shaken and running a hand through his hair.

Chrome's eyes softened. "Yes, Rainbow. He's okay. I stopped you before you killed him."

Fuck.

But another thought slammed into me at his words. "Wait..." I said, my brows furrowed. "How did you stop me? What happened?"

Chrome took a step back. "Honestly, I'm not sure. I think it was one of our joined abilities, like the portal. But I think I understand how I did it. I felt like I was being guided by some outside being... I don't know. But I tethered onto your aura and wielded your element of air. It was dominating you based on your strong desire to deplete Orion."

"You what?" I asked, floored by someone's ability to do that. "You can take control of my power whenever you please?" I did not like those implications.

Chrome shook his head. "I don't think it's whenever I please," he started. "I felt pulled to do it. Like you were subconsciously begging me to help, even if you didn't realize it."

I nodded, then dropped my gaze to the dead grass at my feet. "Thank you."

Chrome wrapped me in a hug, tucking my head into the crook of his arm and gently pressing the side of my face into his chest. The scent of sage and peppermint wafted from his body, calming my senses. "I'd do anything for you, my Rainbow," he said into my hair. The warmth of his breath tingled my scalp, then radiated down my neck and spine, making me quiver.

A flutter rippled in my chest that I tried to stifle. I twined my arms around Chrome's waist and squeezed him. In that moment, he was my anchor that kept me from drifting away in the arms of my emotions.

I sat cross-legged on my bed with my spine straight. My hands rested atop my knees, and I breathed in slow, cleansing breaths to ease the weight on my chest. Fluttering my eyelids closed, I shut out the world around me.

I'd constructed an air shield around my body to create a physical bubble that separated me from the world. I tried to 'go within', as *A Guide to Meditation and Finding Inner Peace for Beginners,* suggested.

After my incident with Orion in the training fields, I'd immediately retreated to the solitude of my room. Shame, guilt, and utter failure nearly suffocated me as the memory of Orion's crimson face lodged in my mind. After the self-loathing thoughts battered me long enough, I snatched the book on meditation from the oaken side table.

My thoughts assaulted me, but the book explained it was to be expected. It said all they wanted was to be acknowledged, heard, and sent on their way. I grew frustrated at the thoughts' bombardment, but I remained focused on my slow breaths in order to release the tight resistance.

For several long minutes, I allowed the thoughts to come to me. At first, they were surface thoughts, such as recent events. However, they soon morphed into deeper, darker sentiments.

The book suggested observing them objectively. Then to ask myself whether they were positive or negative thoughts. If they were negative, then why? Especially when it pertained to thoughts about myself.

Why am I such a failure? I'll never be enough. Or am I too much? I don't deserve happiness. I'm weak. Stupid. Why am I so awkward? How could I be so brainless to never ask questions? To never see what was right in front of me? No wonder my father hated me so much.

On and on the insecurities went. They came one after another, plowing through my soul and cracking me open. Each thought brought a stream of salty tears down my cheeks. The level of self-hatred I held for myself was crushing. My heart broke for itself, knowing I'd always felt this way without ever realizing it.

The spiraling thoughts came to a screeching halt with the revelation I wasn't responsible for them. From a young age, others around me projected their negativity onto me. Others who never held the right to mold my self-beliefs.

As I stood by and watched from an objective perspective how the self-beliefs were formed, I realized I wasn't any of the terrible things I'd been led to believe. They were ministrations designed to control and manipulate me. Only now, I noticed them.

I expanded my consciousness, becoming aware of the patterns that held me back from breaking free from the prison in my mind. Never again would I allow someone to dictate my thoughts or actions.

I was my own person now that I was free from the Royal Domain. Not only was I liberated from the physical confinement, but I could shatter the mental enslavement, truly releasing me from my father's control.

Years of painful emotions flooded to the surface. My shoulders wracked for the little girl who never knew love, but desperately craved it, only wanting acceptance. I hugged the tiny child who'd tried to hide her bruises and broken bones at school.

Gut-wrenching sobs resounded within my air shield for little Gray, who wanted a mother to kiss her goodnight, but instead walked with her gaze to the ground, pretending to not to hear the hateful whispers.

I grieved for the young woman who'd shut down after the death of her first love.

My heart shattered for the weaponized woman who'd been lied to her entire life. I bled forgiveness for the lives she'd taken without ever questioning her orders.

I allowed my suppressed trauma to gush from me, baring myself raw and exposed, to rid my soul of the poison. I realized running from my pain was doing myself an injustice. The only way I'd ever find acceptance from others was if I learned to accept myself.

I wasn't sure how many hours passed with me curled in the fetal position. My tears drenched the sheets, earning myself a slicing headache and swollen eyes.

I couldn't remember the last time I'd truly cried. Perhaps the day I learned of Slate's death? I'd always believed crying was weak. My father had taught me that, which probably meant the opposite was true.

I felt empty, lighter now that I'd eased the weight of the pain that I'd been clinging to for so long. Feeling as if I'd survived a harrowing hurricane, I lay there, staring blankly out the wall window at the dusky autumn fields. I vowed to myself that no person or power would ever control me again, because the only person who could control me...was *me*. And that was enough.

Silence reigned in the expansive public study on the second floor. A few Elementals pored over texts in the early hours of the evening. I needed to escape my room. However, I wanted to be in the presence of other people without actually socializing.

Three days had passed since my incident with Orion, and I'd avoided everyone ever since—even Chrome.

The warmth from another large stone fireplace beside my table soothed me and chased away the ravaging thoughts I fought to counter. My eyelids were heavy, threatening to shut as I willed them to remain open.

The sketched lines of my rendition of the beastie-bear blurred as my vision waned. I was losing the battle of wills.

A book slammed onto the table, making me jolt upright in my seat. My heart pounded in my ears as my hand went to my waist in search of a blade to wield. I came up empty. No weapons were there because I wasn't wearing a weapons belt.

"Chill. It's just me." The clipped, feminine tone could only belong to one person.

"Fucking hell, River. Don't do that," I chided, slumping back in my seat, willing my heart to slow to its normal rhythm.

River shrugged, flicking her sleek ponytail over her shoulder. Her nails were perfectly manicured, and her makeup was flawless. "I heard you nearly killed Orion the other day. You good?"

I groaned, letting my head fall into the cradle of my hands. "Yeah, trying to be."

"Well, it's happened to all of us at some point in our lives. Don't worry about it."

I split my fingers wide enough to peek through the gaps. She sat poised. Her violet gaze highlighted her sharp, russet features. "If Chrome hadn't stopped me…"

"I know," she said, her face not betraying her intent. "It's scary. We've all had some really close calls. But for you, it's to be expected, considering you're like a tot learning to walk."

I snorted. "Thanks for that."

River shrugged again. "Look," she said, the usual tightness around her mouth slackening a fraction as her gaze softened. "I almost depleted my little brother once. I know how you feel."

My heart sank at the implications had she succeeded. It hit too close to Chrome's story. A story few knew. "And what happened?"

River looked away and began chewing on the inside of her cheek. "My mother stopped me. She filled my lungs with water until I passed out."

My brows shot to my hairline. "Wow. That's…intense," I said, thinking of the harsh punishments my lovely father had bestowed upon me.

Another shrug. "That's my family: intense."

"I can relate." I ran my fingers through my hair, the black-and white waves catching between my fingers. "My father once broke all of my ribs because I failed to summon a ball of electricity on the first try."

River scoffed and shook her head. Her narrowed eyes told me she was trying to envision the memory.

"He proceeded to throw me into the deep end of the swimming pool before I had the chance to heal. I blacked out and sank to the bottom. He waited until I was on the brink of death before he allowed a guard to retrieve me."

River's mouth fell slack. A look of pure disgust dripped from her expression as she crossed her arms over her chest, lifting her chin higher. Our gazes met in understanding.

"I was thirteen. My powers had only manifested a week prior." I leaned back in the cherry-oak chair, propping my forearms on the rests.

"That piece of shit really knows no bounds, does he?" she asked, venom lacing her tone. "My parents," she started, remaining stiff in her seat. "They were tough. They pushed me and my brother to the extreme, but it came from a place of love—of belief in our abilities. They knew we needed to be prepared for the world. To be able to survive no matter the situation," River explained. Her gaze went distant. "But your father," she said, scathing. "He's just fucking evil. A heartless piece of shit. And I hope he dies a very slow and gruesome death."

I offered a half smile and held her gaze in solidarity.

I didn't want her sympathy, and she didn't give it. Like me, she wasn't one for showing emotions or opening up about painful experiences. We didn't have to. Some wounds shone on our exterior like armor. They spoke for themselves.

Chapter 43

COTTON

The guards escorted the Kinetic woman with earthy green hair from the metal table in the interrogation room. Obviously, she hadn't been lying; the thermal signature in her chest and other areas would've lit up bright red if she had been.

I wasn't sure how much longer I could pull this off. Every day for the past month, King Forest had me interrogating everyone who'd ever come into contact with Princess Gray, hoping to catch the culprits responsible for aiding in her escape.

When the king questioned me about being seen with her down in the training room, I'd made out that I had been apprehending her to bring her in but she'd overtaken me and fled. It went against everything inside me to lie like that, but it was the only way to protect Scarlett and Hazel. Because Gray and I had never been close, he bought it. But his sights had been set on Hazel and Scarlett since Gray's disappearance, and I'd been running a very risky game in interfering with the investigation.

The chair scraped against the concrete floor as I pushed away from the table, rising to hand over my report of the most recent interrogation. It said the same as all the others: no connection with the princess.

I couldn't ignore the lead weight in my stomach telling me that King Forest was running out of patience.

Thankfully, the king decided to do away with cameras after Devolution Day. We had plenty of Kinetics with the capabilities to run them, but the king said it was a waste of our energy to do so. Instead, he relied on our magic to keep a tight grip on the King's Palace.

I needed to check on Scarlett, my oldest and dearest friend and the one person who had stayed by my side when I stopped speaking. She knew something traumatic had happened but never pressured me to tell her. I'll forever love the shit out of her for that.

The King's Palace was quiet today, which was odd. Usually, people were busy milling about or rushing to get to one place or another. For it to be calm felt eerie. Ominous. I popped my neck as I straightened my suit jacket, a nervous habit.

I knocked on her door, shoving my hands in my pockets. Glancing over my shoulder, a pair of eyes burned into my back, watching and waiting. Or perhaps I was just being paranoid.

After a beat, the door swung open. Scarlett stood with her ruby hair pulled up in a messy bun. She scanned the hallway, clearly feeling the same foreboding as I was. I stepped inside, and she pulled me into a tight hug. I wrapped my arms around her tall frame, relieved to see her alive and well.

"How much longer do you think we have?" Scarlett asked, pulling back to meet my eyes. Her blue gaze swam in worry, searching mine for any answers.

I shook my head, scanning the suite over her shoulder with a pinched brow. Angling my head, I lifted my shoulders in question.

We broke apart and I stepped further into her suite's foyer. After softly closing the door behind me, we moved into the living area where I continued to look around, searching for Hazel.

"I don't know where Hazel is. She hasn't been by today," Scarlett said, deflated, crossing her arms over her chest. "She's not in her suite. I can't shake this horrible feeling, Cotton."

Over the years, Scarlett had learned to be able to read me as if I were speaking out loud. Forest was such an asshole, never providing any support for my disability in speech. He said no one else in the Royal Domain was mute; therefore, he shouldn't have to make accommodations solely for me. Besides, there was no one else around who knew sign language. It wouldn't have mattered if I knew it anyway. The king wanted me silent, so he'd never make it easy for me communicate with others.

Having Scarlett understand me on a level where I didn't have to struggle to communicate was the best reprieve I'd been granted since all those years ago. I had to protect her at all costs.

"What do we do, Cotton? Run? But where to? We don't even know if Gray is alive." Scarlett began to pace, her bare feet wearing a path on the white carpet.

I closed the distance between us, grabbing her by the shoulders to force her to look at me. I wish I had something more optimistic for her, but I didn't. We had to run.

Holding her gaze, I bit my bottom lip and angled my head for the door, searing her with an intensity conveying my intention to flee. Scarlett's eyes widened before she inhaled a sharp breath. With a reluctant nod, she took off to her bedroom, throwing shit into a bag and grabbing any weapons available.

I leaned my shoulder against the doorframe and arched a brow.

She halted. "What?"

I moved my gaze down her body with my lips twisted in skepticism at her cotton shorts and cut-off tank as if to say, *You're going to make a wild escape wearing that?*

Scarlett rolled her eyes. "Shut up. Obviously I'm gonna change. Keep your judgy shit to yourself over there, okay?" she retorted as she returned to tossing her belongings haphazardly about.

An amused grin teased the edges of my lips as I snorted, shaking my head.

Aggressive banging on the door made both of us freeze. Scarlett's eyes blew wide for a moment before reaching for a knife. She tossed me a dagger, and I straightened my spine, tucking the blade up my sleeve.

Giving her a pointed look, telling her to remain in the room, I turned on my heel and strode with faux confidence to the door. My heart pounded a harsh rhythm, adrenaline and fear singing my veins as I looked through the peephole, hoping it was Hazel.

My stomach soured to see that it was not, in fact, Hazel.

Fuck.

Tightening my grip on the hilt of the dagger up my sleeve, I steeled myself for what awaited behind the door. Defeat choked me despite the numerous escape plans running through my mind.

With a clink, the door opened to three stoic guards. "Inquisitor Cotton Sjodin and Emissary Scarlett Kittle, you are under arrest for committing high treason against the Crown for assisting Princess Gray Monroe in escaping her punitive justice for her crimes."

"Cotton, move!" Scarlett shouted from behind me.

I sidestepped just in time to avoid the knife that embedded in the throat of the guard before me.

Shit. Fight our way out, it is, then.

The other two guards lunged, and I swiped my dagger in a clean slice along one's jugular just before he dropped to the floor. The final guard went on the offensive with a dagger of his own, arm raised high and poised to come down on top of me.

I was prepared to fight him off when a blur of red sped by; the guard went slack as Scarlett embedded a knife into the side of his neck.

"Fucking run, Cotton," Scarlett growled, blood coating her hands while splattered all over her arms and neck.

I jumped into motion, grabbing her wrist and dragging her along with me into the hallway. Where the fuck was Hazel?

As if she heard my inner thoughts, Scarlett said, "We need to find Hazel."

I nodded and took off to the elevator en route to Hazel's suite. Scarlett and I didn't speak on the ride up, casting nervous glances at one another.

The elevator jerked to a stop. We held our breaths as the elevator door slid open to reveal Grim Valor on the other side with a hungry sneer. My stomach twisted as both of our magics winked out, leaving me cold.

"Don't even bother. Hazel is already down in the prisons, rotting away with the rest of the filth." Grim took measured steps toward us. "Drop your weapons. You can't win this fight." A sinister grin slowly spread up his pale face. "Unless you want one? In that case, I'll be happy to oblige."

No, we'd find another way out. Somehow, for now, we only had two weapons and no magic. Surely, the guards surrounded the perimeter at this point. We didn't have Hazel, and there was no way we were leaving without her.

I gave Scarlett one last look. A look that said, *we don't have a choice,* followed by the dip of my chin. I tossed the bloody dagger on the floor at Grim's feet, never wavering from his predatory and sickly stare. Scarlett followed as we held our heads high, not allowing ourselves to see this as a defeat.

We'd find a way out...with Hazel.

I lifted my wrists before me, and within seconds, the magnetic cuffs clicked into place before I was blindsided in the eye with a hard blow, making the world go black as I crashed to the floor.

Distantly, I heard Scarlett's scream before I succumbed to nothingness.

Chapter 44

GRAY

A month had officially passed since my arrival at the Hollow, and I still hadn't read the letter that Orion gave me all those weeks ago.

I held my mother's letter, rotating it between my fingers. My heart raced at the idea of finally opening it.

In my lap sat my sketchpad and a pencil, a drawing in progress of Chrome. Shamed soured my stomach as I glanced at it, reality hitting hard how it wasn't Slate I was drawing. Pages and pages of Slate's face filled my sketchpad, especially since his death. I drew him to make sure I never forgot what he looked like, to ingrain his face in my memory. Each one had a tiny bit more detail than the last.

But here I sat, drawing another man. I felt sick.

Slamming the sketchpad shut, I dropped it to the floor.

Out of sight, out of mind.

I leaned forward in my cozy chair by the built-in bookshelf of my room, elbows resting on my knees as I studied the envelope and my Elemental name in elegant script. I slid a finger in the sealed lip's gap, moving to slide it across. But I stopped.

I couldn't do it. Fear wouldn't let me.

Jumping from my seat, I raced through the dimly lit hallway to Orion's office. I needed to know more about my mother. I wanted her only words to me to mean something, to feel tangible. And Orion was the best source for that.

I beat my fist on the door, the letter clutched in my other hand. Orion swung the door open. His face twisted in confusion. "Gray, what's wrong?" he asked, dropping his gaze to the envelope in my hand.

"I can't open it," I said, breathless. "I can't fucking open it."

A look of understanding crossed his face as he ushered me inside. "Come in."

I dropped my shoulders and let out a breath before entering his office. "When I open this, I want to feel connected to her, ya know? Like I can imagine her saying the words written here. Once I read it, I can't read it for the first time again. So, I want to make it right."

"I completely understand. I'm glad you came to me." He moved behind his desk and reached for the framed photos that sat there, facing him. "As I've said before, she was very beautiful," he said, his voice almost a whisper.

I walked over to him and took the frame, studying the three individuals that were the focus. It was the one I saw the first night of my arrival. A slightly younger and much happier Orion was in it, as well as a man I presumed to be King Jonah and then my mother, Queen Lilliana.

She had light blonde hair and blue eyes. Aside from her gilded skin, her eyes were electric blue with white zig-zag lines within, resembling lightning strikes. "She was a highly skilled storm wielder. A very rare elemental ability," Orion explained.

"She could create storms?"

"Yes. Only the most powerful and skilled water elementals can create rain. But nothing else outside of it." Orion rubbed his freshly shaved jaw, giving him an even more youthful look. "But your mother? She could summon lightning with high winds. She could even rain down hail and shards of ice."

"What about her and Jonah? Were they happy together?"

Orion smiled, but it was pained. "They were. Jonah loved her with his whole heart. He cherished the ground she walked on." Longing filled his sea-green eyes. "As she did with him."

My heart squeezed as realization hit me. "You were in love with her, too. Weren't you?"

Orion looked hesitant, then gave a resigned nod. He exhaled. "Yeah, I was. She never knew. She had always been destined for Jonah, ever since we were kids."

"Oh, Orion," I said. Without thinking, I wrapped my arms around his torso. He returned the hug.

"It's okay. Please don't pity me, Gray. I accepted that fate many years ago as I watched them fall for each other as teens. All I'd ever wanted was for her happiness. And she was happy. Which brought me joy to see."

"Your feelings never got in the way of you and Jonah? Did he know?"

Orion took a moment before answering. "If he did, he never let on. I did my best to keep my feelings to myself, just trying to be supportive of his ascension to the throne. I always did better in the background. They were both outgoing; I was more introverted. And I liked it that way. Our father raised us for our roles, but we'd always been close growing up. Did I secretly wish Lilly would see the light and admit her nonexistent feelings for me? Every single day and night. But I never resented them because they were happy and fulfilling their destiny."

Tears filled my eyes for the silent suffering that Orion must've endured for so long. "Oh, gods. I can't imagine what you went through when they were taken."

Orion's throat bobbed from a thick swallow. "It was excruciating," he said, his voice hoarse with emotion. "I couldn't...*save* them. I godsdamned tried, though."

My heart broke for him. "I know you did."

"We were best friends, Lilly and I. She trusted and relied on me. And I *failed* her." His voice cracked, shattering my heart with it. I squeezed him tighter to try to provide some form of comfort.

"No, you didn't. You did what she probably would've wanted you to do. You took care of our people, protecting them. Because of you, Elementals didn't face extinction at my father's hands."

Orion nodded, then shifted to grab some more photos from within his desk drawer. "Take these. Get to know her. She would be so proud of you."

Guilt sank inside. I shook my head. "I don't think so. I've killed too many Elementals, and I fell for Forest's bullshit..."

"Stop that. She would be proud of you. Not for your deeds but for your compassionate heart despite what you've been conditioned to be. You have her empathy and fierce nature. You are most definitely more her daughter than Forest's."

Hot tears rolled down my cheeks at the unfairness of it all. How she'd been taken from me before I ever had the chance to get to know her. To love her. To be loved. But if I couldn't make one parent proud, maybe I could make the other. One much more deserving.

I pulled away just enough to put some distance between us. "I don't think I apologized for almost depleting you that day. I'm so sorry. If Chrome hadn't..."

"Shh." Orion shook his head, his light hair flopping from side to side. "It's okay. It happens sometimes. And you're still so new to the Elemental part of you. No one faults you. Depleting someone could happen to any of us, no matter how experienced we are."

"I'd never have forgiven myself if I'd killed you. You've been nothing but kind and warm to me since I arrived. All of you have. And it's the first time I've ever truly experienced it." His sympathetic gaze had me looking away. I knew he wasn't pitying me, but I hated how weak I appeared.

"I know. And if I could've saved Lilly, I could've saved you from such trauma. I live with that guilt. In a way, I felt like it was deserved."

"What? Orion, you can't seriously..."

"I do. Just know that I don't hold that episode against you in any way. We've all had some close calls."

I reflected on River's comments in the library the other day, how she'd said the same thing. How she admitted she'd almost depleted her younger brother once. But still, the guilt ate at me, anyway.

I wiped my cheeks, sniffling. "Thank you. For these," I said, waving the pictures. "And for being there."

Long-carried sadness glistened in Orion's eyes. I wished I could help ease him of his guilt in some way, but I knew that it would be a path that only he could travel to find his inner peace.

Darkness consumed the hallway when I finally left Orion's office. My path was only illuminated by the coolness of my currents.

I still clutched the letter as I took my time returning to my room. The anxiety about reading my mother's letter had eased since my talk with Orion. In its place came heartache that I would never meet her.

Orion assured me I shouldn't feel guilty for his near-fatal incident in training, but I couldn't help it. Orion had grown into a father figure in the brief time I'd been here. He was my only real link to my mother. The thought of killing someone who genuinely wanted to help me made my stomach feel full of acid.

Thinking over the events, of course, brought back the memory of Chrome stopping me from committing an act that I couldn't return from. I recalled how he'd wielded my magic as if it were his own. The way he'd held me against him as if to protect me from myself made it feel like a baby bird took flight beneath my ribs. Which was why I'd been avoiding him the past week.

Well, I hadn't completely avoided him. We still trained together, but I kept my distance enough to where his devolution symptoms wouldn't return.

I couldn't bring myself to let him in. It was as though the Great Wall of Slate stood between us.

While the gaping hole in my heart that Slate left behind was beginning to mend, I still couldn't allow myself to move on yet. It had been almost two years now. I knew I should move on because he wasn't coming back, but I was scared to let go.

On the other hand, being at the Hollow was doing wonders for my soul. It was the safety to heal while shedding my old skin and stepping into a newer and better version of myself. It would take time to undo a lifetime of trauma, but I felt better already.

The dim, warm light against the dark wooden walls wrapped me in a homey embrace. Soft voices sounded in the distance, most likely a few night owls lazing downstairs in the lounge.

However, there was a beautiful, somber melody floating to me through the night, almost calling me to follow it home. Slow, drawn-out notes of a violin soared high before dropping low and then ratcheting back up into a manic crescendo that built and built, inflicting a sense of a spiraling madness within.

As if in a trance, the music guided my feet toward its origin. I came to stop, finding myself outside of a bedroom with the door cracked a few inches.

I pushed it open, intent on finding the source of this emotional piece that resonated so deeply within me. My breath caught in my throat when I spotted Chrome sitting on the edge of his bed, eyes closed, and brows pinched low, hunched over his instrument as he sawed away at his violin.

The music soared from his hands and fingertips that glided in a blur, keeping pace with his emotions. Before I knew it, he'd brought it back down to the slower, somber notes that drew moisture to my eyes.

I sniffled, and the music stopped. Chrome snapped his head toward the door, eyes wide in surprise. He remained frozen on the bed. *Shirtless.*

I opened my mouth and closed it, feeling like a creep standing in his doorway with him unaware. "Sorry. I heard the music and couldn't help myself," I explained, not sure if I was helping my case or hurting it. "It's really beautiful. I didn't know you could play."

Chrome relaxed, setting his violin off to the side of the bed. "It's okay. You're always welcome in here."

I gave him an awkward smile and glanced down the hall. "I guess I'll leave you to it. I didn't mean to interrupt."

I took a step back to leave but halted when he said, "Wait, Gray." His metallic eyes reflected that deep emotion he held for me, even from across the room. "Stay with me."

Silence grabbed me in a chokehold, but he didn't let that deter him. He stood up and closed the distance.

When only a few inches separated us, he propped his forearm on the doorframe, somehow boxing me in even though I stood in the hallway, free to leave if I truly pleased. "Stay with me, Rainbow," he repeated, his voice low and rough.

My feet were cemented to the floor. I wanted nothing more than to do unimaginably dirty things with him. So many unsolicited fantasies had plagued my mind in recent weeks that it was tempting to cave. The sight of his swirling tattooed marks on rare display and his illuminated, silvery brands were not helping.

A silver lock draped over his eye as his gaze pleaded for me to stay. He inched closer.

I shook my head. "I—I can't." I dropped my gaze to the floor.

"Can't or won't?"

I looked up at him at the challenge, my defiance kicking in. "Can't."

"Hmm," Chrome hummed, disbelieving. "I think you're full of shit, Gray. You want to; I can feel how badly you want to. But you know what else I feel from you?"

My heart stuttered. "What?" I whispered.

"Fear. You're scared if you give in, you'll never be able to go back. You know what's between us is real. Authentic. *Powerful*. And you don't like giving up that control to something bigger than yourself." Somehow, he'd inched closer as he spoke. "Let me in, Gray." His free hand pressed against the center of my chest. "Allow yourself to be worshiped as you deserve to be."

My breath hitched as his lips brushed against my own. The hand on my chest slid up my neck to the side of my face, continuing until his fingers lightly gripped my hair at the back of my head. Metallic eyes smoldered with a heat so hot I couldn't breathe. I was lost to his spell, in a trance like the one his music had held me in only moments ago.

"Stay with me," he whispered against my lips before he claimed my mouth with his own in a gentle yet firm press of his lips.

My element offered no help as my chest constricted. Every cell in my body roared to life with an inexplicable fire, threatening to incinerate me to ashes. The need for oxygen ceased to exist. I didn't need air; I needed *Chrome*. All that mattered was laying my claim on this beautiful man.

Too absorbed in him, my mother's letter and photos slipped from my grip, drifting to the floor.

Fuck it, I'll get them later.

Chrome's full, soft lips nudged mine open, and I welcomed the sensual caress of his tongue against mine. A deep growl rumbled from his chest, igniting a fire low in my core.

I was gone, absorbed in the swirling maelstrom. He was the fire to my ice. And I was melting.

A whimper escaped me as I snatched him closer to my body until only our clothing divided us. His hands roamed down the sides of my neck as he nipped my bottom lip and gave it a wanting tug.

Chrome's hands continued their descent down the sides of my body. He took his time when he reached my breasts, cupping them in his palms before traveling lower. When he reached my ass, he gave it the same treatment.

In that moment, I wanted to give him everything.

Our height difference became uncomfortable. My neck ached from angling upward for so long. Without breaking the kiss, Chrome bent lower and gripped the backs of my thighs, hoisting my legs around his waist. I squeezed my hips around his taut midsection, running my fingers through his hair as he braced his palm on my lower back.

The concept of time and space became an illusion. Nothing else existed outside the two of us and the forces that pulled us together as I greedily swallowed his breaths.

"I've waited so many years to touch you like this, Rainbow," he said between kisses. "And I'd wait an eternity more if I had to."

The door clicked shut behind me, although I was unaware that we'd even been moving. My back knocked into the wall adjacent to the door, Chrome pinning me to it with his body.

Bracing his forearms on the wall on either side of my head, he flicked his tongue against the sensitive skin of my neck as I held myself up, tightening my thighs.

I arched my back, rolling my hips against his, eliciting a nip at the crook of my throat. "Fuck," I gasped.

"Now's the time to back out, Princess. Tell me. I won't move further without your consent," he asked, his voice gravelly and eyes wild through his haggard breaths.

"I want this." I nodded. I needed it. I needed him. He was right. I had been scared to give in to us, not only because of Slate but because of my lack of control of the powerful force between us.

"You sure?" Hesitance shone in his eyes. I wasn't sure what he felt coming from me, but I didn't like it.

"For fuck's sake. You wait any longer, and I might change my mind, Chrome."

He shifted his weight to one arm against the wall so he could free the other to loosely grip my throat. "Be a good girl for me while I make you come on my mouth."

It's like he stole the air from my lungs. He set my unstable legs on the floor, removing the hoodie over my head. I tried to help him, but he slapped my hand away. "No. You do nothing but relax and come when I tell you." The look in his eyes left no room for argument. And for once, I heeded it.

Once I was bare before him, a chill raced over my heated, gilded skin. "You're so fucking beautiful, Gray." He kissed me again before slowly teasing his tongue and lips down my neck, then to my chest. He massaged a breast and then flicked a thumb over the peak. "So perfect," he said, licking my nipple, leaving a coolness in his tongue's wake before he closed his lips around it. He gave it a gentle suck.

I leaned my head back, pushing further into his mouth with a moan as I felt already undone by the pleasure that shot straight to my core.

"That's it, little savage. Let me hear you." He traced a finger up the inside of my thigh as he dragged his lips to the other breast. He moved too slowly. I wiggled my hips, urging him to hurry.

Chrome rasped out a chuckle against my nipple. "You're so fucking impatient. We really need to fix that, don't we?"

Chapter 45

Gray

Chrome lowered himself to his knees at my feet, stopping his finger's ascension to the growing tightness at my center. The sight of someone so powerful on his knees for me shattered the last of any resolve I had.

His quicksilver eyes whirled like a vortex, matching the emotions that he failed to block from me. Feeling twice the passion would be the death of me. I didn't think I could withstand both of our emotions. I wouldn't last long.

I bucked my hips toward him, silently begging for his touch to return.

Chrome chuckled, a husky sound, before he nipped the inside of my thigh. "What do you want, little savage?"

I glared down at him, barely able to breathe. "You know what I fucking want."

A crooked grin inched up one side. "That's not playing very nice." He nipped me again, this time slightly harder. "How do we ask nicely?"

"Please," I gritted out through clenched teeth.

"Please...*what*, Gray?" He slowly dragged his fingertip up again toward my center, teasing me and setting my nerves on fire.

"Please make me fucking come."

"All you had to do was ask. Was that so hard?" He reached my opening, circling around the wetness with his finger. "You're so fucking wet for me."

My mouth went dry from heaving for air. "Please, Chrome..."

He groaned just before he entered a finger inside me. I gasped at the penetration. "Fuck, you're so tight." He worked his finger slowly before entering a second one, spreading me further for him.

"I need...I need...*you*." My chest felt like it would explode. Every time he hit that special spot that put me on the brink, he slowed down, leaving me on the edge for minutes.

Without stopping the motion with his fingers, he brought his face closer to my center, laying a tender kiss to the inside of my thigh. "All...*mine*," he said before flicking his tongue against my clit. Another groan escaped him. Then he took my clit between his lips with just the right pressure, adding his relaxed tongue to massage it as he sucked.

My knees buckled. Chrome's free arm flew up to catch my hand, giving me something to balance on. I suddenly became aware I wasn't being quiet in the slightest.

Chrome tugged on my hand as he shifted from his knees to lie on his back between my legs. "Sit on my face and let me make you fall apart."

My legs could hardly hold me vertical much longer anyway, so with shaky thighs, I gladly lowered myself onto his mouth. His tongue instantly began to slowly lap at my opening. The electricity that already hummed in my veins intensified and shot through my body. I drooped forward, bracing myself against the wall as Chrome's mouth brought me closer to pure ecstasy.

He groaned into my pussy. "You taste like oblivion. I'm forever lost to you." His tongue lazily caressed my opening several times, before dipping in and out, as if he had all the time in world. Pulling my clit between his lips, he applied just the right pressure as he sucked, putting me on the precipice of nirvana. I rolled my hips over his tongue, unable to control my body's needs.

"I'm gonna..." I whimpered.

"Come for my tongue, little savage," he rasped. He pushed two fingers back inside me while never relenting with his mouth.

My core tightened; I was wound up, I couldn't breathe. I threw my head back as I allowed the shockwaves of pleasure to surge through me. My inner walls clenched tight as the euphoric explosion catapulted through my body.

Chrome squeezed my hips, rocking me back and forth over his mouth, consuming every bit of my release.

My body went limp, feeling drained as I worked to even my breaths and ride out the aftershocks that Chrome continued to induce after the fact.

A banging on the door had me bolting upright, adrenaline shooting right through my weakened state as I stood to remove myself from Chrome's face. I cursed, using the wall to hold me upright as I searched for my discarded clothes.

The banging continued. "Chrome!" Blaize's muffled voice yelled from the other side. "I know you're in there. Open up."

Light-headed and weak, it was a struggle to get dressed in a frenzy. "Relax. Go get a shower and get dressed," Chrome said, wrapping his arm around my torso, pressing a tender kiss to my forehead. "I'll be here when you get out."

I sighed in relief. "Thank you."

Like the rest of his room, the oversized bathroom was similar to mine with the natural oasis theme. However, there was a masculine touch that I found made me feel safe.

I took the time in the shower to process what had just happened. How I'd lost myself to Chrome in the heat of the moment. As much as I felt I should feel ashamed, I didn't. Whatever happened between us felt right, natural.

After cleansing my body and allowing the warm water to relax my muscles, I left the shower before I could overthink too much longer. I didn't know what this meant for us or where we stood, but I felt I'd earned a semblance of happiness at this point.

When I returned to his room, fully dressed, Chrome sat on the edge of his bed, his knees bouncing anxiously as he stared at the door.

I froze. "What's wrong?"

Turning to meet my gaze, he said, "Sergeant Hogan is here, waiting for us downstairs. They needed me to let down the wards with Onyx to let them in."

"Oh." I let out a breath, relaxing my shoulders as my mind jumped to the worst-case scenario. "Did he bring the book?" I towel-dried my hair.

Chrome nodded and rose to his feet. "We should get going. Everyone is waiting on us."

"Okay." I found a hamper in the corner by the bathroom and discarded the towel. "Let's go."

I moved to reach the door when Chrome's hand wrapped around my neck from behind, spinning me around to meet his lips in a demanding kiss that claimed me. "Just so we're clear, we're not even close to being done."

I nodded dumbly, desire igniting my veins once again. "Okay," I whispered, afraid my voice would show how much I wanted his promise to hold true. Because *damn*.

Chrome's lopsided grin told me he knew exactly how I felt. He stole another kiss, this one softer, before grabbing my hand and lacing our fingers together before heading to the door. "Let's go."

Before we reached what I'd come to learn was called the War Room, Chrome and I dropped hands. Whatever we were, I wasn't ready to go public with it...yet.

The table housed our group, plus a few human rebels. One face stood out. *Dash.*

I narrowed my eyes at him, to which he flashed me a beaming smile. "Nice to see you again, Your Highness."

Before I could retort, Chrome gestured for me to take our seats at the opposite heads of the table. I took mine at the far end, where River and Aella flanked both sides.

I fought the blush that crept up my neck, fighting the erotic images of Chrome's face buried between my thighs. I squeezed them together, taunted by the memory of his mouth, tongue...

"Princess Gray."

I snapped my head up and cleared my throat, straightening my spine.

"I'd like for you to meet Sergeant Hogan, leader of the rebel militia in the southeastern region." Orion waved a hand toward the muscular, bearded man draped in American military camo. The fabric was old—faded, stained, and frayed—but the name tag beamed proudly on his chest.

Hogan appeared to be in his late thirties. He wasn't an unattractive man by any means. Yet, the hardness in his eyes told me he'd seen too much death to ever be okay again.

"And you must be the princess everyone's pinned all their hopes on." A strained smile, as if he was too tired to muster a genuine one, pulled at the edges of his mouth.

"I am, although I warned those here that it wasn't the wisest choice."

Hogan breathed out a weak laugh. "It's a pleasure to meet you."

"Likewise, Sergeant."

Chrome took the time to exchange pleasantries with the sergeant while everyone chatted amongst themselves before the meeting began. I caught Dash smiling mischievously at me. Before I could say something, River smacked my arm.

She leaned into me, whispering, "About time you two fucked."

I tensed. "Why the hell would you think that?"

River laughed as if I was missing something important. "Honey, everyone in the fucking lodge heard you."

"No..."

"Oh, yes, Princess."

Aella leaned in on my other side. "Don't listen to her. It wasn't the entire lodge."

I sighed but caught her keyword. *"Entire*? You mean..."

"Just River because she was being a nosy bitch."

I shook my head and laughed at River's shameless shrug. "Oh. Well, in that case, was it a good show?"

River snorted. "All I know is I wish someone would make me feel like that while eating my—"

She was cut off by Chrome grabbing everyone's attention, but his intense gaze narrowed on River. "Now that we're all here," he started.

River suppressed a laugh, her hand covering her mouth. "Who was it we were waiting on again?" she mumbled in a smartass retort.

Aella snorted, holding back a giggle while studying her hands in her lap.

I bit my lip, determined to keep a straight face. Chrome cocked an eyebrow, waiting for us to get it together and be serious.

"As I was saying," Chrome said. His severe expression said he wasn't amused, but the twinkle in his eyes said otherwise. "Sergeant Hogan has been kind enough to come to us with *The Book of the Arcane*. We should give him our undivided attention." He speared River with a hard look before his lip twitched.

Hogan cleared his throat. "This book was hidden in D.C. The government had it under tightly sealed protection for centuries, and before that, monarchies and the Catholic Church did. It's been well-guarded."

The sergeant looked to his right, where Dash sat. Holding his palm out, he gestured for the teen to slide the ancient tome to him. Dash pulled it from his lap, carefully setting the thick book on the table before gingerly passing it to the rebel leader.

"It's ancient. It must be preserved by some form of magic because if it weren't, it would be decayed by now," he said as he slowly flicked through its pages. "According to the reports stolen from the Pentagon, there is no known language from our world in this book. But the illustrations are indicative enough." Sergeant Hogan then slid the book to Chrome, whose brows were furrowed as he studied it.

After flipping through several pages, he stopped, pointing at something that caught his eye. "That's the beastie-bear." He looked up to meet my gaze. "Take a look?"

I nodded. Standing from my seat, I rounded the rectangular table to reach him. Once I stood beside him, his hand found my lower back. Warmth flooded me.

The pages were yellowed and weathered, but the ink was still dark and clear. There, right before my eyes, was a sketch of the massive, horned bear we encountered. "Yeah. That's it."

On the same page was a sketch of a regal castle, pointed spires and all. "You said it was supposedly a regal being, right?"

"Yes, that's what I was told."

"Seems that information checks out," I said and pointed to the castle.

Chrome flipped through several more pages. Sigils and runes marked many of them. It struck me as odd how they resembled Kinetic brands and Elemental marks at the same time. "I don't see anything exactly resembling Kinetics and Elementals. Do you?"

Chrome shook his head. "But there's similarities." He snapped his attention to Orion. "You were a scholar, right?"

Orion dipped his head. "I was."

"Do you think you'd be able to decipher this language?"

Orion hesitated. "I can do my best."

"Thank you. I want to..." Chrome stopped on a page, drawing my attention to what halted him.

A black-and-white drawing depicted two individuals that seemed to merge, yet they remained separate. I studied it, trying to decipher the meaning without being able to read the passage beneath it. "That looks like a bond of some kind? If I'm not mistaken, it looks like a spiritual one," I said, noting the energetic fields circling the joined figures. A line connected the two from the sternum like a tether. "The Twin Soul Bond?"

"It appears that way, doesn't it?" He looked up at me as if I were the only person in the room, stealing my breath. I couldn't pull my gaze away as my heart threatened to beat from my chest.

Breaking the tension between us, Orion said, "I'll take the book and see what I can decode. Thank you, Sergeant. We are most grateful for all the trouble you've gone through to get this relic."

"Anything to stop Forest from further destroying humanity. The sooner the bastard dies, the sooner we can rebuild our world," Hogan replied, his jaw set in fierce determination.

"I'll have Blaize show you to the cabins where you can stay for a few nights. They've been prepared for your arrival. Electricity and running water are ready for you," Orion assured him.

Dash's eyes lit up. "What about Katia's pies? Please tell me I can have Katia's pies."

Kodiak grinned. "She'd be delighted to bake one for you. I'm sure she's already got one made for you guys."

Dash clenched his fist victoriously. "Can't we stay here, Sergeant?"

Hogan rolled his eyes. "Don't get spoiled."

"There's another book out there that's in Forest's possession, right? A book of dark magic? What do you know of it?" Onyx cut in.

"We don't know much, but our intel sources at the palace tell us that he's had it for over two decades. And that it contains the key to destroying the veil between realms."

I bit my lower lip. "If there's a source of power that he seeks in Arcadia, then it must be in the book. Surely, it'll have a drawing somewhere."

Chrome's hand began slowly circling my lower back, sending little shocks up and down my spine. "If it's in there, Gray, we'll find it. The only issue is how long we have before Forest decides to make his move."

Chapter 46

CHROME

"It's just us today?" Gray pulled her hair up into a bun, the marbled strands blending to look like stone.

The midafternoon sun did nothing to warm the bitter chill as Gray breathed hot air into her fingerless gloves. "It is. The others are training. Today, we'll spar with each other as if we're enemies. Weapons, magic—everything."

"Good. I never got that fight I was owed," Gray smirked, stretching her arms.

I removed my loose-knit hoodie, exposing my tattoos and brands. "Because you hesitated when you saw my flawless skin and mesmerizing eyes. Gave me the upper hand."

"No, that is *not* what happened," she scoffed.

"No? Then why didn't you slit my throat that night?" A knowing grin taunted her as I twisted from side to side.

"Because I was...I wanted answers first."

"Sure," I said, not believing her for a second. "You forget I can feel when you're lying, little savage."

"How the fuck do I block my emotions from you? Did you ever figure it out?"

I bit my bottom lip, trying not to laugh. "Not exactly. We'll work on that." I stretched my arms above my head. "But, for now, I want to see where you are in your progress. Let's find out if you can keep up with me."

Gray snorted and began to stretch her legs. "I can keep up with you."

"You're my equal, so you better," I challenged, meeting her fierce expression.

We had tried many times to open a portal again. We'd been unsuccessful, just like I'd been unsuccessful in slipping down the bond and taking control of her magic again during training sessions over the past several weeks.

It didn't mean other progress hadn't been made yet, though.

"No rules?" she asked.

"No rules. Except, obviously, we can't actually kill each other," I said, picking up normal human blades.

"What a strange turn my life has taken," Gray mumbled, wielding two daggers and falling into a fighting stance.

I observed her body. "You're not opposed to it. And neither am I."

"You have some perks." She shrugged.

I rolled my head from side to side, easing the stiffness. "Let's play, my little savage." Then I lunged.

Over an hour passed of multiple rounds of sparring. Gray held her own quite well. She had most definitely improved in recent weeks with her awareness and her magic. It wasn't that Gray had been unskilled before, but she lacked specific skills that could cost her life in the heat of a battle. No doubt it was an intentional design flaw constructed by Forest.

I wanted her to be as equally lethal as me. She had the savagery but just needed to tighten up the loose ends in her training. In the event I wasn't there to help her, I wanted her to be able to handle herself, regardless of the number of enemies.

"Don't go easy on me, Chrome." Gray used her air magic to whip three daggers at me in quick succession while she aimed a kick at my head.

I held up my palm to stop the blades and spun away. I grabbed her ankle and jerked her toward me. She crashed to the ground on her stomach with a frustrated grunt just before I straddled her lower back and pinned her wrists in front of me. "How would you get out of this hold?"

A blast of magic hit my gut, but I didn't relent, pressing my weight harder into her. I sensed metal skewering in my direction. Using my element, I halted a knife's blade again but angled it to her throat, lightly resting on her carotid artery. "That would've worked on the average Kinetic Warrior." I leaned in, pressing my bottom lip to the shell of her ear. "I'll count it as a win."

My dick hardened against her tailbone as I lay across her. Having her beneath me like this at my whim had another kind of beast lifting its head within me. I could still taste her from the other day. Her sweetness never left, and it had taken everything inside me to not push for more since.

I skimmed my bottom lip along her jaw. Her breaths became more labored, husky. "Is this part of training now?" she asked, her voice raspy.

"When you beat me, you get rewarded."

"I didn't beat you."

"It counts," I whispered in her ear before finding the sensitive spot at the back of her neck and pressing slow, teasing kisses there, keeping her arms pinned behind her back.

Gray lifted her ass, grinding against me. I groaned, releasing her and flipping her onto her back. "What should your reward be this time, little savage?" I asked, absorbing the heat rising in her rainbow gaze. I released my control of the knife, dropping it to the ground beside her head.

"That's a loaded question, Chrome." Her newly freed hands began roaming up my thighs that straddled her, inching up my torso, then to my chest. I needed to feel her on my bare skin. I needed to be *inside* her. To consume her.

I leaned in and nipped her bottom lip. "Greedy." I kissed down her neck, flicking my tongue out to taste her salty skin. "You can take it all. I'll give you everything."

Gray whimpered, just the smallest of sounds. And that was it for my control.

I grabbed one of her thighs and hitched it around my waist. She responded by wrapping around my midsection and pulling me further between her legs.

It didn't escape me that we were out in the training field; anyone could walk by. I didn't give a fuck. Apparently, neither did she.

"You up for putting on a show, Princess?" I slid a hand beneath her tight tank, finding her breast.

"Let them watch." She pulled her bottom lip between her teeth, a fire burning bright in her eyes. With the slightest tilt of her chin, she said, "You're mine."

A growl came from my chest as a primal need to claim her as my own took over.

Gray's hand found my waistband, and her fingers inched inside. They brushed against the thin fabric of my briefs covering my dick, sending a jolt through my body I hadn't expected. Warmth from her breath caressed my neck, lifting the tiny hairs just as she pressed a kiss against my skin.

A throat cleared behind me. "Sorry to break this up and all..." Onyx's voice broke through the sexual haze. "But there's an emergency, and you're needed."

I didn't care if the world was burning to the ground; I wanted to be buried inside the girl with fierce eyes and ashen hair. "Can't it wait?" I asked, my voice muffled against Gray's neck.

"No."

Gray stilled beneath me, and ever so slowly, her hand withdrew from the confines of my pants.

I dropped my head against her chest in defeat. "If this isn't life or death, I'm going to kill you. Otherwise, Orion or you can handle it."

"This is definitely for you. Both of you," Onyx said. I still hadn't turned around to face him, but I could tell he was uncomfortable by the tone of his voice.

Reluctantly, I sat up and then rose to my feet, pulling Gray up with me. "What's wrong?" I adjusted myself before turning around to face Onyx.

It was rare to see Onyx be anything other than optimistic. Seeing the anxiety dripping from his tight jaw and worried eyes had me reevaluating the situation.

Closing his eyes as if to brace himself to deliver the news, he said, "There's been a breach of the wards by a Kinetic scout."

I tensed, my heart skipping a few paces. "Excuse me?"

"A Kinetic scout made it through the wards. He was apprehended by some guards patrolling the perimeter, but…"

"How?" I asked, my voice devoid of any life.

Gray moved by my side, glancing back and forth between us.

"I don't know, Chrome. I honestly don't." Onyx breathed out in defeat. "I reinforced my magic when Sergeant Hogan and the rebels arrived. You did, too! I don't know how…"

The memory resurfaced from a month ago of the night my contact and I had a run-in with Kinetic warriors outside the speakeasy. Afterward, I continued to drink to chase away intensity of the madness fueled by the bloodshed. My contact had to help me get back to the Hollow. There was a high chance I wasn't in the right state of mind to notice if we'd been followed or not. "Fuck…" I looked away. "Okay. Take me to them."

Gray stepped up beside me to join us. "No, Gray," I said, my voice gentle, but firm.

She reeled back as if I'd slapped her, hurt shining in her eyes. My heart clenched. "The fuck you mean, *no*?" She stiffened her spine and clenched her fists, ready to go to war with me over this. A sharp tug on my heart jolted me, signaling Gray's burst of anger and betrayal.

"No, this is too dangerous. I can't risk you being…"

A fist collided with my jaw, rocking my head back. I stumbled. "You don't get to dictate what I can and cannot do. This is just as much my battle as it is yours."

I wasn't even mad that she hit me. I deserved it. But I couldn't risk her in this. "Yes, it is. But you're not going. This is my Hollow. My rules." I ran my hand through my hair, regaining my senses after the solid blow she landed. "You'll be a liability." The words fell from my mouth, and I wanted to shove them back in as soon as they did.

"Fuck you," she spat before she slammed a blast of Kinetic magic into my chest, shocking me from the inside out. It felt like she'd just fried my organs.

"I'm sorry," I grunted, gripping my torso. "But you need to trust me on this."

"Trust you?" She laughed. "That's funny. Says the guy who..." She bit her bottom lip to stop the words that almost slipped free. "Fine. I'll sit back and look pretty for you. Just like everybody else seems to want from me. But in the meantime, go fuck yourself."

She stormed off, snatching up a few daggers and knives on the way.

The familiar pain of self-hatred crept back into my chest. The last thing I wanted to do was to make her sit on the sidelines, but there were things she couldn't know just yet.

Onyx led me to the dilapidated barn on the outskirts of the Hollow near the farm fields. We could've easily put earth Elementals on the task to fix it up, but we didn't want to make the space comfortable for any potential threats.

The holes in the tin roof made the area freezing and dank, while the piles of hay held tattered articles of clothes discarded from years past. Nobody bothered to remove them.

"He's not speaking," Onyx said as we walked past the empty stalls. "Must say, he looks so familiar, though. I just can't place him."

"Gray can't come here. If someone recognizes her, that could spell disaster."

Onyx looked uncomfortable but nodded anyway. "Got it." A few moments later, he added, "Though I must say, this will make for some awkward-as-hell pillow talk. I mean..."

I smacked him on the back of his head. "Don't..."

Onyx laughed, rubbing the spot I had just hit. "Okay, okay."

Reaching the back of the barn, we came to a halt before a closed stall door. I used my magic to unlock it, then pushed it open. The rusted hinges screeched, forcing me to suppress a cringe.

I pulled out an Elemental dagger as I entered the stall, ready to interrogate the intruder. A shadowed figure sat hunched in the corner, the afternoon sun streaming through behind him. It struck me as odd that a Kinetic scout would be trying to make their way inside the property during broad daylight. That wasn't very wise.

But when I looked at the person in the light, I froze.

"Onyx," I said, my voice hardening. "I'm gonna have to ask you to leave. I need to be alone for this."

I could sense Onyx's hesitation, looking back and forth between me and the scout, probably wondering why I had just given away his identity to this person. It didn't matter. This person knew exactly who Onyx was without me having to tell him.

"You sure?"

"Yes. I got it. Let Orion know that I can handle this. No one is to come here. This person is dangerous, and I'll handle them myself."

Onyx ran a hand through his black hair. "Alright. But don't hesitate to call for help."

"I won't." I didn't take my eyes off the Kinetic scout.

Once Onyx was gone and out of earshot, I dropped my arm to my side. "What the fuck are you doing here?"

Chapter 47

GRAY

I beat my fist on Orion's office door, determined to find some answers in *The Book of the Arcane*. Pissed is what I was. I was determined to prove I was the furthest thing from a liability. I'd find information, anything that would stop Forest.

Then I'd go find out who that scout was myself.

I was done with powerful men, thinking I needed to be in the background. That I was a hindrance when I'd done nothing but prove myself day in and day out since I was born.

And how dare Chrome think just because we shared a fucking soul, he could order me around.

Orion swung the door open with a gust of wind. He sat at his desk, his head buried in the book. "How can I help you, Princess?"

"I came to see if *I* could help. Have you been able to translate anything?" I took a seat across from him, taking controlled, deep breaths to calm my fiery anger toward Chrome so I could focus.

"Only a few letters. Many of the sigils are similar to Elemental ones," he muttered, completely engrossed in what he studied.

"Like what?"

He moved over to a sheet of paper, scribbling an Elemental sigil down, and next to it, he drew one of the symbols from the text. "This," he pointed to the foreign symbol, "is similar to our sigil, meaning soul or life force. There are slight variations in the fine details of the angles, but I'm confident that's what it means."

I leaned forward and studied the two examples. "What image are you looking at that the symbol is associated with?"

Orion pointed at a particular drawing on the page. "This one," he said without taking his eyes from whatever he jotted down beside the tome.

"Anything about the magic poisoning the land? Any drawings resembling that, I mean?"

"No. Not that I've seen yet."

"You mind if I take a look?"

Orion waved a hand toward the book. His brows furrowed as he looked back and forth between two sheets of paper, a pen in his grip.

I slid the book closer to me. The drawing of the suspected soul bond glared at me. I resented it now. A part of me wanted to find a way to break it; that way, I would no longer feel like a burden to Chrome. But I pushed the thought away, realizing that it was stupid thoughts planted by an abysmal man.

I was still livid at Chrome, though. I wasn't sure what he wanted to keep from me, but I would find out one way or another.

Gently, I flipped through the pages, looking for anything that might stand out.

I got close to the end and was beginning to doubt that I'd find anything. With my jaw propped on my hand, I felt my hopes wane as I came to the last page.

As I flipped it closed, something caught my eye. "Orion..." I whispered, feeling my heart rate pick up at the possible small revelation.

After what seemed like a few hours, I kept returning to a particular drawing. It was of a very rough and antiquated sketch of a stone with unpolished, jagged edges. Nothing extraordinary about it stood out. I almost breezed past it for the third time, but something told me to stop.

"What about this?" I asked, glancing up at Orion.

With pinched brows, he took the book for himself, cocking his head to the side. "Hm, I haven't seen this one. I must've missed it, somehow," he murmured, his eyes scanning the text quickly back and forth as he tried to make sense of it. "I can't believe I missed this." Confusion warped his brow, as he scratched his stubble.

"You want a better look?" I asked, sliding the tome to him.

Eagerly, Orion leaned closer to the book, his eyes widening and dancing back and forth over the page.

"What?" I asked.

"It's..." Orion gripped the back of his neck. "It's gone. Disappeared."

It was my turn to lean forward, looking over the page. But it wasn't gone. "No, it's still there."

Orion's eyes grew wider, his head jerking up to look at me. "Now, I can see it." He glanced back at the book. "Only if you're looking at it."

I reeled back, shocked at such a suggestion. "What? Why would that be the case?"

Orion shook his head, not understanding either. "I don't know," he murmured, already seemingly moved past this weird phenomena as he scrambled for his pen. "But I'm going to copy all of this down really quick."

I sat frozen. The world tilted on its axis as I tried to make sense of this strange occurrence.

"Don't move," Orion muttered as he began scrawling on his loose papers. "I'll definitely work on deciphering this. Stones hold all kinds of properties, as you know with black crystal."

"Exactly. If this is what Forest is after, I wonder what kind of power it holds that's strong enough for him to go to such lengths to obtain," I pondered aloud.

"Precisely," Orion said, his teal gaze clashing with mine before returning to the book. "It will take me some time. This language is complex, more complex than the rest of it, which tells me it's of value. Especially since you're the only one it appears for."

Leaving Orion's office had me in higher spirits than I'd been in when I'd first arrived. I felt like I was finally contributing in some way. Hungry, I made my way to the dining hall to grab some dinner. A few hours had passed in Orion's office after the revelation, both of us searching in silence for anything else that might've stood out, particularly if the stone was the source of power that Forest was seeking. We originally suspected it was a weapon, or perhaps a chalice based on folklore within our world with the idea that maybe it had derived from Arcadia centuries ago.

But we came up empty-handed. Nothing stood out.

I found Aella, River, Void, and Kodiak at our usual table. No Onyx or Chrome, though.

Anger flooded me again, remembering how he'd tried to control me earlier in the training fields. I hated how small I felt when he called me a liability, reminding me of how my father always made me feel.

Setting my plate on the table, I forced a smile. "Where have you been?" River asked, pointedly filling her fork and taking a bite.

I stabbed at a broccoli floret and shoved it in my mouth. "Orion's office," I said around my food. "Trying to find something on Forest's secret treasure."

"And?" Void asked dryly.

"And nothing concrete yet, but we found a suspicious-looking stone in the book. Orion's gotta work on deciphering the text about it, so that'll take some time. Although..." I took a sip of water. "It only appears for me."

Everyone at the table looked at me skeptically, their expressions urging me to continue. I explained the phenomena, how it disappeared if I wasn't looking at it, and how we believed that it might be our best lead since it's so well-guarded. River sharpened her features in thought while Void dropped his fork, rubbing his jaw as he chewed his food.

"What are you guys talking about that's got you all looking like you're playing a game of Clue?" Onyx dropped his plate on the table. Naturally, no space was left uncovered on it.

I set my fork down against the ceramic plate as I glared at him. How was he going to act like nothing had happened earlier?

"What?" he asked, already scooping heaps of food into his mouth.

"Where's Chrome?"

He shrugged. "I don't know. Probably his room. Why?"

It struck me odd how no one had said a word about the scout's appearance. "What do you mean, 'why?' What happened with the scout?"

Onyx sighed. "Dead. Chrome killed him." He took another massive bite. "Pretty brutally, in fact."

I gaped. "Are you fucking kidding me? Why didn't anyone tell me?"

"Because he's dead. He didn't know anything. He said he was the only one that knew where the Hollow was. He hadn't had time to report it back to the king yet," Onyx explained casually.

I rubbed my temples. "And did Chrome happen to get the information out of him on how he managed to get past the Hollow's wards?"

Onyx stilled. Silence ensued around the table.

I pushed back from the table, no longer hungry. I snatched up my plate, ready to track down Chrome myself and confront him. Onyx's words stopped me. "Don't do it."

"Why the fuck do all these men think they can keep ordering me around?" I asked the ceiling.

Without looking up from his plate, he said, "I'm not ordering; I'm advising."

I laughed, but it held so much bitterness. "Advising? Because you're Chrome's little lapdog bitch. Always heeling to his orders, huh? You left one mindfuck of an asshole and fell right into the hands of another because, apparently, you can't think for yourself."

Hello, projection.

I knew I had gone too far. And there was no doubt I had been projecting my trauma onto Onyx, who wasn't the target of my anger. I wanted to snatch the words back as soon as they left my mouth as I stood there breathing harshly. I was supposed to be working on my quick temper.

Godsdamnit.

Everyone at the table might as well have turned to statues. Onyx slowly set his silverware down against the plate before rising to his feet. His jaw was clenched tight, and his amber eyes were hard when he looked at me—none of his usual mirth and warmth were present.

Onyx took measured steps toward me. It was in that moment that I truly took in his size. He looked down his nose at me with his lip curled, disgust written all over his expression. "Now, I see it." And then he walked off, exiting the dining hall.

I didn't spare anyone else at the table a glance as regret squeezed my heart and moved into my gut. "Onyx!" I called after him. I jogged to catch up as he shoved the double doors wide open. "I'm so sorry. I shouldn't have said..."

As he crossed the threshold, I dodged through the swinging doors behind him. He whipped around, shoulders hunched forward, hands fisted at his side. Shocked by his twisted expression, I stumbled back a few steps as he closed the distance. "You have no fucking idea what you're talking about, Gray. You're so quick to judge others when you won't even look at yourself when you don't get your way."

All I could do was open and close my mouth, speechless by his shift. "I'm sorry," I whispered. "I didn't mean it."

"No, you're just an entitled little princess," Onyx sneered. "I see why people couldn't stand you. And if you're not careful, the ones who have taken you in will turn on you, too."

A sharp ache struck me in the chest. "Onyx..." Tears lined my bottom lids. "Please, tell me you don't mean that." My hands shook at the possibility of losing someone who'd been nothing but welcoming and kind, all because I couldn't keep my mouth shut and control my emotions.

Onyx shook his head in disappointment. "I don't. But you see what false words do when you're hurt? Perhaps you should think about that next time."

"I'm so sorry I said those things." I dropped my gaze to stare at the dirt caked to my boots. "I just...I'm just so tired of people thinking I'm a liability. A burden. I'm tired of having the truth hidden from me."

Onyx rubbed his face, then gripped his neck. "Come on. We need to talk." He walked away at a brisk pace, expecting me to follow him.

I did.

He led me to his room down one of the hallways on the top floor of the lodge. He held the door open, and I squeezed past him awkwardly.

I took in his room, and unlike Chrome's, his was full of personal items. An acoustic guitar sat propped against the wall by his bed. Onyx took a seat on the luxurious mattress that was probably the same as mine. "Come on. Sit. I won't bite."

I rolled my eyes but followed suit anyways as I propped a leg underneath me and sat down comfortably.

"I understand why you're mad. I remember how you were treated. You're valid in that. But I was just the messenger, Gray."

I nodded, giving him a weak smile. "I know. I was wrong for that." Onyx sighed, tilting his head. He cracked his knuckles and continued, "What do you know about my disappearance?"

I frowned. "Not much. No one does. Just that you disappeared one day. You were presumed dead."

Onyx nodded and gazed out the curtained window. "Good." I stayed silent, waiting for him to carry on. "I assume Chrome has told you the story of when he escaped the King's Palace?"

A knot rose in my throat at the memory. "Yeah."

"I was there," Onyx said. "I witnessed them torturing him, and I wasn't supposed to."

"Oh," I whispered.

"Yeah, it was savage." Onyx ran his fingers through his speckled hair. "I mean, here was our hero, the most respected and valued Kinetic of them all. The man that Forest displayed to the public like a fucking show pony...and he locked him in the interrogation room, brutally torturing him for days on end until he was barely alive. Chrome finally snapped."

Onyx swallowed, a haunted expression entering his eyes. "I saw him kill Peri." Dropping his gaze, he blew out a harsh breath. "He tried to fight it, but he'd been deprived of any replenishment for too long. That's when he killed every single person locked in that room with him. He short-circuited every neuron in their brains.

"I tried to help him escape, but he was so...*feral* at that point. He thought I was deceiving him. He saw the high rank on my guard uniform and assumed I meant him harm. I got him out, though. After he damn near destroyed the King's Palace."

I reflected on the events of that day and what my father had claimed. "Forest's words that day were, 'Griffin Silas, son of the deceased Elemental king, wanted to wipe us out...'"

Onyx grimaced. "When he said that, I knew he was hiding something. A few days after, I overheard Uncle Grim," he said, his lip curling and nose crinkling at the mention of his father's younger brother. "I overheard him talking to Amethyst about Forest's plan to open the portal. They considered Chrome a failed experiment, but at least they had you.

"I couldn't stay at the palace after that." Onyx shook his head. "I would've outed myself. My mother, the cold bitch that she is, would've noticed and turned me over right away. So, I packed my shit and ran in the middle of the night."

Onyx rubbed the back of his neck. "I was on my own, roughing it out in the world for a year until I stumbled upon the Perry Hollow. They held me as a prisoner at first, but Orion convinced them I was genuine after interrogating me over the span of a week. Then, they took me in as if I were one of their own. Chrome hadn't found them yet. But when I told Orion the story, he set out in search of him. A year later, not long after the EMP strike, he returned with Chrome in tow. He was a mess. But over time, Chrome recovered and became the leader that he is now."

I let Onyx's story sink in, piecing together what I already knew. I thought back to the memory of his father's broken demeanor after Onyx's disappearance. "Thank you for sharing your story with me, Onyx," I said, genuinely appreciative of his trust. "Ugh, I can't imagine what it must've been like growing up with Grim as your uncle." I cringed at the thought.

"He is a sick piece of shit who needs to be put down," he spat, hatred twisting his smooth complexion. I wondered if he knew what Grim had done to Chrome. I hoped Grim hadn't committed the same atrocities on Onyx. But I didn't ask. Some things were too personal.

I nodded in agreement. "I wish I'd killed him in my escape."

"He'll get his penance," Onyx stated. "I have no doubt."

"But your dad," I began, remembering I meant to tell him. "Your father helped me to flee. He seemed resistant to my father's rule."

Onyx smiled softly. "Yeah, from what I know of the long, sordid tale involving King Jonas and Queen Lilliana, I can understand why. My dad is a man of honor, and there was no honor in what happened to them."

Chapter 48

GRAY

A weight lifted from my chest while another sank to the pit of my stomach. I was relieved that Onyx and I were okay, but I was still *not* okay with Chrome. And the others were probably pissed at me after my little display in the dining hall.

I needed to talk to Chrome. As much as I tried, the rage toward him wouldn't subside. With each step, my temper rose as the memories of earlier resurfaced. How we'd just been about to fuck in the middle of the training fields when he decided to turn into a sexist asshole, treating me like I was his to command.

My gait picked up to the point I nearly tromped through the lodge on my quest to Chrome's room. I rounded a corner, only to slam into a chest. Said chest was much smaller than I anticipated. Still tall, though.

"If you wanted a hug, princess, all you had to do was ask," a deep voice said.

"Dash." I looked up at the tall, scrawny teenager, doing my best to keep my temper at a minimum. Although, I had a bone to pick with this little shit, too. I crossed my arms. "I shouldn't be shocked to see that you're still alive, but here we are."

"I'm a good shot." A smug expression took over his baby face.

"I recall," I said, my voice dry. "That was really stupid of you shooting the Endarkened, by the way. That could've gone wrong in so many ways."

Dash rolled his eyes dramatically in the way only a teenager can. "God, if I have to hear another lecture about this shit, I'll go out there and hunt down an Endarkened and do it again just to prove a point."

I raised my brows. "Honestly, I wouldn't recommend it. I'd just take the lecture..."

Dash blew out a breath. "Yeah, I'm enjoying the amenities too much. Gotta take advantage of it while I can."

I snorted. "Do you know where Chrome is?" Onyx had said he was in his room, but I'd hate for that to have changed since I'd walked across to the other side of the lodge to find him.

"In his room. I just left."

"You did? You and Chrome are close?"

"I keep forgetting that he goes by Chrome here," Dash muttered to himself, scrunching his face in thought.

I slapped the back of his head. "Focus."

Dash rubbed the offended spot on his head. "Hey! That wasn't very royal of you."

"Are you close to him?" I asked again, shaking my head.

"We're friends. We stuck together while he was waiting to meet up with you." The rebel shrugged.

"Meet up with me?" I deadpanned. "You mean kidnap, right?"

"Semantics, Princess."

I pinched the bridge of my nose. How did Chrome deal with this? I sure as fuck couldn't. "I'll see you around. I gotta talk to Chrome."

As I stepped around him, he nudged my shoulder with his elbow. "Talk," he snorted. "*Right*," he said, drawing out the word. "You're totally gonna bone."

The look of horror on my face must have been the reaction he was aiming for because he burst out laughing so loudly it echoed. "Catch ya round, Princess!" Dash swaggered away down the hallway.

I shook my head, wondering how this kid was one of Sergeant Hogan's most trusted rebels. He seemed a bit risky, in my opinion.

Taking a cleansing breath, I realized that, despite how angry with Chrome I was, and as much as I needed to confront him over the scout situation, I needed to give my emotions some space, instead of doing as I usually did and react rashly. That was growth, right?

Changing course and making my way back to my room, I decided to give myself a night of solitude and relaxation.

Between the conversations with Orion, Onyx, and Dash, I was at max capacity for dealing with people for the day. A hot bath, a strong glass of whiskey, and a book were what I needed for the night.

In the bath, I took the time to process everything I'd learned that day. It was a lot. I needed to breathe and just be with myself, something that was becoming less and less frequent these days.

The Elementals at the Hollow had become my friends, and I wasn't sure when that had happened. I cared about them, and I was under the impression that they might actually care about me. At least, I hoped they did. I wasn't sure if I could handle much more rejection.

All would be right in the world if only Scarlett, Hazel, and Cotton were here, too.

My breath caught as I realized the error of my thought process. I hadn't included Slate in that list. The usual sadness that accompanied my memories of him washed over me like the bubbles filling the tub, but it was more with acceptance.

I contemplated the discovery of the stone in Orion's office earlier that day, trying to work out how it could tie in with Forest's plans. Going off what I knew about the properties of stones, and my father's goals, I wracked my brain for the missing link.

My thoughts drifted to Chrome's affliction. If the Endarkened had some connection to the dark magic in Arcadia, then perhaps there could be a way undo it. What if there was a link to the stone in some way that could offer a solution?

I blew out a breath, convinced I was grasping at straws out of desperate hope to save Chrome from his inevitable fate.

My mind returned to Orion and the stone, my thoughts a maelstrom of wild theories that had nothing concrete to give them credibility.

Thoughts of Orion jolted the conversation we'd had about my mother. The photos. The *letter*. My heart lurched to a stop.

Where the fuck was the letter?

I sat up in the bathtub, the water sloshing over the edges onto the floor. "Shit." Bolting to my feet, I climbed from the bath and frantically dried my body in a rush, my heart ready to beat from my chest.

The last place I'd had it was outside Chrome's room, and I'd carelessly dropped it on the hallway floor. I'd intended to come back for it, but that was before Blaize had interrupted.

I needed to find that letter.

Throwing on a pair of leggings and a faded sweater, I stormed over to Chrome's room on the opposite end of the hallway. My lungs felt restricted, locked down, as my heart raced to a violent beat. I couldn't lose the letter. It was my only link to my mother. It was the only thing I had of her.

As I neared Chrome's door, my head began to feel fuzzy, probably from the lack of oxygen amidst my panic. I beat on the door, causing random Elementals passing by to give me startled and uncertain looks.

My pulse whooshed in my ears, drowning out everything around me, except the fact that Chrome wasn't answering his godsdamned door. I pounded on it harder. The wood threatened to give under my abuse. "Chrome! Answer the fucking door!"

Nothing.

My breaths came in shorter and shorter while my chest clenched too tight. I spun and ran down the hallway, then sped down the spiral stairs, doing my best not to trip and break something vital in the process.

It was too much. Everything was getting to be too much. I'd been working on keeping control of my emotions, but it wasn't working. I had all of this immense power confined within my veins, and yet, I felt as powerless as I had under my father's control.

And the only thing I had to physically hold onto was my mother's letter. And now, it was gone, and I had no idea where to even look. I could only hope that Chrome had it.

And that thought pissed me off because, once again, I was at someone else's whim and mercy.

"Gray, what's wrong?" Aella grabbed my arm and whirled me to a stop, making me come face-to-face with her as I reached the bottom of the steps. "What is it?"

"Where's Chrome?" I grabbed my chest, feeling like my heart would implode any second.

Aella looked taken aback. "I...I don't know. Have you checked the lake? Sometimes, he meditates out there."

"Thanks," I said in a rush and jerked away, sprinting toward the front doors of the lodge.

Icy but refreshing air relieved my lungs the moment my foot touched the wraparound porch. My eyes adjusted to the darkness. A storm approached as brisk winds swirled around. I tossed up an air shield, protecting me from the cold and harsh breeze.

My energy dwindled, my legs feeling like jelly and my arms like lead. I was exhausted, yet I was pushed forward by either fear or hope. I wasn't sure which one.

A shadowy figure sat poised in the grass, his back straight against a tree. "Chrome!"

Slowly, he angled his head to face me, not disturbed by my interruption. "Little savage."

"Where's my mother's letter?" I dropped the air shield protecting me.

Silence claimed the space between us. "I don't know what you're talking about."

I closed the distance, still leaving a large enough gap to keep him at bay. "Where the fuck is her letter?" I repeated.

Chrome rose to his feet. "I don't know what you're talking about. Honestly."

My lip curled, and I huffed in disbelief. "*Honestly?* You? Everything that comes from your mouth is such a fucking lie." My hands shook from the anger and betrayal I felt from him.

The calm and carefree demeanor he'd just exuded was wiped clean, replaced by coiled fury and a clenched jaw. "Watch yourself, Princess."

Somehow, Chrome erased the space separating us, his nose only an inch from mine, his warm breath brushing against my face. "Why? Don't like being called out on your shit? The truth hurt?"

His eyes softened. "I hurt *for* you, Gray. Don't you get that?"

"Yeah." I snorted. "Only because you feel my emotions. Now that you ate my pussy, you think you can control me. Think again." I summoned my electric Kinetic magic, ready to hit him with a strong blast.

It fizzled out before it ever left my palm. He'd countered it with his own form of electricity. I growled in frustration. "Why? Why wouldn't you let me go with you to see the scout? I could've helped with getting information from him. I could've known him and that...'

"Exactly," he snapped. "And if he did know you, Gray, that's the last thing you need to risk. Because if something happened to you because of an error I made on an emotional basis, I'd never forgive myself. That scout could've found a way to alert your father with his abilities."

"That's not your call to make!"

"It is when this Hollow was entrusted to me!" Chrome yelled, his deep baritone echoing off the lake surrounding us. "The Elementals are my people. They're yours too, yes. But you're still new."

"You can't order me around like I'm your servant, Chrome."

"No, but I will if it protects you at times."

"The fuck you will," I seethed. "I don't need anyone's protection."

Chrome fisted the base of my hair, pulling me flush against him and forcing me to meet his molten eyes. "Yes, you do."

I shoved him away, needing to clear my thoughts. Everything about him was clouding my judgment, and I wasn't ready to drop my issues yet. "Don't touch me." I pointed a finger at him.

Pain lanced my heart at the hurt that crossed his face, all his vulnerability shutting down. I breathed out a sigh and ran my shaky hands over my face. "Where's the letter?"

In a clipped tone, he replied, "I told you. I don't know."

"I had it the other day before I went into your room. I dropped it on the floor and planned to come back for it. But then Hogan showed up, and Blaize interrupted..."

"I'll ask Blaize about it."

"He didn't give it to you?" My voice shook, my throat tightening and my face heating simultaneously at the last sliver of hope he might have had it.

Chrome shook his head. "No," he said, his tone gentler than before.

"Don't!" I snapped. "Don't talk to me like I'm a child." I might have been overreacting, but I needed that godsdamn letter.

Once again, I fought to get a breath. It felt like a wall blocked off access to my lungs. "I...I need..." I grasped my chest, panic seizing me in its unrelenting grasp. "Help."

Chrome rushed over to me, wrapping me in his strong arms and slowly lowering us to the ground. "You're having a panic attack."

"I can't breathe," I gasped, squeezing his bicep that caged me against his chest.

"I know." His voice was calm and sturdy as he stroked his fingers through my hair. "What do you need? I'm here. Take whatever you need from me..."

I was going to suffocate to death. I just knew it. "Chrome..." I whimpered.

Soft lips caressed my temple. "I got you," his deep voice murmured in my ear, chasing away the wall around my lungs. "You're safe, Gray. Do you hear me? No one can hurt you anymore. I won't let them."

The copper taste of blood oozed onto my tongue from biting my trembling lip. I was trying so hard to hold back years of suppressed rage and pain from abuse. Chrome tightened his arm around my shaking body.

My anchor.

"Stay with me. I've got you."

Chapter 49

GRAY

M y chest cracked open. Or so it felt.

I screamed; it was raw and guttural and ripped my vocal cords into flayed strips, releasing my anguish into nature's embrace.

Chrome held me tight, anchoring me to the earth so it could absorb my suffering. I was so tired of holding myself on a tight leash all the time, so tired of hiding my emotions from the world.

Harsh sobs wracked through my body as I cried, while I wished I wasn't having this ridiculous meltdown in front of him. It would taint how he saw me. Now, he'd know the truth. I wasn't strong like I portrayed myself to be. I was broken. I'd just hoped I would've been able to piece myself back together without anyone bearing witness to it.

Severing the shackles of a lifetime of brainwashing was excruciating. The toxic patterns and mindset that had been instilled in me since birth were as hard as steel. And I questioned if I'd ever be strong enough to break them all.

The letter from my mother had been so many things to me. Not only was it a physical manifestation of her thoughts and emotions, but it was also the only piece of a loving parent I'd ever held. It was the closest thing to a hug from her I'd ever receive. It represented the stark contrast to my father, to show me that there was good in me after all. That I wasn't just my father's daughter. That maybe, through the letter, I'd be able to recognize the morality in me.

Now, it was gone.

Here I was again, so fucking pissed at constantly being under someone's thumb, but once more, I was lashing out at the wrong person. I wasn't mad at Chrome but at myself. It felt like I'd never be truly free; like every time I began to pick myself back up, my father's fists knocked me back down, reminding me of my place.

I continued to scream until my voice could no longer withstand it. Chrome supported me against him, providing a safe place to unleash it all. The wind whipped around us, mixing between lashes and caresses, mirroring my warring emotional states.

"What do you need, Gray?" Chrome asked again. "I'll do anything." His voice was rough in my ear, full of emotion due to the turbulence he felt from me.

"I need..." I didn't recognize my voice. "I need..." The adrenaline and anger fled my body, replaced by exhaustion instead. My head felt fuzzy, my throat sore, and my body weak. I felt empty as I sagged against him. He held me firm, a pillar of strength. "I need to be reminded of the good parts of myself."

Chrome ran his fingers gently through my hair and massaged my scalp, relaxing me. The wind settled into a calming breeze, and the cold air seeped into my bones with the adrenaline gone. "There's so much good in you, Gray. It kills me that you don't see it. But I'll be more than happy to show you. As many times as it takes."

"How?" I asked, my voice weak.

Chrome pressed his lips to the top of my head. "I have my ways."

"I don't like that you think I'm a savage."

"I love that part of you," he murmured against the top of my head. "As much as you bring me light, I bask in your darkness, too. Because I want all of you. Good, bad, light, and dark. Whole or broken. I want *you* to love the dark parts of yourself because dark and light exists within us all, Gray." His baritone voice vibrated down my spine. "We can't escape it. Running from ourselves never ends well. It's only when we come to embrace our whole selves that we find any sort of peace. I may be a monster, but I'm a monster against other monsters. I'll gladly be a monster for those I care about. My family. For *you*."

Hot tears streamed down my face. "I don't know if I can accept that part of me. It's the part that belongs to Forest."

"Did you not hear what Orion said about your mother? She was a fierce warrior. Powerful and ruthless when she needed to be. But she was also kind, gentle, and loving. Yes, your father molded you into a killer. But we can't allow what he did to dictate our lives, to forfeit our happiness because we don't think we're worthy. Whatever shit he put in your head about being unwanted and unworthy was a ploy to control you, to manipulate you to his own ends." He shifted his arm to trail a hand from the center of my chest and up the column of my throat, cupping me just under my jaw.

"You are so much more special and powerful than he ever allowed you to believe. He wanted you manageable because he saw what happened with me. He needed you on a tight leash. But you're free now, my little savage. You're ruthless, yes, but you're also his worst nightmare because of it. It's one of the most raw and beautiful parts of you, just as much as your compassion, heart, and light. I want to see it all." He angled my head so I'd peer up at him over my shoulder. His ethereal beauty blurred through my tears.

My chest loosened, and warmth flooded my chest at the way he looked at me like I was his everything. His world. "I'm sorry." My voice broke from the emotion he evoked inside me, hitting all the exposed wounds that I tried to hide. "I shouldn't have attacked you over the letter. That wasn't okay..."

"Shh." Chrome's thumb tugged on my bottom lip. "I appreciate your apology, but your defensiveness and anger are warranted. I understand it. Feeling that lack of control reminds you of your father and how you were treated." He stroked his thumb across my cheekbone. "You'll get there,

Gray. It takes time. But in the meantime, I'm here for you to unleash on when you're triggered. I can handle it."

What remained intact of my heart shattered in his arms.

The kindness. The adoration. The strength.

But there was one thing that held me back from falling over the cliff with him. "I hate that I need to be saved, especially by a man. I'm not helpless, Chrome. And I'm not a damsel." My stomach twisted at the realization of how much Chrome had saved me. And then how Slate had saved me all those years ago when I was more than capable of taking care of myself.

"Gray, you're far from a damsel. Why do you think I've pushed you to train and hone all your abilities? I want you to have all your blind spots covered, as well as sharpening your fighting skills in the event I'm not around anymore," he said, letting the notion linger. "I want you to be so fucking deadly that no one *dares* to look at you the wrong way. You're my equal in every single way. No one can come close to challenging me like you do. And I love it so fucking much."

Chrome swiped away the tears. "It doesn't make you weak to accept help. We all need it. Life on a normal basis is hard to do alone. Which is why your father had us so isolated." His eyes zeroed in on my bottom lip, sending my pulse racing for different reasons than before. "If you haven't noticed, you've saved me just as much, Rainbow. You gave me hope. You brought me back from the brink of no return. *You* gave me freedom."

In the same way he'd just grounded me from my panic, now, he sent me soaring through space, forgetting that oxygen was even necessary for survival. Fuck, he was the most beautiful being I'd ever seen. He lifted his eyes to meet mine, and a fiery passion burned within them, making the molten silver in his eyes swirl wildly.

"Everything inside me wants to gut your father and hang his corpse by his entrails for all the world to see for what he's put you through. For every time he made you feel less. For every hair he hurt on your head. I want him to suffer so fucking slowly for it. But I can't rob you of your justice. I will proudly watch you as you take what's yours."

The last of my walls crumbled. I grabbed the back of his head and yanked him toward me. He didn't resist as our lips met, our breaths mingling and tongues dancing. It wasn't gentle from either one of us.

I spun to where I straddled his lap, roaming my hands down his sculpted chest while his hands explored my curves. Greedy. Dominant.

"You're mine, Gray Monroe." Chrome tucked his head underneath the curtain of my hair, kissing and biting down the column of my neck. "You fucking own my decaying heart."

I nodded, unable to speak as my body was set ablaze. I needed him in ways I had been resistant to admit.

Chrome pulled back and grabbed my chin between his forefinger and thumb, making me meet his eyes. "No matter what happens to me, I'll always find you. In every lifetime. In every realm. Because it's always been you for me—ever since I was ten years old."

"I'm yours," I whispered, and I meant it. I could no longer deny the powerful nature of our bond and the ways we complemented each other. The way he understood me and my needs on a level that not even Slate had. It was like he lived inside my soul and knew it intimately. And I could no longer deny the effect he had on my body, even since the night in the speakeasy. My will to fight my feelings for him was officially dead.

Chrome rose to his feet, my legs wrapped around his waist, and his hands cupped under my ass.

I assumed he planned to carry me all the way back to the lodge, but my assumption was proven wrong when my back hit a tree trunk, and his lips found mine once again. I was no longer cold despite the bitter chill sending goose bumps down my skin.

"I'm gonna have to ask you again, Gray. Are you sure you want this? You're vulnerable, and I refuse to..."

I grabbed his cheekbones in my palms, noticing the anxious doubt weaving into his gaze. As if he didn't believe that I could actually want this with him. "Chrome Freyr, I'm yours. Now, fuck me."

Pure, unadulterated hunger roiled in his eyes. "Yes, My Queen." Grabbing the hem of my sweater, he lifted it above my head, stripping me bare before him. "Fuck, you're so beautiful."

He dipped his head of chromatic hair, taking a peaked nipple into the warmth of his mouth. It was a delicious contrast to the cold air. I gasped, a moan slipping from my throat as I locked my fingers in the tree's roots.

With a growl rumbling in his chest, he pulled away, slipping a hand into the waistband of my leggings. "Always so wet for me, little savage." His fingers grazed the sensitive skin along my inner thigh en route to the apex. It was slow and teasing, making me yearn for more as my core tightened in anticipation of his touch.

My back arched, the bark of the tree biting into my shoulder blades, but I could care less. "Chrome..." I whimpered, not giving a single fuck how desperate I appeared.

With two fingers, he swirled the moisture around my opening before dipping them inside, earning a gasp from me. He groaned, "I'm gonna bury myself so deep inside you that you'll feel like you're magic itself."

My lower stomach did a little flip, heat radiating through my body at his words.

He pushed his fingers in and out, stretching me. I cried out as he picked up speed, pumping harder with precision to hit that spot that made it so hard to breathe. "I'm gonna..."

Chrome withdrew his fingers and continued pinning me to the tree with his waist. My heart was ready to pound from my chest when he held my gaze with pure hunger and adoration shining in his eyes as he brought his fingers to wrap his lips and tongue around them. A growl emanated from him, deep and low. "I can't get the taste of you out of my mind. My oblivion."

He grabbed my waist and stepped back, easing me to the ground on unstable legs. I didn't hesitate to drop to my knees. I needed to taste him and bring him to *his* knees. I grabbed the waistband and pulled him closer as I worked the button on his black cargos.

I pushed his pants and boxers down from his hips to his ankles, leaving him long and stiff before me. I leaned a few inches closer and licked his shaft from base to tip, absorbing his bliss.

An animalistic groan came from his diaphragm, sending more shocks of need through my core. I gripped the base of his cock in my fist and slowly wrapped my mouth around the swollen head. My tongue swirled lazily around it as I grew eager to take as much of him as I could. He hit the back of my throat with an uncontrolled thrust. I moaned before continuing to massage the silky skin with my mouth. His eyes rolled back in his head, which spurred me on further.

I ravished him, wanting to consume him in every way I could.

He retreated, erratic breaths coming from his nose. "Have I told you how much I love that dirty mouth of yours?"

"Show me."

Chrome's nostrils flared, and the challenge gleamed in his eyes. He kicked off his pants that clung to his ankles, then knelt before me, tangling his fingers in my hair and bringing me in for a hard kiss, tasting himself on my lips. Slowly, he guided my back to the hard earth, where he hovered above me. Removing my pants, he lined himself up with me.

His harsh breaths clashed against my own. Our lips grazed one another as he bore the weight of his emotions onto me through our bond. Tears sprang to my eyes at their intensity. My heart couldn't contain it all.

I knew the word for it. It flashed big and bold in my mind's eye, but I wouldn't dare say it out loud. His eyes said it all, though, even if he didn't voice it either. "Stay with me," he whispered.

Another piece of my soul split open for him. I nodded, giving myself freely to the man I once swore to kill. I choked on the emotions, unable to speak.

The head of his shaft pushed against my wetness. My nails dug into his biceps as he entered me, his width stretching me more than I'd expected. We both groaned as he seated himself to the base, waiting for me to adjust to his size before he started to move.

It was slow, torturous. I needed more of him. I needed him to let go, to take me in ways our bodies craved.

"I want to hear you, Princess," he said through clenched teeth, working to leash his restraint for my sake. But I wasn't made of glass.

"I want you to stop holding back. I'm not fucking fragile."

Something snapped in his eyes. He withdrew from me and snatched both my legs in the air to prop against his shoulders. "You're right." He curled his fingers around my ankles, bracing his weight as he slammed into me. I cried out, clawing at his legs while I no longer felt corporeal. I was lost—I wasn't even on Earth as he continuously hit that spot from the angle he held me.

"My little savage wants it rough and deep?" His thrusts were relentless as he unleashed in the most euphoric of ways. Chrome pounded me into submission, showing his own inner savage.

Just as I was about to peak, he slowed his pace to achingly slow, causing me to growl at him in frustration. But his molten gaze never left mine, pinning me there. "You take me so fucking good, but we really need to work on your patience."

Chrome cut off my remark when he flipped me over on my front. Snaking an arm around my waist, he lifted my ass in the air, leaving me completely bare to him. The air chilled my heated skin, but the heat from his teasing fingers skating down my spine sent more sparks throughout my body. "So beautiful." He stopped to caress my ass cheek, and I felt his emotions bask in having me served up on a platter for him.

Chrome lined himself up with me again, his hand gripping me around my waist. He shoved himself inside while pulling my hips back to meet his thrust. I took the entirety of him in one stroke. I cried out as I rocked forward. "You're so..." he said through gritted teeth, "fucking tight."

I didn't know how much longer my arms could hold me as he pummeled into me. The woods echoed our sounds, the lake reverberating my cries and moans back to us. Fisting my hair in a tight grip, he slowed his pace with deep thrusts, rolling into me.

I clenched around him, squeezing his cock. "Chrome, I need to...*please*."

"That's my good girl." Then he tugged on my hair, wrapping his free arm around my waist, making me straighten my back against his front. The arm around my torso slid up the center of my chest and cupped the front of my throat. He kept his pace even, steady, holding me on the brink of ecstasy. Leaning forward, he kissed my earlobe, taking it between his teeth. "Come on my cock," His gravelly voice alone was almost enough to send me over the edge.

Chrome's mouth found mine as the orgasm washed over me, swallowing my sounds for himself. Oblivion claimed me as I imploded from the inside out. With it came a blast of air from my body mingled with the blue electricity of my magic. It didn't spare Chrome. A deep, pleasure-filled groan rumbled in my ear, and I watched in awe as he seemed to absorb my uncontrolled magical blast into his body, sending pleasurable tremors down his spine. Suddenly, he withdrew and released me.

Chrome pulled me flush against him as we crumpled to the ground on our sides, facing one another. He peppered me with tender kisses on my forehead, nose, and cheeks just before settling on my lips as he caged me in his arms against his chest. I melted, feeling cherished in a way no one had ever made me feel before—not even Slate.

Something within our soul bond clicked into place. I couldn't place it, but both forms of my magic felt different. More tangible. Secure. The chord that seemed to connect us felt more concrete.

I sensed *him*. I felt his energy in a way that was new like I had an internal Chrome GPS system. The tether connecting us through our bond felt more solidified.

Leaning back, I met his gaze. It swam with warring emotions that I *felt* him trying to mask.

"I feel it, too," he said, almost as if he read my thoughts. But that wasn't it. No. He read me in the same way I read him.

I had a feeling we'd just unknowingly done something irreversible regarding our bond. Something on a soul level that we didn't understand.

Chapter 50

CHROME

"**I** feel you," I said, my voice low. "Not like before, but clearer."

Gray's rainbow eyes were wide as she nodded her head. "Me, too," she whispered.

My energy buzzed, my magic feeling electrified. I noticed the difference during sex, but I wrote it off as just being lost in the pleasure. But when she orgasmed and expelled her powers, which is unusual in itself, I absorbed her magic. Not with my abilities, but into my aura—my soul. As if her magic had somehow merged with mine.

It didn't make sense because I didn't suddenly have her abilities, but my connection to her felt more concrete—like I could pinpoint her at any time.

As a test, I focused on closing off the connection between her emotions and mine. With a simple thought, the tether connecting us closed off, like the slam of a door. Gray jumped in surprise, feeling the bond go mute on her end, too. "Well," I mused. "I figured out how to give you privacy now."

Gray deadpanned. "Surely you can't be a bit gentler than that?"

I nuzzled into her hair, breathing in her scent of vanilla and lavender. "Let's be honest. You don't want it gentle, little savage."

Gray relaxed in my arms. "I just want you." Her lips brushed against the skin on my chest as she spoke, her breath warming me from the chill.

"Just stay with me," I said into her hair, the tones weaving together to resemble marble. "You'll see that I'll always find you." I kissed the top of her head. "I swear on my broken soul."

And I meant it with every frayed fiber of my being.

"I promise." Gray's promise stitched itself into my soul.

After some time just lying in our comfortable silence by the lake, Gray spoke up, her voice muffled against my bare chest. "What all do you know about the Twin Soul Bond?"

I sighed. "Not a whole lot, honestly." Combing my fingers through her hair, I went on, "As I've said before, we share two halves of the same soul. It's a bond that goes back lifetimes for us. And I know there are several steps that need to be taken in order to fully complete it."

At that, Gray lifted her head to peer through her droopy lids at me, her brow furrowing. "What do you mean? What steps?"

"Again, I don't know the details, just that there's like some type of ceremony involved." I hesitated, unsure how she'd respond to what I had to say next, but I wouldn't lie to her about this. "And sex."

"Sex? You mean we just..."

"Partially. We're not fully bonded yet." I bent down and kissed the tip of her nose. "I would assume that's why we feel this new clarity between us."

"And our magic..."

I nodded. "Yes, my magic feels different, too. More powerful and energized by yours."

Gray dropped her gaze to a tattooed Elemental mark wrapping up my neck, her lips pursed as she thought about the new development while I continued to gently stroke her hair. At last, she leaned forward, placing a soft kiss on my chest. And the broken pieces of my soul seemed to find their way back together again.

I awoke in the comfort of my bed, warm and content—at peace. Behind my eyelids, I could tell the soft morning rays indicated dawn. My mattress shifted, dipping from the movement of another body at my side. I peeked a drowsy eye open to find Gray curled into my side, nestled into me with her arm draped over my torso and leg thrown over mine. And as my mind caught up to last night's events, I took note of her essence, of how it was basically merged with mine.

I smiled. My heart felt so full it could burst at the sight of seeing the woman who'd rarely been treated with kindness or respect trust me in this way. To sleep beside me in her most vulnerable state. A man she'd once vowed to kill.

I was honored to see her like this. I felt how much of herself she hid away from those around her, even though she wanted to show it. After being rejected for the majority of her life, who could blame her?

Brushing the hair blanketing her face, the scent of vanilla and lavender settled in my senses as I pressed a kiss to her forehead. She angled her head back to meet my eyes with her sleepy gaze.

"Hi," she breathed, her voice airy and husky.

Still grinning like a fool, I stroked my thumb down her cheekbone. "Hi."

After we returned to the lodge last night, we forewent any activities the others tried to entice us into. No one commented on our close proximity or my possessive hold around her waist, but I saw their knowing looks as they bit back smiles as if they knew what had happened. We simply went to my room, where we fucked hard, gently, and everything in between for hours, just soaking in one another's presence, letting every restrained breath free. No walls. No barriers in our bond.

No fears crept into our night together. Between the rounds, we laughed together. And I loved pulling that husky sound from her throat. And that smile...

As I stroked her hair with my fingers, she looked up at me with that smile again, turning me into a lovesick fool as tears filled my eyes.

This woman brought me back to life. She gave me back to myself whether she meant to or not. If she asked me to, I'd level the fucking world for her. I'd do anything. I loved every shattered piece of her. If I had to sweep each jagged shard up with my bare fingers for her so she could piece herself back together, I'd do it without a second thought. I didn't care if it shredded my skin in the process. Hell, I'd search the winds for the lost pieces.

That smile would be my undoing.

I dipped my head, placing the softest of kisses on her lips. I groaned, feeling her arousal. My dick reacted immediately. I teased her jaw, then her neck. She arched her back. "Don't we have..." she asked, breathless.

"No," I mumbled against her neck. "We stay here all day."

Gray giggled, further hardening my dick. "No, we can't."

"The fuck we can't. We're kinda in charge of the place." I licked the protruding vein on her neck. Chill bumps raised on her body. I smiled against her smooth, gilded skin.

"We have stuff to do. Important things and shit," she mumbled, her voice thick.

"This is important."

Again, she laughed but threaded her fingers through my hair. She jerked my head back, pulling my mouth away from her neck. I met her amused gaze. "Focus."

"I'm focusing."

"Training. We gotta check and see how that's going. Talk to Orion about the book..."

I lifted a finger and brushed it over her lips. "We'll get it done, Rainbow," I said. "But first, we're going to enjoy me being inside you." An unbridled fear rose to my chest. What if this might be the last chance we ever get? It was ridiculous, I knew. But I'd waited for her since I was ten. Sixteen years of waiting. The fear of losing something so precious, beautiful, and special scared me worse than turning Endarkened had been. Because without her, life felt hollow.

My eyes must've reflected my anxiety because Gray's face softened. She slid a hand to hold my face in her hands, searching my gaze. She nodded. "Okay," she whispered before leaning in to take my bottom lip in her mouth.

I shifted to where I hovered above her, kissing down her chest erratically, trying to chase away my panic and reassure myself that she was here. That she would stay.

"I'm here, Chrome," she said, her voice a rushed whisper. "I'm here." Her fingers tugged my hair.

My breaths came in short. "I can't lose you."

"You won't."

Sliding between her bare legs, I threw the sheet off us, lining my face with her pussy. I licked her inner thigh, making my way to her center. She squirmed, and I held her hips down with my forearm. Slowly, I licked up the slit in her center, finding comfort in the fact that her taste was on my tongue. I groaned, locking my lips around her clit and rolling my tongue along it before giving it soft sucks.

After slipping my fingers inside, fucking her with my hand, it didn't take but a few minutes before she was coming hard, all while I devoured her, drinking her in like she was my salvation. I lingered, lazily cleaning her with my tongue, reveling in her aftershocks.

I crawled over her, ready to claim her again. And again, until I felt sure this was real. That this wasn't a dream.

We were real. She was mine. And I was eternally hers.

After two hours, I finally subdued the raging fear enough to be able to leave the room without being an absolute asshole to everyone.

Once again, she lay tucked into my chest. Her fingers traced the black ink that stained my gilded skin from my chest up to my neck. My silver currents glowed vibrantly. "What do the sigils mean?" she asked.

"Different things. They're similar to the Kinetic sigils that we have branded."

"I hate there's so much about Elementals that I don't know."

"I know. Between me and everyone else, you'll know it all in no time." I kissed the tip of her nose. "It didn't take me that long."

"What's this one?" she asked, tracing the one on my heart, right on top of the Freyr family crest. Two swords were crossed, and there was an outline of wings in the center. When I joined the Elementals after I fled, I wanted to cover it up in the most disrespectful way possible as a massive "fuck you" to my cold bitch of a mother by stamping an Elemental mark in its place.

One side of my lip quirked up. "It means *king*."

Gray laughed. "I wish so much that she could see that."

"She will. Just before I fucking kill her." She wanted a monster. Well, the cunt got one, but now that monster was her worst nightmare for what she did.

The wicked grin that slowly rose on Gray's face was everything. "I can't wait to see it."

I pulled her closer to my chest, so grateful to be here. So fucking lucky. "I'll talk to Blaize about the letter. I'll find him as soon as we leave here."

Gray tensed in my arms. "What if he doesn't have it? Then what?" she asked, anxiety creeping into her voice.

"I'll find it," I promised.

Gray exhaled a shaky breath. She started pulling back to look at me. "I almost forgot to tell you what I found yesterday in Orion's office. There is this drawing of a stone..." she started.

My brows furrowed, my head tipping to the side just the slightest.

"It only appears when I'm looking at it. I think it's the source of power my father is hunting in Arcadia."

My eyes widened. "You think so?"

Gray nodded. "Also, I keep thinking about the Endarkened."

I swallowed past the lump in my throat. "What about them?"

"Something tells me that the Endarkened are not the natural order of our species. We know basically nothing of our origins." Absentmindedly, she traced my tattoos and brands as she spoke. "It's just...I feel like maybe, there could be a connection with the stone from *The Book of the Arcane* and the Endarkened."

I forced a smile, not wanting to crush the hope she worked so hard to hide. Her eyes glistened with it. "There might be. We'll look into it more." I pulled her back into my arms, resting my cheek on the crown on her head.

Gray cleared her throat. "So, are you going to tell me who the scout was and why the hell you decided to kill him?"

My heart lodged in my throat. I hesitated, feeling like ice water had been dumped on my bliss.

"Who was it? Did I know them personally?" she asked, her voice quivering.

"You did. But it's better this way. Trust me."

"No, I deserve to know who it was, Chrome. Was it a friend of mine? Because let's be real, I didn't have a whole lot of them back at the Kinetic Palace."

"Not quite." That's all I'd give her.

"Who?" she demanded.

"I'm not telling you. It's better you don't know."

"Chrome..."

"No, Gray. I'm not doing this."

"Was it Scarlett? Cotton?" Betrayal shined in her rainbow eyes. My heart twisted.

"It doesn't matter. They're dead now." I clenched my jaw with a tight smile.

A lone tear slid down her cheek before she broke eye contact with me, gazing out the window. She nodded, swallowing back her emotion.

With my thumb, I swiped the tear away. "I'm sorry. I didn't want you to have to deal with more heartache than you already have."

She sat up in the bed, sniffled, and shook her head as if to rid the emotions. "Doesn't matter. Let's just go check on the training."

Just like that, she shut down her connection to the bond between us as she climbed from the bed. She didn't bother covering her naked body as she walked to the bathroom, her back pin straight and her face a mask of stoic hardness once again.

I'd never hated myself more than I did in that moment.

Gray and I walked side by side as we observed the Elementals training in various groups. Pride warmed my chest as I watched even the non-warriors fought viciously. I loved the Elemental sparring style. It was quick, smooth, and precise, like a dance.

Kodiak and Void trained me, and then I learned how to combine the more brutal and direct style of the Kinetics with the Elementals to form a style of its own. I employed Onyx to prepare them for the Kinetic offensive and defensive strategies, hoping not to leave anyone vulnerable.

Finally, the past couple of months of preparation looked as if it were paying off.

I spotted Orion and Void on the other side of the field. With a nudge of my elbow to Gray's shoulder, I gestured for us to head in that direction.

Gray's demeanor hadn't changed since my room. She was locked down again, and regret and guilt ate away at me. We had been so close only hours ago. Now, a major divide sat between us.

She stopped walking, her stare locking on a couple—two women. One with a sword and one with two daggers. Confused, I glanced between Gray and the two other women. The one with two daggers left her side undefended, earning a slice with the mortal sword. The woman winced and stepped back, recovering her stance with her two daggers.

Gray made a beeline toward them, running to stop them before it went any further. "Stop!" she yelled, moving to stand in between them.

The brunette with the sword was already spearing toward her, spinning in a pirouette to land what would've been the killing blow. She hadn't anticipated Gray stepping in. Gray simply ducked and kicked at her feet, sweeping her while snatching the sword from her grip.

"What the fuck?" the brunette said from the ground, springing back to her feet. "Why'd you do that? Are you stupid?" My brows shot to my hairline, waiting to see how Gray would respond to this.

Slowly, Gray swiveled her head to face the brunette, her face set in cold stone. "I'm going to pretend you didn't just say that." Then, she turned her attention back to the blonde with two daggers.

I couldn't hear what she said, but she took the girl's wrists in her hands, rearranging her grip, and then directed her stance to angle her in a more grounded position. I knew Gray favored daggers, and she had no issue fighting against someone who wielded a sword against her.

When she was finished, she stepped back and smiled at the blonde before walking back to my side, her chin held high.

"I think we should train here with everyone, too," she said as she approached.

I narrowed my eyes at her, wondering what her angle was. "Why's that, little savage?"

With a sigh, she said, "Because they need to see that their leaders train with them in solidarity, not isolated from the rest as if we think we're better than them or something. I'm sure they trust us to be well-equipped fighters, but it's another thing to see it firsthand. To see that we're willing to fight side by side with them if it came to it."

I chewed on my lip, rubbing my jaw. "I think you're right. I'll go get Onyx and River. We'll spar with them, two on two. Me and you against them." A mischievous grin tugged up my cheek. "What do you say?"

Gray mulled it over. "I'd love to kick Onyx's ass," she said with a smirk.

I bent down and kissed the top of her head before jogging off to retrieve Onyx and River, my magic and blood already singing with anticipation to fight with Gray by my side.

Chapter 51

Gray

"This honestly isn't fair," Onyx grumbled about being paired off against Chrome and me. Chrome tilted his head to crack the stiff joints in his neck. "Just think of it as a growth opportunity."

Onyx deadpanned, dropping his arms by his sides from his stretch. He huffed. "Whatever. We'll kick both your asses. Right, River?"

River rolled her eyes before dropping down to grab her ankles to stretch her hamstrings. "If I don't have to carry your ass through, then yes."

I was still hurt by the information Chrome skirted around telling me back in his room. Betrayal stung deep by the possibility of one of my friends turning against me. In all honesty, it seemed very plausible that it was one of them.

But what had me most upset was Chrome withholding that information from me. I appreciated that he wanted to protect me, but I wasn't a child.

Despite being pissed at Chrome, even after the world-shattering night and morning we had, I felt this was a great opportunity to test our enhanced bond. It would also serve as us standing in solidarity with the rest of the Hollow. I needed to earn their trust and respect. I didn't just need to; I *wanted* to because I really liked it here. It felt more like a home than the King's Palace ever had.

With Chrome standing beside me, we fell into offensive stances. I eyed River while Chrome's feline lethality faced off with Onyx.

I'd shut off Chrome's connection to me through our bond, but now, I wanted to see what it was capable of in the midst of a fight.

Even though I'd made a lot of progress in combining my two abilities, neither one of us had been able to mimic what Chrome had done to me on the day that I almost depleted Orion. We'd tried. Based on what he felt compelled to do, Chrome's theory was that it was my soul's way of calling out to him as a failsafe. And it most likely worked the other way around, too. We just hadn't fully figured it out yet, although the theory was strong.

With a simple thought, I lifted the mental barrier I'd placed over the tether. Warring emotions slammed into me that weren't my own, and the chord connecting us hummed with the usual tug. I gave it a moment to settle, focused on his excitement for the fight and the thrill of violence, and let it swim through my bloodstream as it mingled with my own drive.

Like before, I could feel him beside me, almost like an extension of my soul. It was so odd to be connected to someone on this level. It would definitely take time to adjust, but I couldn't help but imagine how beneficial this could be in a fight.

We all wielded human-made swords, the non-lethal type. So, we would, indeed, be inflicting pain without the threat of being poisoned by redfern or black-crystal blades. A lot of blood would be shed between us.

I spun the pommel in my hand, getting used to its weight as I prowled toward River, remembering all her weaknesses—not that she had many. Like all of us, she had them, they were just harder to get to.

Chrome sauntered toward Onyx, his double-edged sword hanging casually at his side. Instead of two blades glowing orange, this sword had one blue and one orange. His gait was relaxed but coiled tight with an intensity that I channeled for myself.

My lower stomach clenched all over again to see him so deadly, violent, and confident. Remembering all the ways he touched me with those lethal hands...

River stalked toward me as she seemingly mentally planned out her line of attack. It didn't take long before she lunged. I raised my sword to clash against hers, steel ringing out across the training fields. River's violet eyes glinted with a ferocity that matched my own, and I loved it.

In my peripheral, I noticed a crowd beginning to form around us as the Elementals in the Hollow wanted to see their rightful leaders in action.

I shoved River back a step, but then she swiftly swerved around the kick I aimed at her side. In the same fluid motion, she swiped her sword in a horizontal arc. It came an inch from slicing across my abdomen. I lurched back.

An air shield would protect me from taking any hits, but it would also prevent me from making any either.

I summoned my air to pull the knives from my weapons belt as a whip made of water coiled around my ankle. Just as the whip jerked my foot out from beneath me, I managed to get a knife free and launched it at River.

The knife sailed the short distance between us, embedding in her thigh. The water around my ankle began to freeze to my skin. I sent a gust at River, knocking her airborne and onto her back.

The ice freezing my foot to the ground began to melt, so I stabbed it three rapid times with a knife, breaking free.

The clash of swords to my left drew my attention to Chrome and Onyx dueling with one another with magic and weapons alike in a whirl of orange and silver currents blurring together. They spun around one another with their swords in a violent dance, making it obvious they trained together more frequently than not.

River jumped to her feet. I sprinted at her, wrapping an arm around her and tackling her hard, dropping my sword in the process. I scrambled to straddle and secure her in a pin. The glint of metal reflected off the sunlight in her hand. She speared me with a look of pure focus, a knife in her fist.

A piercing pain shot through my diaphragm from the punch she landed in my ribs. I gritted my teeth and took a second hit just as I summoned a dagger to my palm. I jabbed it into the space between her chest and shoulder.

An agonized scream ripped through the training field. Knowing she could heal once the blade was removed, I summoned my Kinetic magic, preparing to send a shock to her limp arm.

She turned her focus on Chrome, who stood locked sword to sword with Onyx. Chrome was pushing Onyx back, and it was obvious Onyx wouldn't last much longer as he gave Chrome another inch.

Chrome growled, his teeth bared, and his face contorted in pain as he withstood the invisible magic of Onyx's thermal Kinetic ability.

Within a split second, River threw the knife she held with her uninjured arm. And with Chrome fully distracted, he didn't sense the metal blade flying toward him until it had already sunk into his side. It cost him as he instinctively protected the wound, exposing his other side and weakening his grip on Onyx.

Onyx kicked him in the gut while ratcheting up the intensity of the heat he inflicted on Chrome's insides. Chrome's nostrils flared, and his molten eyes swirled dangerously. I faced River again, punching her with an electrified fist in the jaw and then using my air to lodge another knife in her side.

"Sorry..." I muttered before jumping from her torso. I sensed Chrome, and I spun, finding him on his knees.

Oh, fuck that. He kneels for no one.

I launched an electrical blast at Onyx's back that locked him up as the volts ran through his body. With my air, I sent my fallen sword sailing to Chrome's already open and outstretched palm. He'd *felt* my next move and was ready to catch it to run it through Onyx's gut.

Even knowing that we could heal rather quickly, it still turned my stomach to see people I cared about wounded in such brutal ways.

Chrome rose to his feet, pulling the sword free immediately, bracing his shoulder under Onyx's arm. Blood pooled from his mouth as he wheezed for air. "Fuck..." he rasped.

I whirled around to find River sitting up, wincing as she pulled the knife from her side. I dropped down beside her and slid the dagger free from the juncture between her shoulder and arm.

"Shit, are you okay?" I asked, noting the paling of her dark gold skin.

River nodded, strands of black hair falling over her face. "Yeah. I'll be good."

I felt compelled to apologize, but this type of training was commonplace among both Kinetics and Elementals. I just hated hurting people I cared about.

Movement in my peripheral caught my attention. Everyone on the training field had congregated to witness this brutal fight between their top fighters.

Orion's ocean eyes met mine with a prideful smile. I returned it before pulling away and finding Kodiak standing between Aella and Void. As if sensing my stare, Void made his way toward us and knelt beside River. He wrapped an arm around her shoulder. The silver double rings around his black irises shone brightly in his vacant gaze. "You did well. Looks like you listen to me after all."

If it weren't for River sitting there in pain, I would've quipped something smart-ass to him playfully, but instead, I allowed the pride I felt from his approval bloom in my chest. "Thank you. Still want your lessons, though."

I turned to seek out Chrome and Onyx. I approached them, where they sat in the grass. Chrome glanced up to offer me a quick smile before returning to help with Onyx's healing wound.

After training, I returned to my room, cleaned up, and headed down to see off Hogan and Dash. We'd each thanked them for their efforts and for coming to us with *The Book of the Arcane*. It wasn't a gesture we overlooked.

Dash had made some quip to me about not getting chloroformed again, to which Chrome laughed out loud. I couldn't tell if I would miss the little shit around here or not. It was up for debate.

Once the humans left and were on their way, the group and I made a beeline for the dining hall. I was fucking hungry. Now, here I sat, full and ready for a nice nap.

"You've been here for nearly two months, eating her food, and you've yet to meet my mother." Kodiak shook his head disapprovingly before a playful smile spread wide.

I pushed away from the table, wanting to catch up on some rest after my long and active night with Chrome, followed by an intense training session this morning. Kodiak followed suit.

"Come on. You're going to love her." The earth Elemental grabbed my wrist and pulled me to the back of the dining hall leading to the kitchen. Pushing the swinging doors open, a mixture of delicious aromas of buttery potatoes and savory roast cascaded through my nose. If I hadn't just eaten, Kodiak would've had to restrain me from raiding the place.

We continued through the vast commercial kitchen, noting the wooden spoons stirring inside pots on their own before moving the frying pans on the stove. I was confused until I remembered Kodiak having mentioned his mother was an earth Elemental like himself.

We rounded a corner and nearly collided with a short, stocky woman. A hand clutched her chest, eyes wide with surprise. "Oh! Baby, you scared the daylights outta me!"

Kodiak's low rumble of laughter brought a playful glare onto her face, but she pulled her much larger son into her arms. "Ya think he'd want me in an early grave from the state he puts my heart in each time he scares me," she muttered into his torso before pulling back and observing him to assure herself he was okay. "You and your sister both. Little heathens, I tell you."

"But you'd be bored without us." A sly smirk on his face pulled a reluctant grunt from the brunette before us.

"Says you." A sheen of sweat coated her forehead. As she blew a fallen lock of hair from her eye, a kind, suntanned face was revealed. Her skin and vibrant azure eyes stood out beautifully with the dark hair she'd pulled into a loose, intricate knot at the back of her head.

As if she had just noticed my presence, her eyes widened along with her smile. "Oh, my! It's..."

"Princess Gray Monroe," Kodiak finished for her. "Thought you two needed to meet. Meet my mother, Katia."

"It's just Gray. No need for the formalities, ma'am."

Tears welled in Katia's eyes, and her bottom lip trembled before she jolted forward, wrapping her arms around my neck and tugging me flush against her chest. "You have no idea how long I've waited for you to find your way home, my dear." The embrace was something I always imagined a mother's would feel like. It was something I'd never experienced, making me long for more of it while squirming on the inside simultaneously. She pulled back and held me at arm's length. "Thank you for being here," she whispered as her eyes roamed over my face. "You look just like her. So beautiful."

Heat crept up my neck and cheeks. I ducked my head down to try and hide my reaction. "Thank you," I said, clearing my throat. Uncomfortable from the attention, I added, "So, I hear you're responsible for the fantastic food around here. In my opinion, you deserve to run this place. I'm sure Chrome doesn't hold a candle to your delegation skills."

Katia swatted away my compliment. "Oh, stop it. My son must've put you up to that. I only do what I can to contribute around here."

"Not at all," I assured her, chuckling. "The food is much tastier than at the King's Palace. Theirs is good but lacks flavor."

Katia's chest puffed out. "Well, of course, dear," she said, trying to stifle her pride. "They lack any semblance of a heart."

I grinned. "Those were my exact thoughts when I had my first meal here."

Katia squinted at me, slight wrinkles forming on her forehead. "How are you replenishing, dear?"

Taken aback by the subject change, I stuttered and looked to Kodiak.

"It's a learning process for her, but she's taking it easy," the Warrior General provided.

His mother nodded as if it confirmed whatever suspicions she had and dug in the front pockets of her loose pants. "Take this, Princess. Come to me whenever you get low."

A small tin can pressed into my palm. Its round shape clutched easily in my fist. "What is it?"

"Mushweed," Katia said. "It's an herb that helps replenish you when you're unable to do it from an aura. We all know the risks of going too far, so we hold onto Mushweed as a security blanket to avoid depleting if we get too low on our reserves."

I stared at the tin can, amazed and relieved that this existed, wondering why no one has mentioned this to me until now. "Is this a new development?"

"Oh, gods no. This has been a well-kept secret for millennia, going back as far as when we lived in villages and little clans."

"Do the Kinetics know this exists?"

"No. And we'd like to keep it that way. It's a minor advantage we hold in the grand scheme of the war." Katia's tone took on a hint of warning.

I nodded. "Understood."

The double doors we'd entered through swung open and slammed hard into the wall. Kodiak and I spun to find River's rigid posture with twin Elemental blades in her fists. "The Hollow is under attack. Forest found us." Kodiak was moving before she finished, brushing past her. "Let's go." Gone was the quiet teddy bear; in his place stood the Elemental Warrior General, ready to protect his home.

I moved to follow him but remembered Katia. I turned to find her right on our heels.

"I'm coming," Katia insisted, her kind demeanor wiped clean as fierce determination glinted in her eyes. "My son and daughter fight, so I fight with them. A mother protects her own."

A tightness welled up in my throat, and I simply nodded again.

"Come." Katia grabbed my arm, and River joined us in our hurried rush from the dining hall.

On the other side of the wall window, a battle raged on between Kinetics and Elementals. Magic and weapons flared to life in the dying sun. I ached to join, but River and Katia were going in the opposite direction toward the front of the lodge. "Where are we going? We need to be out there!"

"Weapons! Extra weapons. It was a surprise attack, so some weren't prepared and will be depleted on their reserves if they don't get weapons in time. We need to grab some extra antidotes, too, just in case," River rushed out as we weaved through the lodge and made it through the front doors.

The battle raged out front, too. The Kinetic Warrior Guild had us surrounded. I raised my hand to launch an air attack, but River snatched it down. "Not yet. Save it."

My hand itched to let something fly—anything.

We sprinted to the training facility and stocked up on various blades and syringes of antidotes. It wouldn't be enough for everyone, but these extra supplies could spare a few lives.

Fury lit an inferno in my chest. As long as my father was alive, he'd never let me live in peace. He wanted the Elementals gone for the sole purpose that he knew they were the only ones who could stop him in his quest for power. So many innocent people had died because of him. The asshole had an entire race of people brainwashed to do his bidding.

Elementals were nothing like he'd taught me growing up. I would protect them in any way I could. I was meant to be their leader, and I'd show him tonight that he fucked up by creating me.

Shoving daggers and knives into my pockets, I grabbed four swords. Two went into the holster at my back in the shape of an X while I held onto the other two. River barely contained her rage with her curled lip and sharp expression. Kodiak remained silent as he finished strapping blades in holsters along the Elemental tattoos marking his thick arms. Sweet Katia transformed into a fearsome warrior with not a shred of fear in her eyes.

Without a word, we dashed back outside into the melee, hoping we weren't running into devastation.

Chapter 52

GRAY

I sprinted into the chaos with Kodiak and River flanking me from behind. Katia hung back to take on the intruders on the fringes.

With a sword in each hand, I slashed the throat of a Kinetic locked in combat with an Elemental without slowing my pace. I whacked through any Kinetic Warrior I reached, clearing a path through the mayhem.

Currents and Elemental magic clashed across the entire property of the Hollow. Weapons clanged viciously as the song of death accompanied the crimson painting the grass.

Wanting to hold onto my magic reserves, I relegated myself to my blades for the moment. I sliced another throat, and when the woman's eyes went wide, and her body slackened, I searched over her shoulders for any familiar faces—one in particular—as I felt *him* across the lawn.

I glimpsed Chrome's metallic hair, slinging water droplets from its ends as he fought like a one-man army in his specific death dance in the rain. He was alive and okay. I breathed a sigh of relief as I saw him with my own eyes. I pushed forward, landing a punch in the temple of a man with orange hair before shoving my Elemental blade in the space between his ribs. The Elemental he'd been locked in combat with didn't have a weapon. I tossed one of my swords to him and moved along, sliding a spare one from my back.

I chopped at the backs of knees, impaled warriors from the front, and hacked necks as I held Chrome in my sights. He worked fluidly with his metal element and was throwing his opponents with a blast of some sort. I had never seen him wield his Kinetic ability before. He held it close to himself at all times.

Not far from Chrome, Orion flew—literally—across the battlefield, using his air magic to propel him around to run his sword through skulls and spines. The calm and compassionate Orion I was accustomed to was gone as I saw a thirst for violence and vengeance I never thought I'd see in him. Gone was the sadness in his Caribbean-Sea eyes, and in them stood nothing but cunning rage.

River and Blaize fought together with water and fire magic. The siblings intertwined their elements into a rope that charged a Kinetic that River sparred with. At the last second, the elements parted, the water rope moving up the warrior's nose while Blaize's fire rope coiled around his ankles and licked his body, consuming his screams in flames.

A hot blast of heat slammed into my side. I cried out and ducked, sensing a weapon swinging at my head. I kicked the side of a kneecap.

"Fucking abomination."

I launched an electric blue blast at my attacker. The warrior seemed familiar, but I couldn't place him. He stumbled back a few steps with a grimace, then charged me with a sword raised high.

I let him come. "Your king raped a powerful Elemental to conceive me, so take that shit up with him."

My air element rose to the surface within me, a breeze whipping through my hair. As I prepared to launch a blast at him, the Kinetic's beady eyes widened. I glanced down at the roots, twining up his legs and climbing up his torso and chest before reaching his throat. Looking for the source, I spotted Void a few paces away, shoving his sword into the heart of an opponent.

Grateful for Void's help, I took the opportunity to conjure air to throw a knife from my weapons belt into the Kinetic's eye. "I never fucking liked you." I shoved the blade in deeper with my element. "Sexist pig."

Continuing to run, I spotted Onyx locked in a magically induced Kinetic duel with a blue-haired female. Green currents ran up her arms and neck, indicating her microwave magic.

Fuck.

My boot collided with a woman in the gut before running my blade through her throat. Rain poured into my eyes, the work of the water Elementals. I directed air to push others out of my path so I could help Onyx. Microwave magic didn't fuck around.

The ground shook behind me. I stumbled, dodging a small sonic blast aimed at my head. I spun, finding Kodiak opening a chasm in the ground swallowing Kinetic Warriors before closing the gap. Large rocks from underground flew up and knocked into several attackers, leaving other Elementals to impale or behead them.

Void joined Kodiak to work together with earth magic. Void never slowed with his spear while using the limbs from trees as extra weapons to skewer. The roots responded to his command to wrap around throats, squeezing until the eyes bulged from their heads, and they collapsed to the ground.

Still, somehow, more Kinetic Warriors arrived just as quickly as we wiped them out. And sadly, there were too many gilded-skinned Elementals lying lifeless on the lawn. I remembered Onyx and raced toward him and the blue-haired Kinetic. I recognized her. I was pretty sure that was Onyx's ex-girlfriend. How healthy.

I sensed Chrome before metallic hair and silver currents reflected in my peripheral a distance away. He sliced his double-edged sword clean through the neck of a Kinetic. As the body collapsed, his blood-coated face shone as the rain washed it down his neck.

Our eyes locked. He did a quick scan over my body, pure savagery illuminating his clenched jaw as he gazed at all the blood. Goose bumps raised on my arms. I felt his anger rise, threatening to scald me from the inside out. Without pulling his eyes from me, he held an arm out, releasing a pulsing blast into a threat rushing me that I was unaware of, obliterating them into entrails.

My mouth widened in shock, but he soon threw himself back into battle. Onyx still fought the blue-haired Kinetic, but I caught Aella several feet away, locked in a fight with a Kinetic, who attacked her with sonic blasts. Aella stood on a raised platform of compact air that carried her around, dodging his blasts as she lashed a whip at him. He deflected each strike with small sonic blasts, releasing thundering booms that broke the sound barrier.

A Kinetic sprinted toward me, face twisted in disgust at my gilded skin and rainbow eyes. I smiled, sending a sharp gust of air at his feet, sweeping them from the ground. The Kinetic crashed onto the mud, slipping in a hurry to get back to his feet. He looked *so* familiar, too.

Salmon hair jolted my memory as I recognized Mills, the bartender from my fateful birthday revel. "Ah, Vermillion, was it?" I purred, stalking closer. "I see you've earned yourself quite the promotion since we last met."

Mills spat mud from his mouth to the ground.

I continued to prowl closer, throwing an air shield around my body so I could deal with him. "Going from poisoning drinks to all-out battle. Tell me, Mills. Did I ever do you wrong?"

He sneered. "You exist."

"Ouch," I hissed between my teeth, my hand on my chest in fake hurt. "Not the first time I've heard that."

Orion whizzed in a circle to my right, throwing a well-aimed dagger at a Kinetic with ruby hair. My heart lodged in my throat as I recognized the man as Cardinal Kittle, Scarlett's older brother. Did that mean Scarlett was here, too? Cotton?

Facing Mills again, I conjured an Elemental knife to my free hand, my sword still in the other. "It's too bad. We could've been friends, but no. You chose murder. So, I think I'll return the favor." I threw the knife and watched it rotate until it landed perfectly between his now-frozen eyes.

I looked just in time to see Cardinal slipping away from Orion as another Kinetic Warrior took his place.

Sensing a knife cutting through the air, I sent a breeze to knock it off course. I looked just in time to see Chrome drive the Elemental side of his double-edged sword through the throat of a beefy Kinetic with light gray hair.

As savage as Chrome looked, he couldn't help the dipped brow from the sadness that sat there with the life he took. He knew the man. And when I looked down at the slumped body on the ground, I met the vacant eyes of Scarlett's eldest brother, Granite. The two had been friends. A fissure in my heart cracked for Scarlett and Chrome.

Chrome whirled, punching an incoming attack from behind. Again, when the blow landed, it was like a localized explosion of pressure, blasting the Kinetic back and imploding him into crimson bits.

Chrome was weaponless as he fought three-on-one with his bare fists. Each blow he landed sent a pressurized explosion into his attackers. If he kept using his magic at that rate, he'd deplete his reserves soon. I called out to him and conjured my element for assistance. Without looking, he held out a hand as I sent a sword his way, which he grabbed seamlessly before sparring with the two remaining Kinetics.

Water elementals unleashed their wrath, rinsing away the blood as fast as it drenched us while drowning Kinetics. Still standing in my air shield, I scanned to see if anyone needed help. River's black ponytail caught my attention, and I watched as she began to struggle against a thermal Kinetic who countered her ability while she remained locked sword against sword. In their specific vicinity, rain formed and froze into large shards of ice. Just as it reached the top of the jade hair of a female warrior, the ice melted and turned to steam. River tried again with a different tactic but ended up with the same results.

Electric energy buzzed in my veins. I sent a high voltage of my blue magic into the rain pouring above River's Kinetic opponent. The electricity combined with the water locked up the female warrior in electrocution, leaving River the chance to drive her sword in her gut.

I remembered Onyx in his fight with his ex, and I dashed toward them. Just before I reached him, I was barreled into from the side, taking me to the ground. Too focused on reaching Onyx, I used my air magic to drive my knife into my assailant's side. With a curse, he lurched from my body, and I didn't waste the opportunity to reach for my sword to finish him off. But I instinctively dropped it from the shocks of electricity jolting up the arm that held my blade.

That was all the attacker needed to lurch at me in a split second despite his wound. The male warrior sat atop me, pinning me to the ground. As his blade was about to pierce the skin on my temple, a dagger flew from nowhere and sunk into his carotid artery. A jolt coming from the bond had me opening my palm to catch the hilt of a dagger, my body having reacted before I ever realized what was happening.

Looking behind me, Chrome winked at me with a smirk. I rolled my eyes and pushed the gurgling Kinetic off me, climbing out of the mud. "Fucking arrogant ass," I muttered to myself.

A familiar voice cried out in agony, distinguishing itself from the others' echoing around us. Onyx collapsed to his knees. He looked up at the young woman with a look of betrayal just as the blue-haired Kinetic Warrior shoved a dagger into Onyx's ribs.

I screamed and desperately scrambled through the mud to his side, tossing up an air shield to protect us. I rummaged through his pockets, searching for the antidote, trying not to look at the blood dribbling from the corners of his mouth. "Why is her blade affecting you? It shouldn't..." It didn't make sense but I searched his pockets anyway, not wanting to risk his life. His pockets came up empty. "Where's your fucking antidote, Onyx?"

"Used..." he wheezed, "it." He must not have restocked after the training session earlier.

I dug into my pocket and pulled out one of the extra vials I grabbed from the training facility. Jamming it into his neck, I couldn't help but notice how pale he grew. His currents were flickering, shorting out.

"Come on, Onyx. Don't you fucking do it."

Suddenly, a black cloud appeared beside Onyx's head, the specks of ash slowly piecing together to form a man. After a second or two, Chrome stood in its place.

Shocked, I asked, "What the hell, Chrome?" My mouth opened wide as I looked back at the space he had just been sparring half a football field away only seconds ago.

"New ability, I guess," he mumbled in a rush, seemingly unconcerned. Squatting down, he slid his arms underneath his dearest friend and cradled him to his chest. Onyx was fading as his thick, dark lashes drooped, brushing against his ochre skin. "Let's see if I can do it again without killing us both." And just as he had arrived, he left in reverse, disintegrating into what looked like black ash that floated away on the wind.

"Holy shit," I whispered. With the severe anxiety his final words just brought me, my air shield blinked out.

A flash of gold drew my focus, and not from the Elementals in battle around me. Sneering at me like he was already the victor, Golden Figarro flipped a dagger and caught it, drawing a sword in his other hand. Shoving the dagger into his weapons belt, he said, "Should've killed you back at the palace."

Rising to my feet, I sighed. "Ah, I get it. My death will cement your place as Daddy's number one bitch," I said, adjusting the grip on the dagger that Chrome sent me while reaching for the final sword at my back.

"You can imagine my shock to find that our hero, Chrome Freyr, has been alive all this time, hiding out amongst the enemy. And not only that, but he's an Elemental himself," Golden mused as if we were having a casual chat.

"Yeah, you'd think the king would've said something a long time ago about that, right? Isn't it strange that he hid it from all of us?"

Golden shook his head, unconcerned. "Not surprising. Of course, he'd disgrace such an abomination." His upper lip pulled up as he pointedly eyed my golden skin and unique eyes.

"I honestly pity those who refuse to open their eyes to the truth before them; choosing to be sheep led to their slaughter and allowing themselves to be disposable weapons at the hands of a man on a power trip. He doesn't care about any of you, only those that offer something of value. You look like a clown vying to be his lapdog, Golden," I said, falling into a fighting stance. "Call off this attack. You don't even know what you're fighting for. Because if you did, you might think twice about your goals."

Golden laughed and looked around the Hollow's lawn-turned-battle-field. The numbers were dwindling on both sides. Blood blended with the mud in the puddles staining the beautiful oasis. "You think I'd ever believe anything you have to say? Look at you. I can't believe I ever bowed to you."

He lunged. Closing the distance between us, our swords clashed. Orange and blue glowing blades illuminated the space between our faces.

I shoved against him, throwing my body weight into the motion, then spinning away before using my element to throw the dagger at him. Golden dodged with a sidestep as if he anticipated the move. Instead, he launched a knife of his own before I could see what he was doing.

To avoid it, I dove to the side, landing with a roll. A sting on my thigh sizzled beneath my skin. I hissed and cursed from the cut of a Kinetic blade as I rose to my feet. My element went silent, no longer at my call. My electricity threatened to singe through my currents. I sent a crackling sapphire ball at my nemesis. It must've been stronger than I intended because Golden stepped back in fear. I pursued the advantage, ignoring the poison spreading through my veins.

My arms began to feel leaden as I lifted my sword. Just in time to avoid a fatal blow, Golden's blade knocked mine away. We fell into a rhythmic dance of parrying and deflection. I focused on my footwork, doing every-thing in my power to stay upright and not give him much more advantage as my vision began to blur.

I wanted to scream from the increasing pain of the black crystal pump-ing through my veins. I didn't have long before I was unconscious if I didn't get the antidote in my system soon.

Golden feigned to the right, and through my hazy mind, I bought it. He kicked my ankles from the ground. The air fled from my lungs as I crashed to my back in the mud. A heaviness settled in my chest.

Disappointment. Failure. Shame. He won.

My leg grew numb, and my arm was too leaden. I couldn't even aim an electric blast at him if I wanted to.

Golden straddled my thigh, standing above me. Droplets of water fell from the tip of his nose and jaw. I closed my eyes to prevent the water from dripping into them. I opened my eyes, hating that the last thing I'd see before death was this asshole's face. I could only hope that Chrome and the others would kill Forest somehow if the Hollow still stood after this catastrophe.

Through my tunneling vision, I could barely make out the whites of his gleaming teeth, smiling with glee at this triumph. The reflection of metal whizzed past my line of sight, followed by the sharp puncture in my neck. As soon as the needle penetrated my skin, Golden stumbled back, blood painting his hands that covered his stomach.

Rough, calloused hands gripped the sides of my face, forcing my head to the side to look into metallic eyes. "Stay with me, Rainbow," he murmured, desperation and fear in his voice as he pressed his forehead against mine.

Feeling my limbs ease the weight from them, I lifted my arm, gripping the back of his neck. "I'm here."

He nuzzled the tip of his nose against mine, his warm breath warming the frigidity that the adrenaline had me unaware of until the poison had set in. "Where you go, I go."

Another wave of warmth heated my chest as unadulterated panic shone in his eyes. "I'm here, Chrome," I reassured.

He exhaled a quivering breath. Finally, he nodded before sitting up on his knees. It dawned on me that he'd been sprawled across my body in a way that acted like a shield as he gave the antidote time to work through my system. Initially, my gut instinct was to shove him off. However, after a hazy moment, a piece of my soul softened at the realization that he was protecting me with his life while I lay vulnerable, something no one else had ever done before.

I remembered I had the herb that Katia gave me before River informed us of the attack. Mushweed. "Oh, I have Mushweed. Take some. I can feel your reserves are low."

Chrome's jaw clenched. "Thank fuck. I was struggling not to..." he trailed off, biting his lip and looking down in shame. He was so low he wasn't sure he couldn't refuse depleting. He had one more shot. If he caved, it would be game over for him. For us.

I sat up, inhaling a deep and refreshing breath. "Hey," I said, snapping him from his thoughts. "You got this. I've got you."

Chrome's lips parted as if he wanted to say something, but nothing came.

I looked away, reaching for the tin can in my pocket. "I don't know how much to take." I passed it off to him.

Carefully, he took the can and removed the lid, taking a small pinch of the ground-up herb. He tipped his head back and dropped it onto his tongue. With a bob of his throat, he passed the can back to me. "Here. Just a pinch."

I imitated what he did and swallowed the earthy substance. My mouth was dry, making it hard to push down.

Replacing the lid, I shoved the tin can back into my pocket. Once again, a pair of large, strong hands grabbed the sides of my face. Except this time, a pair of soft lips melded against mine in a desperate and greedy kiss. The rain pooled in the space between where our lips met.

Though caught off-guard, I returned the kiss without question. Just as quickly, he pulled away. Blood and some type of gelatin substance clung to his chromatic strands of hair. It was entrails. Entrails were in his hair.

I was speechless. Even a gory mess, he was the most beautiful being I'd ever laid my eyes on.

"Come on, my little savage. Let's go play."

Chapter 53

GRAY

G olden had disappeared.

Chrome scanned the sprawling lawn for the Kinetic who'd escaped. "It wasn't an Elemental blade, so he'll heal."

"For now."

"I'll fucking carve the skin from his body. Alive." Chrome's jaw was clenched, his fists tightening around his sword.

With a final look at one another, we pushed our way back into the mayhem. The numbers were lower, but the fight for the Hollow's survival was far from over.

Combining the use of our magic and fighting skills, we blasted and sliced through bodies, deftly whirling around Kinetics with speed, side by side. We fought on an intuitive level together, instinctively knowing when one needed a weapon or assistance.

The antidote healed me while the Mushweed rejuvenated my energy, making me feel fresh for the second round of this fight. My magic on both sides surged. Wind acted as a sentient being on my behalf as I held back on my Kinetic powers. The electrical voltage fed off my anger, growing at an intensity so strong that it threatened to explode from my body. I needed a release.

Chrome, having sensed my increasing anxiety, met my eyes. "What do you need?"

"A release."

"Not exactly the time or place for that, but I wouldn't be opposed..." he said, slicing his blade clean through the neck of a Kinetic Warrior. Blood sprayed his face, and the rain washed down his neck.

Heat flooded my core at the fucked-up image that flashed in my head. I rolled my eyes, running my blade through the chest of a neon-haired man before jerking it back, spinning, and carving through the abdomen of a warrior behind me. "Fucking on a battlefield," I said, throwing an elbow into the ribs of a woman. "That would be a first." A punch to my jaw rocked my head to the side, sending a blinding pain through my skull.

In the next breath, the offender was blown to entrails. Frustration bubbled in my chest. "I had that!"

"I know," Chrome said, stabbing the side of a man's neck. "But he hurt you." He whirled. "Pissed me off. Told you I'd kill anyone who ever dared to hurt you again."

I answered with a blast of Kinetic magic from my palm into the face of an incoming man. But the magic didn't want to relent. It wanted out, clawing at my chest, wanting to unleash its wrath on the battlefield. "You might want to move. Something is happening."

The little hairs all over my body raised as static electricity built and built around my aura.

Chrome paused to look at me in confusion but still sent a pressurized blow to a Kinetic he dealt with. "What's wrong?"

"I don't—don't know," I said, wincing from the effort it took to try to hold it back. "My Kinetic magic is—it feels unstable or something."

"Fuck," he said. "What's your energetic source?"

"I don't know," I groaned. Chrome stepped in front of me to fight off the horde as I froze, unable to move.

"What the fuck do you mean you don't know? How do you not know that?"

"I just don't! Mine always worked differently. I draw my energy from all types of wavelengths. Father would never tell me."

"Fucking bastard. It looks like a form of electromagnetic energy. You're gonna have to let it go."

"Chrome, I'm scared."

"I know, Rainbow. But you gotta do it. Trust me."

I hesitated, feeling the electricity promise to fry my veins if I didn't listen. "Okay."

"Good girl," he said. "Let it go. There's no better time than now."

So, I did.

Instead of blue energetic volts, pure white streaks of lightning exploded from my body and into the sky. The light from my magic blinded the battlefield. The release of pent-up energy was euphoric, sending electrified pulses down from my neck to the base of my spine.

Thunderous booms crashed around us as the volts cracked through the air to the ground.

Lost in the power, I didn't think to even try and aim the strikes away from my allies. I froze. The lightning strikes slowed to a stop after several minutes. Turning my head, I came nose to nose with turbulent, quicksilver eyes. Energy poured from his aura, and he was alight with electricity. His currents raced violently in a way I'd never seen.

"What the fuck happened? Are you okay?" I asked, worried and glancing around the battlefield, seeing the fight rage on, although there was a wide diameter opened around us that wasn't there before.

"I just absorbed the electromagnetic energy expelled from the lightning." His shoulders shook from trying to hold it all in. That was an astronomical amount of power he'd just absorbed. Holy shit. "In doing so, I was able to control it for you."

"Share it with me," I said, holding out my hand for him to take. I wasn't sure what we were doing, but something told me to do it. Perhaps the bond? There was no way he could release that amount of energy with his ability. Everything would be obliterated for miles.

He didn't question it. Instead, his hand latched onto mine, and the implosive energy he held in flowed to me. Feeling my hair rise again, I held his eyes. "Ready, little savage?"

I nodded, unsure about what we were about to do, but I trusted him to not allow this unbridled power to kill those we swore to protect.

"Let go, Gray. I got you."

With the power back, I let lightning treat me as its conduit. I had no way of knowing how to control it yet, but that was where Chrome came in by slipping in through the bond we shared and taking control of my Kinetic power. Just like he had that day with Orion. He directed it to strike down Kinetics, turning them into charred black bodies.

The Hollow became home to a wild, vicious lightning storm. Each time it struck, a body would drop. With every strike, it sounded like a bomb went off. It was deafening. Some Kinetics with auditory abilities tried to control it, but the lightning soon smited them all down.

Chrome remained still, squeezing my hands and darting his eyes around the battlefield to pinpoint targets. He directed the strikes as I let the energy flow from me. Multiple strikes would hit at once, leaving behind dropped Kinetics.

As my Kinetic magic waned, gravity seemed to pull against my body harder than usual as exhaustion took hold. Chrome looked at me. "Come on, Gray," he said, grabbing the Mushweed from my pocket. "Take more. Not so much this time."

My eyelids began to droop, and my legs grew weak and cold. I slumped forward, but strong arms caught me. "Take it, Gray. Open that pretty mouth of yours."

I complied. His golden and chromatic beauty blurred in my vision. The bitter herb sat on my dry tongue, and I worked to swallow it down.

Chrome held me upright against his side while I waited for the Mushweed to work its way through my system to restore my reserves.

Once the lightness returned to my limbs and chest, I leaned my head against his shoulder.

"Better?"

"Getting there," I mumbled. "That was fucking intense."

He nodded. "They're gone. The Warrior Guild."

I tensed, pulling away to take stock of the carnage. "Holy fuck..." I whispered as I scanned the front lawn of the Hollow, covered with hundreds of dead bodies. Sadly, there were more Elementals in the mix than I hoped to see.

Chrome clenched his jaw, his nostrils flaring. "I failed them."

I whipped around to face him, taking his jaw in my hands. "No," I demanded. "Stop it. You saved them."

"Look at all the Elemental bodies, Gray! And Onyx..." His head drooped forward, the reflective hair drenched like his morale.

The rain had stopped, but the cold seeped deep in the marrow now that the fight was over. "Where is he? I couldn't...I tried to get to him, but I—"

"It's not your fault." Chrome took a deep breath. "He's with the healers. Hopefully, it's not too late," he said. "I need to get to him and figure out what happened."

"Go. I'll stay here and see what I can do."

"I need to fix the wards. It's a mix of my magic and Onyx's. But mine can work for now until we can move locations."

"Move locations?" I asked, my heart slamming to a stop.

"Forest knows where we are now. The wards will make it a bit difficult, but he knows where we are for the most part," Chrome explained, moving to head into the lodge.

"Wait." I grabbed his biceps, stopping him. "What the hell was that you pulled earlier with Onyx? The little—" I whirled my finger in a circle to indicate the black cloud of ash he turned into.

Chrome raised his brows with a breath. "I don't know exactly. I saw Onyx go down, and I wanted more than anything to be right there to help him. And next thing I knew, I was fading away into the ether and reforming beside him."

"Like teleporting?"

"So it seems." He leaned down and kissed my forehead before taking my lips with his. I melted into him, so beyond relieved that he was alive.

I pondered the possibilities of this new ability, wondering if I'd ever be able to master it. "Go to Onyx."

With another kiss, we parted ways, leaving me to check the dead as I prayed I wouldn't stumble across someone I knew.

After a half hour of separating the Elemental bodies from the Kinetic with my air magic, I stood beside Kodiak and Aella. They both aided with air and earth, levitating the bodies to specific sides of the lawn by uprooting the ground to hold them in a temporary, shallow grave until the funeral proceedings.

Aella worked in stoic silence, her only sounds being the sniffling from the tears she shed.

Orion was with the surviving Elementals who helped in the cleanup effort if not wounded too badly. Those who were injured were in the healing ward of the lodge before any permanent damage could set in.

We took some hard losses.

My heart cracked down the middle at the sight of River, hunched over the body of a boy in his late teens, clutching him to her chest, hoarding him from the two adults on either side of her as if to protect her baby brother from their parents. She wailed into his chest, his dark head rolling limply to the side.

It brought back my own memory of the agony that wrecked me the day Forest told me of Slate's death, robbing me of breath. I broke away from Kodiak and Aella, strolling in the direction of my distraught friend.

I didn't say anything as I approached, kneeling beside River and pulling her into my chest with Blaize squeezed in her arms. Her parents knelt at Blaize's head. It was clear they tried to force their emotions back, determined not to show them publicly, but this kind of grief didn't allow for that. Their mother's face twisted in anguish, tears streaming down her cheeks as she fought unsuccessfully to keep them at bay. The same could be said for their father. Even they couldn't silence the wails.

My own throat constricted as a sob was wrenched from my chest. The fire elemental would never taunt me with his mischievous ways again. Those eyes that flicked with a playful flame were forever extinguished. He was too young.

"I should've been there," River forced out through gritted teeth, her voice muffled as I cradled her head to my chest.

"No." I shook my head. "Don't do that."

"It was my job to protect him."

I glanced at her parents, remembering the story she'd shared with me about when they were children. Of how much pressure they put on her. "You did your best. It was chaos, River."

"I wasn't enough," she whimpered.

I trekked back to the lodge, my body caked in blood and mud. It clashed against my blue currents and gilded skin.

After the solemn clean-up effort, we departed, taking a breath for the first time since the attack. Funeral pyres would be lit for the deceased Elementals. The numbers had been too great. There were too many losses that a cloud of agony hovered suspended above the property. It would be a long night, even with everyone exhausted and mourning.

It was customary to hold pyres for the deceased as soon as possible. As the fire element burned away the old life, the wind carried it away to settle into the earth, and then it was cleansed by the rain. The longer the body sat before the pyre, the deeper the karmic debt accrued in this lifetime. The debt would then burrow into the soul's fabric, making their next life that much more difficult to grow from.

The mass ceremony was set to begin within the next hour, giving everyone time to eat, change, and get cleaned up before the send-off. The deceased Kinetics would be included.

Before reaching the front porch of the lodge, I sensed a Kinetic presence hiding several feet away near a cove of trees. I froze, allowing my magic to rise to the surface. The energy from their energetic magic zinged off my aura, sending tingles down my spine.

Blue electricity sizzled in my palms as I took slow steps toward the hidden Kinetic. I remembered Golden disappearing when Chrome showed up and braced for an attack. Creeping closer, I kept my senses open, the voices of the mourning and downtrodden becoming distant. My heart rate kicked up, anticipating another fight I wasn't sure I had the energy for.

I hated the squishing noise my boots made in the mud, no matter how quiet I tried to be, while a chilling breeze made my bones ache.

Shadows crept over me through the bough of the trees. The Kinetic essence drew closer with each step, but I couldn't place the interloper yet. I wafted a breeze in a circular direction in my near vicinity and brought it back to me. Sniffing the air for a scent, I caught the smell of citrus as the odor of sweat followed.

"Princess," a gruff male voice spoke from behind a tree. A splash of bright ruby stepped into view.

"Cardinal?"

"Look, you gotta listen..."

A dagger appeared in my hand before he could finish. Cardinal looked down at the weapon with unease. Raising his hands up in defense, he said, "I'm not here to fight. I need your help."

I reeled back. "*Help?* You're fucking kidding, right?" He couldn't be serious. "You call all of that coming for help?" I waved a hand behind me to gesture to the massacre.

"That wasn't me. You know your father, how he is. I had to come. I didn't kill anyone." He shook his head.

"How noble of you."

"I needed to know what to believe..." he started, brows furrowing. "But seeing Chrome alive kind of confirmed my fears."

I tilted my head to the side, not trusting him for a second. "And?"

"And I talked to Scarlett."

I tensed. "Is she okay? Is she..."

"She's alive. For now."

Air lodged in my throat. "For *now*?"

Cardinal nodded. "Not for long. Which is why I'm here." My best friend's big brother ran a hand through his hair, just a shade of red brighter than Scarlett's. "The king...he..." he stuttered.

"Spit it out."

"After you fled, he conducted an inquisition. He put Cotton on it with his ability. Naturally, Scarlett and Hazel were at the top of the list of suspects. He tried to cover for them, but Grim caught on. They're all in the prison, set for execution at sunrise for treason."

No. No. No.

"I swear to the gods, Cardinal, if you're just telling me this as a ploy to get me back in my father's clutches..."

He clenched his jaw tight when he said, "I'm not. I swear. I just lost my brother. I can't lose my baby sister, too." Cardinal's eyes shone from unshed tears.

My heart squeezed as I mulled over his words. I was unsure whether to believe him, but I could risk my friends' lives by wasting time. "Prison, you said?"

He nodded. "Yes, I can sneak you onto a train and into the palace if we leave now."

"I need to tell Chrome."

Cardinal inhaled a breath, thinking it over before nodding. "Okay."

Fear and adrenaline pulsed through my body once again. I imagined Scarlett sitting in the disgusting prison cells of the King's Palace, disheveled. I saw Hazel curled in on herself, waiting in the darkness, with bruises on her face. And Cotton, unable to speak or cry out.

I couldn't let it happen. They couldn't die because of me. No.

As I hyper-focused on the dramatic images in my mind, my body began to feel lighter, as if the particles that constructed my life force and physical form were separating and floating away on the breeze. Except there was no breeze.

Black pieces of ash drifted in front of my face, just like when Chrome disappeared with Onyx. Starting with my feet, my body disintegrated into ash. Cardinal's eyes widened. "Gray! What's happening?"

I couldn't respond. By the time I opened my mouth to tell him to find Chrome, my throat and mouth were fading in the wind. Then the world went black as I drifted away into nothingness, being pulled through the ether to the unknown.

Chapter 54

CHROME

Freshly showered now, I stared at Onyx with my fingers laced in my lap. He lay unconscious, his deeply tanned skin pale against his orange currents that raced at a regulated pace. At least his breaths were even.

Blood and dried mud caked his face and hands, the remainder of the gory battle lingering. A bandage wrapped around his abdomen from where he'd been stabbed by Royal. Fucking bitch. I never liked the deceitful girl. Not to mention how she'd try to fuck me to use me to raise her standing in the Kinetic Palace.

Dread sat heavy in my stomach as my mind raced with questions. However, my main question was: *Why did a Kinetic blade affect Onyx?* Had Forest figured out a way to make Kinetic weapons lethal when wielded by Kinetics?

A healer walked into the room with herbs, natural concoctions, and valuable sanitizing items like rubbing alcohol on a tray. "He'll be okay, Prince. It'll take him a few weeks to fully recover, but you got him here in time. Had you not, it would've been too late," the blonde Elemental named Jude assured me. Her gentle smile reminded me of Orion, who was no doubt handling the clean-up of the attack.

The tension hadn't left my body, even knowing that Onyx would be fine. "Is there anything else I can do?"

"Go get ready for the funeral proceedings. The people need you more than Onyx right now." Jude turned her attention back to my best friend, who'd become like a brother to me over the years since finding refuge here. She took a rag and wet it in the bowl full of water at his bedside before wiping his skin clean of the carnage. "But first," she said, straightening her spine and digging in her pocket, "take this. You'll need it soon enough." Holding out her hand, she met my palm with a tin can of Mushweed.

I smiled softly, almost feeling guilty, before shoving it in my pocket. "Thank you, Jude. You're truly a life-saver. Let me know if there's anything I can do for you," I said, sighing in defeat. I stood from the chair at Onyx's side, breathing out an anxious breath. I needed to do something. My energy was restless, and I felt the need to be in action after the battle that had just occurred. I hadn't even begun to process everything that had happened yet.

Jude remained hunched over Onyx but tilted her head over her shoulder to offer me a gentle smile. "You've done more than enough, Chrome. Thank you for everything. This attack will have its ramifications on the Hollow, but with you and Princess Gray, we'll recover and come back stronger than ever."

My chest tightened with emotion in the amount of faith people had in me. I didn't understand it, probably because I had been literally losing my mind for the past several years as I became Endarkened. I held on for them. For the people here that Forest tried to wipe out of existence.

I dipped my head, my throat constricting with so many heavy emotions. "I'm going to help clean up down there. Let me know if anything changes with Onyx."

"Of course," she said and returned to her charge.

I left the healing ward and hurried back to the lawn, hoping to find Orion and the others. I immediately thought about how I should try out the new power I'd just discovered. It had been unintentional, and I hadn't had the time to think much about it. But one minute, I was fighting a

Kinetic when I saw Royal's blade go through Onyx's stomach. And the next, I was fading into ash and floating away in the wind to land beside Onyx. In my urgency to save him, I tried it again, desperation squeezing my heart viciously.

I reached the top of the landing and stopped, imagining the front lawn in my mind's eye again. I pictured the massacre that had taken place right outside my home, imagining the sensation of my body dissipating into nothingness and traveling through space and time in the form of what looked like black ash. I felt it as the bits of ash pieced themselves back together to form my body, which felt heavy after the travel.

The bloodbath had been cleaned up significantly since I left to find Onyx. The deceased were piled in shallow trenches as a temporary holding space while the earth Elementals worked on constructing the pyres.

I scanned the area, searching for my closest friends. Anxiety climbed in my chest, fear taking root that they were one of the bodies in the trench. I stopped a passing Elemental man, irises the color of gold, to ask where everyone was.

He looked haggard, ready to collapse into a deep sleep for two days, judging by the reddened eyes and dark circles beneath them. "They went to get cleaned up for the funeral."

"Everyone is alive, then?" I asked, and he understood who I meant. Everyone knew.

With a nod that seemed to take all his effort, he assured me they were before hurrying inside the lodge.

I focused on the bond, trying to place Gray's essence. It wasn't shut down on her side; I could feel that much, but I couldn't find her. I stood near a copse of trees, spinning in circles as I tried to pinpoint her location. The panic was now effectively taking hold.

Something was wrong; I could feel it. Where the fuck was she?

I kept trying to calm myself by saying she was probably in the shower, but that wouldn't explain why I couldn't sense her here. She'd be too close to not feel. And our bond wasn't shut.

"Fuck!" I yelled to the darkening sky, shoving my fingers in my hair.

I couldn't sense Gray, but my elemental magic sensed the metal of the blade sailing toward me from behind.

I sidestepped and spun just in time to block Golden's attack. He swung his broadsword as his face warped in vicious determination. I didn't have my sword in hand, but I ducked the swing and blocked his forearm with mine. Summoning my Kinetic power, I landed a punch to his gut in the same breath. Compact electromagnetic energy expelled from my fist upon impact, causing a pulsating blast to slam into him.

Fuck, that always felt too good. I knew my magic and its unpredictable nature. And when I was going through my Endarkening, that magic got even more unstable. I didn't want to risk it getting out of control, but desperate times called for desperate actions.

Golden soared backward, not exploding into bits, as I didn't exert much power in the blow. He slammed into a thick tree trunk, his skull cracking against the bark. I needed him alive. For now, at least. Just long enough to get info on Gray because I suspected he had something to do with her disappearance.

The Kinetic pain in my ass lolled his head to the side, a humorless laugh leaving his lips. "I can't wait to drag your head back to the king."

I bit my lower lip, pulling out an Elemental dagger using my magic. "Where. The fuck. Is she?" My voice took on the deep, murderous timber that came out when I spiraled.

I was wound tight with icy rage as it slithered beneath the surface of my skin, waiting for the right moment to strike at this piece of shit. Even if he had nothing to do with Gray's disappearance, which I doubted, then he deserved a slow death for thinking he could lay a finger on her and get away with it.

Golden sneered, already beginning to heal his cracked skull. "She's dead."

It was my turn to laugh, something akin to a demon seemed to raise its head from within me. And it wasn't related to my devolution, although I was beginning to feel the echoes of the withdrawal symptoms wanting to return with Gray nowhere to be seen. "Oh, yeah?" I prowled toward him, honing him in my trap. "Is that so?"

"I slit her throat myself. But not before I fucked her like the little whore she is. It was so thrilling...watching her fight against me. But she got what she deserved, the little cunt."

I saw red. Actually, I don't think I saw anything because next thing I knew, I was straddling Golden, mutilating his severed corpse. I was bathed in his blood, his face a dark crimson, as deep cuts marred every inch of his upper body. The iron from his blood that I extracted blended with the crimson from his face. There was hardly any spot left unscathed that wasn't protected by his armor.

I blacked out in my rage, and I wasn't sure how long I'd been there wasting time carving a very dead Golden Figgaro. My chest heaved, and I pushed away from him. I needed to find Gray. The blackout rages were not a good sign.

Fuck, where was she?

I looked around the trees, noticing the sinking sun, the shadows growing darker and darker—definitely a bit duskier than they had been when I had arrived.

Tremors began to return to my hands from the panic about not being able to find my little savage when she most likely needed me. How long had she been gone? I could always just leave now and try to follow the bond, hopefully leading me to her.

I forced out a breath and planned to do just that when a throat cleared behind a tree near me. I slowly cocked my head in its direction, the predator rising to the surface. I took slow and calculated steps toward it.

The call to violence sang a beautiful song in my heart as I sensed the energy of a Kinetic hiding away. "Come on out..." I cooed. "I know you're there."

A silhouette stepped from the trunk into view. Bright ruby hair caught my attention. My steps hitched, remembering Cardinal from the battle. And Granite, who I'd had to kill. An old friend.

"I really don't want to have to kill another Kittle tonight."

Cardinal raised his hands in the air; no weapons were present, but that didn't matter when he possessed magic. "I'm not here to fight."

"Mhm...then why, might I ask, did you show up here at all if not to kill an entire Hollow of Elementals and your princess, Cardinal?" I drew closer to him, my Elemental and Kinetic magic on the tips of my fingers. I eyed him as if he were a mouse I was about to capture in my paws.

My control was seriously beginning to slip. I needed to fucking find Gray, and not just to keep me from going Endarkened. Because if something had happened to her, I would go Endarkened in a heartbeat. I didn't give a fuck. Without her, I'd be lost anyway.

"I had to, Chrome. You, of all people, know that," Cardinal said indignantly. "I didn't kill anyone, though. Look, Gray needs you..."

My jaw clenched, and my nostrils flared. "Where is she?"

"I don't know! She fucking disappeared into thin air!"

My breath froze in my throat. "She fucking *what*?" I asked through clenched teeth. The tone that left my throat was low.

Cardinal took a step back, realizing I wasn't the same Chrome he knew from back at the Kinetic stronghold. Like with Granite, I'd been friends with Cardinal, too. None of that mattered anymore.

"I was telling her about Scarlett, Hazel, and Cotton being held prisoner at the King's Palace. They're set for execution at dawn. And she just suddenly disappeared. But before she fully faded away, she told me to find you and tell you." Cardinal's words were rushed as he worried about my reaction. As he should.

"Fuck!" I yelled. She was at the King's Palace. That's why I couldn't sense her. She was too far away. She did exactly what I'd done on the battlefield upon hearing the news about her friends' imprisonment.

"I gotta go." I closed my eyes, envisioning the grounds of the hellhole I'd been raised on.

"What? Where did she go?" Cardinal asked, his brows scrunched in confusion at my sudden mood change.

I bit my bottom lip, mulling over which information I should divulge to him. "To the King's Palace."

With the image of the Kinetic Palace grounds in my mind, I focused on my connection to Gray, wanting nothing more than to be next to her. I quickly felt my body begin to dissipate into ash, starting at my feet drifting off into the ether. I was weightless as I soared through time and space to my little savage.

It looked like the king's expiration date came earlier than anticipated.

Chapter 55

GRAY

The familiar stench of the King's Palace prison made me nauseated. It burned my nostrils and throat as I fought constant gags.

It seemed that I discovered the same teleporting ability that Chrome had during the battle. Naturally, I *would* fade all the fucking way to the King's Palace and not just a few feet away for my first time like Chrome had. But since I was there, I decided to get Scarlett, Cotton, and Hazel out.

But the main question plagued my mind: if they were all locked up in the dank cells of the prison, then why did Chrome make me believe one of them was the scout who infiltrated the Hollow's grounds? Who was the scout? And what was Chrome hiding? I wouldn't let this go when I got back.

The complex system of cell blocks made it take forever to find where my friends were being held. I had already scoured every cell on every block for the past forty-five minutes, and I was no closer to placing them than I had been when I arrived. I didn't have my bracelets on, so I was surprised I hadn't been stormed by guards yet. Surely, my father and Amethyst knew where I was.

I tightened the cowl over my nose, but it did nothing for the stench of rot and death. If I didn't find them soon, I would pass out from this shit.

I jumped at every creak and shuffle across the concrete floor, thinking it was guards who'd found me. When in reality, it was only non-Endarkened prisoners, sensing someone in their presence and eager to set eyes on a fresh face. I blocked them out, focusing on finding the energy of my friends' auras.

A gentle breeze wafted through my hair, making me freeze in place. The air down here was as stifling as a thick swamp. I summoned two daggers to my hands with my element and called forth my Kinetic electricity as I dropped into a defensive stance.

Pieces of ash swirled together and began to form a corporeal body, beginning at the feet. As soon as he stood beside me, he grabbed the back of my head and pulled me into a hard kiss with a desperation that ached my heart. The relief from his agonizing fear struck me.

Pulling back to rest his forehead against mine, he rumbled, "Thank fuck." His breaths were frenzied and harsh in his panic.

"Cardinal found you, I see."

"More like *I* found *him* after I mutilated Golden," he growled. His nostrils flared, and he squeezed his eyes shut as he worked to contain his anger.

"Did you kill Cardinal?"

Chrome clenched his jaw and roughly shook his head. "No. Although, I probably should've before I faded here. He's still on the Hollow grounds."

"Fuck," I hissed out before I registered something he'd just said, crinkling my forehead. "Fade?"

"Yeah, it's what I'm officially terming our new teleporting ability."

I mulled over it for a minute. "Makes sense, I guess." I shrugged.

"Of course, it makes sense, Princess. I don't simply *do* things for no reason," he scoffed, almost offended.

I ran my hands over my face, not in the mood to bicker with him right now.

"We need to hurry and get back to the Hollow in case Cardinal has something up his sleeve," Chrome said, his voice returning to seriousness.

I tensed. "I'm not leaving here without them, Chrome."

A grin slowly spread across his beautiful features. "No shit, little savage. I'm not here to save you. I'm here to help you." A heavy weight lifted from my chest, thinking he was going to turn into a caveman as he dragged me back kicking and screaming.

Chrome teased his tongue across his bottom lip. The action was so predatory, with the gleam of violence in his mercurial eyes. "While we're at it. We're going to kill the fucking king."

We didn't speak as we began our search for the three Kinetics. As we passed cells full of rotting Endarkened, the memory of the kneeling, Endarkened woman when I was last here with my father and Grim lit ablaze with a sudden realization.

Even through her descent into madness, her Elemental essence had recognized me as her Elemental queen. Despite the fact that kneeling to royalty didn't seem to be custom anymore, something told me that this was something far deeper than I could imagine.

As Chrome and I made our way through the dim corridor, the darkened cells silenced at our sides. We skimmed inside each one, looking for Scarlett's vibrant ruby tresses or Cotton's snowy hair.

I sought their specific energies using my Kinetic magic, trying to pinpoint Scarlett's potent, bright aura and Cotton's subdued one. Hazel's gentle aura had a subtle nuance that had always made it easy for her to sneak up on me. But they were absent.

We ran on precious seconds with each step. Our fade—as Chrome insisted on calling it—inside the prison had surely tripped the security measures in place, so we didn't have time to waste. My muscles were coiled tight, ready for the unexpected. My hearing was expanded, as I took in any invading sounds.

Chrome grabbed my hand and jerked a sharp right toward a cell.

My heart froze.

A female lay sprawled on the putrid cement floor, a splash of color staining the drab concrete like a pool of blood. Scarlett lay unconscious, her currents repressed by a thick metal bracelet.

Chrome nodded to me, motioning for me to move on and find Cotton while he handled Scarlett. It hurt me to leave her there unconscious, but I trusted Chrome to get her free.

Before I could turn around, Chrome already had the metal bars crumpling at his command to open a gaping hole large enough for him to enter.

I found the next cell and came face to face with a bleary-eyed Cotton. His colorless hair and pallid skin was caked with dried blood and dirt. He strained his neck to see what was happening in the cell beside him, but I grabbed his hand through the bars in silent reassurance.

I looked to the cell beside us and spotted Chrome's foreboding silhouette exiting with Scarlett's limp form draped in his arms, her ruby hair swaying with the movement. I motioned to him with my head to signify I'd found Cotton.

Cotton's olive eyes widened in fear as he launched himself backward at the sight of Chrome, obviously recognizing him as the deceased legend.

I'd never seen Cotton show so much emotion.

I held up a placating hand to calm him. I didn't want to risk speaking, but I would have to if we wanted to get out of there soon.

"Cotton," I whispered. "It's okay. We're here to get you out." Cotton darted his suspicious gaze between Chrome and me, wondering how it was possible. His stare lingered on my bloody appearance. Shit, I probably looked horrific. "I'll explain later, but we gotta go. Now."

I moved out of the way while Chrome warped the metal bars on Cotton's prison cell, as he had with Scarlett's. Cotton hesitated for a few breaths. Each one felt like another second closing in on our lives. "Come on."

Shaking out of his stunned state, he pushed off the cinderblock wall of the cell and hurried out. In the faint light of the hallway, I spotted dark bruises marring his cheeks and jaws, as well as deep cuts and a swollen eye.

"Where's Hazel?" I asked, searching the cells beside his.

Cotton's features fell, and then he dropped his gaze to the floor, a heartbreaking sadness washing over his defined features. I reached for his shoulder, anxious for a response. He raised his sodden head and narrowed his eyes toward a cell across from his. I followed his gaze, my heart plummeting as bile rose in my throat.

My hand covered my mouth. "Hazel...*no*," I whispered. The bronze-haired beauty hung from a noose crafted out of the thick linen of her pale blue dress. Her body dangled, hanging lifelessly from the horizontal beam that supported the vertical bars of the cell door.

Chrome spun with Scarlett in his arms. "Fucking shit," he spat. He squeezed his eyes shut, bowing his head to his chest. "Godsdamnit," he growled to himself.

I felt the onslaught of his warring emotions as they passed through him: anger, shock, sadness...guilt.

The elevator doors ground open down the hall, snapping us out of our moment of shock over Hazel's death. Chrome pivoted to face Cotton. "Can you carry her? I have a feeling I'll need to fight."

We needed to get to Forest, but I wasn't sure how we were going to manage that with Cotton and Scarlett in this state.

Cotton hesitated, shaking out his arms, which I assumed had been injured. He nodded, extending his arms to cradle his closest companion.

I pinned him with scrutiny. "If anything happens to us...*run*. Get the fuck out of here. Do you hear me?"

Cotton studied me with his head cocked to the side, and his eyes squinted in thought. I assumed he was trying to figure out my motives, but he nodded again.

Footsteps echoed down the hallway toward us. I released a small blast of magic with the jerk of my hand while summoning a breeze to carry my electrical strike far enough to hit the suspecting guard. The footsteps halted, followed by the heavy thud of a body hitting the floor.

"Okay, let's go," Chrome said, turning to me. Before he continued onward, he did a double-take in a nearby cell, squinting his eyes into the darkness. Suddenly, he spun around to face another cell. A look of confused shock painted his expression, and then he rotated to face another.

I followed his gaze, curious about what threw him off. A motionless, shadowed figure knelt hunched over in the first cell. Squinting to see through the darkness, I saw that they knelt with their forehead pressed to their knee. I spun in a slow circle, noticing all the remaining figures mirroring the gesture.

The groaning had ceased once we made our way deeper into the prison. The sight was as eerie as they came. Had the Endarkened filling these cells been kneeling this entire time for us? I locked eyes with an unnerved Chrome. "Rise," I said, and they did. "At ease. And go rest." The moaning continued, but the shuffling of feet told me they followed my command.

"Let's go," Chrome said, his voice unsteady, clearly perturbed by the sight of so many kneeling Endarkened.

I nodded and cast one last glance at Hazel's limp corpse hanging from the cell door. I was gutted. It was another Helair taken from this world. My stomach burned at the thought of leaving her here like that, knowing she wouldn't get a proper burial. If only I could've gotten here sooner...

I let the emotion sit heavy on my heart as I began to half-walk and half-run down the corridor with Chrome at my side.

With a glance over my shoulder, I saw Cotton following behind, squeezing Scarlett protectively against his chest as he worked to keep up with our pace.

"We're gonna try and make it to the lobby, and when we do, you run. Do what you have to do to escape with Scarlett. Okay?"

Cotton's expression was hard and focused. If he was at full health and didn't have his magic suppressed, he'd be a huge ally to have on our side. He and Scarlett both, but I wouldn't risk them when facing against Forest and, more than likely, Amethyst, too.

Our new fading ability was untested in many ways. I'd only done it once. And even though I'd witnessed Chrome do it with Onyx during the battle, it wasn't worth the risk in this type of situation.

As we rounded the corridor to the stairwell, a familiar voice that oozed down my spine like dirty oil broke the silence. "Ah, so nice to have you back, Princess. Things have been quite *interesting* in your absence." My magic went cold in my veins, completely shut down while my currents and gilded skin winked out.

The three of us slammed to an abrupt halt. Chrome drew two swords free from the holster strapped to his back. "Touch her," he challenged, a viciousness I hadn't yet heard coming from him. It was hair-raising. "I *fucking* dare you."

Grim Valor leveled his beady black eyes toward Chrome, and an excited smile spread across his gaunt face. A smile like that on a man like him was nightmarish. Nothing good ever came from it. "Ah, well, if it isn't my favorite stepson returned from the dead! Welcome home, Chrome. Or should I say, *Griffin*? I believe we have a fine score to settle for the murder of my daughter."

Chapter 56

CHROME

My chest heaved. It took everything inside me to keep from attacking irrationally. I knew how dirty he was. He wasn't above cheap tricks to get the upper hand. And naturally, my magic was shut down, thanks to his ability to absorb others' magical energy waves. It was Grim's only true weapon in this cutthroat world. A parasite—that's what he was. A godsdamn parasite.

I glared at the man who took what little innocence I had left as a child, wielding sick and twisted abuse in order to accomplish one goal: to break me. And it worked. It was a monster they wanted, and it was a monster they got.

"You know, if I didn't know any better, I'd believe you've missed me and our little *bonding* moments," he said with a sadistic grin. I knew this tactic intimately and wouldn't give him the satisfaction of a reaction. He stalked toward me slowly, like he believed he was a predator playing with his prey. A predator he might've been, but he bred a more dangerous one in me. "Where, oh where, have you run off to hide like the *weak* little bitch you are?"

I lowered my head to hang between my shoulders. A dark chuckle bubbled up from my chest. This motherfucker...The sound resounded off the walls and promised violence of the best kind. Vengeance. "Your arrogance proves how godsdamn stupid you truly are," I said.

In a blur, I latched onto my stepfather by the throat, jerking him off the floor. My Elemental sword glowed orange and remained in my free hand at my side.

Dangling in my grasp, Grim kicked his feet to no avail, attempting to touch the floor as he clawed and clutched at my hand.

I studied the pathetic waste of oxygen that was trapped at my mercy. Cocking my head to one side, my lip curled up at the edges in disgust. Then, slowly, I angled my head to the other side. In the movement, my repulsion morphed into a mocking grin by the time it reached the other shoulder, as if I'd slipped into another personality. This smile felt evil and twisted to its core.

Chosen by affliction, this man's voice had been torturing me for years, begging me to give in to the temptation of becoming Endarkened.

Barely tethered rage that had been twisted for so long finally had one of my abusers in its grasp. My fury was an entity all of its own at this point, and I was more than happy to be its vessel. The only other thing that could make the tether snap was if someone touched Gray.

Grim's dark and beady eyes bulged from the pressure of my grip on his throat. Fear permeated the air around me, and I consumed it. I bit my bottom lip, truly loving seeing this piece of shit helpless and at my mercy.

"What's the matter, Grim? I thought you were more capable than this." I pushed out my lips in mock sympathy, but my dark satisfaction couldn't be obscured from my eyes. "Or are you only capable of controlling children?"

Grim went limp in my grasp, seeming to surrender to his fate. "You should be proud, *sir*," I said, my tone mocking. I clenched my jaw, my voice hardening. "I turned out to be the weapon you so *desperately* wanted."

"Think of Peri," Grim rasped out, wheezing. "I'm her father. She wouldn't want you to...kill me," he pleaded, using one of my only weaknesses to once again try to control me. "She'd never...forgive you."

I didn't give a fuck.

Peri feared Grim. She wasn't blind to his shit. She knew how to placate him and play the sweet and naïve role for her father just as I always insisted. Her death was on his hands, our mother's, and the king's. I was just the weapon that misfired while they played with it.

Movement in my peripheral brought me back to the present. Gray inched toward Cotton, who remained nearby with Scarlett in his arms. I needed to figure out how to get them out. I could level the fucking building, but those three needed to get out first.

I squeezed Grim's throat tighter, causing more choking sounds to gurgle from him. My lip curled back. "Don't. *Ever.* Speak her name to me again."

I lifted my sword, ready to run the blade through Grim and end him once and for all. "I wish I could stay longer to savor the slow death you deserve, but we have places to be."

I shifted the hilt in my palm to drive it through his diaphragm. Grim flailed in my hold, and in the midst, a small blade was jammed in the space between my ribs. Just like old times. It was enough for me to loosen my hold on him.

Grim plummeted to the floor with a grunt.

Gritting my teeth, I groaned from the pain, but anger quickly swallowed it and transformed into a growl in the same breath. I hunched over, clutching the wound that was poisoned with black crystal from his Kinetic weapon.

From the floor, Grim gasped for a breath, a blue blade jutting from his fist.

I risked a quick glance at Gray. A fire burned wildly in her eyes as she bared her teeth. She paced back and forth like a caged animal, squeezing her knife. She looked anxious to jump in and finish Grim off herself, but she was giving me this. Just as I wanted Forest to be her kill, she wanted to give me the same with Grim.

Grim scrambled to his feet, adjusting the knife in his hand and shifting into an offensive stance, no longer running his mouth. Fear engulfed his eyes. He knew he just fucked up because I still lived.

I forced myself to inhale a deep breath and release it slowly, blocking out the searing pain in my side and trying to tame my heart rate. It wasn't my first Kinetic blade wound, and it wouldn't be my last. I had several minutes before it got unbearable, so I needed to be quick.

Straightening my shoulders again, I dropped my bloody hand that protected my stab wound. "You think a simple stab wound will slow me down? Remember how you used to cut and stab me with your blades when you'd rape me because I cried? And then said, if I didn't find a way to heal, I'd prove how weak I was and didn't deserve to live?" I laughed, devoid of anything decent left inside me. "Yeah, you trained me well." I lunged and spun in a pirouette.

The action was so quick that Grim wasn't able to process what was happening until it was too late. At the last second, his beady eyes widened in horror just before my blade sliced through the bone and tissue in his neck. It was the most satisfying sound.

Grim's head slid from his neck and dropped to the floor with a thud, his face forever frozen in fear. His body crumpled seconds later to join it.

My shoulders sagged in relief, and my breathing was labored as I stared down at Grim's severed body, then spat on his bleeding corpse at my feet. I had only one regret. "Well, that was too fast," I said, instilling the sight into my memory so I could savor it for years to come.

An odd sense of lightness filled my chest. Even seeing the bloody spurt from his neck, it felt surreal that he was truly gone. I wondered how long it would take for that to sink in.

With Grim's death came the return of our magic. I sighed as my currents raced up my arms, the taste of metal flooded my senses while grounding me, and my gilded skin gleamed once again.

Gray walked to my side, a hand sliding from the bottom of my jaw to rest on my cheek. She forced me to meet her watery gaze. Through our bond, I felt her pride swell for me. "You did it. He's gone." Rising up on her toes, she pulled me in for a final, desperate kiss.

I broke the kiss, resting my forehead against hers. "I really wanted to hear him scream. Just once."

Gray chuckled and pulled away, turning to face Cotton again. He still cradled Scarlett's limp body in his arms.

Cotton's eyes darted between us in nervous confusion, probably trying to figure out what the hell was going on.

"I'm sure you've got a lot of questions, Cotton, but we need to get out of here," Gray said and looked at me as we tried to figure out which direction to go next.

I knew all the nooks and crannies of this forsaken hellhole. I'd find a way to get us out. "Follow me." I turned and headed back down the corridor we came from when Grim ambushed us. We passed by the Endarkened, who were lying down after Gray's order.

Odd.

Gray and Cotton followed. I could feel Gray's worry over Scarlett growing as she walked next to Cotton. "Redfern poisoning?" she asked from behind me. Cotton didn't verbally answer her, but I felt Gray's relief, so I assumed he shook his head in response.

A hand latched around my bicep and snatched me to a stop. I faced Gray, her jaw set, and eyes narrowed. "What? What's wrong?"

Rolling her eyes, she slapped an antidote syringe in my palm. "Were you planning on taking care of that or just waiting until you damn near died from the poison?" she demanded with a raised brow.

In my rush to get them out of the King's Palace, I'd push aside the wound. I didn't have any antidotes on me but thank fuck Gray did. She must've had it left over from the battle.

"There you go, saving me again," I murmured with a small upward tilt of my lips as I exposed my neck to her.

Gray rolled her eyes as she removed the plastic encasing on the needle before thumping the tube. But I saw the smile she fought to hide. "Of course, I'm saving your ass. Don't forget it," she said as she plunged the syringe into my carotid artery.

The antidote's effects worked through my veins, soothing the rising burn that had been quickly building. During my time here, the king had ordered part of my training to be cut and stabbed daily with Kinetic blades.

Sometimes, they'd bring me to the brink of death to see how far they could push me, so it was almost too easy for me to forget the wound in my rush. Because the pain wasn't new to me, I'd grown somewhat of a tolerance to it. Still, it sucked until I got the antidote.

I breathed in deep, savoring the cooling of my veins. "Thank you," I whispered, brushing a strand of hair from her bloodstained face.

Gray leaned into my palm. "Anytime." She rose up on her toes and pressed a quick kiss to my lips. "Let's go."

Cotton stood behind us, looking haggard and exhausted, especially after refusing to put Scarlett down.

"Got a plan?" Gray asked as we continued rushing through the maze of the underground prison.

"Sort of. Just gonna ask that you trust me," I said, directing a pointed look at her out of the corner of my eye.

Gray snorted but remained silent otherwise. I sensed she wanted to ask me something, yet she held back.

For once, I decided not to push the issue. Now wasn't the time.

At the end of one of the cell blocks, a familiar door came into view. I rushed toward it.

"Chrome," Gray said through gritted teeth. "What the hell? We're *not* going into the interrogation room!" she hissed.

I didn't acknowledge her protest; instead, I walked faster. There was a way out in there. I wasn't even sure that Forest knew it existed, but since I'd spent so much time in there during my youth, I'd discovered every crevice in that room when left alone in there for days at a time.

I heard it before I saw it. A blade split the air apart as it sailed toward Cotton's throat. It slammed into a compact air shield just as Cotton launched sideways with Scarlett in his arms. He stumbled but managed to stay on his feet.

I summoned my double-edged sword to my hand, searching for the intruder, but I knew exactly who it was by the poignant and cold energy that approached us from an adjacent corridor.

I worked my jaw tight, the cold savagery returning to my soul as I jerked my head to face the source of the knife that Gray had thwarted. Sharp heels clicked along the concrete floor in the shadows until the light of the main hallway exposed her sharp features and dark lips.

As if she had been waiting in the shadows, Amethyst sauntered into view. Her violet hair pulled tight at the top of her head in a pin-straight tail that kissed her lower back.

It had been years since I'd last laid my eyes on my mother. She hadn't changed a bit. Still cold. Still a fucking cunt.

"It's a shame about Grim," she said about her now-beheaded husband, feigning the faux pity that she'd mastered at birth. "But he was growing quite tiresome." She snapped off her silver bracelet, her energy assaulting me.

Had she been following us the entire time, anticipating the perfect moment to strike?

She speared Gray with a cunning stare, her empty eyes twinkling with victory. "The king's been waiting for you. Nice of you to return willingly."

I needed to get them out of the building. If my mother was nearby, that meant Forest wasn't far behind. Those two had always had this strange symbiotic relationship like that.

An idea popped into my mind. It was a long shot, but it was worth a try. I felt compelled to try it, and if it failed, then I'd find another way.

Amethyst slid free a dagger, igniting the sharp, blue symbols embedded with the metal. Immediately, I snatched the blade with my element and put the edge tight against her throat. My mother simply smiled.

I spun around, levitating my sword by my side. Like last time, I took hold of Gray's hands in mine, squeezing them while focusing on the urgency of getting these three out of the King's Palace. I held Gray's confused rainbow eyes.

In the distance, within my mind, my mother's cold laugh echoed throughout the corridor. I was beginning to lose hope that nothing would happen.

Gray's eyes lit with understanding, and she nodded.

A deafening crack reverberated off the stone walls, Glancing down at our hands, a white light encompassed our hold, sealing them together.

To my left, the air began to ripple to life. The shimmering curtain of the portal to Arcadia came into clear view, responding to the urgency and desperation that we'd felt with the beastie-bear. It had been a suspicion of mine for a while after many failed attempts in training with Gray but I had no way to truly test it until now.

"Cotton! Go through it! Someone will be there to get you to safety," I said, looking at the skeptical, silent Kinetic. Poor guy had way too many surprises tonight. "Hurry!"

Cotton jumped into action, clutching Scarlett in his arms as he stood before the portal. He looked over his shoulder at me and Gray's clasped hands.

I tossed a glance at Amethyst to be sure she hadn't gotten away from the knife at her throat. It wouldn't kill her unless I kept the blade lodged there long enough.

My stomach sank at the look of glee on her face as she saw the portal. *Fuck, she needs to die—and fast.*

Cotton took a step across the veil, disappearing on the other side, Scarlett's deep red hair being the last thing we saw of them.

I turned to Gray. "You go, too."

Gray reeled back as if I'd slapped her. "Excuse me? Hell no. I thought..."

"I know what I said. But I have a plan, and I need you out of here in order to do it."

"No. I'm staying. Don't fucking try me. Forest is *mine*," she growled, the little savage within her coming out to play.

I couldn't help the slow grin that overcame my face. "That's my girl."

Gray and I dropped hands, the portal quickly closing behind. I snatched my sword from beside me. "This is my kill," I said in a low tone for her to hear.

Amethyst seized the knife at her throat and threw it at me with deadly speed and accuracy as it grazed my biceps. Fuck. My Elemental magic went cold.

I charged her, spinning the sword with ease. Her red currents illuminated the eerie hallway, and her lip curled as she braced for my attack, holding only a dagger she pulled from her weapons belt.

Before I reached her, the low-grade burn of her ultraviolet magic began to radiate along my skin. I fought to block it out, my jaw flinching as I sliced my sword at a downward arc toward her diaphragm.

Amethyst sidestepped the blow. Instead, she dropped to the floor with a spin and swiped at my ankles with her stiletto. "No weapons, son. This wouldn't be a fair fight, would it?"

I stepped aside, avoiding the kick. My skin was beginning to blister, and my heart rate climbed high. I growled from the agony.

A random blast of blue magic hit Amethyst in the gut, knocking her on her ass. It was small, not enough to do much damage to her, but enough to make the burn subside.

I stalked toward Amethyst, who lay sprawled on the floor. If I had my Elemental magic, this could be over already. If I trusted myself not to lose my shit, then I'd finish her off with my Kinetic power.

I loomed over her, my lip curled in disgust at the woman who birthed me. The orange blade of the sword angled downward as I held it above my head, ready to drive through her chest.

In another quick move, Amethyst sat up enough to sling her dagger in a perfect throw. Her icy stare focused on Gray.

The blood drained my face, an icy fear sinking its teeth into my heart and churning my stomach.

I whirled to face Gray. My horrified gaze fell to the dagger that was sunk into the hilt in her torso. I froze.

It happened so fast, so unexpected, that Gray hadn't had time to defend herself. If she'd had a fucking shield up...

Why the fuck didn't she have a godsdamn shield up?

"No!" I bellowed, my breaths coming in frantically, desperately.

Then, the demon that existed inside me rose its ugly head, a numb, steely calm overcoming me. I turned ever so slowly and fixated my wrath on Amethyst.

She'd risen to her feet, a victorious smirk painting her sculpted face. I hated that we shared the same feline eyes. "Now, it's just you and me, son."

Chapter 57

GRAY

F ire tore through my insides from the poisoned blade. My Elemental power stuttered, winking out.

"She'll die from that," Amethyst said with a shrug. "And you'll die from this." Her lip curled back as she raised her palm toward Chrome. "I know you're poisoned and can't use that vile Elemental magic of yours to protect you."

Chrome stumbled back, groaning in pain. He clutched his sword tighter. She was searing him alive with her magic. I cried as I dropped to one knee, weakened by the poison spreading through my veins and engulfing them in white flames. "Chrome!"

Chrome continued to back away, his free hand going to his burning face. An anguished, raw scream echoed throughout the hallway. His legs, growing too weak to withstand his weight, collapsed beneath him.

Amethyst advanced on him with calculated prowess. Despite the pain and my better judgment, I noted he'd inherited that trait from her. "You think this is bad?" she said and then smirked at me. "Just wait until your father gets a hold of the two of you." I couldn't think past the pain. It was unbearable. I collapsed on my side, hugging my torso in the fetal position as I curled in on myself on the filthy, cold floor. I couldn't breathe. And I could imagine Chrome was in the same condition as I.

I opened my eyes to find a blurry pair of black, polished loafers almost touching my nose. Then, I was hit with the poisonous magic of gamma rays. My organs felt like they were being soaked in acid.

Tears streamed down my cheeks. Only one person that I knew of could wield that form of magic.

My stomach twisted with intense nausea, adding to my agony. I didn't even try to fight it. I couldn't.

I vomited, my cheek pressed against the cold, dank floor.

My insides felt flayed to shreds. Dissolved.

"*Finally*, you learn your place, Daughter. Face down in a puddle of excrement. Weak. Dribbling at my feet like the useless whore that you are." He lowered himself to a squat, a dark chuckle reaching my fading mind. "I knew you'd be back."

I lifted my head from my chest. It was so fucking heavy, but the pain receded with each passing second.

We sat in the interrogation room at the end of the prison corridor.

A deep rumble growled from beside me. I lolled my head to the side to peek at Chrome in the same condition, glaring under a hooded brow. I followed his glare, feeling my body lighten from the agony, easing up on the strain of my neck.

My father stood in his immaculate glory, his vibrant green beard manicured to perfection and not a hair on his coifed head out of place. Forest swiped the dark sleeves of his suit so no speck of dirt was to be found.

I tested my body with the shake of my arms. Cold, magnetic cuffs bound my wrists to the bolted-down metal chair while the dented table pushed against my belly, leaving me no wiggle room.

My mind snagged on Cotton and Scarlett. I hoped wherever they went, they were safe and that Scarlett would recover. I couldn't handle losing her after Hazel.

"Finally." Forest's refined voice broke through my confused state. "Now, we can get started. Unfortunately, we needed you two to be healed in order to proceed." I noticed two empty syringes sitting beside two full ones, presumably the antidote to the redfern in the Kinetic blades.

Chrome jerked his arms in the chair, unable to contain his seething rage. He tried to lunge at the king but was instantly jerked back in his seat. "You have *no* fucking idea what the consequences could be if you succeed!"

Forest leveled him with a blank expression. "I don't care. This world has always been fucked." He looked down at his navy suit jacket, straightening the lapels as if that was the most important thing.

"What if nothing is left?" Chrome asked through a clenched jaw.

"Well, let it burn, then," Forest said with a shrug. "It's not like I'm the one who caused the EMP. Isn't that right, Chrome?" He turned to me with an arrogant, knowing smirk.

Aside from the heaving breaths, Chrome stayed silent. I'd never seen him look so pissed.

It took a second for me to process what my father had just said, my brain skidding on the brakes. "What?" My dry mouth turned to sandpaper.

Forest's face lit with a bright grin, his deep brown eyes sparkling with wickedness. "Ah, she doesn't know, does she?" he scoffed. "Of course she doesn't. She never was bright enough to see the truths right in front of her."

I ignored the condescending jab and furrowed my brows, turning my head to face Chrome. "What is he talking about?" My voice was almost unrecognizable. No doubt I'd shredded my vocal cords with my screams.

Forest chuckled. "All the time you've spent with Chrome, and you have yet to discover the truth behind Devolution Day? My gods, you *are* fucking dense, Daughter. Must've been a trait from your mother."

"What the hell are you going on about? No need for theatrics, Father," I snapped. I'd had enough.

Forest crossed his arms and stood at ease on the other side of the table, a satisfied grin on his features. "It seems Chrome only divulges the truth when it benefits him." He stroked his beard in thought. "Well, since he won't be forthcoming himself, I'll spill the tea instead. Chrome here is the one who—"

"I did it," Chrome said, interrupting. His lip twitched as he bore his glare into Forest. "I am responsible for the EMP on Devolution Day. I *was* the EMP. But I did it to stop *you* to spare Elementals from being eradicated. You had the human military set to wipe us out with their technology. And if that wasn't enough, you had the worldwide help of Kinetics. I had to take down the grid to stop it all. And it worked. I don't regret it for a fucking second."

I gawked at him, not understanding how I hadn't put that together. EMP, electromagnetic pulse. The ability to control and manipulate electromagnetic waves. The memory of his pulses during the battle surfaced. How he kept saying his magic was unstable.

Holy gods. Chrome wiped out three-quarters of the human population in a single pulse.

I felt like a dumbass for not figuring it out. Even so, for him to take down *all* the power grids worldwide in a singular pulse required an unfathomable amount of power. So, it never crossed my mind that he could've been capable of such a feat unless...

"You had to deplete a second time to do it, didn't you?" I asked, the rest of the pieces falling into place. He'd told me he'd depleted *twice*. Once, when he depleted Peri, but he never divulged about the second time. It must've been to take down the power grid in a last ditch effort to save his people.

Oh, Chrome.

Chrome dropped his head to his chest in silent admission.

Why hadn't he told me this? He could've told me, and I would've understood. The fact he'd kept a monumental secret like this from me said he still didn't trust me. Not the way I'd come to trust him, and that hurt.

"I'm sorry, Rainbow," Chrome mumbled from beside me, still bound to his chair.

I didn't respond; I just stared at the madman who reveled in our discord.

"Now that we have everything out in the open, let's get on with it." The king pushed to his feet and walked to the other side of the room to a table pressed against a wall. Placed on it were various items, but it didn't look promising. A hand-crafted bronze bowl the color of Hazel's hair—marked with uneven indentations around the sides—sat next to a sharp knife and an old tome.

The cracked, black text was ancient. Dark energy seeped from the book, its noxiousness poisoning the air in the confined room.

Forest retrieved the book with care and flipped through the pages until he must've landed on the one he sought. He came before us, holding the tome sprawled across his hands with the air of a pious leader gracing his disciples. "Isn't this gift so lovely?" he asked with a maddened grin. "It was a precious gift from a sweet little sorceress before you two were thought of."

"You mean a Tempest?" I asked, my brow raised, taking note of the fact he'd apparently been working with the Tempests from Arcadia for over two decades.

Forest sneered. "Yes, Daughter. A Tempest, those lovely little sorceresses in Arcadia. Maybe you're not that daft after all." He shrugged. "This book has been great for weakening the veil over time. But when you two came together, your powers weakened it that much more, allowing for the portal to open. But there are other useful spells." Forest lifted his gaze to land on me. "Such as a nice, little protection spell that will keep your harmless little blasts from touching me once I activate it." He smirked as he returned his attention to the book.

From the back of the room, Amethyst swayed toward the table, no doubt observing it all with barely concealed glee. She grabbed the bowl and the cloth beneath the knife before taking her place at Forest's side.

Skimming his eyes between Chrome and me, he began reciting a passage in a foreign tongue.

Amethyst walked to my side and dropped into a crouch; the butcher knife in her hand glistened with malice. I thrashed in my seat.

Amethyst leaned into my ear. "I've always found your eternal short-comings so amusing. This one, though? Definitely tops the list." She snatched my handcuffed arm to expose the veins on my wrist. I writhed in my chair, tossing a stream of colorful curses as I did.

Amethyst's elongated, plum nails dug into the joints of my wrist with an unyielding, sharp pressure, causing me to lurch forward with a cry. The edge of the table jammed into my diaphragm.

Forest never ceased the chanting, even when Amethyst carved a deep gash along my vein. I gasped as my blood cascaded to the dark, gray floor.

Amethyst reached for the bronze bowl from the tabletop to catch the flow of blood in its belly. I could feel my life force fleeing my body, but just as quickly, the cut stitched itself back together now that the redfern was being cleansed from my system.

Once the wound healed enough to the point it no longer provided a strong blood flow, Amethyst stood. Although, not before she swiped the blade across my cheek in a stinging gash.

With a victorious smirk, she sashayed with her cunning prowess to her son's side. I grunted and nursed the cut she gave me, letting out another slew of curses her way, knowing she did it for no other reason than simply because she could.

Feeling an unfathomable rage set my body alight, I cast a sideways glance at Chrome. He fumed with a deadly silence, never veering his furious gaze from my chanting father. He knew they had us at a disadvantage and was simply biding his time until we could get out of the cuffs. Chrome didn't put up a fight against Amethyst. He sat there as she sliced open his arm like she did mine, refusing to let her see him struggle.

When she stood, she stared at him, her expression trained on her son longer than expected. The tightness around her eyes softened, and her throat bobbed as if to swallow a fleeting emotion.

I narrowed my eyes at the momentary lapse I didn't think she was capable of feeling. But she had. Rage burned through my body. *Now* she felt remorse for what she did to her son?

Fucking bitch.

As if she knew I'd caught her, Amethyst cut her eyes to me and curled her lip into a wicked grin before spinning to join Forest. He continued his chant, dropping a few small items from the table into the bowl. One by one, stones of varying shapes and colors, along with herbs I couldn't identify, thunked into the bowl of our blood.

Smoke billowed from the surface, and my panic set in. Whatever he was doing couldn't be good if it included our blood and began to smoke like that.

I didn't know what else my father needed in order to complete this ritual, but my mind raced with potential escape plans.

My thoughts immediately went to the bond that Chrome and I shared. We didn't know much, just that it connected us on a spiritual level and allowed us to do what other Kinetics and Elementals couldn't, such as feeling one another's emotions and taking control of one another's magic. Oh, and opening a portal to an entirely new fucking world. No one really knew the full extent of the bond's power yet, but maybe it could help right now.

Perhaps our bracelets only suppressed the magic *within* our bodies? The magic never left, it only laid dormant. But what if there was a literal tether connecting our souls? And what happened to that tether once we had sex and our magic seemed to intertwine?

I stared at Chrome's devastatingly gorgeous profile as an idea formed. It was a long shot, but maybe it could work just this once. If I could free him somehow, then he could wield his metal element to set me free in return. I closed my eyes, trying to find a place of peace in the chaos.

He'd told me when he took control of my magic that he'd latched onto my aura, so that's what I planned to do. I opened my eyes, ignoring the gut-wrenching signs of him accepting defeat, and focused on seeing the faint light surrounding his body instead.

Feeling the energetic fields around others had always been easy for me since I awakened my magic, but seeing them wasn't common. Even amongst our kind, my vision had been superior. Now, knowing that I was a hybrid, I understood why.

The energy was bright around Chrome, yet swathes of shadows on the edges swallowed that light. My heart sank. He was on the edge, so close to letting the Endarkening process consume him and take what it was owed.

I shoved the fear away as I searched for a tether binding the two of us. Forest's chant wound down as his voice rose in volume. I focused on the space between us, desperate to find *something*.

There was nothing at first, just air. The more I focused, the more frustrated I became. So, I pivoted to a different tactic. I remembered a technique I'd learned while meditating. Exhaling a heavy breath, I closed my eyes again and searched for the inner peace within me, grounding me while waiting for the anxious thoughts to move along.

I released all resistance and shut out my surroundings.

Opening my eyes once more, I held onto the blank state I was in. Without the energy of my thoughts and emotions clouding my sight, I spotted a faint chord of light connecting our heart chakras.

I dove back within myself and sought my well of magic. In my heart's center, it sat nestled in a shimmering ball of blue-and-white light. I guided it to the entry point of the chord and gave it a sharp nudge, sending it down the bond to Chrome, shocking him from within with a pulse of my electrical energy combined with my air element.

Chrome gasped and jolted upright, his eyes wide with confusion. By sending a bit of my magic through the bond to him, it shocked his well of slumbering magic awake, even with the magnetic cuffs on. I could see the euphoria set in as he tried to hide the effects of feeling his magic return. It would be temporary, so he needed to act fast.

He turned to face me. A mixed expression of surprise, gratitude, and determination settled on his defined features as relief washed through him. His customary dark grin inched up the sides of his face as the cuffs connecting his wrists to the chairs clicked open.

Then mine followed.

Forest chanted, lost in a trance to whatever perverse language he guttered out with harsh breaks. Amethyst....

Amethyst was gone, no longer standing at his side.

Chrome rose to his feet with calculated restraint. No doubt, he'd already concocted a plan the moment he arrived at consciousness.

His black hair had returned to its natural chromatic state, as had the golden skin and the ignition of his silver currents.

Standing from my seat, I startled as a sharp point poked the skin on my neck, right above my carotid artery.

I stilled. Icy fingers slithered around to cup the back of my neck. "You do anything stupid, son, and she dies. It's a full syringe of redfern and black crystal combined."

Chapter 58

CHROME

I couldn't pull my eyes from the needle pressing into Gray's neck. Time stood still while I contemplated every possible way to lodge a knife in my mother's throat. I knew she'd follow through on her threat; she never had been one to make cheap promises. I needed to be smart. "Put that poison in her body, and you'll wish I had never been fucking born...*Mother*." Never mind the fact that she'd already made that abundantly clear since I was able to form memories.

"Don't interfere, Chrome," Amethyst warned. Was I imagining things, or was there a hint of caring in her voice?

No, I was definitely imagining shit.

I locked eyes with my little savage princess. No, my savage *queen*. Her chin was held high, and her eyes were as cold as ice. It was her choice whether she wanted me to interfere or not. The last thing I wanted to do was to step in and potentially fuck shit up if she had a plan of some sort, but if not, I'd be more than happy to help.

I was the deliverance of eternal wrath. I wouldn't hesitate to carve the veins from anyone who touched a fucking hair on Gray's head, but I would give her the chance to defend herself if she was in a position to.

Gray closed her eyes and dipped her chin in the slightest of movements, giving me the go-ahead to step in.

My shoulders shook from a rage so fucking intense that it consumed me. I thanked the gods for her giving me the go-ahead because I couldn't hold back much longer. I could feel her resolve through our bond; she would play her part while I unleashed hell.

"Stay with me," she whispered. I barely heard her, but I felt her plea, begging me not to lose myself in the fight to win this battle.

My lips twitched at the words that had become my mantra with her.

While Gray tossed up a tight shield around her body, I used my element to launch the knife from the table at Amethyst's head. As expected, she ducked, giving Gray the chance to throw one of her electrified blue orbs at her. My mother flew across the room, slamming into the wall.

Forest needed to be subdued—and fast. I wasn't sure what the hell he was chanting, but I was sure it was bad for us.

The one thing the king hated most was chaos, especially if it wasn't his doing. The control freak that he was, he couldn't stand it if one person stepped a toe out of line.

Well, what did I happen to be best at causing? It was too soon to kill them. There were still other factors at play. I needed answers, and I needed to get Gray shielded.

Once again using my element, I made all of the metal in the interrogation room go airborne. Weapons, tables, and chairs levitated, even the ones bolted down to the floor, as I removed the screws.

The room became a maelstrom of debris, spinning wildly around at erratic speeds. I was sure to hold it high enough so as not to accidentally hit Gray. Honestly, it wasn't hard to do with her vertical ineptitude.

I kept my focus on Forest, who stared back at me, a slow, vicious grin appearing on his face. "It's done!" He laughed. "You're too late!" More unnerving laughter peeled from his chest as he looked up at the ceiling, watching my chaotic outburst.

Agony ripped through my lower chest cavity, almost blinding me. It felt like someone took a sharp metal hook and forced it to latch onto my diaphragm and then tugged. I gasped for breath, but it hurt too much. I stumbled back a few steps, desperate for it to stop. "What..."

I spun around to find Gray hunched over with a hand pressed against the top of her diaphragm. The pain began to subside, allowing me to try and make my way to her. As soon as I reached her, she straightened, her breaths ragged.

After assuring me she was okay, I noted my mother clambering to her feet, dusting off the dirt from her pristine clothes. I stripped her of any weapons and sent a small, pressurized blast at her, just enough to keep her out of the way. I wasn't done with that bitch yet.

I turned back to face Forest, who couldn't contain his gleeful grin.

A strong gust of wind blew past me and crashed into his chest. Knocking him off his feet, he spun several times before skidding across the concrete floor. He lifted his head, a menacing gleam in his dark eyes. "I've fucking had it with you, you little bitch."

Gray sauntered to my side, a viciousness of her own encapsulating her aura and sending it like a straight shot to my cock down our bond.

When Gray didn't deign him a response, only a scathing look of absolute abhorrence instead, Forest snapped. Apparently, he was not used to blatant disobedience and respect...from his daughter, no less.

"The bond is complete! There's nothing you can do now to stop it." Forest rose to his feet, his perfectly styled hair thrown askew and his suit disheveled.

"What bond?" I asked. My initial thought went to the bond between Gray and me, but I doubted that was what he was referring to. Gray and I met each other's alarmed eyes.

Forest rumbled with another chuckle, getting off on the joke Gray and I weren't privy to. It only served to piss me off more. At last, the king spoke. "The Syphon Bond."

"Explain," Gray demanded. She showed no fear, nothing but pure savage beauty stared down her father.

Forest appraised Gray with a look of amused disgust. "Tell me, why are you so bloody?"

Gray sighed, "Oh, don't be cute, *Father*. Two legions of Kinetic Warriors that you garnered from fuck knows where just ambushed the Elemental Hollow that happens to house Chrome and me. You can't contain your arrogance enough to point it out." Now, it was Gray's turn to smile. "Did you know it was a bloodbath? Did you think this blood on me was mine?" An unhinged laugh escaped her, and once again, my dick hardened. "I'll fill you in on a little secret, Your Majesty..." She took three bold steps to close the distance between them and whispered, enunciating each word. "They're. All. Fucking. *Dead*."

The daughter and father stood motionless, tense, and glaring at each other as if their looks alone could make the other drop dead. I was prepared to step in if needed, but as much I hated Forest for everything he put me through, I hated him more for what he did to Gray. I had stayed in the shadows, hidden away from her, unable to do anything while I felt every fucking horrible emotion he made her feel for sixteen years.

She deserved this kill.

At last, Forest smirked. "As predictable as always. I knew you'd both make your way here, so the palace is cleared out of everyone. Anything you two have planned won't make a difference. The Kinetics of the Royal Domain are rallying others around the country."

Forest was extra chatty. I imagined after twenty plus years of strategically planning these events, his ego wouldn't allow him to contain his pride. He thought he'd won.

Gray ignored him, continuing on as if he didn't speak. "You can't kill me," she said in a low, menacing voice. "You need me. You may have hated me because of my Elemental side, but the fact that you needed me to accomplish your goals made you hate me more. Because you're a weak-ass man who uses others' powers against their will because you lack it." Gray started to laugh, a sexy, raspy sound. "You're jealous."

Forest nodded, chewing on the inside of his cheek as he turned and casually strode toward the table where his set-up had previously been. He looked up at the levitating objects, reaching for a sword. I held strong to my grip on it, refusing to let him have it.

"Let him have it," Gray said, not taking her eyes off her father. "I won't be a coward like him, just his worst nightmare."

I relinquished my hold on the sword while Gray summoned a sword of her own that levitated. Judging by the sigils engraved on the blade, it was a Kinetic sword, but she didn't need a weapon to kill him. In fact, she could easily disarm him with her element, but she was bloodthirsty, and she had something to prove to herself. I was all too happy to watch her unleash her inner savage onto the man who'd taken so much from her.

Forest sneered as he approached his daughter. "I *created* you and all that power. Don't forget that."

Gray chuckled. "More like spawned me."

I bit back my own laughter at her smart-ass mouth that I loved so much.

Amethyst's seedy energy tickled the edges of my awareness, rousing from the hit she took from my magic, but I kept my eyes on Gray and Forest, knowing my mother would try and sneak-attack me from behind. I'd let her think she could, allowing her arrogance to get the better of her.

"I gave you everything, Gray. You were fucking royalty, for fuck sake, you ungrateful little shit. I may have hated everything you stood for, but you were *mine*. You'd be nothing without me," Forest spat.

A growl climbed from the darkest depths of my chest. Gray didn't belong to anyone. Above all else, she was her own person. But I had her heart, her soul. She was mine to protect and serve. Not to fucking own.

Forest snapped his attention to me with a sneer. "Ah, you have your little protector now? I see there's another bond at play here. I wonder how this will play out."

"What's the Syphon Bond?" I demanded.

"You'll see soon enough."

My mother's ultraviolet magic started its pesky burn along my skin again. She crept up behind me. I'd give it to her; she was silent, but I was even more trained since I was last here, thanks to Void's sensory awareness training.

I waited until she was right on me, clenching my jaw against the rising burn. I felt the air move against my neck, and I ducked just as she was about to jam a syringe full of the redfern and black-crystal mix.

I spun on my heel and kicked her feet out from underneath her. She crashed to the floor but jumped back to her feet without missing a beat—agile as always. At least I got something beneficial from the bitch.

We circled each other, and when I reached a point where Gray was in my line of sight, I saw her in the midst of a fierce battle with Forest. Their swords whirled and streaked through the air before clashing against one another. I believed in her. She could easily take him, but he was dirty.

I trained my attention back on my traitorous mother, who sold me out to her sadistic husband. Her sadistic, *dead* husband.

I summoned a sword from the ceiling. The second the hilt brushed my palm, I lunged at my mother. She was weaponless. I body-slammed her with a brutality that had bones cracking. I held the tip of my sword at her throat. She splayed her hands wide at the sides of her head, looking dazed from the impact. "Please. Chrome, don't." She coughed. She'd heal if I didn't hurry.

"That concussion has you all sorts of fucked up if you think I'd let you live." My teeth were bared, taking everything within me to keep from skewering her throat to the floor and then retrieving my Elemental blade to stab every godsdamn vital organ in her body. I wanted her to suffer, to feel a fraction of what I felt as a child.

I glanced up to check on Gray to see where she was with Forest. He was bearing down on her—hard. Using brute strength, advancing on her with every swing that she was forced to defend. She was already exhausted after the battle, then drained from the ordeal down in the prison from Forest's gamma poisoning and Amethyst's ultraviolet magic. She was beginning to panic as her strength dwindled. I felt it.

Fuck.

"I'm..." Amethyst coughed. "Sorry."

I snapped my head down at her with an astonished look. "Shut the fuck up." And I looked up just in time to find Forest running his sword through the base of Gray's spine. Her mouth widened in shock as she looked down and saw a quarter of the sword protruding from her diaphragm.

As the time seemed to slow, my heart stopped, splintering into the fragile shards of ice that composed it.

Turning her head, she met my eyes with a look I'll never be able to scrub from my mind. Her sword slipped from her hand, clanging to the floor just before she collapsed to her knees, blood pooling from her mouth. *"Help,"* she guttered out.

Smirking, Forest casually spun on his heel and returned to his table.

In haste, I released a small pulse at my mother's chest to keep her subdued. Nothing else mattered as I sprinted toward Gray, sliding on my knees across the concrete floor, taking her face in my palms. "No, no, Gray. You're gonna be okay. You hear me?"

She shook her head, eyes wide in fear and pain. "P...po...poison."

I searched her eyes frantically before shifting around to her back. I reached for the hilt, but I noticed that the blade was precisely lodged in her lower spine. If removed incorrectly, she could be forever paralyzed if the antidote wasn't given to her in time. And where the fuck were the antidotes, anyways? Fuck, fuck, fuck.

I forced my mind to slow, to allow the inner beast to rise to the surface, even calling for the affliction. I needed to be able to fucking *think.* I moved back to her front, gently lying her down on her side, careful not to jostle the sword, and placing her head in my lap.

She looked up at me with fading eyes. What remained of my soul shattered.

Hot, angry tears burned down my cheeks. "Don't you fucking leave me, Gray Monroe. I swear to..." I bent down and peppered her with urgent kisses. "Stay with me." My voice broke, choking on clawing panic. "You promised to stay with me!"

The light waned from her rainbow eyes with each labored blink. She gurgled on her poisoned, obsidian blood with each breath. "I'll fucking find you. I promise," I whispered against her blackened lips.

My chest heaved, as I went to the darkest place I'd gone yet. I wanted the fucking world to burn. If she wasn't in it, then the world didn't deserve to stand.

As Gray's lashes fluttered closed and her breaths came to a stop, I slowly lifted my head. The affliction was back. I embraced it this time. I wanted its help. Except the voice was no longer Grim's; it was Gray's. A twisted version of it, but it matched what I felt, so I didn't question it.

Kill him. Look what he did to me, Chrome.

"*Forest!*" My voice boomed off the walls in the interrogation room. Gently, I laid Gray's head ever so softly on the floor. I checked her pulse with my fingers. It was faint, but her heart remained beating.

"What did you do to that sword?" I stalked toward him. "Black crystal shouldn't affect her that fast."

Unconcerned with my fury, Forest chuckled, standing with the black book back in his palms before he snapped it shut. "Ah, yes. I dipped that blade in redfern and black crystal before you two woke up."

I nodded, not surprised in the slightest. I needed to know what was necessary to heal her in time. But Forest needed to die first. This was the only way I'd take this kill from her, was if she couldn't do it herself. I'm pretty sure she'd forgive me for this.

I summoned a knife from the ceiling and launched it at Forest's head at the speed of light. But it bounced off an invisible shield, clinking to the floor. "What the fuck?" I growled.

Forest's smug grin taunted the feral beast inside me. "Oh, that nice little spell I was telling you about. Protects me from any attacks." He boastfully waved the book at me. "I knew you'd lose your fucking mind again like you did when you killed Peri. You still don't have any control. What a fucking waste."

Any shred of restraint I had snapped. I honestly didn't know how I hadn't yet. I was trying to hold on for Gray's sake, using the beast to my advantage. But this motherfucker...

I whirled around, my nostrils flaring, sensing the strong magic of my mother standing at the back of the room, observing everything from afar.

I let the energy of her magic lull me to it. It was *intoxicating*. I didn't fight the desire this time. My mind slipped further and further away with each step I took until I closed in on her.

Her deep purple hair was disheveled, and her blue eyes widened in fear, the realization of what I was about to do clicking into place. "Chrome...no..." she whispered, shaking her head. "I never wanted to do it. You have to understand...It was..."

I didn't give her a response. As I did when I replenished my Elemental magic, I absorbed the energy from her aura. Like the other two times I depleted, this time felt euphoric—except better. It was everything I'd been missing out on. I needed more. I need it all. I felt the strength of her power stitch into the fabric of my soul, bolstering mine.

My mother gasped for air as if I had robbed her of it. "I'm sorry. I love you, son."

At those words, memories of her checking to make sure Grim carried out his punishment of rape floated through my mind. I replenished my magic, letting it build to an unfathomable limit. It fueled power through my veins, reigniting something that had just died inside of me. I watched the life force leave her eyes as she crumpled to the floor. Gone. My mother was dead, and I felt nothing but joy.

My mind, body, and soul overflowed with power, which was the point. I needed to destroy something. What was I supposed to destroy?

Feeling full and whole for the first time in...ever, I turned around and faced Forest again. That smug grin from before was beaming wide. "Perfect!"

I looked down at the girl impaled on the floor. *Gray.*

I scanned the room, searching the debris for any antidotes left behind. Through the wreckage of mine and Gray's magic, I began to lose hope, thinking that there was no way that Forest would have one for us. But if he needed us alive like his plans indicated, then it would seem he wouldn't risk our deaths.

Five seconds passed. Ten. Fifteen. My eyes darted in every direction while Forest straightened his suit. Finally, I spotted one discarded in the corner amongst the pile of papers and other useless items. I sprinted, retrieved the syringe, and ran back. Fading would actually take longer in this instance, although the thought occurred to me.

Crouching down, I carefully removed the sword from Gray's back, gentle not to sever anything vital. "I got you, Rainbow. You hear me? It's gonna be okay," I whispered, wondering if she could hear me. I should've felt remorse for what I'd just done to Amethyst, but I didn't. Not when I knew what I had to do next would require the amount of power I'd just obtained. It was the only way.

As soon as the blade was free from her body, black blood gushed from the wound like a broken faucet, covering my hands. I pressed my finger over the hole in her abdomen, trying hopelessly to staunch the flow. With my free hand, I stabbed her carotid with the syringe full of the antidote mix for both races, praying on my forsaken soul that it wasn't too late.

With a final whisper of a kiss to her forehead, I rose again to face Forest. I felt Gray's awareness spark back to life, and I released a much-needed breath.

Something dark and twisted braided itself into the stitches of my essence. I was a time bomb, and I wasn't sure how much longer I had before it all went to shit. My mind might have been intact at the moment, but it would soon fade. The question was, how long did I have before I forgot Gray entirely and became a mindless, rotting creature with the sole intent of depleting?

My hand hitched in its movement as I dragged it down my face. The dark gray veins appearing beneath my gilded skin made my heart stop. I was Endarkened. Fully. There was no going back from that. I needed to make sure Gray was okay, kill Forest, and then get the fuck out of here before I turned on the only part of my soul that existed.

"Looks like you managed to escape becoming Endarkened after all," Forest intoned. "You're welcome."

I angled my head, narrowing my eyes at him. "What are you talking about?"

Forest chuckled. "It never ceases to amaze me how ungrateful you and my daughter have always been." He ran his hand through his obnoxiously green hair, fixing its messy state. "You're bound, now. You're more than an Endarkened. More than any of us. You're an Infernal."

I closed my eyes, clenching my jaw. "What the fuck is that?"

"You'll be informed of the details soon enough."

A groan had me snapping my head in Gray's direction. She was stirring, the antidote taking hold.

Come on, Gray. Get up.

"And it's only a matter of time before she is an Infernal, too," Forest said, keeping his eyes on his daughter. "She's bound. Just like you."

"You're fucking dead," I growled, an inhuman sound escaping my throat.

"You get to keep your mind! You should be thanking me, boy!"

Instead of entertaining his narcissism, I returned to Gray's side. Her eyes fluttered open, then widened at something she saw on my face. "No..." she rasped. The veins.

"Come on, Rainbow. You gotta get up," I said, bending to help her to her feet.

Once she was steady, I peered into her shattered eyes. I felt her heart fracture, which made this more difficult. My soul was being stripped to fragments of glass while my heart felt like it was the permanent home to a dagger. I was being flayed alive from within. "Stay with me," I whispered, my voice cracking from the emotion clogging my throat. I blinked away the moisture blurring my view of her perfect face so I could commit it to memory, holding her face in my hands.

The only minute comfort I took was that she had a family now and she was more than capable of protecting herself.

I needed her to have a shield, a powerful one. "Shield yourself." My voice was so soft that Forest wouldn't have been able to hear it. "Now."

Gray closed her eyes in resignation, a sob breaking free despite her effort to stifle it. After the first one broke free, she didn't try anymore. Her shoulders shook as she gave into reality, each sob ripping me open more and more. "I love you." I melded my lips with hers, coated in black blood. I absorbed her salty tears, taking anything of hers that I could.

I felt her air shield go up, then I reached down the bond we shared and added my newfound strength to it.

Still connected to her kiss—tasting her for the last time—I focused on all my pain, my losses, the injustice of whatever was happening to me. The emotion fueled the immense well of power as it built up to unimaginable levels. I absorbed all of the electromagnetic energy being emitted around me, including in the entirety of the King's Palace and compressed it into the tightest, most compact ball in my core.

In a single pulse, I exploded it from my body.

Unlike when I knocked out the grid, this one would cause physical damage.

I went deaf briefly at the initial boom that was the equivalent of what I imagined nuclear bombs sounded like. The walls of the King's Palace blew out in every direction. In one breath, the building no longer stood. One second it was there intact, and the next, debris thrashed violently around us in volatile gales. The shield protected Gray, while the debris dodged me altogether as I directed it to. I didn't even have to break from Gray's kiss to know what happened around me. I *felt* it. Controlled it.

I pulled her harder against me as the debris swirled around for several minutes. It was impossible to orient ourselves, so I kept my lips pressed to hers through the maelstrom. This was what I wanted her last memory of me to be. If I was going to bring the world to ruin, I'd do it with her in my arms, even as she wept into my goodbye.

After what felt like minutes, I broke the kiss, studying the woman who'd saved me from myself. "I'll always find you." With my thumb, I wiped the wet streaks from her face before I tore my gaze from her. Against everything inside me, I turned around, clenching my jaw tight against the agony in my heart. My feet crunched in the rubble, leaving her broken and alone in the wreckage as I walked away from my destruction.

Where was I going? I didn't know. I just need to be anywhere other than here. Something dark slithered beneath my skin with an intensity worse than ever before.

Corrupted. I may have escaped becoming Endarkened, but I knew I was something far worse now.

Chapter 59

GRAY

The pieces of my shredded heart drifted to the ground with the ash that rained upon me. The landscape was a barren wasteland. What had been a deserted and ruined city was now reduced to rubble. It was difficult to see through the thick cloud of dark debris blanketing the sky, but I could see enough to know the city blocks were gone. The abandoned skyscrapers were gone. And all that remained was my wrecked body and tattered soul.

I couldn't breathe as I remained glued to the spot Chrome had left me, watching his silhouette disappear into the early morning rays of dawn. My jaw trembled, and the ringing in my ear wouldn't relent. Gasping for air, I clutched my chest, wishing I could reach inside and snatch it out. I'd do anything to make the pain stop.

I refused to accept what had happened. I couldn't. I couldn't accept that he was now Endarkened, even though dark gray veins protruded from his warm, golden skin.

Even more, was the fact he sacrificed himself...to save me. And I really wished he hadn't. This was exponentially worse than when I lost Slate.

The memory of how he looked at me just before the kiss, so much love and regret shone in his metallic eyes. Yet, he couldn't hide his shame or his broken heart from me, no matter how strong he tried to portray in those final moments.

The explosion was nothing like I'd ever known was possible for a single person to be capable of. The depths of his power were terrifying. I wasn't even sure how far the blast reached, but there was nothing for miles.

Unable to withstand the weight of my agony, my legs collapsed, my knees catching me in the pile of rubble. I felt cleaved in two. But I couldn't give up on him. I wouldn't.

Something rustled in the debris. Snapping my head to attention, I scanned the shaded area, the falling ash and dust blocking out the morning sun. I didn't have much left in me. I was beyond exhausted. I wasn't even sure how I'd get back to the Hollow. I was almost drained, but I had enough of my magic reserve, thanks to the antidote Chrome gave me to fight off a threat if needed.

Rising to my feet, I crunched across what, minutes ago, had been the interrogation room. Since it had been underground, the blast had leveled the ground to give a new elevation for miles to see.

I felt lightheaded, and my entire body ached, but nothing compared to the anguish in my soul. I shut down, numbing myself in order to seek out the threat. Wiping the wetness from my face, I noticed my hand came away with black liquid smeared on it.

My poisoned blood from Forest's sword.

Chrome saved me. He sacrificed himself *and the world* to fucking save *me.*

My heart twisted into a tight knot as I struggled to swallow the onslaught of my devastation.

A muffled cough rang out nearby in the rubble, snagging my focus. I stumbled to the source. A flash of green clashed against the graying landscape. Unrepented wrath replaced any sense of shock and grief.

"You're too late," Forest coughed out, trying to rise to his feet. How the fuck did he survive that blast? The only reason I did was because of my shield that Chrome managed to reinforce with his power. "Once again, you failed."

"How are you still alive after that?" I approached him, determined to make him give me answers before I killed him...slowly.

"That book has so many wonderful secrets forgotten in Arcadia. One of which included creating a shield composed of the magic weaved into the veil between our world and Arcadia. That shield could only have been broken by a magic powerful enough to destroy the veil. And because the shield was part of the veil, it, in turn, destroyed the veil." Forest laughed, wheezing as he straightened his spine. Covered in gray soot and ash, he looked comical. Had it been any other situation, I would've laughed.

The world spun to stop, registering what he'd said. "What does that mean?"

Brushing off his sleeve, Forest smiled, blood trickling down his temples. "Arcadia is here, merged with our world."

"Why?" I whispered, unsure of what that meant. Dread sank further and further into my gut the more he spoke. I almost decided to kill him already so I wouldn't have to hear anymore. But something told me there was more I needed to know.

"Why else, Daughter? Power. There's an ancient object of great power in Arcadia, and I want it." Forest shrugged. "The only way for me to get to Arcadia was for me to destroy the veil altogether."

The stone?

In my silence, he continued, clearly proud of himself. "My end of the bargain is complete. With you two now bound to Arcadia and Terragard, nothing can stop me." He puffed his chest out and ruffled his hair, looking far too happy with himself.

I scrunched my face in confusion. "What the fuck is Terragard?"

Forest rolled his eyes, annoyed. "Our world. It's the name of our realm."

"How are we bound to the different realms?"

"Your questions are getting on my nerves. I feel like I've given you more than your insolence deserves," Forest drawled, bored.

I was weaponless. With the blast, there was no way of me even having a slither of hope of finding one. As I processed all the information he'd just told me, everything clicked into place.

"You orchestrated everything that just happened? You wanted him to become Endarkened so that he'd be powerful enough to blast through the veil. And you knew you had to make him snap in order for him to..." My head began to spin at the level of cunning in my father. Even I underestimated him. He couldn't have played us more perfectly if he'd tried. All the way down to the attack on the Hollow and sending in Cardinal, who had a familial bond with Scarlett. He'd lured me in with the threats on my friends, knowing Chrome would follow.

Reeling from the total mindfuck of it all, I reared back and punched him in the jaw. His head rocked to the side, but he simply smiled, rubbing the spot my fist hit. "You'll never win." His deep laugh ignited another roaring flame in my chest.

"Watch me."

As I went to summon my element, Forest's hand lurched out, wrapping his cold, thick fingers around my throat. "The Tempest will be so pleased to finally meet you." He tightened his grip, squeezing my airway and blocking off my ability to breathe.

The pressure in my head built while I beat on his forearm, trying and failing to land a blow anywhere on his body. He had me trapped any way I moved, threatening to break my neck. A smile continued to pull up the edges of his lips, his triumph gleaming brightly in his dark eyes.

As my vision began to wane, I called on my element again and summoned my Kinetic volts to my palms. The blue electricity flickered to life, struggling to gain strength, but I managed to latch onto his wrist.

Forest flinched enough to loosen his hold, giving me the chance to increase the power of the electricity circling my hands. I electrocuted him, and finally, he dropped my throat. I gasped for air and summoned my element, allowing it to soothe my lungs, bringing me comfort with it.

My dwindling magic reserves begged me to deplete him, his strong aura enticing me to take it for myself. Remembering the gray veins on Chrome's body and everything he'd sacrificed for me, I forced the urge away despite my nihilistic mood.

Once again, I commanded air, shoving an influx of oxygen deep into his lungs. A silent gasp came from him as his hand grasped his diaphragm. I watched as his face turned red from the pressure that streamed into his lungs, inflating them like a balloon.

He wheezed, trying to pull in a breath that wouldn't come. Forest's eyes bulged from his head as he clawed a desperate hand at me. I took another step back, dodging his hopeless attempt.

Gritting my teeth and feeding on his suffering, I sent all that remained of my Kinetic magic at him, encapsulating his entire body in a voltage low enough that wouldn't immediately kill him. I wanted to drag this out as long as he could physically withstand it.

I felt nothing but pure euphoria as I watched him collapse to his knees. "You've taken everything from me! My mother, a decent childhood, my freedom, Hazel, Slate!" Tears welled in my eyes, my throat constricting. "*Chrome.*" My voice broke on his name. I wasn't sure I'd be able to hear it or say it in the foreseeable future. How the fuck was I going to get through this? Again? This time would be even worse than the last.

I surged another burst of air into his lungs. Unable to fight back with his magic, Forest rolled over onto his side, hugging his chest as his mouth gaped wide. He suffocated on the amount of air I overstuffed him with as I denied him the chance to exhale. I slowly kept increasing the flow, reveling in his suffering. It would never be enough.

Whispers of Chrome's touch taunted me in my mind. I imagined that smirk, hearing" little savage" roll off his tongue in a way that only he could deliver. I'd finally found a semi-healthy place of peace within myself, opened up again. Began to love again. Only for it to be snatched away. "Now bow before your *fucking* queen."

Conjuring my element, I lifted Forest from the rubble, and positioned him on his knees before me, forcing his ruby face and convulsing body to kneel.

I sneered down at him, white hatred filling my heart like the air that filled his lungs. "Long. Live. The King."

His eyes widened even more as I sent a final surge of air into his lungs, about to implode them from the inside out within his ribcage. An agonizing pain sliced through my chest. My heart chakra felt like it was being singed—poisoned—by a blackness that doesn't exist in this world.

Something was happening through the bond, and the torment was blinding, bringing me to my knees with a throaty scream that tore through the wasted land.

The chord felt like it was dissolving. No, not dissolving, but morphing. The nature on the other side twisted into something evil.

Chrome.

I was losing him. Not in the flesh, but everything that made him who he was. Each second that passed changed the essence of our soul bond, turning it into something darker. Chrome was still there, alive and present. I couldn't place his location, but his essence was black.

The transformation was excruciating. "No!" I screamed, hardly registering that it was my own voice. *"Chrome!"* My head swam, my vision tunneled, and I begged for reprieve. I couldn't live like this. I didn't want to live in a world without *him.* "Come back," I whimpered, my wet cheek pressed into the soot.

A shadow loomed over me as I lay curled in the fetal position. The brutality tearing through my chest didn't allow for me to move despite how hard I tried.

"Unsurprisingly, you failed again," Forest grunted. I wished the fucker would just die, but I missed my chance.

A sharp pain pummeled my ribs from the hard kick he landed, cracking the bone and robbing my breath. "Go...fuck...yourself," I wheezed.

"I wish I didn't need you alive, but Celanea insists."

Celanea? Must be the infamous Tempest.

"She'll be along shortly to collect us. Thankfully, she was able to get all the Endarkened before Chrome wrecked my home," he grumbled to himself.

Thankfully? Since when did he give a fuck about Endarkened?

I gritted my teeth and squeezed my eyes shut through the pain, wishing I would just black out already. For what would come next, I didn't want to be conscious.

Sliding his forearms beneath my torso, he jostled me, making my broken ribs scream. I was depleted, unable to heal to fight him off. But I'd fucking try. I squirmed, throwing every bit of energy into a kick.

"Stop, you little bitch..." my father growled and then dropped me when I clamped my teeth hard on his bicep.

I collided with the hard ground. More pain. Another blow, this time to my jaw, before he snatched my head back by the roots of my hair, forcing me to meet the black depths in his eyes. Fuck, he was gonna take a chunk of my hair.

I bit my cheeks until they bled to deny him the satisfaction of my cry.

His hot breath stung my nostrils as he leaned in close, his voice just as poisonous as his magic. "As soon as Celanea is finished sucking your magic dry, I will personally rip out your throat and make Chrome watch with a smile on his face."

Another blow to the ribs, this time with his fist.

"Touch another fucking hair on her head, Forest, and see what happens..."

I must've been hallucinating because there was no way that voice was here. Not now.

Forest stilled, fear briefly flashing across his features. His eyes widened as if he'd seen a ghost. Perhaps, it was.

"You're supposed to be dead," he seethed.

A knife whizzed over my head and embedded in Forest's shoulder, knocking him on his ass. He scrambled to get away.

"Close your eyes, Gray," the deep voice said from behind me. No problem. My eyelids were so damn heavy. Too much today.

Through my closed lids, a bright light illuminated. Light Kinetic. Who the...

No. That's not possible.

"Back the fuck up, Forest."

That voice again. I couldn't process everything happening.

My body jostled again, this time in gentler arms with a familiar scent. One I'd almost forgotten, bringing another onset of tears to my eyes.

"Slate?" My voice broke as I cracked open my eyes.

"Nice to see you again, Princess," he said, his tone soft as he scanned my abused body with a grimace.

"How?" I whispered, scared if I spoke too loudly that it would all come to an end. Surely, I'd blacked out and was dreaming. This couldn't be real.

"Long story. But I never died."

My heart couldn't handle anymore. What the fuck did he mean he never died? Where the fuck had he been? And why did he abandon me like that?"

"Shh," he said, struggling to reach into his pocket. He came up with a small tin canister. "Chrome just gave me this. Said you would need to take it so you can fade us back to the Hollow." Gently, he adjusted me in his arms, as desolation consumed me. "Forest took off. We need to go."

Chrome? Excuse me?

My already ravaged world tilted over the cliff, careening out of control. He might as well have just stabbed me twice more in the heart with as much of a betrayal that was.

"I can imagine you're pissed but I'll explain everything once we get the fuck out of here. Celanea will be here to collect you. We gotta go."

He dropped the pinch of Mushweed on my tongue, and kept scanning the barren wasteland anxiously while we waited for it to take root enough for me to fade. Once I felt cognizant enough to realize that this was not a horrific nightmare and that Slate had been alive this entire time, I envisioned the Hollow.

"I'll never forgive you for this," I forced out through the tears steadily trailing down my cheeks. My throat was too tight, making it hard to breathe.

I felt my body begin to disintegrate, catching the flash of hurt in his eyes.

"I know," Slate whispered. His words were carried away on the wind as we turned to ash, drifting through time and space while leaving my mangled heart and beaten soul in the rubble of the King's Palace.

Chapter 60

CHROME

Excruciating pain ripped through my soul from a black poison hellbent on overtaking everything within me. It dominated, forcing its will upon me as it sought out every crevice and square inch of my fractured being in a methodical fashion.

My mind remained untouched, but it was only a matter of time before the decaying energies of those I'd depleted dug their steely claws in and stole my memories and entire identity. The evil flourishing in my veins would transform me into something unknown.

I collapsed to my knees with a guttural cry to the sky as the internal flaying engulfed my chest. My vocal cords threatened to shred and disintegrate while my fingertips dug in and clawed at the creases between muscles in my desperate attempt to rip free the blackening poison. Hollow breaths rasped from my burning throat as I dropped my head in defeat. I couldn't fight my way out of this battle.

Another sharp pain raked through my chest. And with a stilted gasp, my back arched of its own accord as if the blackness consumed and molded me from the inside out.

I struggled to breathe past the pain, sending a silent thanks to the gods that I'd been able to hold on long enough to make the fade away from Gray in time.

I clung to the image of her in my mind. Soft rainbow eyes were hidden behind the hardened wall she'd formed to protect herself from a world that never showed her kindness. Her button nose that always tempted me to kiss it, and her angled jawline that allowed the perfect grip in my palm to tamper down her warring nature. The scent of vanilla and lavender that always seemed imbued in her hair wafted through my senses as if she stood beside me, ready to fight off this inevitable power coursing through my soul.

In the moments after I depleted my mother, I'd never felt more powerful. It was the intoxicating and infallible feeling that I'd been chasing all these years since Peri's death. In that moment, I thought myself to be the bringer of justice, an archangel sent from heaven to smite the world of the darkness forced upon it. I felt like the god of wrath, all-powerful and all-consuming.

Walking away from Gray and leaving her devastated in the wake of the chaos was the hardest thing I'd ever done. At least she had Slate.

I sucked in a broken breath as the black poison offered me a reprieve. Not wanting to waste any time, I rose to my shaky feet, my legs weakened like jelly while acute pains lanced through my bones and tissues. I embraced the physical pain like an old friend, better than the emotional pain of walking away from Gray.

Already, I felt hollower, like I was missing parts of myself that were crucial to who I was.

Memory flashes of Slate finding me just before I faded out of sight crossed my mind. He'd done well at staying hidden since Gray's escape from the King's Palace. As my informant via Hazel from the King's Palace, as well as Arcadia—where he'd been hiding all this time with an ally powerful enough to open a portal for him to travel to and from—he'd been vital.

There were moments where Gray almost sensed him, but thankfully, he'd been too far away for her to pinpoint. My cousin's loyalty was unfounded. He protected Gray all the years I couldn't, all while he tried to uncover Forest and my mother's motives. He'd done just as I'd asked him to when Forest's orders of my treatment began to escalate. I saw what was coming, even though I didn't know the full extent of their plans yet. And I knew it was only a matter of time before they turned to Gray.

Everything worked according to plan until he'd been caught snooping, which led to Forest planning an ambush on the Guilds' mission that Slate served on. Except, Forest never knew that Slate had been working with me in the shadows for the past year and a half after his "death".

When he found me before the fade, I slipped him the Mushweed I'd hidden to pass along to Gray, knowing her magic would be completely drained. "Get her back to the Hollow. Guard her with your life. Then, you're gonna be there for her."

Slate pierced me with a saddened gaze, knowing what I'd done and the fate I was doomed to. And I trusted him to follow through no matter what it cost him. "I will not be in a relationship with her this time. It would be too cruel after everything she's been through."

I shook my head in a nod. "Good because she's *mine*." I knew he was also suffering from the loss of his sister due to a pact they'd made with one another long ago. A pact that if one of them were to ever get caught within the king's grasp, they'd take their own lives to avoid spilling secrets under his torture.

Swallowing thickly before he went on, he said, "Try to fight it. If anyone can do it, it's you."

I was born and bred to fight. And I would fight this transformation as long as I could withstand it. I didn't know what being an Infernal meant, or how much different it was from being Endarkened. But it felt similar to the devolution symptoms. Forest had said I'd keep my mind, but I was already beginning to lose memories.

I held onto Gray, though, clinging to her like a lifeline.

Guilt burned within me alongside the blackness that spread its toxic essence along every bone, muscle, tissue, vein, and cell. But I didn't regret sending Slate to Gray all those years ago to be close to her; to be her friend, her support, and show her what she was capable of.

I never expected them to fall in love, but she had been happy, and I'd had zero claim on her, seeing as the only time I'd spoken with her was when we were kids. But I'd had to endure her heavy, intense emotions, which were similar to my own. And I couldn't stand not being able to do anything about it.

Right before I faded, I'd envisioned the tattoo parlor in Macon. Where I stood now, hours south of Buckhead, looked nothing like the tattoo parlor Gray and I once fought at. The wasteland of ash and sand around me indicated my power stretched further than I ever believed possible.

Fucking hell. I did that?

More sharp pains clawed at my chest, working higher and higher until it reached the middle of my throat. I wrapped my fingers around my trachea, half-screaming and groaning at the same time. I stumbled to remain on my feet.

Each wave of pain pulled me further and further away from myself, as the ravenous hunger for more power clouded my vision.

I opened my eyes once the pain receded again, the little breath I had in my lungs freezing on an inhale. Facing a different direction, the view didn't fit the barren wasteland. It was...*otherworldly.*

Behind me, sat a dark forest. Even if Macon still stood, the forest shouldn't exist in that spot. It had once been a busy city, bustling with vehicles and hurried humans. I staggered backward several steps at the eeriness of the wood, the wrongness it exuded.

The sky above was azure and clear of any clouds, yet an unnatural darkness radiated from within. A poison that called to me, coaxing me toward it like I was tethered to its composition. I staggered forward, each harried step harder than the last as I willed myself to the wicked darkness.

The gnarled branches of a tree drooped low, beckoning me to its twisted and blackened ends. The wood curled around itself in an attempt to snuff out all life and light, reminding me of snakes that squeezed their prey to death. Inky fluid seeped from the crevices, dripping down the wood like decaying, foul sap. The dark leaves were almost as pitch as the thick, black substance. With razor-sharp and jagged ends, they dared anyone to touch its malice.

Something tugged on my diaphragm, pulling me forward. Between the dark chord and the poison, the pain was unbearable, but my feet moved of their own accord. My mind was still intact, but the further I went, the more I felt comfort in the darkness.

The tug on my diaphragm jolted me to stop. Oppressive silence snuffed out all life—there were no signs of life or magic. It was completely devoid of anything natural as the foul odor of sulfur and death choked me.

Somehow, it felt like home.

Leaves crunched, and no echoes followed. The soft footfalls padded in my direction. It was too dark, no light making its way through the tree boughs. I waited, tapping into my Kinetic magic that was now heightened to unfathomable strengths. At the feminine cackle, I snapped my head around.

"I wouldn't do that if I were you," she crooned in a sing-song voice. "Oh, your magic is absolutely delicious, King Freyr." She had an unrecognizable accent, something ancient and wholeheartedly evil. It called to me.

I couldn't speak, physically unable to as I waited for the woman to come into view.

"Come to me," she ordered, her tone hardened.

I obeyed, finding myself wanting to follow her, serve her. My feet carried me, the tugging on my diaphragm subsiding to barely noticeable. I came to a stop before a black cloaked figure, long raven hair pooling at her waist. This must've been the Tempest that Forest had mentioned. "It's so wonderful to meet you at last. You must be burdened with so many questions."

Still, I couldn't bring myself to speak as if something pinched my voice box shut. I simply stared at the woman; her face obscured in the shadows of her cloak.

"To answer you succinctly, you are *mine*. I own you. You and your magic are bound to the energies of Terragard and Arcadia for my kind's magic to feed from. You are the first Infernal in over a millennium." She began to pace in front of me as she appeared to think over her next words carefully. "Fucking Celestials wiped my precious creations from the realm," she said, then followed it with another unhinged cackle. "I ended up cursing them twofold." She sighed, looking up into the blackened sky with wistful reminiscence.

"You see, child, Elementals and Kinetics were once one race called Celestials." The woman spit the last word like it was a venomous thing. "And Celestials were being naughty and interfering with my plans. Long story short, a long-fought war broke out in Arcadia, and I needed soldiers that could fight against the might of the Celestials' power. So, I did what anyone would do; I cursed them and then bound them to me, bending the will of a Celestial to my control. They became my children, my pets, these beautiful Infernal beings."

The Tempest stopped pacing, and through the shadows within the hood, I could see her pale lips pushed out into a pout. "But then, the Celestials took away my children. So, I cursed the Celestials by dividing up their power into two separate beings. And then I had them cast out of Arcadia. Along with the curse, came the Endarkened. My own little special brand of fuck you." She began to pace again. "After the Celestials were cast out and split up, I had the veil locked down, where they could never return. Cursed to live in a world that didn't have magic, and their power weakened by not being at their full strength. They reproduced, and the Celestial bloodline died...until you and the little queen came along that is." Yellowed teeth peeked through the shadow, forming a gnarly and wicked smile.

"You're my first reborn child. Here to help me set things right for my kind. Once the curse fully sets in, you'll never look back. You'll fight honorably for my cause and help me restore Arcadia to its rightful place where darkness reigns, but I need power to do so. And you're everything I need in order to get it there. The queen will follow, turning Endarkened in her grief. The Twin Soul Bond between you two will deteriorate, and she will go mad, desperate to deplete in order to fill the gaping hole the bond left behind, even if it hasn't been fully anointed yet. But your physical union solidified it enough."

My heart palpitated in my chest, thinking of Gray. Fuck, I couldn't do anything. I couldn't warn her. I wondered how much longer I'd be able to think of her like this.

"Now," the Tempest said, clearing up from her history lesson. "It's time to complete your transformation. We have much work to do."

Another set of footsteps crunched through the leaves toward us, not stopping until Forest's sneering face was before me, wiping the soot and ash from his pristine suit.

My breath guttered, fearing the worst for Gray if he was still alive. Fuck, she was supposed to kill him—or the blast was. What the hell happened?

With a sardonic laugh that got swallowed by dead energy surrounding us, he said, "Welcome home, boy."

Afterword

If you enjoyed A Touch of Gold and Madness, please help other people discover the series by scanning the QR code below to leave a review. Word of mouth is so important for independent authors and helps more books like this get written!

Acknowledgements

Wow. Honestly, I don't know where to begin. This book has been in the making for almost a decade as I struggled to find the right way to tell this story. After a series of life events, it finally came to me in the form of Gray and Chrome one day during maladaptive daydreaming.

It has been healing for me in so many ways, and I hope as a reader you were able to resonate with it on some level. Gray and Chrome saved me. Point blank. And through them I was able to begin healing.

This book wouldn't be here without the help of so many people. Seriously, it takes an army to publish a book. To start, I want to thank my parents for their support throughout the whole process. If not for them, I would still be daydreaming of this story.

Slate (the real-life Slate), your confidence and support were monumental. (Still find it crazy that the character came along before you did). The belief you had in me when I wanted to pick this story back up is something I'll never forget, and I'll be forever grateful. You never even questioned me. It's all I needed to commit to finally finishing this story and getting it out into the world. And thanks for listening to me drone on and on about it when you had no idea what I was talking about.

Tory, my *parabatai*. We've been writing together for years and talking about the day we'd finally get books out there. If not for you, I would've given up in defeat a long time ago. The alpha reads through the roughest of drafts were immense. You've been here through it all during this journey and my gratitude is unending. It's crazy to think how we started out roleplaying Harry Potter next-gen in our early twenties. Thanks for putting up with my insane ideas and not judging me for them. It was also your belief and confidence in me to achieve dream that kept me from giving up. You have no idea how much I appreciate that. Now, it's your turn to one out there.

Eezy. Those comments back on Wattpad gave me life. Thank you for sticking around all this time with your encouragement. It was Nova and the emotional chords you yanked on that inspired Chrome and this story. This story wouldn't have manifested if not for you. Your excitement and enthusiasm are what motivated me to keep going.

Amarah, I thank you for opening my eyes and saving me from making a devastating mistake. You saved this book. Thank you for all the advice, and our great talks of emo music and kids. And for being my first author friend when I dove back into this story. You have been instrumental in more ways than you can know, and I'll be forever grateful for you.

Kendra, thank you for everything you've done. There was a time I would've been absolutely lost and totally screwed without you. You've done so much in helping me getting this book right with the beta read, as well your reactions brought me life. Your role with the ARC team has been incredible, and I'm so honored to have met you and be able to call you my friend. Your undying support and excitement has been unfounded. Hopefully we'll all get together one day and celebrate.

Samantha. Thank you. First, thank you for being my author bestie. Second, you should look into line editing on the side. You saved my ass so much in helping to integrate edits. So, I thank you endlessly, my friend. I wonder how Chrome and Vesryn would get along. I can only imagine the dramatic antics they'd be up to together. (This is a thought that frequently goes through my mind.) I'm so excited for your writing career and can't wait to see how The Aelfyn Archives continues to blossom.

Kirsty, thank you for your attention to details and helping me shape this story. I'm so grateful for your help and kindness. Your insight into helping me make this story land was beyond beneficial and I cannot thank you enough. It was the fact you seemed to see and get my story from the start that made me know you were the editor I *had* to work with to get this book where I envisioned it. And you did. So thank you so much.

Rebecca Quinn, thank you so much for your advice. I'll never forget your kindness and willingness to share your knowledge. I'm in awe of you and I'm so honored to call you a friend.

All the authors and editors in The Avengers Assemble Discord group, thank you for providing the support during a very difficult time in this process. Thank you for providing the resources and knowledge I needed when I was so lost. Most importantly, thank you for helping me to get my mind right so I could get this story where I always envisioned it.

My Fellow Trauma Queens. Your knowledge and your willingness to share it has saved me from making further mistakes as a baby author. Thank you so much. Let's continue to break hearts, shall we? K.C., thank you for being the sweetest. Julia and Lacey, I will forever refer to you as my writing twins. N.R., I will forever credit you for giving me the term, Murder Muffin to refer to Chrome. T.A., thank you for being so supportive from the moment I joined IG.

My ARC team and bookstagrammers/booktokers who've been carrying the torch for A Touch of Gold and Madness like it's the next Fourth Wing, you guys are everything. I truly don't have words to describe how much you mean to me. Every time I began to think no one would want to read this book, someone would message me expressing their excitement. It's brought tears to my eyes more times than I can count. I'm honored to have found you guys and have you on my team. I'll never take any of you little savages for granted. The kindness that the bookstagram and booktok communities showed me from the start is something I'll never forget. You guys are the heroes. I thank you from the bottom of my heart.

I feel like I'm leaving out so many who've helped me in some way or another, and I wish I could name everyone. Thank you to anyone who offered any advice, guidance, support or encouragement. My gratitude is limitless.

Go join K. L. DeVore's **The Little Savage Squad Reader Discord** where you can engage with other readers of *A Touch of Gold and Madness*.

https://discord.gg/xs4tuFn

About the Author

K.L. is a dark fantasy romance author who lives for complex plots, characters, and worlds. When she isn't writing or editing, she is either reading or drawing realistic charcoal portraits. As a mother of two excitable boys, she values the quiet evenings when she can focus on her work best while drinking a mug of sugar-free hot cocoa.

While she loves writing a spicy slow burn and lots of fight scenes, her books depict dark themes of trauma and healing that she hopes will resonate with other readers.

You can follow K.L. for updates and content regarding *The Celestials of Arcadia* series on her social media accounts where she is interactive with her readers.

Instagram: @authorkldevore
TikTok: @author_kldevore

Made in the USA
Las Vegas, NV
07 September 2024

94938645R10319